"Sir! You intrud...
she turned...

The man moved quickly, and Kit had no chance to grab the dagger hidden among her clothes. She did not wish to reveal the weapon's existence yet. Better to be civil and await the opportunity to gain her knife without a struggle.

"I hesitate to apologize," he said, still unable to see her face due to her cloak's large hood. "I was unaware of your presence here until a moment ago, and I will not deny that I enjoyed the few glimpses you allowed me."

"Unbeknownst to me!"

"You are cold."

"The man is a scholar," she muttered to herself as he came even closer.

Kit refused to be intimidated by his size. He was a big man at a distance and absolutely massive close at hand. She knew he could have her flat on her back in seconds....

Dear Reader,

Entertainment. Escape. Fantasy. These three words describe the heart of Harlequin Historicals. If you want compelling, emotional stories by some of the best writers in the field, look no further.

We think Margo Maguire is one of the best *new* writers in the field. Her debut book, *The Bride of Windermere,* is a captivating marriage of convenience tale set in medieval England. A knight, Wolfram "Wolf" Gerhart, has been sent by King Henry V to escort the beautiful Kit Somers to court. En route, Kit and Wolf waylay at his lost estate, where they begin to fall in love. Court intrigue, a surprise inheritance and passion abound from start to finish!

Silver Hearts is a charming new Western by Jackie Manning. Here, a doctor turned cowboy rescues a feisty Eastern miss on the trail, and their paths just keep crossing! *Joe's Wife,* by the talented Cheryl St.John, is an emotional Americana story of a bad boy turned good and his longtime secret crush, now a widow, who proposes a marriage of convenience.

Rounding out the month is *My Lord Protector* by newcomer Deborah Hale. Set in 1742 England, a young woman forced to wed ends up marrying her fiancé's uncle, who'll "protect" her until his nephew returns. Unexpectedly the two fall madly in love!

Whatever your tastes in reading, you'll be sure to find a romantic journey back to the past between the covers of a Harlequin Historical®.

Sincerely,

Tracy Farrell, Senior Editor

Please address questions and book requests to:
Harlequin Reader Service
U.S.: 3010 Walden Ave., P.O. Box 1325, Buffalo, NY 14269
Canadian: P.O. Box 609, Fort Erie, Ont. L2A 5X3

THE BRIDE OF WINDERMERE

MARGO MAGUIRE

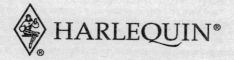

HARLEQUIN®

TORONTO • NEW YORK • LONDON
AMSTERDAM • PARIS • SYDNEY • HAMBURG
STOCKHOLM • ATHENS • TOKYO • MILAN • MADRID
PRAGUE • WARSAW • BUDAPEST • AUCKLAND

ISBN 0-373-29053-5

THE BRIDE OF WINDERMERE

Copyright © 1999 by Margo Wider

Printed in U.S.A.

MARGO MAGUIRE

lives in the Detroit area with her husband and three school-age children. She's worked as a critical-care nurse for years, writes when she has time and is an active volunteer in her local schools and community. After returning to college to earn a degree in history, Margo came to realize that an awful lot of history was stranger than fiction. She decided it would be fun to put the two together.

To Mike and our three wild ones.
Everything is possible with you.

Chapter One

Northumberland, England
Late April, 1421

Damn the man! Damn that fool, Baron Somers!

Wolfram Gerhart Colston strode through the forest, toward the lake, away from his men. How could Somers possibly think he could defy the king's orders? Who in kingdom come did he think he was? The monarch had sent Wolf to fetch the man's stepdaughter and fetch her he would! He was damned if he'd go back empty-handed, and there was little time to waste. It didn't matter how hard Somers tried to withhold the girl, Wolf would get her to London.

The huge knight deftly sidestepped a fallen branch in the dark and continued on his route to the lake, hoping for a few moments of peace near the dark water. It was near midnight and he'd been unable to sleep, so annoyed was he with the recalcitrant baron, a mean and lazy drunkard. Edith, his lady wife, was just as bad with her cloying ways and batting eyes.

Wolf had to admit he was more than a little exasperated by the entire situation. What in God's name could King Henry V possibly want with little Kathryn Somers? Henry had only recently returned from France with his bride, Catherine of Valois; Wolf could not understand what was so important about this one girl in Northumberland. What's more, Wolf resented the fact that *he* had been the one sent to this remote county to collect the child.

Wasn't Wolf known for his cold precision, his prowess in battle and his immunity to all the superfluous nonsense that went on at court? There were so many more important duties for Henry's lieutenants, who had just recently returned to England, that Wolf resented having his talents wasted this way.

Wolf hoped this wasn't one of Henry's ridiculous practical jokes. On second thought, that was doubtful. Since inheriting his father's throne, Henry had become respectable and a whole hell of a lot more responsible than he'd been in his reckless youth. No…this was no joke.

The one and only consolation to this trip was that Wolf now traveled as the king's emissary. Before delivering young Kathryn to London, Wolf intended to visit Windermere Castle and meet his cousin, Philip Colston, the current Earl of Windermere.

And Wolf would make every effort to see that the fraudulent earl was unseated.

The knight was certain that Philip was responsible for the violent deaths of Wolf's father, Earl Bartholomew Colston, and of his older brother, John. It was twenty years since they'd been killed. Twenty long years, and Wolf intended to travel to Windermere in order to unearth whatever evidence was necessary to expose Philip's treachery.

The only complication to Wolf's plan was Lady Kathryn. She was the reason why he'd been unable to travel to Windermere directly from London. And now, he'd have to take the child to Windermere with him, as well as to any other estates or manors he visited. There were hints and rumors that the Scots might try to steal the girl, and Henry said he wanted her safely in Wolf's hands.

* * *

It was still a bit too cold for swimming, but Kit Somers immersed herself in the chilly lake and washed quickly, before old Bridget could realize she was gone. It wasn't that she was ungrateful for Bridget's concern, but Kit was twenty years old now, well beyond the age of needing a nurse and Bridget did hover so.

The old woman, a distant cousin who had also been her mother's nurse and companion, was her only ally against the loneliness and brutality of the last fifteen years since her mother's death. But Bridget had become such an infernal worrier. Now she had taken to fretting about the smattering of King Henry's soldiers camped out in the fields beyond her stepfather's manor house.

A quarter moon hung over the lowest of the trees and a hazy mist hovered over the ground, giving the forest an otherworldly appearance. The lake was the perfect place to be alone and try to devise a plan of escape. It was a puzzle, though. She had no desire to comply with King Henry's order to appear in London, but Kit knew she couldn't openly defy him. However, if she happened to be away and never received the royal command, she couldn't be accused of ignoring the king's order. Unfortunately, she was certain the damnable escort would somehow manage to ferret her out of any hiding place. She had seen their leader at a distance, a huge, well-muscled knight with a head of dark, untamed hair, and he didn't appear to be a man who would easily accept her refusal to accompany him.

Perhaps she could just keep him on the run, she thought. She was as good on horseback as any man in the vicinity, and her skill with a bow was better than most. There wasn't any reason why she couldn't stay in the forest and evade the king's soldiers for weeks at a time. Yet thinking of the dark knight, she had to admit, she might not succeed.

And what of her stepfather? If he ordered her to go and she openly defied him… Kit shuddered. His reprisal would be swifter than that of the king. It was better not to think about those consequences just yet.

Kit left the deeper water and walked back towards the shore. She stood up in the shallows and unpinned her light-blond curls to let them fall where they may. How she loved the cold air hitting her naked body like this. She stretched her arms out, then overhead and reveled in the primitive pleasure she derived from the frigid air.

Perhaps a solution to her dilemma would come to her while she slept that night. Even better, maybe Rupert would return from his duties in London. After all, it was possible—all right, she admitted to herself, *remotely* possible—for him to arrive and rescue her from whatever fate King Henry had in mind for her. As one of Henry's knights, Rupert might be able to intervene on her behalf.

Against her optimistic nature, Kit had to recognize the fact that few things had ever gone in her favor, and she had better quit hoping for a neat rescue. She was better off relying on her instincts and her unpredictable nature to see her through. She had managed to avoid countless beatings by her stepfather by keeping him off balance, doing the unexpected to divert his attention.

She wondered what the baron would expect her to do now.

Wolf sat on a fallen log at the edge of the wood facing the lake, lost in thought. He believed that Philip Colston had arranged for his family to be ambushed as they journeyed to Bremen to join Lady Margrethe, Wolf's mother. Earl Bartholomew and his son, John, were savagely killed before Wolfram's eyes, along with all but one of their attendants. Of their entire party, only Wolf and a young squire, Hugh Dryden, had survived.

Furthermore, in case the ambush failed, Philip managed somehow to implicate Bartholomew in an assassination attempt against King Henry IV. Philip quite tidily ensured that his uncle's name would be dishonored, and Bartholomew Colston would have been outlawed in England by some miracle if he or his sons had managed to survive the attack.

Philip and his coconspirator father, Clarence, had no idea that anyone had survived the ambush in Europe. To their knowledge, all of Bartholomew's entourage had perished. However, not only had Wolf survived the attack in Germany, his identity was kept secret through the years to protect him, as well as to give him the advantage when he was ready to return and unseat Philip.

Wolf was so absorbed in his ruminations that he didn't notice another presence nearby until he'd been sitting awhile. When he looked up toward the water, he thought the pale moonlight and mist were playing tricks on his eyes. Coming from the depths of the lake was a maiden, like one from the old tales he'd heard as a child. His feelings of annoyance and bitterness dissolved instantly, and he was intrigued.

The maid's skin shimmered in the filmy light and her hair, as she loosed it around her, seemed made of the finest golden silk. The night was cool, and Wolfram thought he could almost see the goose bumps rise on her. The tips of her well-shaped breasts had certainly risen, and Wolf's palms fairly itched with desire to touch her.

His eyes traversed her length, appreciating her shapely legs, her hips and slender waist as she came out of the water towards him, unaware of his presence. He was unable to draw a breath when she stopped and stretched herself in the ankle-deep water, throwing her head back, reaching for the moon. He almost expected her to give out a haunted call to whatever other spirits were lurking about this night.

Her face was averted from his gaze, but Wolf easily envisioned it. He rose up, as if in a trance and stood mesmerized by her, conjuring up images of her soft and gentle features. The fairy stepped out of the water and went over to a pile of clothes that lay just beyond the bank. She began to dry herself, but upon suddenly hearing steps behind her, the ethereal beauty yanked up a long cloak and hastily threw it on, covering herself as decently as possible under the circumstances.

"Sir! You intrude!" Kit gasped as she turned and saw him. The man moved quickly, and Kit had no chance to bend down for the dagger hidden among her clothes. She did not wish to alert the man to the fact that she had a weapon. Better to be civil and await the opportunity to gain her knife without a struggle, she thought.

"I hesitate to apologize," he said, still unable to see her face due to the hood she'd pulled so far forward. "I was unaware of your presence here until a moment ago, and I will not deny that I enjoyed the few glimpses you allowed me."

"Unbeknownst to me!"

"You're cold."

"The man's a scholar," she muttered to herself as he came even closer.

Kit refused to be intimidated by his size. He was a big man at a distance and absolutely massive close at hand. She knew he could have her flat on her back in seconds. If only she could get to her knife, she thought. She didn't dare stoop down for it because he would surely knock her over, and she'd be defenseless.

She needed to get away, yet the dark giant was clearly not of a mind to let her leave. This would never do! Maybe she ought to try simply running. She was fast and knew the forest paths well. A man of his size would probably be slow, but what if she was wrong? What if he managed to catch up to her? What if he discovered the cottage, her only refuge in the woods? She couldn't run all the way back to Lord Somers' house wearing only her cloak. Her stepfather's men would surely—

"Where do you live?" his voice was gentle. "It isn't safe for a gentlewoman out here alone. My men are camped nearby and I couldn't vouch for the manners of any of them, coming upon a maid alone in the dark."

God's blood, he was a gentleman. Kit breathed a sigh of

relief and offered up a silent prayer of thanks. Chivalry demanded that he give her due respect. "Thank you for your concern, sir," she said with relief. A change of tactics was needed. If she used a bit of honey, the way her stepsisters did so annoyingly, perhaps she could get him to go away. "I will just gather my things and be off—"

"Where is your home?"

"Not far." Her voice was as sweet as she could make it.

"I cannot allow you to go unescorted. There are dangers in the night, my lady."

Kit wanted to scream at the man but held her temper in check. A ladylike argument was more likely to win her cause than screeching like one of the banshees of Bridget's tales. "Please sir, allow me to pick up my clothes, and you may escort me to my cottage," she said sweetly.

Chivalry was all fine and good, but who could tell how a stranger would behave? Even Lord Somers, her own stepfather, was mean and brutal with her. Kit almost groaned aloud when the man swept down and picked up all of her belongings at once. Now she'd never get her dagger. And there was a good chance she wouldn't be able to outrun him, especially without her boots. No, she could see he moved too well for a man his size, with grace and purpose.

"You mystify me, my lady," the knight said.

"Oh?" Kit turned away and tried to calm herself as she walked towards the cottage.

"At first when I saw you I thought you were one of the nymphs of old." Was there a hint of amusement in his voice? "Now I tend to believe that you are made of flesh and blood yet you have little fear of me. Why?"

If only he knew she was trying to figure a way to get hold of her knife so she could slip the blade between his ribs. "Naturally, I am wary, sir. I realize just how vulnerable I am. I'm ill at ease having to rely on your sense of propriety and chivalry. I would hope, by all the saints, that you intend me no harm." She wanted to gag. If her stepsisters could only see her, they'd be on the ground, laughing.

The cottage was almost in sight now, though the soldier would be hard-pressed to see it, since the night was so black and the building lay within a thicket of trees. Her stepmother had had it built, ostensibly for the use of the family, but Kit knew she used it for other purposes. Fortunately, Lady Edith was not there tonight with any of her gentleman friends. Kit would be able to slip inside, bar the door and outwait the knight in warmth and comfort.

"Here we are, sir." Kit stopped and turned to dismiss the soldier, but the man seemed incapable of taking the hint. "My…my mother awaits me," she lied.

He moved towards her, and though Kit couldn't actually see his face in the dark, she sensed that he was looking at her intently. She felt exceedingly uncomfortable to be so scrutinized, especially by the man who had just watched her as she bathed. It was absolutely indecent.

"Sh-she is ill, you see…er, and will worry overmuch if—"

"Who are you?" His voice was soft, a caress. He came closer.

His nearness was intoxicating. Kit's mouth went dry. Though the knight was huge, she was suddenly no longer afraid. An alien curiosity filled her as she realized that no man had ever affected her in the way this man did. "I…er…"

Before she could answer, he dropped the clothing he carried and took her face in both of his hands. His mouth brushed hers, a gentle caress of lips that made her tremble. He groaned as his mouth touched hers again, gently at first, then gradually more demanding until his lips were slanting over hers, leaving her breathless and bewildered. His hands slipped under her cloak and moved onto her shoulders, then down her bare back until they reached her smoothly rounded bottom. He pressed her tightly against him. She felt his hard, clothed body against her naked flesh and a knot of pleasure wound itself up tightly in her pelvis. She had never experienced anything like this before. Not even Rupert had ever—

Kit broke away from him in shock. "Please!"

"Who are you?"

"Let me go!"

"My name is Wolf." His hot breath seared her ear, and his lips brushed against her lips again.

Kit tried to pull away. She'd never been kissed this way before and was shaken to the core.

"Who are you?" he repeated.

"No one! I am no one! Let me go!" At that, she pulled away and ran to the cottage, her cloak billowing out behind her. When she was inside, she dropped the heavy beam across the door and leaned against the rough wall until her breathing slowed, until her heart stopped its wild pounding.

Wolf knew with certainty that she didn't want to be found with him, but he considered risking all to touch her and taste her again. She was unlike anyone he'd ever met. Beautiful, seductive, intriguing. He was shaken by his own reaction to her, and one taste of this goddess wasn't enough. He wanted her as he'd never wanted anyone before.

But the truth of the matter was that he couldn't risk offending the local nobility while on this errand of Henry's. He'd have to put this woman, this delectable "no one" out of his thoughts for the time being.

Wolf finally turned and headed back into the thickest part of the forest towards camp. He was a patient man. He would come back for her when all was settled at Windermere.

Kit couldn't sleep all night. She sat in the dark with a blanket around her and still she shivered, though she couldn't really complain of the cold. It would have been nice to go out and retrieve her clothes, but she was afraid *he* would be out there waiting.

"Wolf." It suited him, she thought. He was certainly big enough to lead a pack of wolves and though he'd been gentle with her, she sensed that he could be brutal as well as kind. In the moonlight, she'd been able to see his wild mane of shaggy dark hair and light gray eyes that almost seemed to glow in the dark.

She really needed to try to consider a feasible way to evade King Henry's army in the morning, but all she could think of was Wolf. His lips, the way his tongue slipped in and out of her mouth, his hands touching her shoulders, sliding down her back, her bottom...

Rupert had never even kissed her. He'd gone off with King Henry over three years before, without even the benefit of a betrothal, promising to return after the French territories were regained. But here it was, ages since the fall of Normandy and Rupert had not returned. How long did he expect her to wait?

Kit could practically feel herself growing older by the day. Her stepsister, Margery, would be betrothed soon and Eleanor was likely to follow in another year or so. Kit longed to be off with Rupert to become his wife and the mistress of his home. And she yearned for more now, too.

Feelings like the ones the knight aroused must surely be sinful. Just thinking about what had happened caused that hot, pulsing knot to tighten in her belly again, and she squirmed at the memory of Wolf's touch. *Rupert's* touch, she meant. It would be just the same with Rupert, even better, she told herself, when she was his wife.

Just before dawn, Kit climbed out the narrow window on the far side of the cottage. She sneaked around the corner, straining her eyes in the predawn light to see if anyone lurked about in the dark. Wolf was gone, so she grabbed her clothes and quickly ran back to what she considered to be the safe side of the cottage. She dressed quickly, then hastened back to her stepfather's house.

Although Lord Thomas Somers' house was large, Kit knew she would never be believed if she said she'd been inside all night. Not that her stepfather would care where she was all night; the only thing that mattered to him was that she keep his household running smoothly, and that she be there to take the blame when it did not. However, it would give him the excuse he needed to bring her to her knees, which seemed to be one of Lord Thomas' favorite pastimes. Anyway, Bridget would have torn the whole house apart looking for her, and Kit experienced a pang of guilt for causing her cousin trouble and concern. Bridget hadn't been in the best of health lately, though Kit was hard-pressed to put her finger on what was wrong.

She ran through the yard and into the stable. There were plenty of likely spots for a youth to sleep, and it wasn't the first time Kit had spent the night there with the horses.

The sun was high when the ruckus in the yard woke her. It would be the man from King Henry, no doubt, and here she was with nary a plan. Her heart jumped to her throat when she recognized the angrily booming voice. It was the voice of Wolf, the man at the lake. "Explain yourself, Somers!" he demanded. "Where is she?" There was no gentleness to his voice now, she thought, though he had used it like a caress last night.

Her stepfather staggered into the yard. Kit looked up toward the sun to gauge the time. It was not yet noon, but Lord Thomas had already imbibed too much. His clothes were rumpled and soiled, and he wore the stubble of the night's growth of beard. His face had taken on that look of meanness so familiar to Kit, and he could barely stand. No wonder the knight was impatient. He probably hadn't received an intelligible response from the baron since he'd arrived.

"She was here, I tell you, and I will get the twit back." Somers' eyes narrowed, and Kit recognized the signs of drunken vengeance. She didn't want to be caught by him while he was in this state.

"I will return in one hour," the knight said, his annoyance matching the baron's anger. "At that time, I will col-

lect young Kathryn and depart immediately. Have her here
and ready or suffer the consequences of Henry's wrath.''

Wolf turned and moved away with a grace that belied
his massive frame. He was every inch a soldier, and Kit
had a quick opportunity to study his face and body before
making her move. His features were sharply defined and
altogether too pleasing. Even a ghastly scar which ran from
the right upper corner of his forehead, slashing over his left
eye and into his left cheek did nothing to diminish his powerful magnetism. His cool gray eyes were hooded by thick
black brows, the thickness and darkness matching that of
his unruly mane.

Kit watched the man rake his hand through the dark hair
in frustration and knew she had to move quickly. She was
not about to be caught by any of her stepfather's men, nor
was she going to allow herself to be vulnerable to this Wolf
and his soldiers. She would hide and wait for Rupert, and
after he'd claimed her, only then would she deign to travel
to London to please the king. After all, if she left Baron
Somers' holding now, how would Rupert ever find her? For
he must certainly be on his way north to claim her.

Kit slipped out the back of the stable leading Old Myra,
a horse her stepfather had recently acquired from a neighboring estate. Kit hoped that with the proper encourage-
ment, Old Myra would head for home, some seventeen
miles east of Somerton, and Baron Somers' men would
follow the horse's trail. In the meantime, Kit had no intention of accompanying the mare to her former home.

Undetected, she led the horse down the hillside to the
cover of trees, pointed her eastwardly and gave her a good
crack on the rump. Old Myra took off as though she had a
bee under her bridle. And Kit ran as if she had one in her
britches as well, but in the opposite direction.

When she got closer to the village, she stopped to scoop
up a handful of dirt to smear on her arms and face. If any
of the baron's men happened by, she was certain she could
pass for one of the villagers. If not, the baron's retribution

would affect not only her, but the people of Somerton as well. With a sigh and a prayer, Kit moved swiftly through the woods, hoping that her ruse with old Myra would keep the baron's men off her track.

Unfortunately, Old Myra had plans of her own. After tearing away in the direction of her former home, she ran into an obstacle, a small creek which had swelled with the spring rains, and it caused her to turn back much sooner than Kit had hoped.

Without the diversion of Old Myra's trail, the baron's men found Kit easily. She thought she'd been so clever heading for Somerton village, never considering that the baron's retainers would go there first. Why couldn't Old Myra's trail have fooled them? Why hadn't she thought to climb into one of the trees and wait them out? They never would have looked for her in the high boughs that were so familiar to her.

Kit was outdone, but only for the moment. It was a long way to London, she thought as they dragged her roughly back to the house. Plenty could happen before she reached the city, and Kit vowed to work out some plan that would enable her to rendezvous with Rupert.

"Oh, my child, my wee girl," Bridget wailed as Kit was dragged into the courtyard. The baron's men were unduly rough with her, especially in view of the fact that she had acceded to them. "I've been so worried, not knowing—"

"Hush, woman!" Lady Edith admonished angrily. This business with her stepdaughter had disrupted her life enough without having to listen to the rantings of Kathryn's deranged cousin. She turned to Kit. "I see you've outfitted yourself as becomes your station, Kathryn."

Margery and Eleanor snickered behind their hands.

Kit gulped. She knew she was a mess, but she refused to improve upon her present appearance for the benefit of Lady Edith or anyone else, for that matter. She straightened her back and drew herself up proudly. Her pride and her sense of humor were about the only two things they hadn't taken from her. She bolstered her courage by thinking of Rupert and how he would come to take her away. If only her true father had lived, he would have protected her, cherished—

"Where is the little wretch?" Lord Thomas drawled, coming into the yard. As he came around the corner and saw Kit, a cruel gleam entered his eye. The baron's men recognized Lord Thomas' mood at once and made no move to help or protect Kit. She had refused each of their attentions too many times to expect help from any of them.

Kit refused to cower, even when Baron Somers lashed out and backhanded her across the face. The blow split her lower lip and sent her to the ground, but she got to her feet immediately and began to run. It was disheartening to hear the cruel laughter behind her, then the footsteps following, gaining on her. They were going to play with her the way a cat teased its prey. It was not a new game, chasing her about the yard, letting her wear herself out, then dragging her back to the baron for whatever brutality he had in mind. Kit wouldn't have played along willingly, but the instincts to escape, to protect herself were too strong.

This time, the baron only blackened her eye, though the blow knocked her senseless. Someone dragged her to her room and locked her in. It was several minutes before Kit regained her senses.

"Oh, darlin' girl," Bridget cooed, tears streaming down her face. "What has he done to ye this time? If my Meghan were livin' none o' this would be happenin'."

Kit opened her right eye, the unswollen one, to see Bridget's little face looming over her. "What happened?" she whispered. It hurt to move her lips and when she pressed her fingers to them, she knew why. Dark blood still oozed from the gash Thomas inflicted.

"Ye must go with the king's men," the old nurse said. "At least ye'll be away from the devil baron. Ye'll be safe from his infernal temper for once."

"But Rupert—"

"Rupert won't be comin' back, don't ye know? Can't ye understand?" Bridget argued, exasperated. Frustrated. She'd tried to convince her young charge of this over and over again. "Sure and I love the lad, but he's been gone too long. He can't expect ye to be waitin' for him still, with nary a word in three years. The only way we've heard about him has been from the few travelers who've—"

"Oh, Bridget, my head hurts." She didn't want to think about Rupert not returning for her. Nor did she want to think about Wolf coming to take her away.

"He knocked ye good this time. Come, lass. Ye must trust in Monmouth. King Henry Hereford's son can't mean ye any harm. The father was just, and ye've heard as well as I that the son is a righteous man."

Bridget helped Meghan's daughter to get up.

Kit looked askance at Bridget. Her reasoning was sound, but Kit's heart leapt to her throat nonetheless, when she heard riders approach the manor house.

Wolfram ducked to clear the door frame and enter Baron Somers' house. A cheerful fire burned on the hearth and Wolf spied the baron sitting on a large, comfortable chair nearby, drinking from a wooden goblet. Four cronies lounged about, also drinking. None of them rose in respect due an emissary from the King.

"Come in, sir," Lady Edith said as she led Wolf and three of his men to the group.

"I trust you've found the girl."

"She's with her nurse and won't come down." The baron's speech was much more slurred than it had been earlier in the day. He rubbed his sore knuckles conspicuously as he spoke.

"Then I suggest you get her." He had no desire to drag a tearful child from the arms of her nurse. It would be much better for one of her stepparents to fetch her. Baron Thomas looked to his wife for assistance, but she backed away in protest.

"Ungrateful little witch—she won't obey me," Edith protested. "Never has. I won't go."

"Doubt she'd come with me..." the Baron remarked, smirking.

Wolf's patience snapped. He'd been going round in circles with these people long enough. By the almighty, if they wouldn't get the girl, he'd fetch her himself, regardless of the consequences. He headed toward the stairs and took them two at a time. "Which room!" he called back angrily. One of them damned well better answer, he thought.

"Third on the right," came the lazy reply from the baron. "But you might need..." But Wolf had already stormed down the passageway, "...the key."

The bloody door was locked! He'd be damned if he'd go back there and ask anything else of that drunkard downstairs. He put his shoulder to the stout wooden door and crashed it into the room.

Wolf looked around, but all he saw was a skinny old woman cowering in a corner and a filthy lad whose lip was torn and bleeding. One of his eyes was blackened and swollen shut. There was no girl child here. The miserable baron had lied to him! He was going to have to go round again with that fool!

"Where is she?" he roared. He thought he heard laughter from below.

The battered boy moved towards Wolf. His worn, brown hat was pulled down low over his forehead, completely covering his hair. Wolf noticed that the undamaged eye was an uncommonly beautiful shade of moss green, fringed in thick dark-brown lashes, and threatening to run over with tears. The boy blinked several times to clear his vision, and Wolfram didn't miss his slight wince of pain.

"I am Kathryn."

Wolf glanced around the room, certain he had mistaken his own hearing. He could have sworn it was the *lad* who'd said he was Kathryn. His voice was pleasing, with a huskiness to it that could only be...a girl's.

"'Tis true, sir," the old woman said in a weak voice. "She is. I've packed her things into these two satchels."

"You?" Wolfram was astonished. Henry hadn't told him exactly what to expect when he arrived, but it certainly wasn't this. A dainty little miss, perhaps, but not this. Not a grubby, battered urchin.

He looked around the room once again. It was bare of furniture, with only a mattress stuffed with straw in a corner of the room. Fresh rushes were on the floor, though and a pleasing, spicy scent emanated from them. Fresh flowers stood in a large clay pot underneath the window, and a wooden crucifix hung on the wall over the mattress. He wondered if this young…person was responsible for the appearance of the main hall. Wolf thought it likely since no one down there seemed to be minutely capable. Even in her stark surroundings, this young Kathryn had made a cozy haven for herself in what seemed to be otherwise hostile territory.

A vague understanding of the girl's situation presented itself to his mind, and Wolf realized he wouldn't mind the opportunity to lay the girl's stepfather flat. For God's sake, if the lousy drunkard couldn't stand to have her about, why didn't he marry her off?

"I have but one request, sir," Kit said. She lifted her chin proudly, obviously having difficulty in asking a favor. "That my nurse accompany us. She has always been with me and since the death of my mother—"

"As you wish," he said abruptly. He wanted to get away from Baron Somers' holding as soon as possible, even if it meant having an additional burden. "Gather your things, woman. You have little time."

"Patience, sir knight," the girl said, looking him directly in the eyes. "A few moments more will hardly matter."

He didn't leave them alone for a minute. If the baron battered the girl any more, their trip would be delayed indefinitely. Besides, Wolf didn't want her to disappear again. From the ragtag look about her, she might just manage to

elude them the next time. He was unsure whether it was
she or the baron who resisted answering Henry's summons,
but he was not about to take any chances. He would get
her to London if he had to bind her to her horse.

As it happened, Baron Somers refused to release a horse
for Kathryn's use. Wolf was ill-disposed to beg and as he
had intended to carry the child Kathryn before him on his
mount anyway, he reverted to his original plan. She was a
bit older than he'd assumed, but his warhorse, Janus, could
bear both their weights and more. In due time, old Bridget
was mounted on a packhorse and finally brought up the
rear with two of Wolf's knights flanking her.

"I can't imagine what the king wants with such a worth-
less, filthy ragamuffin," Lady Edith remarked, loud enough
for Kit to hear.

Wolf felt her body stiffen, but the girl made no reply to
her stepmother's intentionally unkind remark.

Baron Somers lumbered out in the bright sunlight and
leaned against the door frame of the manor house next to
his wife. He shrugged and squinted against the bright sunlight and watched the departure of the king's party.

"I want 'er back!" he called.

Kit felt Wolf grunt a negative reply, obviously not intended for the Baron's ears.

"You hear me?" Somers slurred. "When the king's
through with 'er I want 'er back! Need the brat to run the
place."

It was well past the noon hour when they finally departed
Somerton. Wolf hoped that when King Henry had finished
his business with Lady Kathryn, he'd not be the one responsible for returning her to Baron Somers.

Chapter Two

"You may loosen your grip, sir knight," Kit fumed. "Your mount's back is as broad as a barge. I don't see how you could possibly think I might fall."

Kit had never been wedged quite so intimately between a man's thighs before. It was a disturbing experience but she ached so very badly and was so weary from the long, sleepless night in the cottage, that she actually leaned back against Wolf's hauberk. He loosened his grip nominally and grunted his displeasure.

She knew she had to be wary of him. He was a *man* after all, and she'd had plenty of experience with the men of Baron Somers' entourage. Besides, Wolf was the one who'd taken advantage of her the night before.

It was reassuring to know that Wolf didn't recognize her as the nymph at the lake. She decided it would be easy, as well as prudent to keep up her disguise all the way to London. She was aware of the value of being a filthy, unattractive urchin, as opposed to a clean, well-groomed young lady. Her stepfather and his ornery men had taught her that lesson one rainy afternoon several years before. By sheer luck, Lady Edith had arrived and inadvertently interrupted the incident. Kit had come out of it unscathed and far wiser.

She hated to admit that it wasn't unpleasant to have the knight's strong arms around her now, even if he did hold her too tightly. She might even allow herself to believe he felt a bit protective of her—something no one had ever felt before. It was a strange sensation, imagining someone caring for her.

As they rode, she wondered what King Henry wanted with her, a homely, countrified girl of Northumberland. The king had been so busy fighting the French and gaining a French wife, she couldn't imagine how he would even know of her existence, much less have the time or inclination to think of her.

All Kit knew of her own background was that her true father had died before her birth. Her mother was Meghan, daughter of Trevor Russell, the late Earl of Meath in Ireland. How her mother had come to be married to Thomas Somers was beyond Kathryn's knowledge, but somehow it had happened and Kit had become the man's daughter. She had vague recollections of Lord Somers before Meghan's death, and the baron hadn't seemed so slovenly or brutal then. In fact, it was only after the baron married Lady Edith and had daughters of his own, that the baron had started drinking overmuch. And Kit's life had begun to deteriorate.

In view of Kit's existence up to now, she couldn't understand the sovereign's reason for having her brought to London. Bridget seemed particularly certain that the best course for Kit was to follow the king's command and to put Rupert Aires and Somerton behind her. The old nurse desperately wished for a change of circumstances for her young charge.

Kit hadn't seen a mirror in years, and she was well aware she did not possess a comely face. Edith and her daughters made certain that Kit knew their opinion of each and every one of her features and flaws, from the miserable devil's dent in her "too strong" chin to her hair—"lacking in color, just like the hay in the fields," though it was curly and absolutely unruly. The rest of the Somers family towered over her, and they made it clear they thought her small stature inferior to their height. Her eyes were too green and her skin as pale as the thick cream they skimmed off the top of the bucket. Thanks to her stepfamily, she knew there was nothing right about her. No wonder Rupert hadn't come for her yet. But he would, Kit reassured herself. He would.

Homely as she was, the servants liked her and did her bidding easily. Kathryn became accustomed to running the household since her stepmother had no interest in it. Kit had a good memory and an even better head for figures, which served her well in handling her stepfather's accounts. When the baron's steward had died three years before, Kit stepped in to deal with the income from the demesne and to oversee the peasants' workweeks. It became unnecessary for Lord Thomas to replace the steward, and Kit realized the value of being needed. She consciously worked to become essential to Baron Somers.

She hoped that if he needed her badly enough, he wouldn't kill her in a drunken rage.

As well as her unusual academic skills, Kit also learned a great deal about healing plants and herbs from one of the monks who came to Somerton regularly to trade for the abbey. In fact, Kit maintained a garden of medicinal plants, right beside her precious rose arbor. She often went with Brother Theodore on his healing missions among the villein and townspeople at Somerton and developed considerable skill in the medicinal arts.

Bridget decried Kit's favorite pastimes. Kit loved to ride her horse *astride,* wearing breeches. Nothing was more invigorating than racing horseback through the meadows and feeling the wind on her face and in her hair. She enjoyed shooting her sling or her arrows and testing her skill against that of the huntsmen in Lord Thomas' forest. To Bridget's severe disapproval, Kit climbed the trees in the forest and sometimes lay across the branches high above the lake to watch the reflections of the clouds as they played across the surface of the water.

* * *

Wolf guessed she was asleep. Her back was slumped into his chest, and he'd been supporting her for several miles to keep her from sliding off Janus. Wolf considered how old she might be. Sixteen perhaps? The damnable rags she wore made it impossible to discern whether her figure was that of a child or a woman. Certainly old enough to be married, though why wasn't she? The situation with Baron Somers and his family was obviously not good for the girl, yet she'd remained at Somerton with her stepparents.

The flaw must be her lack of feminine abilities. Her mode of dress was appalling for a maiden. Why, he'd never seen a lady gotten up in such rough woolen breeches and tunic before. Looking at her now, he couldn't fathom whether Kathryn had been guilty of provoking Baron Somers into beating her, or if the man merely gained some perverse pleasure from mistreating the girl. Wolfram gave Kathryn the benefit of the doubt and faulted Lord Thomas with an overblown temper. Wolf never did hold with drunken men who beat women or children, and he couldn't deny his satisfaction in removing young Kathryn from the baron's vicious clutches. Let the man, and others of his ilk, come to blows with men their own size.

Lady Kathryn, however, was obviously no saint. She was altogether too independent for a lass. How she'd managed to run away from him twice was impossible to understand. The girl was demanding, insisting on bringing her old nurse and giving orders to his men as though she were in charge. She was worse than filthy...yet she didn't smell like any wayward urchin he'd ever had the misfortune to be downwind of. In fact, she smelled like flowers. Roses, he thought, though he was no expert at horticulture. Her scent was fresh, he realized uncomfortably, perhaps it was even womanly.

The girl moved slightly, causing her hips to press more closely, and his thoughts turned to his experience at the lake the previous night. Wolf shifted Kathryn's weight as he recalled the beautiful golden woman he'd only just tasted.

He reminded himself that he was a man with a mission. He had to concentrate fully in order to regain Windermere, as he'd set out to do. He'd been in Henry's service for several years now, and gained the king's respect and trust. Now, all that was left was to find hard, physical evidence of Philip Colston's treachery. Henry would then be compelled to accept Wolf's claim and restore Windermere and his good name to him.

Even so resolved, Wolfram couldn't deny that he'd been strongly affected by the woman at the lake. She was every dream he had ever suppressed, every yearning he had ever denied. But Wolf well knew the pain of loving and losing, and he vowed never to fall into that trap again. He'd lost his brother and his father to fate. And while those losses and Wolf's drive for justice gave him a cold, reserved self-possession, it was his mother's apathy that had tormented his soul over the years.

Wolf had survived the fatal attack, but Margrethe Colston hadn't spoken to him in twenty years. She hadn't even acknowledged his existence. It didn't matter that she was beyond response, incapable of speaking to anyone—it was the fact that Wolf's survival hadn't given her even a glimmer of hope. Wolf's life had meant nothing to her.

"Gerhart."

Though she dozed comfortably as they rode, Kit heard a rough voice as one of the soldiers rode abreast of them. She saw no reason to make them aware that she was awake, which she barely was, anyway. She needed to think about getting away and returning to wait for Rupert somewhere near Somerton. Kit tried to keep track of their progress so she'd be able to find her direction when the time came. However, it was difficult to pay attention because she was so drowsy, her head ached and her eye socket throbbed abominably.

''It will be dark soon,'' the man said, speaking to the man she knew as ''Wolf.'' Kit wondered why the soldier called him ''Gerhart.'' ''The old woman is nearly falling off her mount.'' His words were strangely accented, though not unpleasant to Kit's ear. He was a tall man, quite powerful in the saddle, and he was as blond as Wolf was dark.

Kit repressed the urge to turn and see how Bridget fared. Wolf didn't respond to the soldier immediately, and Kit wondered if he was trying to decide whether or not to let her old nurse fall by the wayside.

''We'll stop soon,'' Wolf finally said. ''Send two men ahead to scout a likely campsite.''

Kit felt a long sigh escape the man. He must be in a terrible hurry to get to London to be so irritated by this slight delay. Didn't knights need to rest, too? Weren't they hungry as well? She felt his arms tighten securely around her. In contradiction to her thoughts, Wolf didn't seem weary at all. She thought he must have the stamina of a workhorse. Kit was weary, though, and while her spirit was tenacious, she knew she couldn't keep up with this Wolf. At least not now.

It seemed so safe and secure in his arms that Kit snuggled back into him. Maybe later she would think about escaping to get back where Rupert could find her. She dozed off again until some time later when Wolf spoke.

''There was a woman last night at Somerton.''

At first, Kit was astonished, thinking he'd spoken to her. But before she could reply, she realized that the man who had addressed Wolf before was riding next to them again.

''*Ja?*'' the man replied. Kit wanted to get a better look at him. She continued to feign sleep instead.

''After we get the girl to London and I settle with Philip, I'm going back to find her.''

''Who is the woman?''

''I don't know. But she was…interesting. Intriguing.'' Wolf seemed at a loss for words.

The man laughed. ''I've never seen you quite

so...*intrigued,* Cousin." He waited for Wolf to explain but got no response. "Ladies have fallen at your feet for years yet you—"

"Not this time," Wolf interrupted. "It was strange. She was...different." Kit could hear puzzlement in his voice. She experienced an odd sense of satisfaction as a result of her effect on him. She couldn't think of any man, other than Rupert, who had ever found her interesting, much less intriguing. On the other hand, the thought of Wolf coming back to Somerton for her was alarming. He was not a gentle or charming man like her Rupert.

"What was her name?"

"She wouldn't say."

"That's promising." Through her lashes, Kit saw the man's eyebrow go up. "I'll assume it wasn't the charming and seductive Lady Edith."

"Hmph." Kit felt the sound he emitted, more than heard it.

"It's likely to be months before we finish our business, Gerhart," the man said with amusement. "Do you suppose she'll be waiting for you?"

"What difference whether she waits or not? She'll be mine," replied Wolf with utmost confidence, and Kit's sense of satisfaction vanished. How dare he assume she would fall at his feet when he arrived?

She gritted her teeth to master her irritation and refrained from speaking out. The conceit of the man was unsurpassed. Why, the man thought that because he'd kissed her once, he could begin to think of owning her. He didn't even know her! And he wasn't going to know her, either, she promised herself.

"And you say you don't know who she is?"

"Nay, Nicholas, she would give me no name."

"Mayhap if you described the woman, your little Lady Kathryn could name her."

"Mayhap."

His Lady Kathryn! How many women was this wolf allowed? Kit reined in an urge to slam her elbow into the man's gut. But she knew he wore an iron hauberk, and she would only bruise herself.

"I think it best you keep your thoughts on Windermere and not on a prospective wife. Besides, there is Lady Annegret. When you wed her—"

"Wife?" Wolf laughed coldly. "I made no mention of a wife."

Nicholas chuckled, and Kit was infuriated. When he found out she was the woman at the lake, he'd... Kit resolved never to give him half a bloody chance to discover who she was.

"Ah, Lady Kathryn awakens," Nicholas announced as Kit moved restlessly. She was so angry, she was unable to pretend to sleep any longer. "Did you rest well, my lady?"

"Tolerably."

"Your voice—it is difficult to tell much about you under that layer of dirt and those rags you wear—but your voice seems not to be that of a child. We thought we'd been sent to collect a child." Nicholas looked at her more closely, trying to discern her features beyond the filth and bruises.

"You are correct. I am not a child." She couldn't mask an irritable tone as she gazed at the handsome warrior who rode alongside.

"And you expect us to believe you are fully grown?" Wolf asked in laughing disbelief.

"I don't expect anything from you," Kit shot back angrily. "Except an unwanted trip to London."

"Ach, so the journey riles you?" Nicholas laughed.

"How is Bridget? She must be near to collapsing. She is unused to riding."

"The old woman is weary," Nicholas replied. "We'll stop shortly for the night."

"How do you intend to keep us safe the night through? It is said to be dangerous traveling these roads—"

"Please, my *lady*," Wolf's tone mocked her, "nine of

my men are here and would be loath to hear you malign their talents so.''

"*Nine!* You have only nine?''

"Our number will be sufficient. Now cease. Enough of this prattle.''

Kit bristled with the resentment of having this crass brute in charge of her person. He had no right to order her about. And she didn't care much for the way he scowled at her, either.

A short time later, when they came over a grassy hill, they spotted the two men who had been sent ahead to seek a sheltered spot to camp for the night. They had already scouted out a likely area and a small fire was crackling merrily in the clearing.

It was with great relief that Kit dismounted and went to help Bridget. The old woman was bone weary and though she was not usually particularly quiet about her aches and pains, she was more circumspect than usual tonight. The two women wandered off to the trees to take care of their personal needs and while there, found a stream with cool, fresh water. They stopped to drink their fill.

"Ooch, yer eye, child,'' Bridget said, taking a good look at Kit's face. "Let me wash it for ye.''

"Nay, Bridget. I prefer to remain filthy as a vagabond whilst we're in the company of these clods of Henry's.''

"Clods ye say?''

"Clods, Bridget. Boorish clods.''

"Oh, of course. Ye, dearie, having been to France and to court and so many fashionable places, would recognize a boor instantly, I suppose.''

"Don't tease, Bridget. It takes little experience and less brains to know this man—''

"Who? Sir Gerhart? The leader?''

"What do you know of him?''

"Well, Sir Clarence and Sir Alfred talked a wee bit,'' Bridget said as she stretched her aching back, "to keep me awake and astride that beast, I think. They said a few things…''

''For example?''

''*For example,*'' Bridget's ire was up, and Kit knew she was testing the old woman's patience, ''Alfred said that Sir Gerhart and his cousin Sir Nicholas are the grandsons of some German prince—''

''Ha!''

''—though Gerhart also has some obscure English ties. The two of them have been invaluable to King Henry and 'tis rumored that they'll be given titles and estates upon their return to London.''

''I can guess just who started that rumor.''

''''Tis not like ye to be so disrespectful, Kitty.''

''''Tis not like *you* to swallow such a yarn, Bridget.'' Kit started walking back to camp. ''They're naught but common soldiers, come to take me to London, and *the reason why* is the only obscurity here. The rest is perfectly clear.''

Bridget shook her head dubiously.

''Also clear is the fact that Rupert will never be able to find me now, and I intend to remedy that situation as soon as possible.''

''And how do ye propose to do it?''

''I don't know yet. Just promise not to worry about me,'' Kit said.

Darkness fell slowly, by degrees. They'd eaten a meal consisting entirely of dried meat and when through, the men scattered about the fire to find comfortable places to spend the night. Wolfram backed up to a tree, wrapped himself in his cloak and closed his eyes. He could hear the regular, even snores of the woman, and he knew the girl hadn't moved in ages.

As he was about to doze off, Wolf caught sight of a slight movement from the other side of the fire. It was the girl, and she had turned over. Now she was quiet. Too quiet. And her position didn't seem to be an entirely comfortable one for sleep. Wolf could see that she was holding her breath. The idiot was going to make a move. He was completely alert instantaneously.

She eased herself up in stages, looking around to see if her movements disturbed any of the men. If they did, none of them, not even those on watch, showed any signs of it. Finally, she was on her feet, crouched down, near to the ground. She backed away from the campsite until she was completely in the dark, then stood and ran.

Wolf was up in a second. He couldn't believe the girl's foolishness. Where in blazes did she think she was going? He signaled to the men on watch to remain in place, then traced the girl's path through the woods silently.

Wolf increased his speed when he heard a loud thud and a muffled shriek. He had orders to get the girl to London in one piece, and she seemed intent on making that simple task a difficult one. It was so dark that Wolf had a hard time seeing down the shallow gorge into which she'd fallen, even though he knew he stood on the brink, towering over her. Kathryn was definitely down there, still unaware of his presence, and he listened to the disparaging sounds she made under her breath. He couldn't help being vaguely amused by her cursing.

"Ow!" She tried to stand, but her ankle wouldn't bear her weight and she fell again. "Damnation!" the lady muttered. "By all the martyred saints, my eye, my lip *and* my bloody ankle are ruined. Now I'll never—"

"Let me see your ankle," Wolfram said as he stooped down next to her. She squealed and jumped half out of her skin when he spoke. "Easy, now. It's only me."

"*Only* you? You're the last person I wanted to see," she cried. He smiled at her blunt honesty. Not much like the ladies he'd known at court, he thought, but she was still young. She'd learn.

"Probably a sprain," he said gruffly as he pressed the ankle. She winced in pain. "It's already begun to swell."

Kit groaned.

"What did you expect?" She was certain she heard irritation in his voice. He slid one arm under her legs and the other behind her back, then picked her up. She was a bit surprised that he didn't just throw her over his shoulder like a sack of rags. "You can't tear through the woods at breakneck speed in the dark and not expect disaster. Especially a *woman,* and one as obviously inexperienced as you."

"Oh, *really?*" she remarked disdainfully, refusing to allow him to gloat.

Wolf felt the girl tighten her grip around his neck as he moved quickly through the woods. He realized he was intentionally showing her up, demonstrating how perfectly he could move in the dark without mishap. The girl had grit, and he admitted to a grudging admiration of her spunk in spite of the fact that, but for her, he would still be wrapped up warmly in his cloak, asleep. As her fingers moved around the back of his neck, the bizarre thought occurred to him that her scent was every bit as fresh and appealing as it had been earlier in the day as she rode with him. The thought nearly made him drop her.

"Slow down, Gerhart!" Kit commanded harshly. "I have no wish to sprain the other ankle."

"As you command, *my lady.*" She was damned confident. And impudent.

No one spoke as Gerhart sat down where he'd been before, with his back against a tree, pulling Lady Kathryn into his lap. She turned to move away, but found his grip on her wrists like iron manacles. His silvery eyes bored through her, allowing for no further mischief.

"You will remain close to me for the night."

Kit gasped, but kept her voice low. "You cannot be serious! It is entirely improper!"

"No less proper than allowing you to run off and kill yourself falling into a ditch somewhere."

He gathered his cloak around them both and lay his head

back. He pulled Kit's head against his chest and let her bottom slide to the ground between his thighs. She was much softer than she had seemed before. Perhaps she really was full-grown as she'd implied, and not some hell-bent adolescent.

"By all the bloody saints, I'll not stay here!" She tried to get up, but Wolf pulled her down by the waist until she was nose to nose and breast to breast with him.

"You will." His teeth were clenched tightly.

Wolf forced his attention on her dirty, bruised, misshapen face because a pair of unmistakably, disturbingly mature breasts were pressing into the soft wool of his tunic. He could actually feel her nipples harden against his chest. His body threatened to mutiny against his better judgment, so he forced himself to concentrate on her obstinate, unpleasant temperament.

He was a man of discipline and discerning tastes. He was certainly not in need of this unruly, undisciplined, unappealing, filthy urchin. He had never been one to take a woman just for the sake of having one, and he knew he could do much better when he returned to find the woman of the lake. And soon, he supposed, there would be Annegret. Certainly, he had no need of this overdeveloped adolescent who was determined to cause herself harm.

Kit slid back into place. Her face hurt, her shoulder and hip throbbed from her fall and now her ankle felt as though it was on fire. She lost all interest in having it out with King Henry's knight. Besides, the damnable brute wouldn't loosen his grip. In spite of him, and to his surprise, Lady Kathryn pulled her hood over her ragged hat and fell asleep.

Chapter Three

Wolfram slept little. Lady Kathryn managed to curl herself up like a kitten and sleep soundly through the night. However, her movements, her little sighs and groans and the way she pulled at his cloak all night prevented him from sleeping much. What was it the old woman had called her? "Kitty?" It suited her. He could almost hear her purr in comfort as she tangled herself up on his lap. No, he hadn't slept much at all.

It started raining around noon and Wolf's mood, which was already foul, didn't improve any. Wolf paced the troop so the old woman could easily keep up, but he saw that she was having difficulty nonetheless. "Nicholas."

Wolf's cousin was drawn out of his own sodden thoughts and looked up.

"See to her." Wolfram gave a nod of his head indicating the rear of the train.

Kit moved so she could peer around Wolf's back and saw Nicholas take Bridget up with him on his mount. He settled her in front and pulled his cloak over them both, so she could ride as comfortably as possible. Kit would have thanked Wolf for his kindness toward Bridget except for the fierce look in his deep gray eyes. The man certainly was moody, and she didn't want to set him off. As it was, she was grateful to be securely situated in front of him with his thick cloak covering them and enough heat generated from his body to warm them both. The all-pervading smell of wet horse, wet wool and wet leather was strangely quieting.

The light drizzle turned to rain and still they went on through the hills towards Cumbria. Kit had difficulty understanding why they were veering west since she knew the direction to London was to the south and a bit east.

"You realize you've been taking us in the wrong direction for hours, Gerhart?" She used the name all the men called him and not "Wolf."

His reply was merely a rude grunt.

"I thought you were taking me to London," she said. "Had my stepfather known of this detour, I doubt he would have permitted me to come traipsing around the entire countryside with you and your soldiers."

"He's a good one for seeing to your welfare, isn't he?" The sarcasm wasn't lost on Kit. However, she had her pride and refused to allow him to think that she had been raised as anything less than a lady.

"He promised my mother he would care for me like his own daughter. He has provided well for me—"

"He beats his own offspring as well, then?"

Kit refused to allow him to humiliate her, so she shrugged and did not answer.

"How old are you?"

Kit hesitated before replying. She was somewhat advanced in age to be unmarried, and it was embarrassing. She wanted to lie but couldn't bring herself to sin outright.

"Twenty," she finally admitted.

"Why aren't you wed? Or at least betrothed?" He had no doubt that Baron Somers would have difficulty finding anyone willing to take on this unkempt urchin who probably had no feminine skills at all. Nonetheless, he couldn't see the sense in keeping her around Somerton manor when she obviously irritated the baron to the point of violence.

"I am betrothed! Well, nearly so, I mean."

"What, some local swain has begged for your hand?" The incredulous sound to his voice angered her. He acted as if she were completely unmarriageable! What did the big oaf know of it?

"It just so happens that he is one of King Henry's guard!" she snapped angrily.

"Who?" Wolf demanded. He knew all of them.

"Rupert Aires."

Wolf laughed out loud. Rupert Aires was a young, handsome knight in Henry's service, well known for his amorous adventures with the ladies of the court. He was always embroiled in one escapade or another. Surely Kathryn was mistaken about a future betrothal to him. His loyalty to Henry was unquestioned, but otherwise the fellow was a scoundrel. An unprincipled skirt chaser.

"I don't suppose you know him?"

"Of course I know him." His voice was irritable again.

"Well...?"

"He is a competent soldier."

"Is that all?" Kit's voice rose with indignation. "A competent soldier? We've heard tales in Northumberland about Rupert's bravery in battle, his prowess with—"

"Has Sir Rupert ever seen your face?"

"What has that to do with anything? Naturally he's seen my face. We grew up together. We—"

"I mean without that amusing coating of grime."

"What coating of—? Oh." She raised her chin a notch. "Rupert knows me as well as he knows his sisters."

Another rude grunt.

"Rupert told me that as soon as he's given leave from court, he'll come for me. Don't you see, Gerhart?" she asked earnestly. "That's the reason I had to try to get back to Somerton. Rupert won't be able to find me if I'm away from home. He's the only reason I had for staying." She turned to look at him and found his face only inches from hers. He was scowling again, but Kit couldn't help but notice how beautiful his gray eyes were, framed in thick black lashes. The realization was unsettling. Her gaze dropped to his mouth.

''We're going to the king, Lady Kathryn. Don't you suppose you'll see Sir Rupert in London?'' Gerhart's voice was harsh. He didn't like having her unwavering gaze trained on him. She was too direct for a woman and her eyes, at least the uninjured one, were altogether too distracting.

Kit shook her head and looked away. ''I don't have any idea how to find him. By all accounts, London is huge and Rupert might even now be on his way to Somerton for me.''

At least it was an explanation for the previous night's misadventure, although it riled him unexplainably. Somehow, it didn't seem fair that Lady Kathryn should be fretting and risking her neck over Rupert Aires, a man who had some of the most beautiful, as well as the most faithless women in England at his beck and call.

If Aires had some commitment to Kathryn Somers, he had a fine way of showing it. Wolf knew that all of Henry's guards had been given liberal leaves upon their return from France two months ago. Apparently Aires hadn't seen fit to travel to Somerton to claim his bride. Perhaps if he had, Henry wouldn't have deemed it necessary to send Wolf all the way to the north country to collect this naive chit of a girl.

''None of Henry's guard are on leave now,'' he offered. He wasn't certain that was true, but if it reassured Lady Kathryn so that she'd quit trying to run back to Somerton, the small lie was well worth it.

''Are you sure?''

''Relatively.''

''That's a relief,'' she said. ''Now I'll just have to think of a way to find him when we reach London. *If* ever we reach London. You still haven't told me why we are not heading south.''

''We're not going directly to London.''

"We're not? Where are you taking me?"

He was not accustomed to being questioned by anyone, particularly a ragged, impertinent, insignificant girl. He let out an irritated sigh and gave her a curt response. "Windermere Castle."

"Windermere! But that's in Cumbria! *Miles* out of our way!"

"Thank you, my lady, I am very familiar with the location of Windermere—"

"But that will take ages. And Rupert—"

"I'm beginning to see merit in Baron Somers' disciplinary methods."

"Why didn't you go to Cumbria first and come for me last?" Kit's exasperation, at the very least, matched Wolf's.

"Because that would have contradicted my orders."

"Why?"

"The king was quite specific. He wanted you in my custody as soon as possible."

"But why?"

"Take a nap." Kit didn't mistake his gruff tone nor his now-familiar scowl, and knew their discussion was at an end.

"But, Sir Gerhart—" She persisted.

His gaze hardened, and Kit realized she'd have to leave her questions for another time. She had no interest in testing whether Wolf really thought Baron Thomas was justified in beating her.

Their timing was worse than Wolf thought. The group still hadn't reached Windermere Castle and night was falling fast in the rain. It was easy to see that the old woman wouldn't last much longer, so he sent a couple of the men ahead to search out a sheltered spot to camp for the night. The scouts rode quickly out of the soggy dale and over the hill, out of sight.

It was completely dark when Wolf and his company caught up to the scouts who had found a small inn called the Crooked Ax, at the edge of a tiny village. There were three rooms available, and Wolf's men engaged them. There was also a hot meal to be had in the common room, for which Kit was grateful, since the dried meat they'd been eating did little to satisfy her hunger pangs. She also hoped that the roast fowl as well as the bread and cheese would help to cheer poor Bridget, who was definitely the worse for wear.

Kit's ankle caused only minor discomfort when she walked, giving her to believe it was merely bruised, and not sprained as Wolf had said. The long day spent sitting in the saddle, off her feet, did much to speed the healing process. She was able to climb the stairs carefully after supper and get Bridget settled to bed. The old woman's voice was raspy, and her breathing sounded congested as a result of the long hours exposed to the cold damp air.

"Wash the mud off yer face," Bridget said when they'd reached their room. "If only ye could see yerself, lass. It's runnin' down in streaks. 'Tis unseemly for a lady of quality to go about in such filth."

"I don't want to look like a lady, Bridget."

"And why not, I'll be askin'?"

"The less everyone knows about me, the better."

"I suppose by that ye'll be meanin' the grandsons of the prince?"

Kit rolled her eyes and turned away as the old woman washed her own face in the shallow basin provided.

"Grandsons or no, Rupert's waiting for me in London." She turned back to Bridget just as the old woman was seized by a coughing attack. Kit immediately felt guilty for riling her.

"I won't be askin' ye to put on any o' the gowns I brought for ye, but would ye mind just cleanin' up a bit and lettin' me have a look at yer eye and yer lip? It'll do ye no good to have either one festerin' under all that filth."

Kit gave up and gingerly washed her face. The gash at her mouth hardly bothered her at all but the eye still hurt dreadfully. It wasn't swollen so much anymore, but the bruise had turned to a deep purple with an outer perimeter of green.

"Sure and it matches the color of yer eyes," Bridget joked about the discoloration. She gave Kit a brief hug about the shoulders. "Ye don't know how glad I am that we're away from Baron Thomas and his wife. That man—"

"Yes, we're away," Kit started, returning the old woman's brief hug. She wanted to talk about this trip to London and somehow sensed that her kinswoman might have an answer to her question. "Bridget, dear old mother, why do you think King Henry sent for me?"

Bridget looked directly at Kit and was about to answer, then turned away. "I...I'm not sure as I know, Kitty. Mayhap he knew yer parents, one or t'other."

"Why do I have a suspicion that you know more than you're telling?"

"Ye've a suspicious nature is all, I suppose." Bridget turned away, seemingly peeved with her young charge.

Kit had asked plenty of questions about her parents before, yet hadn't ever received a satisfactory answer. She knew she wouldn't get one now.

By morning, the rain had let up to a steady drizzle and Kit decided, with a shiver, that she would not proceed another mile until Bridget was better able to travel. The old woman had been up coughing most of the night, and Kit knew she didn't feel at all well. Kit braided her hair tightly and pulled the old brown hat down low on her forehead, covering her hair completely. She ordered Bridget to stay abed, then she wrapped herself up in her short cloak and went out in search of breakfast.

Though she knew the men had split up between two of the three rooms they'd let, Kit saw none of them about now. The only person in sight was the innkeeper's wife, who greeted Kit stiffly, obviously unimpressed with her rough appearance.

It mattered not. All Kit wanted was a bit of porridge for herself and Bridget and to find out where Wolf had gone. She needed to talk to him before he decided on his course for the day.

"Sir Gerhart is in the stables," the woman informed her curtly. Her manner clearly indicated that if it had been her place, she would have advised the powerful knight to leave the ragged girl somewhere.

Kit paid no attention to the slight. She just wanted to talk to Wolf as soon as possible.

Wolf pulled Janus' cinch tight and dropped the stirrup back over his steed's side. When he looked up, he saw Lady Kathryn approaching. At least he thought it must be Kathryn, though he couldn't be sure for her face was clean.

Except for an ugly bruise around her eye and a scab in the middle of her lower lip, it was an amazing face. Not a dainty or beautiful face by any means, but a fascinating face. A strong and willful face. Framed by rich, thick lashes, her bold green eyes, one blackened and more than a bit bloodshot, met his gaze with a directness that was unusual in a woman. Pale, shapely eyebrows arched gracefully over them. High cheekbones gave way to a well-formed nose and full lips. The slightest hint of a cleft dented her chin. When he realized he was staring, he turned back to Janus and let his breath out slowly. Where in hell was the ragged little urchin he'd left asleep at the inn?

Why couldn't she have been the child he had expected to find, or more like the ladies he'd known at court? Either one would have been easier to deal with than this headstrong, *disturbing* girl they'd found at Somerton. She was too impulsive and unpredictable by half. He was never sure what to expect from her, and now with her face washed—

''Gerhart.'' Her commanding voice was direct, as well as her gaze.

She was disturbing, all right, and annoying.

He wondered where the meek girl was who'd been beaten by her stepfather only two days before. He walked around Janus and picked up each of his hoofs to examine them in turn, trying to ignore her presence.

''We cannot go on today.'' Her speech was direct and imperious, as usual.

''Oh?'' He controlled his reaction, refusing to be riled by her. God knew she managed to have some effect on him every time she spoke. He had resolved to be immune to her as they approached Windermere Castle. He wouldn't let her aggravate him, nor was he going to be taken in by any feminine wiles she may possess, scant though they may be.

''Bridget is ill. She cannot travel.''

''We leave in half an hour.'' His voice was firm. ''Several of my men have ridden on ahead. If you have not yet broken your fast, then I suggest you do so now, because you will not have another opportunity.''

The dolt obviously hadn't heard her! ''But Bridget is sick! She cannot go on in the rain!''

''She can and she will,'' Wolf replied with controlled calm. ''She will ride with Nicholas, as she did yesterday. The alternative is that she remain here at the Crooked Ax.''

''You do not understand! I am responsible for her. I—''

''You? I thought it was the reverse. I thought your nurse came along to see to you.''

''Of course not! Bridget hasn't been able to do anything for me these last few years other than patch up my—''

Wolf's fierce look stopped her.

''—well, that is to say, Bridget is getting old now and cannot possibly work like she used to. She has been with me since I was a baby and as my mother's distant cou—''

Gerhart held up one hand to stop her. ''Enough!''

''—cousin, I will not allow her to—''

''Halt!''

"—travel in her con—"

"According to the innkeeper, Windermere is a mere two hours' ride from here." His annoyance was clear in his voice. "I will see the woman myself and judge whether she is fit to travel." He started to walk away, but hesitated long enough to chide her. Turning and raising one finger to punctuate his statement, he said, "You would do well to consider curbing your argumentative nature. It would make life a lot simpler."

His remark was enough to make Kit want to give him a good kick as he walked past, but then the man did the unthinkable. He patted the top of her head as he would a dog and further remarked, "You ought to wash your face more often, too, Sprout. It isn't such a bad one."

"Why, you overbearing, black-hearted, thick-skulled—"

He didn't stay to acknowledge her indignation at being so treated.

Wolf found Bridget in the room she'd shared with Lady Kathryn. The old nurse had a steaming bowl of porridge before her and Wolf paced the room, asking questions regarding the woman's health. She did look pale and had a terrible, rattling cough. For a moment, Wolf considered giving in to the girl's wishes. He did not want to cause the woman undue discomfort, nor did he wish to be responsible for the worsening of her condition. However, the old woman insisted she was fit enough to travel. That is, if she could ride with one of the soldiers.

Since it was to be a short ride, Wolf deemed her capable of making the distance. But he cursed the fate that made him responsible for two *women*. What did he know of the silly creatures? He was a man of war, not a nursemaid.

"Sir Gerhart," Bridget said tentatively as the knight started for the door.

He stopped and turned, giving her the opportunity to continue whatever she wanted to say. He hoped she'd be quick about it so they could be on their way. Windermere was only hours away.

"About my Kit—she's a good lass. Never meant to trouble nobody."

"No," Wolf replied, turning to leave. He found the old woman's statement somewhat at odds with his experience.

"Ye don't understand," Bridget said. "She's had to be strong. Independent. She's had no one to look after her and there've been times…"

"Somers?"

The old nurse nodded. "He's come close to killin' her twice. Only things stoppin' him were the fact that he couldn't run the estate without her. And the baron never knew when one of them knights would come from King Henry to check on her."

"Knights?"

Bridget nodded.

"From Henry?"

"Baron Somers never could figure the reasons for those visits. Seemed to be just social calls but the baron was always suspectin' they came to see Kit for some reason. Never failed to ask about her…"

"When was the last time Somerton was visited by one of these…knights?"

"Well, it's been some years now. I don't believe our new King Henry has sent anyone himself, though."

"And what about the estates? You say Lady Kathryn helps Baron Somers run his estate?"

"No. She doesn't help him," Bridget replied.

Of course not. He had just misheard the old woman before. Wolf turned to leave, but stopped dead at Bridget's next words.

"She does it all herself. She's used to takin' charge, like."

There couldn't be any doubt that Lady Kathryn was concerned about her nurse. During the entire two-hour journey, she looked back every few minutes to see how the woman was managing, and Wolf sensed her impatience with the time. Not once, however, did he anticipate the hellion who deftly slipped out of his grasp and off Janus the instant they reached the inner bailey of Windermere Castle. She went immediately to Nicholas, who was still mounted and supporting Bridget.

"Come, come now! I'll need help with her. Just slide her down…" Kit took charge immediately. Nicholas glanced over at his cousin, who watched with puzzled amusement. The older woman came down, and Kit supported her. "Easy now…" She looked up at Nicholas, then at Gerhart. "Well?" she asked impatiently. "I don't suppose one of you could lend a hand?"

Nicholas dismounted at once and helped Kit to support Bridget who was now wheezing audibly.

"All will be well now, old mother. Have no worry," Kathryn cooed to her nurse, reversing their appointed roles. Bridget was quite obviously ill and needed warmth and rest. Kit was also of a mind to find the local healer or herbalist, but before she was able to inquire, two of the men sent ahead by Gerhart approached them. Hugh Dryden and Chester Morburn came from the yard, having waited for Gerhart and the others to arrive.

"Greetings, my lord," Chester spoke. "The housekeeper informed us that the earl is away from the castle until this evening." The small group began walking through the yard, toward the stone steps of the keep. Bridget's weakness kept her from moving quickly, and Kit hovered protectively about her. She didn't give a hoot for Chester's report and only wanted to get Bridget to bed.

"In spite of the earl's absence, Mistress Hanchaw has provided rooms and provisions. The men are well situated and you and Lord Nicholas have been given suitable chambers. I believe Lady Kathryn and Madam Bridget will be sharing chambers. There are other guests here, as well, due to Windermere Fair, which begins on the morrow."

Gerhart seemed preoccupied and paid little attention to the man's report. However, Kit noticed some unspoken communication go between the knight and his man, Hugh Dryden. The soldier gave his lord a nod and headed for the stables with Chester.

Kit stepped slowly and carefully, so as not to tire Bridget. But the mincing little steps annoyed Wolf and without conscious thought, he lifted Bridget with ease and carried her up the steps and into the hall.

Kit was grateful for his help, certain that Bridget would never have been able to make the grade on her own power. The stairs, the castle and all of its surroundings were massive.

Kit had never seen anything like it. If not for Bridget, she would have stayed outside gaping at the huge stone fortress which was unlike anything she'd ever seen before. The stone walls had been more than imposing from a distance, but Kit's preoccupation with Bridget had interfered with her appreciation of them. The drawbridge, portcullis and moat were also worthy of her consideration, and she determined to get a closer look at the first opportunity.

The great hall was decorated with magnificent tapestries adorning the walls and colorful banners hanging from the vaulted ceiling. Several long, narrow windows were cut into the stone walls and there was a stained glass window at the head of the arch. The late afternoon sunlight filtered in through the filmy windows, giving a warmth to the huge room.

Glancing a bit more closely at the banners and the rushes under her feet, Kit detected a shabbiness to the hall, as well as a stale odor, likely due to the refuse left under the tables and benches for the dogs.

Kit vowed that when she and Rupert were married and she was mistress of her own hall, she would never allow such slovenliness. The rushes would always be fresh and the hangings in good repair, just as she'd kept them at Somerton. And she'd have flowers. Vases and pots full of flowers. These conditions in such a magnificent fortress were unforgivable.

"Sir Gerhart, I presume?" They were approached by a woman somewhat older than Kit, dressed in a tidy gray gown and apron. Her hair was completely covered by a white linen wimple, so Kit couldn't tell if it was yet touched by gray, but her face was lovely with only a few soft lines about the eyes.

Gerhart merely nodded in her direction. Kit sensed a hostility in his mood, but couldn't reason why. So far, she thought they'd been treated well, except for the earl being away from the castle. She couldn't believe Gerhart would take offense at the earl's absence. After all, he'd had no advance warning of Gerhart's arrival and was expected back by evening. Surely whatever business Gerhart had with the earl could wait until supper.

"Follow me. I am Mistress Hanchaw, housekeeper for Lord Windermere." She wrinkled her nose most unpleasantly and looked Bridget over.

"Madam," Kit said as they crossed to yet another staircase, "do you have a gardener about? Is there someone here familiar with healing plants and herbs?"

"What ails her?" the housekeeper asked, clearly disturbed at having to welcome a sick person to the castle, even if she was with a party of the king's men. "Not the morbid sore throat or con—"

"Merely a cold in the chest. I'll require—"

"Pray, who are you? I was told to expect the King's emissary, escorting Lady Kathryn Somers and…" She narrowed her dark brown eyes as she looked Kit over more closely. Kit saw the woman grimace over her attire. She quietly thanked the saints that, at least for now, her face was clean.

"You are speaking to Lady Kathryn, Mistress." Nicholas spoke for her.

"There's no time for idle chatter now," Kit said exasperated. "Please bring the gardener round, or just have him send me cowslip petals and leaves, and iris root if he has any. Whatever he has for fever would be good…"

The housekeeper looked more closely, and quite disapprovingly at Kit now. "But *my lady—*"

"Please do as I say. My cousin is very ill, and I must get her settled and see to her well-being." Moving quickly down a dark hall, the group finally reached the chamber that Kit was to share with Bridget. Mistress Hanchaw pointed out the rooms across the corridor which Gerhart and Nicholas would share, then turned back to open the door to Kit's chamber.

It was dark and gloomy, with shuttered windows, thus the only light in the room emanated from two candelabra on the chest, which Nicholas and the housekeeper proceeded to light. Gerhart lay Bridget gently on the thick velvet coverlet of the bed which was also heavily laden with dark velvet curtains. Her wheeze was worse now, between bouts of coughing spells, and Kit was anxious to do something for her. She placed cushions under Bridget's back to prop her up and ease her breathing.

"I think she should have starwort and yarrow, myself," the housekeeper announced after Bridget quieted for a moment.

"Madam, the request was clear, was it not?" The impatience and hostility in Gerhart's tone was unmistakable now. Kit was thankful that he intervened again, since his intimidating tone had an immediate effect on the woman. The housekeeper turned and left quickly. When she was gone, Kit wondered anew what it was about the place that made Gerhart so antagonistic. While she had already noticed he didn't possess the most affable of temperaments, she had yet to see him behave unjustly.

"My thanks, sir," she said to him.

He barely nodded, acknowledging her thanks. There was a disturbing depth, an almost haunted look, in his eyes.

"The nurse is your cousin?" he asked, and Kit's fleeting impression of a man tormented disintegrated with his words. In his place was a powerful man, coolly controlled.

"Well, yes. Distant, though. She is...a gentlewoman."

Her voice faltered as the full effect of his altered gaze slammed through her. She glanced down at his lips as he spoke and recalled the heat and taste of his mouth. His presence suddenly flustered her. He was so very appealing, and he had come to Bridget's aid with such ease. "She is my...my mother's second cousin. A Cochran of County Louth..."

"Hold," he raised a hand to stop her. "I daresay I know more of your family than I could ever wish to."

Nicholas saw the flash of anger in Kathryn's eyes. "Can you manage on your own now, Lady Kathryn?" he quickly interjected.

Kit damned Wolf silently for making her feel like a child and turned to speak to Nicholas. "Yes. Of course."

"Then until later, my lady..." Nicholas left her with Bridget to go seek out his own quarters. Wolf was already gone.

The gardener came up along with the local priest who dabbled in herbology. The two decided on a decoction of iris root and willow bark, which they gave Bridget along with several of Father Fowler's best blessings and prayers for a speedy recovery. Since their prescription did not differ much from what Kit had planned to give Bridget, she allowed them to proceed without interference. Who could tell? Perhaps the priest's prayers would do her more good than the medicinal powders.

The two men had scarcely left when servants arrived with buckets of hot water which they poured into a stout wooden tub. The younger one, a dark-haired girl, added wood to the fire and fanned it, bringing up a cozy flame.

"'Tis a mite cold," she said, glancing over at Bridget, asleep in the big bed. "We'll keep it nice 'n toasty for the lady there...get the damp out."

"Thank you." Kit took off her hat and began to loosen her hair from its long, confining braid.

"There's a special banquet planned for this evenin', milady," the dark-haired girl said. "I doubt Mistress Han-chaw could be bothered to tell—"

"Maggie!" the older girl cried. "'Twill never do for ye to be tellin' tales about the mistress. Of course she was goin' to tell the lady."

Maggie snorted.

"Well, she was, I tell ye."

"Annie, you know as well as I, nothin' that wily witch likes better than to watch a sweet lady squirm." Maggie poured a pail of hot water into the tub. "Remember how she baited Lady Clarisse—"

"Hold yer tongue, ye fool! Or yer blathering'll get you set out but good! And me as well!"

"As I was sayin', milady." Maggie turned back to Kit with great dignity, ignoring the other girl. "There's to be a grand celebration tonight for the beginning of the fair. It opens tomorrow in Windermere town, and all the barons and squires from hereabouts will be attending. All their ladies, too, so you'll want to be at your best."

Annie started to gather up the linens they were meant to deliver to the other Windermere guests. "Tall Lawrence will fetch ye for supper—"

"'Tis a shame about your eye," Maggie said, lingering, studying Kit's face. "All green and yellow now. No way to conceal it, I don't suppose…"

Kit shook her head and sent the maids on their way with assurances that she could manage her bath alone. There were certainly more pressing matters for them to attend to, if there were guests at the castle.

Bridget was breathing easily and regularly, soundly asleep. Kit eased herself back into the hot water and washed away the grit and grime of her journey, thinking of the two maids and their argument.

Kit wondered who Lady Clarisse was, and why Maggie's words had upset Annie so. This was a strange place, this Windermere Castle. Kit thought it even stranger than Somerton Manor where Lord Somers spent his days in a drunken haze while his wife bedded every neighbor and visitor who passed through. At least at Somerton, a person knew her status—or lack of it.

Even Wolf had seemed to quickly gain an understanding of the situation at Somerton. His distaste for Kit's stepfather was quite clear, and his disgust at Lady Edith's infernal flirting was obvious.

It should have been easy to relax in the tub after her days in the saddle, yet thoughts of the taciturn Wolf plagued her: the way he could make her melt with just a glance of those intent gray eyes, then turn around and use words that made her feel like a child, chastised, castigated, effectively put into place.

She wondered what would happen if he discovered she was the one at the lake. She'd wager her boots he wouldn't call her "Sprout" again.

How could he do this to her? Gerhart made her so confused, she could just kick something. He was a tyrant who treated her like a child and even had the gall to call her "Sprout." She had no use for such a man as Wolf. She had Rupert.

Rupert, who was never overbearing. He was easygoing and fun and always smiling. He never frowned or scowled the way this Gerhart-Wolf did. Rupert had known her for so many years, he'd be satisfied with her, even though she lacked the sophistication of court. Besides, Kit had loved Rupert for years and as soon as she arrived in London, she would find him and marry him. This marriage was what she'd planned, what had kept her sane while she waited for him to come for her at Somerton. And nothing could change that.

It was some time later, as she sat in front of the fire drying her hair, that Bridget awoke. "How do you feel, old friend?" Kit asked.

"As though Edmond Grindcob's huge cow Mathilda had sat on my chest."

Kit laughed. "And well you should. You have a terrible

hack and a wheeze as well. But we shall have you cured before long.''

''What did those old goats give me?''

''Nothing I wouldn't have given you myself.''

''Good. Don't let 'em near me without ye,'' she wheezed.

''I wouldn't, ever.''

''Sure and I know ye wouldn't, Kitty. Come sit by me.'' Bridget patted the mattress and coughed. ''I fear it will be some time afore I'm cured.''

Kit got up and sat on the edge of the bed. ''Nonsense. You'll be fine soon enough. And ready to go on to London.''

''Ye must dress for dinner with the earl.''

''I suppose,'' Kit replied. She knew Bridget was going to insist she wear something presentable and Kit didn't have the heart to argue with her now, while her cousin was so pale and weak.

''Wear the deep green velvet, Kit,'' the nurse said, ''along with the cream wimple. It does suit ye so.''

''What? And not the white?'' The white gown with its delicately embroidered bliaut had been her mother's, saved all these years by faithful Bridget. Kit was surprised her cousin hadn't suggested wearing her finest tonight.

''Ye must save the white and gold until ye are presented to King Henry. Promise me.''

''All right, old mother,'' Kit laughed as she began to dress herself, ''I pledge to you that I will wear the white and gold only as you wish.''

''And behave yerself,'' Bridget exhorted.

''You know me, my dear,'' Kit said in an attempt at reassurance.

Bridget merely rolled her eyes.

Wolf remembered Philip Colston well. Though his cousin was in his late thirties, Philip had not changed much over the years. The same mustache was thicker now, and neatly trimmed, as was the small pointed brown beard which covered the end of his chin. There were hints of gray at his temples and a deep crease between his brows.

He still had a cruel twist about his lips.

It was difficult for Wolf to sit peacefully in the great hall over which his father had presided so long ago. He remembered every detail, down to the last dingy pane of stained glass in the windows and the banners, now tattered, hanging from the huge oaken beams of the ceiling. He could almost envision his brothers, John and Martin, coming in with the earl after a hunt or a trip into the village, Wolf being too young yet to accompany them.

Most vivid in his memory was Martin's coffin being carried out of the main doors, and his mother's weeping form supported by his father as they followed the body of their middle son to the family crypt. It was the last time he saw his mother with any expression.

Wolf painfully recalled the summons from Germany in the fall of 1401. Margrethe, Wolf's mother, had been on an extended visit to her parents after Martin's death. The messenger informed Bartholomew that his wife was lying ill at Bremen, perhaps even dying, and that the Earl was to come at once and bring her two remaining sons to her.

En route to Bremen, highwaymen overtook them, viciously attacking, butchering, hacking; leaving them all for dead.

Wolf's injuries were massive, and he survived only because of his brother's last heroic act to protect him—an act that cost John his life—and the quick thinking of a page not much older than Wolf.

The page was a youthful Hugh Dryden who managed to patch Wolf sufficiently after the attack and get him to a nearby abbey. There, the monks healed his wounds, all but the terrible one that left a scar across his forehead and eye. Weeks later, the two boys were taken to Bremen and reunited with Margrethe and her parents. But Margrethe Gerhart Colston, already in despair due to Martin's death, never recovered from her losses. She sat in her solar, day after day, staring out into the courtyard, straining towards death. The fact that one son remained to her made no difference at all.

His father and elder brothers now dead, Wolfram was the new Earl of Windermere, though unable to claim his title. His family name had been completely discredited in England, and it was up to Wolf now to find the proof he needed to restore his family's honor. It had been necessary for Wolf to assume his grandfather's name in order to return to England. Only Nicholas Becker and the page, Hugh Dryden, knew his true identity. Wolf had no intention of allowing his identity to be discovered until the evidence he needed was safe in hand. Only then would he reveal himself to Philip and personally see to it that justice was served.

Wolf knew that Philip inherited his treacherous nature from his father, Clarence, but there was a perverse aspect to the cousin's nature that the uncle had lacked. Wolf felt his bile rise as he recalled Philip's acts of cruelty—always perpetrated on someone smaller and weaker than himself, and always in secret. Only the children knew, and a few of the smaller servant girls, and none of them ever dared tell their elders. Yes, Wolf well knew of Philip's penchant for inflicting pain. He still bore faint marks from a few painful encounters—until he'd learned to stay clear of the older boy.

Tables were set up, and servants began to bring the food into the great hall under the direction of Mistress Hanchaw. All of Wolfram's men were assembled in the hall, as well as Philip's retainers and many local noblemen with their ladies. Wolf recalled hearing of the recent death of Philip's young wife. It seemed a tasteless blunder for Philip to be hosting such a festive gathering so soon after young Clarisse's death.

Yet Wolf knew Philip's true character. The man and his father had been responsible for butchering his family. Philip was capable of any abomination, and Wolf girded himself against the surge of anger that threatened to disintegrate his calm facade.

''It is interesting—and unusual—for King Henry to send emissaries far and wide throughout the land, is it not?'' Philip asked.

''You mean to say you have not been visited before?'' Nicholas countered, answering for Wolf. He sensed his cousin's seething anger and gave Wolf the opportunity to master it.

Philip looked suspiciously at the two huge men sent by the king. There was something vaguely familiar about the silvery-gray eyes of the one called Gerhart. ''Should I have been?''

''Why, of course,'' Nicholas replied. ''It is merely a courtesy extended by our sovereign. His majesty has long been abroad. How can he know how you fare without—''

At this juncture, Lady Kathryn was escorted into the hall by a gangly footman. Nicholas finished whatever it was he was saying to Lord Philip, but Wolf didn't hear him. He was stunned by her unexpected transformation. Though her head and hair were completely covered by a soft linen headpiece trimmed in green, she was clothed now in women's garb. A deep green velvet gown draped her feminine form from her neck to her toes. The gown was elegant in its simplicity, though even Wolf could see that there was some stitchery of considerable skill embroidered along the deep sleeves.

The gown itself revealed little of Kathryn's form, though the grace of her movements was undeniable. Her hands and wrists were now clean, and he saw that they were small and delicately shaped. The damage done to her face was healing, and he was strangely pleased to note that she did not alter the directness of her emerald-green gaze to suit her position as a guest of the earl in the great hall of Windermere.

There was a vague awareness, tugging at the edges of Wolf's consciousness, that Lady Kathryn had the bearing of a duchess.

Chapter Four

Wolf's powers of speech returned when he was forced to introduce Kathryn to Philip. She greeted the earl, tipping her head almost regally. She then took Philip's arm when it was offered, leaving Wolfram and Nicholas to follow them to the dais. Several guests were milling about, waiting for the earl in order to be seated and begin the meal.

Kit noticed that though Wolf wasn't exactly frowning at her, his expression left something to be desired. He appeared completely astonished to see that she was what she said.

A woman.

Fully grown.

The word ''Sprout'' popped into her mind, and her chin rose a notch.

''You grace my hall most delightfully, my lady,'' Philip said as he seated her on his right. Wolf and his German cousin sat some distance from the earl and Kathryn, but they were still able to hear most of their conversation. Wolf thought Lady Kathryn appeared somewhat small and vulnerable with her bruised eye and the healing gash on her lip. His muscles clenched reflexively, knowing that she was exactly the kind of victim Philip relished.

''It has been many months since Windermere has been

blessed with the charms of one so lovely,'' Wolf heard Philip say to Kathryn.

''Our condolences on the loss of your lady,'' one of the barons said.

''Oh, my,'' Kit's eyebrows came together in concern for the earl. ''Your wife has recently...died?''

''Yes, Clarisse died last November, poor girl,'' Philip muttered.

The name ''Clarisse'' shot through her like an arrow. What was it Maggie had said about her?

Wolf didn't detect a bit of emotion from his cousin when he spoke of his dead wife. In fact, Philip seemed altogether too enthralled by Lady Kathryn, and Wolf didn't care much for it. Any normal man would have been able to produce at least some outward sign of grief for the young wife who'd been dead a mere six months. Instead, Philip hung on Kathryn's every word, and hadn't yet let go of her hand.

''How dreadful for you, my lord,'' Kathryn said, recovering herself. ''Was it sudden?''

The trenchers were finally brought to table as well as trays of meat and fowl. Everyone started to eat, forcing Philip to stop touching Lady Kathryn. Wolf noticed the look of concern in Kathryn's eyes over the bereavement of the earl. He knew she couldn't possibly understand Philip's true character on first meeting, but Wolf found her sympathy for Philip irritating, regardless.

''No,'' Philip answered Kit. ''My wife had been ill for some months... A stomach malady.'' He waved the meaty rib of beef he was holding as if to dismiss the topic. Kit thought the earl's attitude too callous. She knew little of the world beyond Somerton, but she felt certain that some expression of sorrow would have been appropriate. There was no doubt in her mind that the Earl of Windermere was a cold man, and his strangeness caused a slight furrowing of her brow. She could not know that her expression would be interpreted as sympathetic rather than simply puzzled.

Philip paid almost exclusive attention to Lady Kathryn

and that fact was remarked upon by many of the guests at the tables nearby. Lady Kathryn's bruised eye was duly noted, though it was said she'd suffered some mishap prior to setting out from her home in Northumberland. No one knew quite why she was traveling to London or exactly what her relationship was with King Henry, though speculation was rife that the king had made her his ward and she was under his protection. They also said he would likely choose a husband for her.

Wolf said nothing to quell any of the rumors regarding Kathryn, since he himself had no idea why she'd been summoned to court. Besides, Wolf decided the rumors and theories would be to her benefit. He suspected the less anyone knew for certain about her—especially Philip—the better.

Kit was exhausted when Philip finally walked her to her chambers. She wanted nothing more than for the clinging, lecherous nobleman to release her arm and let her enter her room. He had dogged her all evening and now, his face was close to hers and his breath reeked of old ale.

Because she was a guest in his home and since she'd promised Bridget to behave, Kit did not trounce on his foot or jab her knee into his groin when he slid a wayward arm around her waist and flattened his sweaty hand across her buttock. "Such a sweet little morsel…" he muttered, even though Kit tried to move away.

"My lord, release me. Now."

"You please me, Kathryn," Philip drawled. "Young, tempting. What ruse must I use to lure you—"

Kit slapped his hand away and was considering doing worse harm when Sir Gerhart suddenly appeared in the corridor, carrying one candle and staggering slightly, singing a bawdy little tune under his breath. He came toward them, lost his balance and knocked into the earl's shoulder. Kit was surprised by his awkwardness, for though he was a large man, she'd noticed that he always moved with agility and purpose.

"So sorry, m'lord," Gerhart slurred. "Wunnerful wine, marveloush party."

"Back off, ungainly oaf!"

"Please, my lord," Kit stepped between the two men before the earl was able to draw his dagger. It wouldn't do to have the two fighting in the gallery outside her room. Nearly in a panic and hardly able to think what she should do next to appease the earl's unreasonable temper, Kit spoke in her best conciliatory tone. "My escort has...has...merely overindulged in your good wine...and...your hospitality. Allow me to help him to his chambers...er...so he does not further embarrass our party."

She took the candle from Gerhart and pulled at his arm, moving him away from the earl. "Come along, sir knight," she said, then turned to Philip. "Good night, my lord." With that, she put her arm around Gerhart's waist to support his drunken frame and led him down the hall. A quick glance behind her verified, to her immense relief, that Philip was not following. "Pompous ass..." she muttered.

Wolf was really too large for her to support much longer. His chamber would have to be nearby or there would be no choice but to let him crash to the floor right there in the gallery. "Which is the door to your room, Gerhart?"

"This one... No, p'rhaps...down here a bit..." He was leaning too heavily on her. They were both going to fall. "You smell like roses again, Sprout," he said, weaving slightly.

Kit was surprised he'd noticed. She always bathed with rose-scented soap, but thought it was too subtle to be noticed by anyone but herself.

"Here. This is it." He staggered into a door which swung into the room under his weight. By some miracle, neither one of them fell. Kit now found herself with Gerhart's arm around her rather than her arm around his waist where she distinctly remembered having placed it. In his drunken state, he had somehow succeeded in keeping her from falling. He was holding her quite closely now, and Kit's breath quickened. His head moved down, bringing his lips precariously close to hers, nearly touching, and Kit had no control over her body's traitorous response to him. She knew it was insane, but she yearned for the touch of his lips again, wanted to feel—

A drop of hot wax from the candle hit her hand, and Kit jumped. She came to her senses and pulled away from him at once.

"Can you manage now, or should I call for someone to help?" she asked, somewhat breathlessly.

"Why would I need help?" he asked, all traces of drunken speech remarkably absent.

"Why would…? You're not drunk at all, are you?" she asked, seeing the amusement in his eyes and realizing that he had been toying with her.

"Of course not, Sprout. I never drink too much," he said, puzzled by his own behavior. He had never feigned drunkenness before, nor any other condition. Wolf told himself that he'd felt compelled to follow when Philip had taken Kit from the hall only because it was his sworn duty to protect her. And after witnessing his cousin's lecherous looks at supper, he didn't trust that the lady would be safe with him alone in the dark gallery.

"Why, you…you…deceitful lout!" Kit cried. "Roses indeed!" She looked for something to throw at him, but seeing nothing readily at hand, Kit whirled about and tore out of his chamber, leaving him in darkness.

When she reached her room, Kit closed the door more gently than she would have liked, in deference to Bridget, who was sleeping. Her blood was pounding in her ears. Kit wasn't sure if her upset was from anger, annoyance or fear of what might have happened if she'd let Wolf kiss her. Would he have recognized her as the woman at the lake from one kiss?

Standing there in the gloom, her distress simmered, but her worried lips gave way to a slow smile as she thought of Wolf feigning inebriation. The act had been contrived entirely for her benefit. If not for Wolf's interference in the corridor, Kit would either have had to submit to the earl or do something equally embarrassing. Neither option was acceptable, and Wolf had saved her from having to make the choice. She grinned. His method of rescue had been perfect. Perhaps he wasn't totally lacking a sense of humor.

Kit pulled off her concealing veil and wondered if he had merely played the diplomat, or had the sight of the earl pawing at her given him the impetus to intervene? The thought intrigued her as she sat down on the bed next to Bridget and felt her fevered forehead. No one had ever seen fit to rescue her before. Not even Rupert.

The fire in the grate had all but died as Kit undressed by candlelight and slipped into a thin white gown. Though the chamber was deep in shadows, Kit knew there was a small bed in the far corner. She intended to spend the night there so as not to disturb Bridget's sleep. As she lifted the candle and turned, a strange sound came to her ears from the depths of the shadows. Kit stood still to listen for it again. Finally, she heard a voice speaking in a harsh, laughing whisper. It was an eerie sound.

"The rooster's found another pretty little hen to decorate his roost!" Kit raised the candle a bit in order to better illuminate the room. A deeper shadow moved in front of the fire, and Kit knew the speaker was there. Too frightened to approach the apparition, she set down the candle and went back to the bed where Bridget lay. Her knife was concealed under the extra pillow. She didn't know what the intruder wanted, but Kit planned to protect herself and Bridget.

"Who are you? What do you want?"

"Methinks the wolf this time will thwart our bird and serve him up for supper."

Bridget moaned a little in her sleep, the sound startling Kit nearly out of her skin.

"You speak nonsense! Come into the light and let me

see you." The last thing she really wanted was to see whatever demon was speaking, but Kit bolstered her courage and demanded a confrontation.

The little bent-over figure moved slowly away from the fire and approached the chest where Kit had set the candle. When finally it stopped near the light, it turned. Kit saw it was nothing but an old woman, bent by a hump on her back, and cloaked in some coarse, dark cloth.

"Ahh! 'Twill be good to see him brought low!" the woman clapped her hands in glee.

"Who are you?" Kit whispered again.

"I?" She looked incredulously at Kit, unable to believe that anyone might not know her. "I am the Countess of Windermere." She threw her head back and laughed silently. It was a bizarre laugh causing chills to move down Kit's back as she watched the wretched old thing going through the motions of laughter with no sound.

"I...I thought the Countess...died last spring... You are not, you could not be her...her ghost? Could you?"

More infernal laughter. Kit trembled, certain she was poor Clarisse's ghost.

"Agatha."

"What?" Kit whispered, completely confused now.

"I! Me! *I* am Agatha. Wife of Clarence the Usurper."

"Who is Clarence?" Kit asked, now totally confused.

"Clarence was the father of the peacock who now struts about Windermere Castle. Philip, he is called."

The riddles were giving Kit a headache, and she was beginning to suspect that this Agatha was no more an apparition than Bridget.

"What do you want?"

"Take care. He needs a new hen to breed him some chicks. The last could give him no brood."

"I don't understand you! Can you not speak plainly?"

"Your wolf will find all he needs if he has the time and knows where to look."

"My wolf—" She realized with a shock that the woman

meant Gerhart, who was never called Wolf. "Who do you mean? What are you saying?"

"Silver eyes. Black thatch. Rightful earl." Her words were said as though they were part of a song, an oft-repeated song.

"Do you mean Sir Gerhart?"

"Ahh, is that what he is called? Born of Bartholomew and Margrethe. Finally come for his birthright." The strange silent laugh came over her again.

Finally, the old woman turned and hobbled back into the shadows. And then she was gone.

Kit stood still for a moment, afraid to move. It had been the oddest experience of her life, and she had no idea what to make of it. Had the woman just vanished into thin air? Where else could she have gone? The door hadn't opened, and she couldn't possibly have left through the window. Kit finally gathered her courage and went over to light a candelabra. With more light, she verified that the old woman was truly gone.

It was a long time before Kit fell asleep. Awakening early to the sounds of Bridget coughing and wheezing, she got up to administer more of the medicine to her old companion and was unable to go back to sleep. The room was chilly, so she added wood to the fire and then wandered about, puzzling over the events of the previous night.

Unfortunately, not much was clear about the old crow's visit the night before. She'd said she was Agatha, that much Kit understood. The old earl was Clarence, and Agatha claimed she had been his countess. If that were true, why did the old lady hobble around in the night, appearing and disappearing out of thin air, and babbling riddles like a madwoman? What self-respecting earl would allow his mother to go about in coarse rags, pestering the castle guests?

Kit opened the shutters to see that it was just barely dawn. It seemed a pleasant spring day, the rain having let up sometime during the night. It was still overcast, but the haziness only made the tree trunks seem blacker and the leaves more green. Even the grasses in the distance were more vibrant than Kit remembered. It was a beautiful land with neatly tilled rows on the hills and a good-sized town in the distance.

She poured water into the basin and began washing, when she saw a tiny gray mouse skitter across the room and disappear under a huge tapestry which hung from ceiling to floor. Kit hadn't paid much attention to it before, for the cloth was darkened and obscured with age, making the details unintelligible.

Wondering about the mouse hole, and thinking to block it up, Kit went over and pulled the tapestry aside enough to search for the crack. Instead, she found more than a mere crack. The tapestry covered a false stone wall, which concealed a door hanging on hidden hinges. A small round hole, just big enough for two fingers was carved into the stone door. Kit put her fingers in, and the catch turned noiselessly. The door swung in heavily.

It was too dark to see into the dank, musty passageway, so Kit lit the candelabra, threw a blanket around her shoulders and went through. She found that the passage was small, only large enough for a narrow spiral staircase, which she began to ascend. Just when Kit was certain the steps would go on forever, the stairs finally ended at a stone door identical to the one in her own chambers. She turned the catch and found herself standing behind a large tapestry. Peeking round it, careful to remain silent, Kit perused what was obviously the bedchamber of Lady Agatha.

The old woman was snoring loudly in her bed which was as heavily draped as the bed in Kit's own chamber where Bridget now slept. The room was dark as well, with Kit's candelabra casting long darting shadows along the floor and walls. As she moved into the room, Kit began to reconsider the prudence of breaching the chamber of a sleeping madwoman.

Before she was able to withdraw, however, Agatha's dark eyes opened and focused on Kit. "Well, well."

"Yes, well, I...I wondered how you got into my room..." Kit said awkwardly. She felt like an intruder yet the old woman had intruded into Kit's room only the night before.

"I waited for you."

"For me?"

Agatha sat up in the bed and crouched her head down into her shoulders. She smiled, displaying more pink gum line than teeth. "For you. Of course."

She swung her legs over the side of the bed and slid down to the floor. Nodding her head, she hobbled over to the window. Drawing the shutters aside, Agatha looked down into the courtyard three stories below and satisfied herself that no one was about. While Kit stood watching, Lady Agatha went across the room to a little wooden footstool and carried it back to the window. She turned and winked at Kit, then stepped up, reached out of the window and struggled to pull a loose chunk of granite free of the outside wall.

"I can't do it. You'll have to get it out."

"What?"

"The stone!" she cried impatiently. "The stone! What he needs to—ach! Here, reach thus." She got Kit to stand on the footstool, and now the old woman was making her reach outside the window. "Pull and tug gently. Your fingers will find the prize."

Agatha's antics were beginning to annoy Kit, and she wished she had never come up to the old lady's room. To humor the old woman, Kit played along, although she couldn't help but wonder where this game would lead. Then, as she was about to pull her arm back inside, her hand happened upon the loose brick.

Carefully, Kit pulled the stone away and turned around to hand the heavy piece to Agatha.

"That's it! That's it! The rooster will broil for lunch!"

Kit reached back outside and put her fingers into the gap. There, she felt a canvas cloth holding something solid, heavy and metal, about the size of a large coin. She pulled it out to see that it was a large, ornate ring: a seal on which was engraved a peacock, its feathers fully extended.

"Whose signet is this?"

"'Tis the seal of Bartholomew Colston, once lost, once stolen, only to be made anew and different, too."

"Your riddles baffle me, good woman. Can you not speak plainer?"

"Show it only to the wolf and no other, else harm will come to you."

Exasperation finally overcame her efforts at good will. "Well, I think I'll just leave this little treasure here," Kit said as she returned the seal to the niche in the wall. Why the woman was hiding it from Philip was no concern of hers, and she didn't want to get involved in their dispute.

"No!" Agatha hissed. "You must take it! Conceal it and show it to no one but the wolf."

"Please, Lady Agatha," Kit said even as she reluctantly retrieved the seal again. "I have no wish to enter into your personal affairs with your son. I—"

"Do not call that vulture my son! He is not of *my* blood!"

"Well, whoever he is, perhaps you ought to give him back his seal, if that's what this is." Kit tried to hand it to the woman, but she closed Kit's fingers around it.

"Why do you refuse to understand?" Agatha demanded in frustration. "Take it! Hide it! The wolf will know what to do with it!"

Kit sighed. She took the iron seal, picked up the candelabra and wrapped herself again in the blanket. "All right, Lady Agatha," Kit said reluctantly. "I'll do it." Returning to the hidden door, Kit turned back to Lady Agatha, who appeared satisfied.

"I've waited so many years... Tell him to seek Tommy Tuttle in London. Mayhap he will tell more..."

"Who is Tommy Tuttle?"

More silent laughter, but no answer. "Let no one know of this passage," Agatha admonished.

Kit turned and slid behind the tapestry and out the door. Within a few short minutes, she was in her own bedchamber with Bridget. It was as if she'd never left.

The gash on Kit's lip was practically gone, and she smiled broadly at the sights and sounds of the fair as she rode into town with the earl and his party. The bruise about her eye was a pale greenish-yellow color, and was not as fierce looking as it had been only the day before. Lord Philip lent her a horse, and though she was compelled to ride sidesaddle due to her gown, it was a pleasant day to be out of doors, moving about freely.

She had never traveled beyond Somerton, and the markets held there had been small and quite unremarkable. The fair that day at Windermere was amazing to Kit, though not unexpected, since everything about the earl's holding was large and lavish. The town was wonderful, full of noise and color, music and entertainment. The smells of food being cooked in the open air made her mouth water, and the sight of excited children running about through the stalls was exhilarating.

The richly garbed earl rode beside her, and Wolf was some distance back with Nicholas, Hugh and a few of his men. Kit couldn't help but notice that the townspeople and yeomen kept their distance from her and his lordship. The people's eyes remained downcast and they held their tongues. Once the earl passed, they put their hands to their mouths and muttered quietly among themselves.

The hostility of the people was not lost on Wolf, either. He knew that when he finally managed to wrest his title and estates from Philip, it would be a difficult task to right the wrongs done in the intervening years. He remembered Philip well enough to realize that the wrongs would be many and fierce.

Kit was assisted from her mount by the earl. Wolf watched the two walk toward the nearest of the stalls, where a merchant stood selling intricately tooled leather belts and purses. She hadn't spoken to him at all since the night before, and Wolf found he missed her annoying chatter. Her head was modestly covered again today, and she wore a concealing cloak over a wine-colored gown with long, flowing sleeves. Though her clothing only hinted at her feminine form, one thing had become perfectly clear. Lady Kathryn Somers was no child, and her lack of courtly style only enhanced her mystique.

The urge to kiss her last night had been a powerful one, and he had to admit Kathryn was more compelling a woman than the intriguing blonde he'd thought he wanted at Somerton Lake. Just the thought of holding Kit again as he had in his room last night was enough to send a painful ache through him. He scowled at his own lack of discipline. She was just a woman. And she belonged to Rupert Aires. Wolf's task was only to get her to London. Nothing more.

To Wolf's immense satisfaction, it seemed that Kathryn was not pleased to be forced into the earl's company. She moved away from Philip frequently to converse with the other lords and ladies, but the earl always managed to take her arm again to draw her away from the others.

"My dear Lady Kathryn," Lord Philip said, "come this way. I must show you a shop down this lane."

As the earl and Kathryn wandered down the muddy lane, a couple of young boys came running through, kicking a large round stone, each trying to keep the other from getting it. The game grew rough, and one of the boys took a tumble. He slid through an immense puddle of mud, and inadvertently splashed Kathryn.

Philip was incensed. Wolf watched as the earl lashed out at the boy, picked him up by the ear and held him in a vicious grip until one of his men, an evil-looking fellow called Ramsey, came to take charge of the lad. The boy, only about ten years old or so, began to cry.

"P-please your lordship," he wailed, "I'm sorry. I—I never meant—"

"You unruly beggar! Have you no sense? I ought to hang you and the miserable, flea-bitten dogs who spawned you…"

Wolf was angered by Philip's exaggerated reaction to the offense. True, a goodly amount of mud had slopped onto Kit's cloak, but Philip was slapping the boy senseless. Surely this kind of treatment was unnecessary and would only breed resentment in the townspeople. Talk of this type of incident spread like wildfire.

"I want him punished! Nail him! See to it!" Philip shouted as two more of his evil-looking cronies started for the lad.

"What can you do?" Nicholas asked, sensing Wolf's anger.

"Nothing, damn it. Nothing," Wolf clenched his fists and stood fast.

"If you interfere, Philip will take offense and then Henry—"

"Bloody hell if I don't know it, Nick!" Yet he somehow had to stop Philip from maiming the child. The boy would soon find his ear nailed to a post, or his foot or hand impaled if Wolf didn't act. It was an untenable situation! He had to—

"Mercy!" Kit herself intervened. She wrapped one arm around the boy's shoulder and chest from behind and kept him from being taken away by the guards. "Please, my lord! Hold!" she pleaded.

Wolf watched as she protected the boy with her own body, caring not a whit for the mud smearing onto her own clothes from the boy's, nor the threat of Philip's guards. Several of the earl's party had caught up now and were observing the incident with interest.

"My lord, since I am the victim, will you not allow *me* to punish the culprit?"

"Culprit? You call him merely 'culprit'?" Philip sneered. "I say he's a menace and ought to be—"

"Please, my lord..." she said sweetly, her tone belying the loathing she felt for the earl at that moment. The evil gleam in his eye was reminiscent of that which Baron Somers always had, just as he was about to lash out at her. Her heart pounded at the memory, and she gathered her courage to speak up for the lad. "Let me determine the boy's fate."

"Why not, my lord?" this from a voice from within the earl's group.

"Yes, how amusing. Let Lady Kathryn determine the lad's penalty."

Philip gestured his guards away.

"What have you in mind?" the earl asked, attempting to appear as if this turn of events was perfectly acceptable. His nostrils flared, his upper lip quivered and Kit was not fooled by his mild tone. He was a perfectly hateful man.

Wolf watched as Kit turned the boy to face her. He could see that she was trying to calm him with a kind look, yet she needed to appear stern for the benefit of the earl.

"Since the lad has nothing better to do than harass unsuspecting ladies," she said firmly, "let him follow along as my page. He shall carry my packages, run my errands, tend to my whims." A murmur of assent went through the group. Few of them believed the lad deserved nailing for his offense. "It should be more than enough punishment for a boy who, I'm sure, would much rather play on a day as beautiful as this."

Wolfram could almost see Kit holding her breath as she waited for the earl's decision, and something in his chest twisted as he watched her quiet torment. Had he been closer, he'd have had to guard against kissing her for her sense of justice and her attempt to keep the boy from suffering such a brutal penalty for merely being a careless child.

"So be it! You heard the lady," Philip finally declared. "Stop your sniveling, boy, and get to it!"

Kit's heart was pounding so hard, she was certain Philip could hear it. "Thank you, my lord," she breathed. She gave the boy's shoulders an almost imperceptible squeeze and when she released him, asked his name.

"Alfie, milady." His voice was very small. "Alfie Juvet."

"Very good, Alfie. Your first task will be to help me scrape off some of this mud. Come. Take me to your good mother. Excuse me, my lord," she said to Philip. "I'll rejoin you shortly." The boy followed as Kit left the group. "Do you live nearby?"

"Yes, milady," he replied, taking the lead. "Down this lane."

"Is your mother at home?"

"I—I don't know for sure, what with the fair and all..." She thought he was going to cry again and put a gentle hand on his shoulder to reassure him. He had lost his hat in the mud, and he tossed his head back to throw the long, dank hair out of his eyes.

"It's all right, Alfie. We'll manage." She turned around to be sure they weren't being followed by the earl or any of his party and was startled to see Wolf. She hadn't expected the tall, dark knight there. What's more, she didn't particularly want to see him. His mere presence forced her to think about Countess Agatha's words and riddles, and Kit had too many other things to worry about right now. His lordship, the earl, was the first of those worries. Kit sensed that Philip was a dangerous man, and she knew she had to keep her wits about her as long as she remained in his presence.

"Right here, milady." Entering the modest but well-equipped kitchen of an unassuming house in the lane, Alfie went ahead, calling for his mother.

No one replied.

"Apparently she is not in," Wolf remarked when he caught up to them. "Water and clean rags will do nicely, lad. Fetch them for the lady."

"Yes, m'lord." Alfie scrambled to search through his mother's cupboards for what was needed, then poured fresh water from a pitcher into a basin. Alfie saturated one rag, squeezed it out and started to work on Kit's cloak.

"I'm sorry for ruining your cape, milady. I didn't mean—"

"I know you didn't mean it. And don't worry. It'll come clean when it's properly laundered," she said. "You know, I recall a few blunders of my own when I was your age." She didn't mention that she also understood the punishments that resulted.

Alfie looked up at Kit, hardly able to believe her words. Looking at her now, he couldn't imagine her running through muddy streets under any circumstances. "Yes, milady."

"I have a name, Alfie," she said. "It's Kathryn, though I'm called 'Kit' by my friends." She began washing her hands in the basin and feeling more at ease in the humble little kitchen than she'd felt in days.

Wolf picked up the other clean rag and dampened it. He took Kit's chin in one hand and turned her face towards the light so he could clean the mud off her cheek and nose. "You might have mentioned to Philip that you're partial to wearing mud," he remarked.

Kit blushed and tried to ignore the huge knight and the sudden thudding of her heart in her chest. She was speechless. He made her nervous, even if he was only jesting with her.

Kit spoke to the boy. "When we return to the earl, you'll have to be particularly respectful, Alfie. I fear he will not be pleased to have you trailing us, so try to remain unseen and—"

"Hold still, will you, Kit? I've no wish to hurt you," Wolf said gruffly, demanding her attention.

Kit held perfectly still and studied the stonework of the fireplace. Then she dropped her gaze to the rough-hewn table. She thought Wolf was being immensely gentle with her already and wondered how he could be any more careful with her bruised cheek and eye. She should have expected his kindness when all she'd known from this man was gentleness—even when he'd been angry at her. But she hadn't experienced much kindness before.

Dear God, how was she supposed to keep a clear thought when Wolf was standing close enough that she could smell the leather hauberk he wore and his clean, masculine scent? She knew if she looked up to his eyes, she was near enough to see the flecks of silver in the gray and practically count each of his long, black lashes.

"—'tis the best I can do, mil...er, Lady Kit," Alfie said, standing away to check his work. The cloak was far from clean, but the worst had been washed off.

"This will be sufficient, Alfie," she was nearly breathless with Wolf's nearness. If only he would touch her again...kiss her... She trembled at the impertinent thought but quickly gathered her wits. "Now, do you have a clean tunic to put on?" Kit looked up briefly into Wolf's darkening eyes and saw a puzzlement brewing there to match her own. For the life of her, she couldn't remember the color of Rupert's eyes.

Chapter Five

The earl proudly showed off the town as though he were personally responsible for making it so fine. He gloated so much over every little stand of bricks, every little nook and bridge, that Kit was very quickly weary of his company.

Not to say that she'd been particularly fond of the earl since meeting him the night before. Besides the man's obvious arrogance, Kit sensed a coldness to him that nearly made her shiver when he was near. It would have pleased her no end to be able to leave Windermere straightaway, but there was Bridget to consider, and she needed rest in order to become well again. And there was Wolf, too. Kit didn't think she'd be able to sway him into leaving until he was ready.

Alfie followed her about the fair all day, carrying everything faithfully and maintaining a respectful and contrite bearing. She tried to reassure him many times and smooth over his little blunders. But Philip reacted to Alfie with a meanness that stopped just short of cruelty, and it chilled Kit to think how the earl would behave if left alone with the boy.

Wolf kept himself occupied at the fair. Kit caught herself looking around frequently to see if she could catch sight of the baffling man, and often found him talking with the merchants, yeoman and other townsmen. There was an ease with which he got along with the people he met, and Kit could see that they liked and respected him.

Much to her dismay, Kit noticed several ladies in the earl's party who tried to catch Wolf's eye. When they succeeded, his rewarding smiles were devastating, even to Kit, who was never the recipient. Kit was all too aware that he didn't have any smiles for her. Only frowns and scowls. And puzzled looks. She knew she was merely an annoying curiosity to him.

It irritated her unreasonably when the knight gave his unwavering attention to Lady Christine Wellesley, the daughter of a neighboring baron. Christine was a red-haired beauty, with deep blue eyes, and dimples in her cheeks. Her elegant gown was close-fitted and fashionable. The lady's hair was exposed, with only the sheerest of silk veils partially covering it. And when Wolf smiled at her, Kit wanted to murder the woman.

But why? She was the first to admit she had no claim on Sir Gerhart, and she knew she couldn't possibly compare to the lovely Lady Christine. But it riled her inexplicably. Kit turned away from them and reasserted to herself that she belonged to Rupert Aires. And she was anxious to reach him in London before he went searching for her in Northumberland.

When they returned to the castle, Philip wouldn't allow Kit to go inside. He took her arm as she reluctantly moved along the paths with him through the gardens, some distance away from the castle. More than anything, she wanted to go up to Bridget. But no matter how she pleaded with the earl, he wouldn't allow her to part company just yet.

"You're so quiet, Kathryn," Philip said as they reached a pretty garden pond. It was a lovely setting, with a carved wooden bench nearby and several twisted paths leading out in different directions.

Philip guided her to the bench and had her sit, then stood looking down at her, placing one booted foot on the seat next to her. He leaned an arm across one knee.

"I'm quiet because I'm a bit fatigued, my lord. It's been a long day," Kit finally answered. She hoped he would take the hint and let her go. "Besides, my cousin is ill and I—"

"There is a matter at hand about which I'd like to speak...though I'm not quite sure whom to address," he said, frowning. "Just who is your guardian, Kathryn?"

He was talking in circles, and Kit didn't know what he was getting at. It was irritating that he had no appreciation for her worry over Bridget's welfare.

"Is it your father, Baron Somers? Or the King, as rumor suggests?"

"I'm sorry, my lord, I myself don't really know. No one has told me of any change in guardianship, though I've heard Sir Gerhart say that I'm under King Henry's protection."

"Hmm." He stroked his pointed brown beard with the tips of his fingers.

"I'm in need of a wife."

She almost choked.

"As you know, Lady Clarisse expired some months ago..."

"My lord, you have taken me completely unawares. I had not anticipated—"

"Yes, yes, well, I appreciate all that but whom do you suppose I should petition? Henry? Your father?"

By God, he was callous indeed. Poor Clarisse, Kit thought. The woman was barely cold in her grave, and her husband was already trying to replace her. Angry now, Kit stood abruptly and moved a few paces away from him. In view of his indelicacy, she saw no reason to indulge in any form of diplomacy. He had been rude and unfeeling all day, first with the boy from town and later, when some of the townsmen tried to speak to him. His behavior had been embarrassing, but this was the last straw. Kit was fed up with the arrogant earl.

"I don't think—" Her pointed response was interrupted by a group of men ambling down one of the paths towards the pond, who were talking and laughing loudly. Their last jest was particularly funny, judging by the uproarious laughter that overtook them when they reached the pond. Kit recognized Hugh, Edward and Douglas, all of them Wolf's men, who tried, amid tearful regressions into laughter, to apologize to the earl for interrupting his peaceful afternoon. Egbert, Ranulf and Claude hung back sheepishly, apologizing and turning to go.

Their hilarity was infectious, though, and Kit found herself smiling, then nearly laughing out loud at Wolf's men. They posed a ridiculous picture—six great knights, all guffawing and slapping their thighs. The earl, however, did not appear amused at all, and practically dragged Kit away, muttering angrily. She suppressed a chuckle, thinking that the jest this time was on the earl. And she couldn't think of anyone more deserving.

Smiling at his irritation, she followed along obediently until they reached the castle entrance, where Wolf stood on the steps, casually tying a leather thong to one of his saddle packs. He barely looked up as they passed, only enough to meet Kit's eyes for a second. However, with a growing suspicion, she noticed that he put away his work as soon as she passed by with the earl. She also didn't miss the fact that Sir Wolf wore a vague expression of satisfaction as well, not unlike the one worn by the cat that swallowed the field mouse.

Blanche Hanchaw greeted the earl anxiously as he entered the great hall with Kit.

"Yes, yes, Blanche." Philip was unmistakably preoccupied. "We're back."

"If I might have a moment…"

Philip still held Kathryn's elbow and was about to guide her somewhere when the Hanchaw woman attempted to draw the earl away.

"…'tis a matter of some importance…er…one of your…*guests*…my lord…"

The housekeeper's words and manner caused the earl

some hesitation. He released the grip he had on Kit's arm, though he kept her hand and kissed it. There was a disturbing glint in his eye when he looked at her, and Kit repressed a shudder when his cool lips met the warm skin on the back of her hand. "Until we sup, my lady."

Thankfully, Kathryn was dismissed, at which point she tore up the staircase in a rather undignified manner in order to get to her chamber. She had worried about Bridget all day and felt guilty about leaving her with only the maids to tend her.

Kit rounded the corner at full tilt and drew up short, for Wolf was standing in the corridor near his door, his arms folded over his broad chest, the saddle pack draped over his shoulder. He looked dark and ominous as well as handsome and terribly masculine in the dim hall. Kit was sure that at the moment, she embodied everything he meant when he called her "Sprout."

"I wondered at the commotion on the stair," he said, turning to face her. "You make quite an entrance, Lady Kit."

And he was quite a presence, she thought, with blood rushing to her cheeks. She let her skirts fall back to cover her ankles, then straightened her wimple as well as her spine. She doubted any of the ladies at court ever blundered quite so spectacularly before the mighty Sir Gerhart. "I suppose I should thank you for rescuing me *again* just now."

"That's thrice by my reckoning, my lady."

"Thrice?"

He merely inclined his head, content to let her figure it out.

"When do we leave Windermere, Sir Gerhart?" she asked, ignoring the tally.

"Weary of the place?"

"'Tis the company that tries my patience," she replied with a sigh. "Windermere itself is a wonderful estate. And the town...it's more impressive than any I've ever seen."

Satisfied by her answer, Wolf told her to be prepared to leave two mornings hence.

Bridget's condition had worsened while she was gone. Kit sat on the edge of the bed and felt the old woman's brow. It was cool and damp.

"I won't be denyin' it," Bridget said to Kit, "I feel a mite worse…than just a cold on my chest." The old woman was quite short of breath, and the words didn't come easily.

She was suddenly taken by a spasm of coughing, and Kit was alarmed to see that she was coughing up blood. Kit pulled the blanket away from Bridget's feet and saw that they were swollen as were her ankles, and legs, halfway up her shinbone. She put her ear to Bridget's chest and listened to her heart beat, just the way she had been taught by Brother Theodore.

The symptoms indicated that Bridget's heart was failing. It was beating erratically, and Kit could hardly feel the throb of it in the old woman's wrists.

"Maggie, go and fetch the gardener, Will Rose, for me. Quick!" Kit ordered. "If you can't find him, try to find someone who can get some of his foxglove powder."

The old woman was lethargic and hard-pressed to stay awake. Kit experienced a sense of panic, knowing full well that only a miracle could save her old friend.

"Bridget, how long have your feet been swelling?"

"Oh…" The old woman tried to think of some evasion, but was unable to, not with her Kit looking her straight in the eye. "…some months now…Brother Theodore…he's been giving me something to help it." She seemed so frail now. Her eyelids were practically transparent, and Kit could even see thin blue veins running through them. "Did ye…enjoy the fair?"

"Yes, it was lovely." Kit was so distracted, she hardly knew what she'd answered. How could she have gone away and spent the day at the stupid, frivolous fair while Bridget lay here—

"And the earl...what...kind of man is he?"

"You must save your strength, Bridget," Kit implored her friend. "I'll tell you of the fair and the earl later, when your strength has returned."

Bridget nodded once, then drifted off to sleep again. Kit slid down to kneel on the floor next to the bed. She picked up Bridget's cool hand and laid her head on the bed next to her. There she waited for Maggie to return.

Will Rose himself returned with the maid. Kit hovered around him whilst he examined poor Bridget and agreed with Kit's opinion that the foxglove was needed. He drew Kit away from the bed to talk quietly while they mixed the powdered leaves with water.

"'Tis poison, as ye well know, milady," he admonished her. "Give her only this much and no more, else her heart will stop altogether."

"I know."

"Give her this. I'll fetch the barber." He also brought Father Fowler to administer Extreme Unction, the last rites of the church.

Bridget drifted in and out of consciousness all evening. The bloodletting performed by the barber caused no immediate improvement and Kit sat on a stool next to Bridget's bed, holding her hand, waiting, soothing the old woman whenever she awakened. A footman came to light Kit's way down the steps to dinner, but Kit instructed him to give her regrets to the earl. She did not intend to leave Bridget again until she was well.

It was soon thereafter that Wolf appeared, having missed Kit in the great hall. She didn't realize he was there until she felt a gentle and unexpected hand on her shoulder.

"How does she fare?" His tone was quiet, just more than a whisper.

Kit had been composed until he asked her the question, but the gravity of Bridget's condition brought her close to tears. She swallowed the lump in her throat, looked up at

Wolf and shook her head, hardly trusting her voice not to crack. "It's her heart. She never told me."

Bridget awoke for a moment and saw Wolf standing behind Kit. She smiled weakly at the tall knight. "Ah, 'tis ye, sir... Take care...of my Kitty."

"I will." The answer was so simple. So final.

"Don't let her...go back...to the devil baron."

Wolf shook his head reassuringly, and Kit implored Bridget to rest.

"He will kill her... One time...next time...he'll surely kill her."

"No," Wolf said quietly.

"She tried to run...once..."

"Quiet now, old mother," Kit said. "Save your breath..."

There was little that Kit could do for Bridget as the night wore on. Maggie slept in a chair near the fireplace while Kit kept her lonely vigil. Sometime near midnight, Bridget awoke again and spoke.

"I must...talk to ye now." Her words were whispered painstakingly, her breath so short that Kit had to strain to hear what she said. "...I know why King Henry...wants ye... The secret...well-kept these many years... Meghan's wish...but now...ye must know."

"Rest, Bridget. Tell me tomorrow when you are better."

"Now." The urgency of her tone silenced Kit.

"Yer mother...met Henry Hereford...King Henry's father...in London...when he became King... She was young...a bonny lass...inexperienced... Hereford was...taken with her...riding on the wings of his success."

Her breathing was so labored, Kit wanted her to stop, but Bridget insisted on continuing.

"They...they..."

"What happened, Bridget?" Kit urged her to continue. "What must I know?"

Bridget experienced a severe coughing spell before she

was able to speak again. ''Hereford sent her to Somerton...to marry Lord Thomas... It was remote...but far enough...from Scottish raids... He knew ye'd both be safe...''

''Who? Mother and Lord Somers? Mother and I would be safe?''

Bridget tried to speak again, but though her lips moved, no words came.

Kit wanted to question her further, but it was obvious that Bridget's strength was ebbing. Kit felt lost, truly lost for the first time in her life. Tears rolled down her face unheeded as she took Bridget's hand in hers, bent over it and wept quietly.

Wolf didn't know why he had to be so preoccupied with that hellion girl, ministering to her old friend alone in that dark, dreary room. He was at Windermere for the first time in twenty years, with his enemy at hand, and all he could think of was how Kit was dealing with old Bridget's illness. What did it matter to him? Wolf knew he had to concentrate on Philip and not allow anything to distract him from his plan.

It was nigh on midnight by the time the ladies retired from the hall, and several of the gentlemen were enjoying a glass of wine near the fire before retiring to their beds. Wolf prodded Philip into recounting the story of his ''dishonorable'' Uncle Bartholomew. Philip asserted that Bartholomew had been one of King Richard's sympathizers, positioning himself against the Lords Appellant, including Henry Hereford, who would soon wrest the crown from Richard to become King Henry IV.

''My dear Uncle Bart was foolish enough to engage some cutthroat to murder King Henry during the Owen Glendower affair. Oh, yes, the Mortimers and the Percys were involved, but none so stupidly as my uncle.''

''I am unfamiliar with the case, my lord,'' Nicholas said. ''How was it proved that Bartholomew sent an assassin to kill Henry? Didn't the late earl and his sons die abroad near the time of the Glendower revolt?''

''The assassin failed, of course,'' Philip sneered.

''But the villain escaped being caught, as I recall,'' Baron Wellesley remarked, shaking his head sadly. ''The bumbling fool somehow dropped his purse containing the gold he was paid as well as an incriminating writ from Bartholomew, duly signed and sealed by the earl himself. It made no sense at the time, and I vow I'll never understand it.''

So this was the evidence used to involve Bartholomew in the plot, Wolf thought, a writ sealed by his father's stolen signet. There was no question that it would have incriminated Bartholomew in treason.

''I'd heard that the earl's seal had been stolen some time before.''

''Naturally, my uncle circulated that story,'' Philip was swift to reply, ''knowing full well that he would soon use our family's noble seal illegally.''

An elderly baron, standing near the massive fireplace, warming his backside, furrowed his brow. His long white eyebrows came almost together. ''I seem to remember that Bartholomew had another seal cast. Different from the old seal. What was it?'' he asked, frustrated that the memory had eluded him.

''Never could understand why Bart wouldn't have used the new signet,'' said another of the barons, ''to authorize that cutthroat—''

''Yes, yes, well, that was lost as well.''

''Right,'' the old man said. ''It was never found after the earl and his sons were overtaken on the road and killed in Europe.''

''Was it ever determined who was responsible for that?'' Wolf asked in a controlled voice.

''Bandits. Highwaymen. No one knows.'' Philip shrugged.

"Your father, Lord Clarence, investigated, did he not?" Wellesley asked Philip.

"There were no answers to be found. No one survived the attack." Philip drained his cup. "It seems we've dragged out all the old ghosts tonight. Let us move on to happier subjects."

The following conversation, having to do with plans for a hunt on the morrow, was of no interest to Wolf, so he soon left Nicholas in the company of the earl and the barons, and went in search of food. He knew Kit had missed dinner, and he thought to take her something to eat. It would be a long night for her.

When he tapped on her door, there was no answer, so he let himself in and set the platter of bread and cheese on the chest. His heart wrenched in an unfamiliar way, seeing her crumpled over her friend, weeping silently. Bridget lay unconscious, her breathing less labored now, but just as noisy. Soldiers called it the death rattle, and Wolf knew Lady Kathryn's old companion wouldn't last the night.

The fire in the grate had all but died, and he went over to revive it. Then he went back to Bridget's bed, crouched down next to Kit and slid a gentle arm around her shoulders to pull her away.

"Will you eat something?"

She shook her head but leaned back against his arm. Wolf couldn't remember a time when anyone had needed him like this.

"Has she awakened at all?"

"Once."

"You've done what you can, Kit." He tightened his arm around her, and she melted into him. He swallowed hard, well aware that she was even more alone in the world than he was. A strange sensation of protectiveness moved through him, and he wished he could shield her from the pain of losing old Bridget. He understood the pain of loss, but had no experience in giving comfort.

"Will you try to rest now?"

''I remember when my mother died,'' she whispered, ignoring his question. ''Bridget stayed and stayed and wouldn't come out to me. I thought she must love only my mother; not me.''

''Come away and eat something.''

Kit had no appetite and shook her head at Wolf's offer of food. She remembered something suddenly and went over to the chest. Opening it, Kit drew out a long, brown woolen stocking that was weighted by something stuck in the toe.

''A strange old woman gave me this today,'' she said. He heard none of the usual brashness or vitality in her voice. ''She told me to show no one but you.'' Kit handed the sock to Wolf and went back to sit next to Bridget.

When he peeled away the soft wool of her stocking and saw his father's seal, the one that had been stolen, Wolf was astonished by how little effect it had on him. A small voice in the back of his mind urged him to question Kit about the old woman who had given her the seal, but it all seemed unimportant now. A new voice, a strange and much stronger voice, told him that his present task was to somehow provide comfort and support for the young woman who was about to lose her oldest friend, likely her only friend, the woman who had been a mother to her.

Chapter Six

Bridget stopped breathing well before dawn.

Kit watched, detached, as Wolf pulled up the soft linen sheet to cover the old woman's familiar features; the cheerful face that had laughed and scolded and cried over the years. Kit knew she must have wept, but was hardly aware of it. She felt sick at heart, nauseated and exhausted. There was a stale taste in her mouth, her joints creaked and all her bones ached.

Wolf drew her into his arms and sat down with her in the big chair next to the fire. He stretched out his long legs and propped his feet on the stool. Kit sat nestled comfortably, securely, feeling the slow, steady thump of his heart in his chest.

Wolf watched the sun rise and pulled Kit closer. She was so unlike any woman he'd ever known, he thought with a sigh. When had he started thinking she was beautiful? She dressed in rags that none of Queen Catherine's women would have allowed in the same room with them. She submitted to beatings from a drunken stepfather, yet ran away from Wolf's protection on the road to return to Somerton and faithfully await Rupert Aires. Just yesterday, Wolf had caught her scampering up the stairs like a kitten on the run. She'd intervened on the Juvet boy's behalf like one of King

Henry's justices, and ministered tenderly to her dying cousin.

How could he think of her as anything but beautiful?

"She never had children of her own," Kit remarked quietly. Wolf's arm tightened around her shoulders momentarily. "Rupert and I were all she had. He should have been here."

Her words slammed into his consciousness.

Rupert. He'd get her to Sir Rupert, by God. As fast as Janus could get them to London.

The funeral Mass and burial took place before the noon hour. For all the earl's pompous posturing around Kit, she noticed he didn't bother to attend the requiem for her kinswoman. He'd gone hunting.

She was grateful to Wolf and his men, all of whom attended, as well as the few servants who'd had contact with Bridget. It was also a surprise to see young Alfie attending, with several of the people Kit had spoken to in the town.

When the funeral was over, Kit returned to the room she had shared with Bridget. It suited her to be alone, but not cooped up in the musty old room, her eyes drawn to Bridget's deathbed whenever she looked up. There was a great emptiness inside her, begging to be let go.

She changed into her old traveling clothes: the brown breeches and rough woolen tunic along with her cloak and the hat that concealed her hair so well. All was quiet as Kit went through the great hall, and she met no one on the way to the stables. A mare was saddled for her, and Kit headed out past the drawbridge and into the meadow beyond the castle walls.

Wolf looked for her soon after she left. Finding her room empty, he asked various servants regarding her whereabouts, but none had seen her. Thinking she might have returned to the cemetery, he went there, but didn't find her. Worry turning to alarm now, he hastened back to the stable to have a groom saddle Janus for him.

"Goin' out after Lady Kathryn, are ye, sir?" the boy asked.

"Lady Kathryn? What do you know of her?" Wolf demanded.

"Nothin', sir, just that she rode out of here some little while ago."

"Alone?"

The boy shrugged his shoulders.

"Where? Which way was she going?"

The boy pointed out the direction.

Wolf took off at a full gallop in search of Kit. Being alone outside of the castle walls was dangerous for a woman. It was unwise—no, downright foolhardy for her to be out riding in unfamiliar territory, he thought angrily, and with the fair going on in town, there were strangers about. Wolf was personally responsible to the king for her safety, but his sense of dread went deeper than that. Though the sensation was an unfamiliar one, the fear that something might happen to her went beyond having to answer to the king for it.

He rode a long way through the meadow where he had played with his brothers twenty years before. So many hiding spots here, so many pitfalls for the unwary rider. Wolf's worst fears were realized when he saw a saddled horse, wandering riderless near the small lake where he used to fish with his father and brothers. Gripped by panic that she'd been thrown from her horse and was lying injured somewhere in the grass, Wolf dismounted.

An uprooted tree lay across the still waters of the lake, and Kit climbed up its huge root system to walk across the long, thick trunk. Scrambling around a branch which jutted vertically from the trunk, she sat down on the tree with her back resting against the branch and dangled her feet over the lake. It wasn't long before she had her shoes off and was dipping her toes in the clear, chilly water.

She had been sitting there for some time before she heard

the steady approach of a rider. It took a while before he finally came on foot to the water's edge, and Kit was relieved to see Wolf.

He appeared to be searching for something in the grass, and Kit was a bit disappointed that he didn't seem to be looking for her. She thought of the way he had helped her get through the night, sitting quietly with her. She had never expected such a thing from anyone, much less Wolf.

The sound of a whistle startled him. It was unlike any birdsong he'd ever heard and when he looked up to scan the area, his eyes finally lighted on Kit, perched on the edge of a huge fallen oak, two fingers poised at the corners of her mouth, ready to whistle again. Her britches were rolled up above her ankles and she dipped her feet casually in the icy water, without so much as a grimace or a shiver due to the cold. He thought immediately of a mysterious water nymph, raising her arms to the moon, but quickly shrugged aside the notion.

Wolf stepped up onto the trunk and walked across to Kit, then sat down on the opposite side of the branch which she used as a backrest. He'd had every intention of throttling her for making him worry so, but looking into her sad eyes, Wolf couldn't bring himself to upbraid her. She was working too hard to keep her spirits up.

''Your boots will get wet,'' she said, watching him lower his long legs towards the water.

He adjusted his legs so that wouldn't happen.

''Were you looking for something?'' Kit asked.

''You.''

She was pleased, even though he seemed cross. She looked over at his profile. How could a man be so beautiful, she wondered. Even with the terrible scar that cut across his forehead, he was achingly handsome. She didn't want him to be angry with her. ''Looking for me? In the grass? By all the saints, Gerhart, I could swear you were searching for toads.''

"Not toads," he said. "Just a kitten, strayed too far from the yard."

"That's what Bridget used to call me," she said, blinking back tears. "Kitten. Or Kitty."

"I know."

"Rupert was the one who started calling me 'Kit,'" she said. "What about you? Do you have many names? Or are you always Gerhart?"

"I suppose I'm many things, Kathryn," he replied tersely, having been reminded of Rupert, "and only sometimes am I Gerhart."

"What of your parents?" she asked. "What do they call you?"

"My father is dead. But my mother used to call me, *'mein Sohn,'* which means simply, 'my son.'"

"*Used* to call you?"

"A long time ago."

"She's still living, then?"

He nodded.

"Do you see her ever? Your mother?"

"Not in five years," Wolf replied. He didn't need to have seen her for twenty years to know she was the same. Staring out her window at her father's palace at Bremen, eating only what was fed to her, hearing nothing... "But I know she is well enough, and secure."

"I hardly knew my mother. I was only five when she died." She dipped one toe in the water. "Bridget told me last night that the old King Henry sent my mother to Somerton to marry Thomas Somers. I'd always wondered why my mother married Baron Somers and I wanted to ask Bridget more, but her breath was so short, she could hardly speak."

"She told you this before she died?"

Kit nodded and swung her foot back into the water. "She said there was something she *had* to tell me. That was it." She shrugged. Perhaps Wolf, having been sent from King Henry, could add to what Bridget had said.

"Not much of a deathbed revelation," Wolf remarked. "Hmm."

"The question is *why* Henry sent your mother to Somerton. The king must never have met Thomas Somers."

Wolf obviously knew nothing regarding her mother or her marriage all those years before.

"Seems I'm to be the recipient of all sorts of information here at Windermere," she said at last.

"You mean the seal?"

"I've expected you to ask me about it."

"I daresay I've been more or less preoccupied," he replied. It was true. For all its importance in the body of evidence against Philip Colston, Wolf was more interested in Kit's welfare right now than in the signet stolen from his father. He wished he could force himself to care less about her, but found it an impossible task.

"A strange old woman gave it to me. At first I thought she was a ghost or a spectre of some kind," Kit explained, "but I found she had slipped into my room through a secret door."

"Secret door? I know of no—I mean I've never heard of any secret passages in Windermere Castle." He thought he knew every nook and cranny of Windermere. Yet it had been many years since he'd been here. He was only a lad of nine when he'd left for Bremen that last time. It was possible that the castle held secrets not open to a young boy.

"Well, it's there. I'll show you when we go back."

"Who was the old woman? Did she tell you her name?"

"Agatha, she said."

"Agatha!" he exclaimed.

Kit looked over at him in astonishment.

"Agatha was the second wife of Clarence, Philip's father." Wolf was clearly disturbed by the information Kit gave him. "It's been thought, these many years, that she was dead."

"I don't believe so, Gerhart," Kit contradicted. "I myself saw her in the flesh twice, the second time in her own chambers. It was there that she had me pull out a loose piece of granite outside of her window to find the ring. She had it stashed there.''

''And she told you to give it to me?'' he asked. He watched as she pulled her feet gracefully out of the water and put her soft leather shoes back on.

''She said I was to give it to the man with the silver eyes and black hair. That could only be you,'' Kit told him, omitting the fact that Agatha had called him ''the wolf.'' As they walked across the log and back onto land, she wondered what the importance was of the hidden seal and why Agatha had wanted Wolf to have it. The woman's ramblings were so muddled, Kit thought perhaps Agatha had chosen Wolf at random from all the guests at Windermere to be the recipient of the ring. Maybe Lady Agatha merely liked his looks. They were certainly pleasing.

What was it Agatha had said about the ''rightful earl''? Kit couldn't remember for certain. Anyway, it didn't matter now. Philip was earl, and the old woman was obviously not in full possession of her senses.

''Tell me…who else at the castle has been imparting information to you?'' They walked back toward the tall grass where their horses were grazing.

''Just Lord Philip,'' Kit told him. ''He said he's going to petition Baron Somers or perhaps even the king for my hand.''

''*What?*''

''You may find it difficult to believe, Gerhart,'' she said, stopping to face him to emphasize her point, ''I may be plain, but I am not as unmarriageable as you seem to think.''

''Why, I've never said you were not a marriageable—''

She laughed. '''Twas not what you *said,* exactly.''

''I implied it?'' Well, first impressions were not always accurate. Wolf thought of Kit's regal entrance into the great hall of Windermere the first night and again of the masterful diplomacy she'd used in handling the earl during the incident with young Alfie. He thought of how well she fit with him on Janus, and now, the way her bare feet had gracefully, even seductively, swept the chilly waters of the lake. Her lips were full, sensuous. Her eyes were an incredibly wicked shade of green framed by the longest lashes he'd ever seen on a woman. She was anything but plain or unmarriageable. "Impossible," he said quietly.

The heat in his dark gray eyes was disturbing. Kit experienced a vague sense of danger to her equilibrium in those eyes, and quickly turned away to walk on. "'Tis a shame about Windermere," Kit said at length.

"A shame?"

"Windermere is Philip's heritage, is it not?" she asked. "Yet he keeps a steward who has allowed the housekeeper to rule and the castle to fall into disrepair. His bailiff abuses his rights and the reeve abuses the villein. The lord's demesne is—"

"How do you know all this, Kit?" Wolf asked, astonished at her perceptions.

"Well, I've eyes and ears, and the good sense I was born with," she said. "It doesn't take a great deal of intelligence to see what is going on here, or what needs to be done to repair matters."

"What would you do, Kit, if you were Lady Windermere?"

"Well, I don't know about being Lady Windermere," she said with a snort, "but if I were Philip's steward, I'd conduct hallmote and bring charges against the bailiff the people whisper about. The reeve, whatever his name is, would also answer to a few charges himself. Then I'd send the housekeeper packing—she had no business harassing Lady Clarisse—and hire tradesmen—"

"What do you mean, harassing Lady Clarisse?"

"Oh, some of the servants believe Mistress Hanchaw gave her no rest."

"Hmm," Wolf mulled that over. "And what about tradesmen?"

"I'd hire some. To begin repairs on the castle."

"And Philip?"

"Oh, well. Philip… I was thinking about a Windermere without Philip in charge. I doubt he could ever be convinced to sack his housekeeper or the steward."

"Bridget told me there was no steward at Somerton."

"Bridget loved to talk."

He thought of the clean rushes, the flowers in the house, the baron's productive fields and the neat little town and knew with a certainty that Kit was responsible. Neither the slovenly, drunken baron nor his wastrel wife would have the necessary skills to manage an estate the size of Somerton. No wonder the man wanted Kit back when she was finished in London.

"What happened when you tried to run away from Somerton Manor? Your cousin said the baron would kill you if you ever tried to run away again."

"I… It was…nothing." Kit shuddered. She didn't want to think of Baron Thomas and the evil light that came into his eyes, the hateful grin he wore when he hurt her. Bridget had been right. It was best to have gotten away from him.

"Surely there was some incident?" He had no idea why he wanted to press her for the knowledge. But for some reason, he felt compelled to know.

"It was years ago. The baron was in a drunken rage…" she finally said. "There had been a visitor from the king, a knight whose name I don't remember now. But he had already left the manor.

"I…I'm still not exactly sure what my offense was, or what he *thought* it was, but he cuffed me and…and knocked me down the steps." She felt dangerously close to tears again as she recounted the events of that day. The baron had been particularly vicious, and she had been more afraid than usual. "I m-must have been unconscious for some time, because the blood from the wound on my fore-head was dry already..."

"What happened?" Wolf seethed with anger as he re-called the long, wooden staircase at Somerton Manor and pictured Kit at the bottom of it.

"My head hit something as I fell, and it gashed open," she replied. "But when I could finally get up and move about, I realized the pain in my shoulder was more than just a bruise. My...my collarbone was cracked." She in-haled a long, shuddering breath, remembering the shooting pain that had coursed through her shoulder and down her arm.

"How old were you?" Wolf asked through clenched teeth, infuriated.

"I was eleven...mayhap twelve years..." she replied. "I didn't know where Bridget was, but I thought if I could just get to the village, I would make my way to the road and find that knight who had been to see Baron Somers. He had seemed a reasonable sort, and had even questioned me about my welfare at Somerton. I hid in one of the cotters' huts. I thought I'd wait until dark, then..."

"Then what?" Wolf asked, becoming angrier with every word. Baron Somers was fortunate that Wolf had been un-aware of any of this when he was at Somerton.

"He burned two cottages before I realized what was hap-pening."

"He knew you were being hidden by the peasants?"

She shook her head. "I don't think so," she said. "He j-just wanted someone to tell where they'd seen me, w-where I'd gone."

"So he threatened the people—*his* people—by burning down their dwellings?"

Kit nodded.

"What a fool," Wolf muttered. "Go on."

"When I realized what the baron was doing, I came out and b-begged him to stop."

"And did he?"

"Yes. He dragged me back to the manor and told me he would kill me if I ever ran from him again," she said. "He was furious that I'd run. He s-struck me again. A lot. I thought he would kill me right then, but his wife interfered. She screamed at him and pulled him off me."

"Lady Edith was fond of you, then?"

"No. She was warning him about something—I think it was about the knight who had just left Somerton. I'm not sure. I've never understood it."

Wolf vowed that Kit would never be returned to Baron Somers. Even if he had to drag Rupert Aires to the church for his own wedding.

"Why does he beat you?"

"Please, Gerhart, I—"

"Why? What drives him to hurt you so?"

"I don't know, Gerhart," Kit answered. "But he never missed a chance at it."

They returned to Windermere's great hall together.

"Come," Kit said, delaying him with her touch on his arm. "I want to show you something." She drew him up the stairs, around the corner and down the corridor to her room.

Kit took him inside and bolted the door behind them. Then she lit the candelabra and led him to the secret door behind the tapestry. Releasing the catch on the door, Kit led the way up the concealed staircase until they reached the chamber where she had found Agatha.

It was empty. There were no furniture, no rugs, no little stool, nothing. It was a cold and empty tower room.

"She was here!" Kit said, hardly believing her eyes. "I swear by all the saints, she was here!"

"Your Agatha?"

"Yes! There was a bed...there!" She pointed. "And a chest, a chair and stool... What could have happened?"

"Are you certain—"

"Of course I'm certain! How else would I have known

this place was… Look here.'' Kit opened the window and reached out. Her fingers finally found the loose rock, which she pulled out of place and handed to Wolf. ''This is where she had the signet hidden.''

He reached out and felt the gap in the stone, then searched the space with his fingers. Finding a leather pouch, he carefully drew it out, then fit the loose granite back into place.

''She was here, Gerhart. Truly, it is not my imagination—''

''I believe you,'' he said, the look on his face darkening. ''Look here.'' Wolf opened the pouch and found a few loose coins inside along with a withered, yellowing piece of parchment. A seal had been imprinted on the paper, but Wolf did not recognize the pattern. Most of the written message was obscured by weather and time, but it was clearly enough addressed to Clarence Colston and dated 22 August, 1401.

''What happened to Agatha? This pouch wasn't here before. What do you suppose—''

''Kit, we've got to get you out of here.''

''Why?''

''Philip doesn't want Lady Agatha's presence known. He's moved her out of this room, so he must have some idea that she spoke with you…'' Wolf started to plan. ''Perhaps if he thinks you believe she was a ghost…''

''But she wasn't a ghost, Gerhart, she was as real—''

He took her by the shoulders. ''Kit, we can't trust Philip.''

She looked at him quizzically.

''I'll explain later. For now, you'll just have to believe me. I'm going to tell him you were visited by the ghost of some old countess and that experience, coupled with Bridget's death makes you anxious to leave Windermere. That way—''

''Anxious to leave Windermere?''

''As soon as possible.'' Wolf glanced outside to gauge

the sun's position in the sky. "We'll be able to ride four or five hours yet if we leave straightaway."

"But we're expected to stay until tomorrow. Won't Philip suspect—"

"Not if I tell him you're upset by the ghost and demanding to be taken away from here," Wolf replied. "If he suspects you've spoken with Agatha, and you've not mentioned the strangeness of meeting his stepmother—"

"I understand. He'll think I'm hiding something. But if I tell him I saw her and believed she was a ghost—"

"Right," he said. "It will keep us ahead of Philip for the moment."

"What about the signet? Whose is it? And what is this parchment? It wasn't there when I found the ring. What does it mean?"

Gerhart latched the window and drew Kit back to the secret door. "Let's get you safely away from Windermere, and I'll explain what I can."

While his men packed the horses and accepted supplies of additional food from the earl's kitchens, Wolf spoke to Philip. He wanted to be the one to explain their reason for their precipitous departure and not leave it to Kit. She was always so forthright, he doubted her ability to lie effectively.

"Lady Kathryn is most distraught over the death of her cousin, and anxious to move on," he explained. "Disturbing as it was, the lady experienced yet another shock."

"Namely…?" Philip eyed Wolf menacingly.

"Apparently, there is a ghost in the castle," Wolf said most earnestly.

"A ghost?"

"Yes, some old Countess of Windermere appeared in the lady's room…" Wolf left the sentence unfinished, giving his cousin an opening to explain.

"…Ah, yes. *That* ghost." The crease between Philip's brows deepened slightly.

"You know of this spirit?" Wolf spoke quite seriously.

Though there were many who believed in haunts, Wolf did not. In spite of that, he hoped he'd be able to convince Philip that he and Lady Kathryn were both believers.

"I have heard of this countess-ghost, but I have never seen her myself," Philip said, stroking his beard. "They say she speaks...?"

Wolf shook his head. He didn't want Philip to know that Agatha had spoken to Kit. "Lady Kathryn said the ghost mumbled some gibberish. Nothing intelligible. Terrifying."

Philip let out a long, steady breath and picked at his beard.

"The visitation has upset the lady considerably, and she cannot abide another night at Windermere."

"Perhaps I can persuade her to stay. She may have another chamber if—"

"I'm afraid not," Wolf said. He intended to keep Philip as far away as possible from Kit. "I've already discussed the matter with her, and she is determined to go."

"Then I will bid the lady adieu," Philip said. "I would be gratified if you would accept a Windermere escort. The roads are not the safest—"

"Thank you, but no, Lord Philip. My men are quite capable—"

"I insist," Philip said.

Wolf had no intention of taking any of Philip's cronies with him. He did not care to be scrutinized by Philip's men all the way to London and he felt particularly vulnerable, traveling with his father's signet and the document he found in the niche outside the tower room.

"His majesty appointed this troop of men himself," Wolf argued. "It would not do to insult the king by adding to the escort without his consent."

"As you wish, Sir Gerhart," the earl said peevishly. Wolf knew Philip was attempting to come up with another means of getting around him, but was interrupted by Kit's appearance. "Lady Kathryn," he addressed her, taking her hand and dismissing Wolf. Then Philip spoke to a page who stood nearby and sent him on an errand to the stables. "I hardly recognize you in these traveling clothes," he said, referring to Kit's rough costume.

"They suit me well on the road, my lord."

Wolf went over to a chair near the fire and tightened a bootlace while his cousin made his farewell. "I hope this…ghost…hasn't put you off Windermere entirely, my dear lady," Philip said.

"Of course not," Kit replied. "Normally, I might have found the experience…er…fascinating, but not just now. My cousin's death—"

"I quite understand, my dear," Philip walked Kit to the main entrance of the hall, putting his hand on the small of her back. "I am certain it will not be long before we meet again, and I anxiously look forward to that day."

"Thank you, my lord." She saw Wolf go out ahead of them to mount Janus. The train of men and packhorses were ready and waiting for her.

"Allow me to present you with a small gift, a token of my admiration for you," he said when they started down the steps. A stable boy had brought around the mare Kit had been riding that afternoon, fully saddled and ready to ride.

"My lord, I cannot accept such a valuable gift. I—"

"Of course you can," Philip said. "She will bear you many miles in safety and comfort. I hope one day she will bring you back to Windermere. And soon. Come. Let me assist you—"

Wolf rode up at that moment and reached down to sweep Kit up into the saddle in front of him. "Lady Kathryn will ride with me."

Philip opened his mouth to protest, but Wolf cut him off with a curt explanation.

"We'll cover more miles this way," he said. Then he smiled. "But—allow me to offer his majesty's thanks for the horseflesh. She's a comely beast."

* * *

Their horses cantered at an easy pace, and Kit was comfortably situated with her back resting against Wolf's iron chest. At first Kit had thought she'd have preferred riding the mare given to her by the earl, but quickly decided that she liked riding with Wolf. She wondered if she would ever ride this way with Rupert and if it would feel so secure and easy with *his* arms around her, and not Wolf's.

The afternoon was warm and sunny, and Wolf rode without gauntlets. Kit studied the backs of his roughened hands where the dark hairs grew thickly over tanned skin. There was strength in those hands, and a gentleness, too. A gentleness she doubted he even realized.

"'Tis a long story," Wolf began, "and one which I can only partially tell."

"Hmm," Kit said sleepily. It was quite pleasant to ride along safely with Wolf on his huge horse. The last days had taken their toll, and Kit was more than willing to be lulled by Wolf's deep, melodic voice as he told the story of the mysterious signet. She was half dozing when he began the tale.

"Philip's father was Clarence Colston, the younger brother of Bartholomew Colston, who was Earl of Windermere before him. Bartholomew's wife was Margrethe, a daughter of Margrave Rudolph of Bremen. Bartholomew and Margrethe had three sons." Wolf was surprised at the ease with which he spoke to her of his family. He had never recounted this story to anyone before.

"The people of Windermere town still hold Bartholomew Colston in high regard. They say he was a fair and just lord, reasonable and well-liked by townsmen and cotters alike, with a worthy steward, a fair reeve and a sensible bailiff. There was prosperity and contentment in his lands. They say that Windermere was never short of laborers or yeomen to work on new projects. The only difficulty came from Lord Bartholomew's brother, Clarence, who liked to harass the farmers and townspeople. It is said he criticized

Bartholomew for eliminating certain traditions like the *merchet* and *heriot*.''

''But every worthy lord has dispensed with those archaic payments,'' Kit said. ''They caused such a strain between the landlords and peasants. Even Baron Somers, well...''

''You're right. Even the most backward lords had dispensed with them. And there were other unpopular traditions which Bartholomew eliminated as well, causing the people of Windermere to have an even greater loyalty to him.'' Kit had never known Wolf to be so long-winded and his telling of the story surprised her. Soothed by his pleasing voice, she listened to his words as merely a story, and wrapped up as she was in her own worries, she didn't realize the personal stake Wolf had in it.

''The ring Agatha gave you belonged to Bartholomew. It was stolen twenty or more years ago, never to be seen again—until now. There were rumors when the seal disappeared, that Clarence or Philip was responsible for the theft, but nothing was ever proven.''

''Why would the earl's brother want the seal?'' Kit asked sleepily. ''What would he be able to do with it?''

''He should have been able to do nothing with it,'' Wolf replied. ''But I have a suspicion that Clarence—or Philip—used it illegally in order to implicate Bartholomew in a capital crime... Treason.''

''Why do you think Agatha gave me the ring?'' Kit asked. ''What possible significance can it have now?''

''It could shed light on the events surrounding the deaths of Bartholomew and his sons.''

''Such as...?''

''I don't really know, Sprout,'' he lied. ''But I intend to look into it when we reach London.''

''What do you think Agatha meant when she said to look for Tommy Tuttle in London?'' she asked, yawning.

''She said what?'' Wolf was startled.

''I didn't think to tell you before. Agatha said to look

for a man called Tommy Tuttle in London. That he could explain…'' She shrugged.

''What else did Agatha say? Try to remember everything, Kit.''

''There was something about the rightful earl coming to claim his title,'' Kit told him, ''but the woman spoke in riddles. I couldn't understand her meaning at all.''

Silver eyes. Black thatch. Rightful earl. As Agatha's words came back to her, Kit suddenly became more alert, more aware of the implications of Wolf's story. Was it possible that Wolf was a son of Bartholomew Colston? Didn't he say the sons had died twenty years ago?

''Tell me, Gerhart, what were the names of Bartholomew Colston's sons?'' she asked, controlling her voice.

''The elder two were John and Martin. The youngest was called Wolfram.''

Chapter Seven

At dusk, Wolf called a halt near a clump of trees which backed up to a rough rock formation, offering some protection from the wind. He wasn't particularly concerned about highwaymen, since they were said to be scarce in the area.

The men started a small fire and prepared a meal with some of the food that was sent along from Windermere. Kit ate only a few bites, then wrapped herself up in a blanket and settled down to sleep near the fire. Wolf's men finished eating, then found comfortable places for themselves, though several remained on the alert.

Kit couldn't fall asleep. Vowing not to weep again and trying not to think about Bridget, she considered the story Wolf had told about Earl Bartholomew and his stolen signet ring. Even with her limited contact with Philip, she could easily believe that the present earl had had something to do with the seal's disappearance. She wished she could recall whether old Agatha had said anything specific about Philip Colston. Her words were so confused, Kit wasn't sure she could believe anything the old woman had said.

Yet she had no doubt now that Wolf—Wolfram—was the rightful earl, a surviving son of Bartholomew Colston. And for some reason, he had to keep that fact hidden. It occurred to her that Philip might still pose some threat to

Wolf, though that was difficult to understand. Wolf was perhaps the most powerful, most controlled man Kit had ever met. She couldn't imagine any reason why he would allow Philip to continue holding the earldom.

Kit wondered how many more estates they would visit before reaching London...and Rupert. It seemed so long since she'd seen him. Only three years and yet she could hardly remember his face. Of course she remembered that his hair was light brown and he had pleasing hazel eyes, but his features had faded in her memory over time. It crossed her mind that Rupert had never roused her senses the way Wolf had, just by his nearness. She almost wished for a prolongation of her journey to London, afraid that Rupert wouldn't be—

Everything was suddenly very quiet. Kit noticed that Wolf and his cousin were no longer talking with Hugh, but sitting quietly, looking at the fire. They didn't appear relaxed at all, though. None of the other men seemed at ease, either. In fact, when she watched closely, she realized they were all readying their weapons, quietly, unobtrusively. A chill ran through her, and she sensed the same danger they did, though she didn't know how or why.

In an instant, men were moving all around her in the dark. Men she didn't recognize, as well as Wolf's men. Kit jumped to her feet and ran back to where the horses were tethered. The clanging of metal on metal was all around, and Kit watched as Wolf's men fought desperately. By Kit's count, the bandits outnumbered them by four—herself included, of course.

She remembered that her sling and a packet of stones were in one of her satchels. If only she could find where Egbert and Claude had put them when they'd unpacked the horses, she might be able to even the odds. She hoped Wolf wouldn't mind. Kit was certain that if he were here, Baron Somers would beat her for interfering, but she had to hope Wolf would appreciate her efforts to help his men.

Forcing herself to remain calm, Kit slipped away from

the fray. Locating her bags, she dug through her belongings to find her little weapon. It was really only useful for killing small animals—hares and squirrels, sometimes foxes—but could easily stun a larger animal if her aim was good. That was all she intended now—to stun a few of these outlaws.

Kit slipped the packet of stones into her belt and climbed up on the gentle mare Philip had given her. From her elevated position, she'd have a clear shot at the attackers.

The battle raged on, with Kit taking shots whenever she had a clear view of her target. Her concentration was focused so single-mindedly on her efforts, she didn't realize that the brigands had discovered her. One of them circled around behind the horses to sneak up on her. He yanked her roughly off the horse and dragged her away from the fray.

''There's a knife at yer throat, yer ladyship, so's I wouldn't be callin' out if I were ye,'' the bandit said in a harsh whisper.

Finally halting near a small river, Kit's assailant shoved her down on the ground. A second later, he was on top of her, cutting her clothes away. She screamed when she felt the cold iron against her flesh.

''Shut up!'' He struck her in the jaw hard enough to make her see stars. ''I promise I'll cut ye first and have ye last!''

Kit struggled with all her might. If the man intended to kill her anyway, what difference did it make whether she struggled or not? She was certainly not going to die without a fight. She got one hand loose and managed to get hold of her knife, but her attacker quickly knocked it out of her hand. When Kit felt him rip her clothes savagely away, she finally knew true panic. She kicked and struggled with a vengeance, desperate to get away from the foul man. She managed to get in a good kick, which only infuriated him. He struck her hard again, bringing tears of pain and desperation to her eyes.

Then she heard Wolf's voice in the distance, calling to her.

"Damn the bastard!" her attacker muttered, gripping her even more savagely, pulling fiercely. Kit screamed again and struggled with all the force she could muster, trying to buy a few moments' time.

When Wolf finally reached her, it was over quickly. The hateful assailant was dead on the ground next to her, and then Wolf had her in his arms and was carrying her away from the site. He took her over to the little brook whose gurgling she had heard before, then sat down with her on a raised piece of flat rock, cradling her as she sobbed. It was the second time in less than a day that she'd sat thus, cuddled into Wolf's arms, weeping like a child.

Wolf dismissed Hugh Dryden, who had come to assist if necessary. The attack back at camp was over now, with none of Wolf's men lost, and only two injured. Most of the assailants had been killed, though two ran off when they realized they stood no chance of victory against King Henry's seasoned soldiers.

The odds had turned to Wolf's favor shortly after the battle began, and he got only a quick glimpse of Kit in action before his attention was drawn by yet another swordsman. Unbelievably, it was Kit who was responsible for influencing the outcome of the exchange.

Unsure of Kit and what she might do next, he waited for her sobbing to stop. When it finally did, only to turn into hiccups and sniffles, Wolf waited again. He'd seen his share of battles, but seeing Kathryn wield her small weapon was something entirely new. She had done it again. Taken him completely by surprise. He wondered when her little surprises had ceased to annoy him.

He smiled, amazed at her spirit. And her skill with the little leather thong.

"This must be four," she said between sniffles.

"Four...? Aye, it is," he smiled, understanding her meaning. She was all right, he realized as a sense of tre-

mendous relief rushed through him. "But we'll call it
even." He brushed his lips across her forehead, marveling
at her. For all her terrifying experience, she hadn't even
lost her hat. And she still smelled of roses.

"We will?" She looked up at him with large, wet eyes,
enough to make his heart lurch in his chest. The thought
that she might have been harmed pierced him to the core.
She was trembling now, and he hugged her tightly to his
chest.

"You'll have to show me that little weapon of yours,"
he said.

She nodded against his chest.

"Do you think you can walk back now?"

"Of course," she replied shakily, sliding off his lap,
holding her shredded tunic together. Her knees buckled almost immediately, and she would have hit the ground had
Wolf not moved quickly to catch her. She slipped her arms
around his neck when he lifted her and looked up at him.
He wasn't scowling at her now.

"Kit." His voice was a rasping whisper. He could only
think how good it felt to have her safe and secure in his
arms.

He hesitated for a moment, but then his mouth found
hers, and Kit trembled with a desperate sensual reaction to
his touch. Her nails bit into the back of his neck and he
intensified the kiss, sweeping his tongue inside her mouth.
Kit's entire body responded, and she groaned as she melted
in his arms. Oh, how could he affect her like this? How
could she let this happen?

Wolf sat back on the rock ledge and moved his lips down
the delicate column of Kit's throat. Her tunic was in tatters
and Wolf's fingers easily found the peak of one full breast
which he caressed first with his thumb, then his tongue. Kit
cried out in pleasure as one of his hands moved down her
back to her buttocks, then her thigh. She squirmed and
kissed the back of his neck while he teased her nipple and
slid his fingers up between her knees.

"Sweet Kit," he whispered, moving his mouth back up to hers. "So incredibly beau—"

His words brought her back to reality, and Kit pulled back abruptly. "Oh, no," she whispered as she clamped her legs together. "Rupert," she cried in dismay. "I've betrayed Rupert." Kit slid away from Wolf and buried her face in her hands. She couldn't bear to face him now, not after he'd touched her so intimately. And she'd let him.

"You haven't betrayed Rupert," he said quietly, shakily. "This sort of thing is—is natural after what happened tonight. In the aftermath of a battle, it's easy to lose control...."

"Yes," Kit said quietly, embarrassed. "I understand." She still believed she'd broken faith with Rupert. God in heaven, it took only one of Wolf's kisses to do it. Just the man's touch set her trembling, wanting more.

Yet Rupert awaited her in London. And Wolf, the son of an earl, grandson of a German prince, had his *Anna-someone*...waiting somewhere.

"Have a look, cousin," Nicholas said as Wolf and Kit approached the camp. He showed Wolf a leather purse taken from the body of one of the attackers.

Kit was still shaky from her experiences by the brook. Both of them. She picked up her blanket and wrapped herself up in it, then followed Wolf to the fire. "There was a merchant at Windermere Fair selling those purses. Robert atte Cross was his name," Kit said. "Look—even the cross in the heart is tooled into the back."

"You're certain you saw these pouches at Windermere?"

"Yes," Kit replied. "I remember Baron Edward's wife remarking on the device of the cross in the heart. I remember thinking it very clever that the man worked his name into his sign."

"These men carry too much gold to have been desperate

for our coin,'' Hugh said. ''In fact, I don't believe they wanted our coin at all.''

''Good. It just adds one more nail to his coffin.''

''Whose coffin, Gerhart?'' Kit asked.

''Philip Colston sent these cutthroats after us,'' he said. ''Do you remember he tried to send some men with us?''

She nodded.

''No doubt to eliminate us whilst we slept.''

''But why?'' Kit asked. ''Because you have the signet ring? Or the paper? How could he know?''

''He knows you've seen Agatha, and he can't be sure of what she may have told you,'' Wolf replied. ''Agatha must have been party to Clarence and Philip's conspiracy against Bartholomew. Philip can no longer trust her.''

''Are you saying that he sent these men...to kill me?'' Her voice was barely a whisper.

Nicholas nodded, while Wolf was loath to confirm her worst fears. Kit looked over to where the horses were tethered. Her brown canvas satchel still lay open on the ground with some of its contents spilling out. She started to tremble again.

''The man who d-dragged me into the woods...he knew I was... He called me 'milady' or 'your ladyship'. H-how could he have known I was anything but a lad, dressed as I was?''

''But he did know, my lady,'' Nicholas countered, voicing and verifying their suspicions. ''Somehow, he did know.''

Kit eventually curled up with her back toward the crumbling rock formation and tried to sleep again, but as before, it eluded her. Worse yet, she was shivering—probably from shock—and couldn't seem to stop.

Wolf, aware of the trembling mass under Kit's blanket, went over to her and dropped down to the ground next to her. Without a word, he hauled her up against him, covered them both with his thick wool blanket and settled down to sleep. Her back curled easily into his warmth and he draped his arm across her waist, as though it belonged there. Before long, her shivering stopped, and she fell asleep.

Somewhere deep in her unconscious mind, Kit was aware that the birds had already been singing for quite some time. Dragging herself to full wakefulness, she lay quietly, enjoying the peace of the moment and the heat and power of the man who lay entwined with her.

Man? Entwined?

She pulled her legs away and sat up abruptly to face Wolf, who was lying comfortably on his side with an elbow bent and his head resting on his hand.

"Good morning, my lady," he said quietly. "I trust you slept well?" His eyes strayed to her lips, then dipped down, unable to resist a glance at her softly curving form.

Kit glanced down to see that her tunic was gaping wide from the gash that had been torn in the fabric, giving Wolf a glimpse of soft white skin and lush, pink-tipped breasts. She pulled the edges of the cloth together for modesty.

Wolfram swallowed hard. He sat upright and pulled a blanket around her shoulders. "Find something decent to wear," he said gruffly. "We'll be on our way soon."

Kit wore women's clothes for the next three days and kept well-covered in a wimple and her old mud-stained cloak. Wolf remained quiet as they traveled, barely answering Kit's few questions. He was sullen and preoccupied, and Kit believed he frowned at her more since he'd kissed her than he had in the entire time she'd known him. She wondered why he was so dour, but all her attempts to draw him out were unsuccessful.

Men! she thought. How was she ever to understand them?

Wolf told her that they would make only one other stop before reaching London, at the estate of John Beauchamp, the Marquess of Kendal. He didn't mention that the Marquess had been Bartholomew Colston's closest friend and had made several attempts in the court of Henry IV to make inquiries into the deaths of Bartholomew Colston and his sons, only to be thwarted at every turn. There had been a wary and suspicious climate at court at the time of Bart's death, and Henry Hereford had been unwilling to entertain any reconsideration of the charges against the earl.

Wolf intended to take the Marquess into his confidence and attempt to gain his support and assistance, which would be invaluable when he presented his case against Philip to King Henry V. Perhaps *this* Henry would reopen the case and judge it for himself.

Relegated to the back of Wolf's mind was the awareness that they would soon reach Westminster and he would have to turn Kit over to King Henry. And to Rupert Aires. The idea did not sit well. The fact that she could have such an effect on him was acutely disturbing. No, it was downright impossible. No woman had ever dwelled so much in his thoughts, nor had he worried about anyone the way he had about Kit. It would have to stop.

When she arrived in London, there was no telling what King Henry wanted with her. Perhaps he would allow her to wed Rupert, though it was possible that Lady Kathryn Somers had some obscure political connections. Perhaps Henry wanted her to marry for diplomatic reasons. Whatever happened, Kathryn would be on her own, at the mercy of the king's benevolence, no matter how much Wolf wished otherwise.

Wolf's thoughts drifted to Annegret, the daughter of a German margrave with whom his grandfather sought an alliance. So far, Wolf had managed to avoid an actual betrothal to Annegret, a pale, meek girl who was quite a contrast to Kit, but both families were strongly in favor of the match. He knew he'd soon have to make a commitment.

As they rode to Kendal Keep, Wolf laid his plans. He would ask John Beauchamp to come to London and make discreet inquiries into the existing evidence against Bartholomew Colston. Perhaps now, Henry Hereford's son would consider investigating Bartholomew Colston's role in the alleged assassination attempt on his father. Wolf believed he would be able to refute whatever spurious evidence existed against his father in the *Curia* files. After all, he now had the old signet ring, as well as Bartholomew's remade signet, not to mention the withered parchment which bore Clarence's name and a mysterious seal.

Wolf also hoped to locate Tommy Tuttle whom Agatha had mentioned to Kit. He wondered how common that name was in London, and if he would ever be able to find him, a man with an obscure connection to a twenty-year-old crime. He vowed he'd go back and find Agatha herself and take her to testify before Henry if need be.

Lastly, Wolf knew he had to get away from Kit. She was a threat to his controlled, well-ordered life, and the last thing he needed was to fall any further under her impudent spell.

They reached Kendal Keep just before nightfall and were greeted on the stair by a round little woman, richly dressed in a blue gown and head covering. Wolf recognized her as the Marchioness, Lady Mary Beauchamp.

"Welcome to Kendal," Lady Mary greeted them warmly, her words bubbling over one another. "'Tis lovely to have guests, and we so rarely do. You look weary, my dear. You must have traveled all day. You're likely hungry and thirsty and wish to rest. We will see what we can— Oh my, here I go off again," she said, putting a conscious stop to her rambling. "How do you do?" she took Kathryn by the arm and steered her away from the knights. "I am Lady Mary, Kendal's wife. Oh, it is so good to have you here. If only Charlotte, my daughter-in-law, were here." Kit smiled at Lady Kendal's effusiveness and went along with her. It was pleasant to escape Wolf's sour company for the moment, though she wondered if Lady Mary would ever give her the chance to speak. "Lady Kathryn, are you not? The man-at-arms informed me..."

Wolf hardly listened to the woman's chatter as he followed Kathryn and Lady Kendal into the hall. Kit seemed at ease, and Wolf knew Lady Mary would see to her comfort while recounting every event in the lives of the Beauchamp family for the last three generations.

Nicholas and Wolf crossed the hall and followed one of the Marquess' knights who took them to a curving stairwell at the rear of the castle. They climbed one flight of the stone steps to reach a small room in the tower, John Beauchamp's office. It was a circular room with long narrow windows cut into the stonework. The lighting, which would be more than adequate in full daylight, was augmented by a low-hanging chandelier.

The Marquess of Kendal was not a very tall man, but he was solidly built, obviously a man of action in his younger days. His hair was gray at the temples, though it was a sandy brown over the rest of his head, just as Wolf remembered. He had a friendly gleam in his penetrating blue eyes and was as reticent as his wife was outspoken. Wolf was wondering how to broach his true reason for visiting Kendal Keep when the Marquess finally spoke.

Looking directly at Wolf, he said quietly, "Did you take me for a doddering old fool, boy, not to recognize the name *Gerhart?*"

Chapter Eight

Never had Wolf considered the possibility that Lord Kendal would remember the name of his German grandfather, and he was chagrined to think that the Marquess was offended by the deception. He wanted the man on his side, not alienated from him.

"Would you be John or Wolfram?" the Marquess asked. "Obviously, at least one of you survived the attack. My guess is that you're Wolf, though all three of you boys had your father's look about you." Lord Kendal sat back in his chair and studied Wolf. "If memory serves, you're a bit young to be John."

"John died with my father," Wolf said quietly.

Though he had to have known and accepted it as fact for twenty years, the Marquess was clearly disturbed by Wolf's words. "Why are you here now? What are your intentions?" Lord Kendal asked.

"I hoped to convince you to help me regain Windermere and clear my father's name," Wolf replied carefully. "I wasn't sure how—"

"I'll help you," the Marquess said without hesitation. He braced his hands on the arms of his chair and stood up. "I've always believed there was foul play involved, and not just bandits on the road, as we were led to believe. There is no doubt in my mind that your uncle Clarence contrived to have your family eliminated in Europe. I am also certain that he, or perhaps Philip, was responsible for that business of trying to kill King Henry Hereford during the Glendower uprising.''

''Do you have any evidence of this?'' Wolf asked, astonished by Lord Kendal's revelation.

''No,'' Kendal shook his head, ''but I knew your father and his brother very well in our youth. Clarence coveted the Windermere lands and the titles. Couldn't stomach the idea that none of it would be his. I never doubted that Clarence was capable of betrayal—worse, murder—to take what he wanted. And he wanted Windermere.''

''We've just come from Windermere,'' Wolf said.

''Have you, now?'' the old man raised an eyebrow. ''You ought to be very cautious around your cousin Philip. He is as twisted as his father was, you know, though Clarence's deeds were usually motivated by jealousy. He hated your father.''

Wolf knew.

''Philip is a different beast altogether,'' the Marquess remarked as he came around to the front of his desk. ''There were some nasty incidents, all hushed up, of course.''

''My lord, Agatha Colston is still alive,'' Wolf said.

The Marquess was intrigued. ''We heard she'd died years ago.''

''She gave this to Lady Kathryn Somers,'' Wolf said, taking the leather pouch containing the signet and the letter from his hauberk. ''Agatha told her to see that I got it. Then she disappeared.''

''How so?''

Wolf explained the manner in which Kit met Lady Agatha. ''She must have been involved in the plot against my father from the start,'' he concluded. ''But I don't understand why she's willing to betray Philip now.''

''I wonder,'' the Marquess mused aloud. ''I would venture to say that she must be a virtual prisoner in the castle.

I don't believe her relationship with Philip was ever a particularly good one. So when she saw you at Windermere, she probably took her chance.''

"But how did she know me?"

"You couldn't possibly realize it, of course," Kendal remarked thoughtfully, "but you're the very image of your father."

"Why didn't Philip recognize him, then?" Nicholas asked as Wolf placed the signet ring on Lord Kendal's desk.

Lord Kendal shrugged. "It's been twenty years. I doubt it would ever cross his mind that one of Bart Colston's sons would return from the dead." He studied the image carved into the ring. "'Tis Bartholomew's stolen seal," he said, looking up. "Agatha had it?"

Wolf nodded. "Agatha had this hidden as well." Kendal sat down at the desk and frowned at the crumpled, faded parchment laid before him.

After studying the ancient paper for a moment, he sat back in his chair. "This will be ridiculously simple," Kendal said, grinning. "When do you leave for London?"

Kit hadn't seen Wolf or any of the men since they'd arrived, and she wondered where they were. She missed her sullen escort and wished for the opportunity to chide him for his poor company the last two days. She wasn't going to allow him to ignore her any longer.

It was terribly unfair—just when he'd started to behave civilly towards her, he had to kiss her. Now, not only did their budding friendship suffer, her heart twisted within a tangle of confusing emotions.

The circumstances were difficult at best. Words couldn't describe how she felt about losing Bridget, and her grief overwhelmed Kit at times. She frequently felt on the verge of tears but did her best to squelch them, knowing full well that they had no place on the road with a bunch of insensitive soldiers for company. And their leader was the worst of them. Dark and brooding, he put up a formidable wall between them and she couldn't bear it any longer.

Wolf hadn't even mentioned her skill with the sling, either, not since his initial curiosity about her ''little weapon'', as he called it. It was as if their kiss had driven a wedge between them.

Kit dressed for supper and went down to the great hall. There, she saw Wolf standing near the huge fireplace with another man.

''Well now, Gerhart,'' the man said as he leveled his full attention on Kit, ''neither you nor my father bothered to remark on the lady's considerable attributes.'' He took Kit's hand and bowed gallantly over it.

''I don't believe your father has met the lady yet,'' Wolf replied tersely. He set his jaw and introduced her to William Beauchamp, Lord Kendal's son. ''Allow me to present Lady Kathryn Somers, ward of King Henry, *betrothed* to Sir Rupert of the king's guard.'' He barely glanced at Kit as he spoke, but he was very much aware that William continued to hold Kit's hand.

''Sir Rupert?...Aires?''

''Yes, my lord,'' Kit replied curtly. How dare Wolf bring up Rupert's name now, if not to remind her of her duplicity?

''I know him. A fine soldier,'' William remarked. ''I wish you well.''

''Thank you,'' Kit replied, glowering at Wolf.

''My brother, Robert, is in London with his wife and son. Perhaps you will—''

''Ah! There you are!'' It was Lady Mary, making her entrance into the hall with her husband. ''I see you've met William—where are the others?'' She took barely a breath and looked about the hall. ''Sir Gerhart, your cousin will sup with us, will he not? Cook has prepared a special meal that—''

''Wife! Will you see to the goblets? William has been remiss.''

"Of course," Mary replied. "Wonderful cask of wine decanted just for this evening. We…" her chatter continued, but only for her own benefit since the sound was lost in the tremendous expanse of the hall.

Kit had planned to speak to Wolf during dinner about his shabby treatment of her, but between her conversations with William and his father, and the fact that Lady Mary never released Wolf's ear, the opportunity did not arise. They finished the meal, and the men left the hall without even a parting word. Kit's frustration with the situation mounted.

"Where did they go?" Kit asked Lady Mary as they walked up the stairs to retire. It was late, and Lady Mary stifled a yawn before she replied. Kit noticed, with some relief, that fatigue decreased the woman's ability to chatter.

"Oh, you know. Men like to go around and see for themselves that all is secure. My husband likes to walk the battlements and see that his guards are alert and prepared."

They reached Kit's chamber door, and the hostess bid her good-night. "If you find yourself unable to sleep," she added as an afterthought, "Cook has some mulled wine in a tureen belowstairs. It helps to soothe the nerves after a long day of travel and excitement."

"Thank you, Lady Mary," Kit said, "I'll bear it in mind."

Kit had barely put her candle on the chest in her chamber when she decided to leave the confines of her room to go in search of a cup of the warm, spiced wine. Though it was late, her restlessness had not abated, and she knew it would be a long time before she was able to sleep.

Having found the wine, Kit poured herself a generous portion, then made her way to the fireplace in the great hall where a fire still smoldered. She sat in one of the big chairs that faced the fire and curled herself up into it like a cat. She sipped her cup of wine and was swallowed up by the long, wavering shadows in the hall.

Kit was determined to inform Wolf on the morrow that

she resented being ignored. She wasn't a child after all, and the very least he owed her was common courtesy. They would both do well to forget the incident near the brook, and he could very well quit taunting her with Rupert's name. Didn't he understand how confusing it was to be betrothed to one man yet still have strange, unwanted feelings for another? How could he be so callous?

Finally satisfied with the content of the lecture she would give the errant knight, Kit drank a second cup of wine and relaxed. The fire warmed her skin as the wine worked on her blood, and soon she was dozing comfortably in her chair. She wasn't at all aware of the men returning to the hall and taking their leave of Wolf, who was not yet ready for sleep.

He went over to the fire and stood looking into the flames, considering his good fortune as well as the prudent planning which brought him to Kendal.

Kendal's magnifying glass helped them determine that the parchment contained nearly irrefutable evidence against Philip and Clarence. Lord Kendal insisted on accompanying Wolf to London, and Wolf knew the Marquess' advocacy in King Henry's court would prove invaluable. Wolf would soon win back his title and see Philip punished for his part in the conspiracy against his father.

For a man without a future, Wolf suddenly had more of a future than he'd ever really anticipated. As they walked the battlements, the Marquess made a few remarks that caused Wolf to consider what lay ahead when he regained Windermere.

There was a multitude of problems that would have to be corrected. The castle itself was in need of repair, and from what he saw in town, Kit was correct about the reeve and bailiff. The people were neither prosperous nor content with their situation. Who knew how many atrocities had been quietly committed over the years under Philip's lordship?

Wolf wondered if Stephen Prest, his father's steward,

could be found. If so, the man would be a tremendous help in setting things to rights and returning to the precedents set by his father. Wolf would have to name a new reeve and bailiff, and he would choose just men, such as those employed by Bartholomew. Aye, there would be a great deal of work to do when he returned to Windermere.

He wondered again whether his grandfather would press for his marriage to Annegret now. Wolf tried to convince himself that it wouldn't matter one way or another. He needed a countess for Windermere, and heirs, and he tried to make himself believe that one woman would suit as well as another. But it was impossible not to think of Kit's touch, her soft lips, and her sighs when she was in his arms…

Not until Kit had he considered developing an emotional attachment to his future wife. He knew it was a foolish thought, making a man vulnerable. Annegret was a likely candidate for his countess. Even though she was so painfully shy and quiet around him, once she became accustomed to him, she would undoubtedly make a good wife, a pliable and obedient wife. One who would be predictable—

A gentle sigh interrupted his thoughts, and Wolf turned to see Kit asleep in the chair behind him, with her feet pulled up under her and her head resting on her arm. She was so beguilingly childlike, so spirited. He knew she was angry with him, and she had every right to be. Though she had tried to get him to converse with her numerous times, he had rebuffed every attempt she'd made to draw him out. He'd even thrown Rupert in her face when he knew very well that she thought she'd betrayed him.

He knew he had been treating her abominably these last couple of days, but he saw no alternative. She was fast becoming his weakness and after the night they were attacked on the road, he vowed not to let that happen. He would get her to London and into King Henry's care. Then he could go about the business of retrieving Windermere without any distractions. Once Windermere belonged to him again, he would begin to repair the damage done over the last twenty years. When the time was right, he would wed Annegret or some other likely maid. One who was calm and sedate and predictable.

Kit stirred in her chair and opened her eyes slightly, only to close them again. Suddenly aware of Wolf's presence, she opened her eyes again, came more fully awake and stretched, covering a yawn.

"You should be abed," Wolf remarked quietly.

"I wasn't tired," she retorted saucily.

"So I see," he said.

"At least you're speaking to me for a change," she said sarcastically, her green eyes flashing.

He did not reply and was more than a little amused by the fact that she was not in the least intimidated by him.

"You realize you haven't said more than twenty words to me in the last three days?"

Wolf picked up her empty cup and sniffed. He suspected she'd had more than enough wine.

"It is very unkind of you to ignore me the way you have, Gerhart," she chastised. "Even Baron Somers acknowledged my existence."

Wolf was taken aback to be unfavorably compared to that scoundrel, Somers, and his shock must have showed on his face.

"Are you angry with me?" she asked on seeing his changed expression. All notions of giving him a piece of her mind fled. She was afraid she had unknowingly offended him and the thought worried her. Willing her voice not to crack, she quietly asked, "Have I done something—"

"No, Kit," Wolf replied gently, unwilling to wound her any further with his unkindness. "Come. I'll help you to your chamber."

"Perhaps I'm not in need of your help." She was back to being defiant.

He smiled. He could deal with an audacious, insolent Lady Kathryn, but not a hurt little sparrow.

Kit stood, a bit unsteadily, and started to walk towards the stairs. If he was going to be curt with her, she saw no need to observe the courtesies which dictated that he escort her and assist if necessary. She didn't need him, nor want him, nor—

"Well then. I'll just walk along with you since I'm going this way anyway."

"Don't bother seeing to me, Gerhart," she said as she staggered up the steps. "I'm perfectly capable of—"

She stumbled, and he caught her around the waist to prevent her from falling down the stairs.

Frustration welled up in her and hot tears were about to spill over when Wolf turned her roughly in his arms and crushed her mouth with his own, never giving her a chance to pull away. He moved his lips on hers until they fit perfectly, then opened them, silently demanding that she do the same. Kit obeyed and when his tongue met hers, she was caught up in a fiery heat so intense her knees buckled. She would certainly have fallen if not for his rough hold on her.

He pressed her closer, fitting her softness to his hard length as she raised her hands and encircled his neck. She opened her mouth to him with a fervor and eagerness that frightened her, yet she had no power to hold back. Twice before had he kissed her, though Wolf's effect on her was even more devastating this time. She shuddered. She was burning with a need she couldn't understand and the need was growing and bursting within her. Wolf's mouth consumed hers and as their tongues mated, Kit understood that she wanted him. She wanted his hands all over her.

Wolf's hands moved up from her waist and slid to the sides of her breasts. Cupping their fullness and finding the nipples with his thumbs, he brushed across them, pulled them erect and let her breasts fill his hands.

He knew he had to force himself to stop. He tasted her

incredible sweetness and was driven by need as her body pressed against his heat. She was going to make him insane with wanting her, yet he knew it wasn't possible. She was the king's ward, and Wolf was supposed to protect her, not ravish her. He couldn't possess her, not with Rupert and King Henry waiting. Not with his decision to stay clear of her. This was merely a mistake, a lapse in his control. He had to think of Kit and her welfare. He had to consider Windermere.

And there was his tentative commitment to Annegret...

Wolf pulled away. Her mouth was swollen from his kisses, and he wanted to carry her back to the hearth and make love to her. The urgency of his desire was completely foreign to him and he knew that it could only lead to heartache. It was clear in her eyes that she desired him as much as he wanted her. He *had* to call a halt, an irrevocable halt. There couldn't be any turning back. She could never be his, not when Rupert waited.

He swallowed hard, then donned a rakish smile to disguise what he felt. He took her hand and kissed her palm sensuously. "I...have no decent excuse for my rudeness tonight, Sprout. I suppose I've been so long without a wench—"

Shocked by his cruel words, she slapped him hard across his face, then turned and stumbled up the stairs as quickly as her legs would carry her. When she reached the landing, she took one of the lit tapers on the table and muffled a sob, then continued up the steps. She hoped to God he hadn't heard her agonized cry.

Wench was it? Or whore?

She swore he would never get that close to her again.

Chapter Nine

After crying herself bitterly to sleep, Kit spent the following day with Lady Kendal. She saw Wolf briefly only once, when she broke her fast in the hall with the Marchioness. Kit remained aloof, refusing to meet his eyes and allowed herself to be fully engaged by Lady Mary's chatter.

It was years since Wolf had felt so miserable. Kit Somers was by far the most desirable woman he'd ever known, responding to his kiss like wildfire, like the golden woman at Somerton Lake, but more real. Kit was flesh and blood, heart and soul, with an impetuousness that he had to admit was strangely appealing. And he wanted her.

It pained him to see how wretched she looked, sitting at the table with Lady Kendal. Her eyes were red and swollen and, while he knew she had more to weep about than his insult of the night before, he felt duly guilty for having added to her burden of the last few days.

Resolved as he was to keep her at arm's length, and even encourage her animosity, there was nothing he could do to ease her agony. As there was nothing he could do to ease his own. Wolf spent the day with Lord Kendal and his son, William. They rode across the Kendal lands and wasted away the afternoon fishing, with Lord Kendal regaling Wolf with story after story of his father's youthful escapades when Bart and Kendal fostered together at Castle Peak.

Though Wolf should have found himself spellbound by tales of the father he'd hardly known, his thoughts gravitated towards Kit time and time again. How could he possibly let her affect him so? There wasn't a woman in all of England worth the trouble she was giving him.

"—really set on marrying Rupert Aires?" William asked.

Wolf realized his thoughts had drifted. He nodded in the affirmative, even though he hadn't heard the complete question. He'd seen William's reaction to Kit's presence clearly enough to understand what was being asked.

"She's a redhead, isn't she?" William asked, but before Wolf could respond, the Marquess' son continued eagerly. "I knew it. With those green eyes, she'd have to be. I'd like to—"

"She's not available," Wolf snapped. *Was* she a redhead? He'd never seen her without a head covering though he supposed she'd uncover it soon enough in London when she saw the fashionable ladies of the court. She'd probably lower her neckline and tighten her bliaut, too, he thought with a grimace. He thought her perfect as she was.

"What does Henry want with her?" the Marquess asked.

"Damned if I know," Wolf replied. "Likely wants her to wed Rupert as soon as possible and put a stop to his shenanigans at court."

"Hmm. She's committed to Sir Rupert, then?"

"I just said she was," Wolf grumbled.

Wolf felt as though he'd been torn in half. Part of him wanted to stay away from the hall so he wouldn't have to face Kit at supper. The other part wanted nothing more than to see her with his own eyes, to reassure himself that she would be all right. Damnation, it was irritating. How could he have been so callous with her the night before? He reminded himself that he'd said the cruel words in order to make her despise him so there'd be no turning back. And he'd done a fine job of it.

Wolf realized that within a day's time, Kit would be on her own in London. She would marry Rupert Aires and return to Northumberland to the Aires family estates. And Wolf would spend God knew how long trying to forget her, trying not to measure every other woman he met—including Annegret—against her.

''Greetings, Sir Gerhart,'' Lady Kendal said as the family and guests assembled together for supper. ''You've made yourself scarce today. So have my husband and son. I don't believe I've seen Lord Kendal quite so pleased with guests in a long time. In fact, he seems over-anxious to leave me alone on the morrow and travel in your good company.'' Though she sounded petulant, Wolf was aware that she was chiding him good-naturedly and didn't intend that her complaints be taken seriously.

Lady Kathryn sat next to Lord Kendal again and concentrated on the food before her. Hardly listening to Lady Mary's chatter, Wolf saw that Kit pushed her food around the trencher and ate very little of it. Once she looked up at him, but lowered her eyes almost immediately.

Her obvious distress bothered him tremendously. Her eyes were bright with unshed tears, and he knew if she cried, he'd be up in a second, dragging her into his arms, apologizing and begging her to forgive his words.

He couldn't let that happen. She would fare better as the spirited, quick-witted woman he had become accustomed to, rather than the hurt, downhearted girl he saw before him.

The conversation at the table turned to the attack Wolf's group had suffered on the way to Kendal. Nicholas boasted of the prowess of the men in routing the attackers, and Wolf took the opportunity to provoke a little temper from Kit.

''Lady Kathryn managed to throw a lucky stone or two, felling a couple of the brigands.''

''What?'' Kit muttered, having difficulty believing what she was hearing.

''They were so surprised at being hit, the lady gave our

men a momentary advantage, even though we were out-numbered, and—''

"They were more than surprised, sir." There was indignation in her tone.

"I beg your pardon, my lady?"

"I daresay I did more than merely surprise them," she said, hardly able to believe the way he belittled her contribution to the battle. She had saved their wretched hides!

"True. They were distracted from their attack and my men—"

"Would have been slaughtered if I hadn't felled the villains!"

"Lady Kathryn," his tone was patronizing, "we all appreciate your efforts—"

"Chester Morburn would have been sliced in half, and Douglas Henley would surely have fallen if not for my 'lucky stones' as you call them!"

The Marquess observed quietly as the argument continued and wondered what made Wolf goad the girl so. She was rightly angered by his belittling of her assistance during the attack, and Lord John found his curiosity piqued. What was going on between them now? Why did he taunt her so? The Marquess intended to find out, if not here in Kendal, then in London.

"...and furthermore, 'tis unseemly for a lady to stand astride a horse's back," Wolf had taken to lecturing her pompously, "taking random shots, hoping to remain unnoticed by the enemy. Had I not seen you being taken away into the woods by that brigand, you may have suffered more than—"

"I managed to *endure* your rescue!" Kit bit out the words. "Given a moment more, I would have freed myself and escaped. It was only—"

Wolf chuckled indulgently, infuriating her all the more. Lady Kendal reached across her husband and put her hand on Kit's forearm in an attempt to calm her.

"Shall we ladies withdraw?" Lady Mary asked. "We'll leave the gentlemen to their own devices for a while."

The trip to London was deplorable. Kit insisted on riding her mare, refusing to consider spending another hour in Wolf's saddle, near him. One of the men always rode next to her, but never Wolf. If he happened to speak to her, which was rare, his tone was curt. He raised a mocking eyebrow whenever he looked in her direction and dared to be impatient with her when she requested a halt to take a private trip into the woods.

The man was insufferable, and she couldn't wait to reach London and be rid of him.

Yet she was miserable when she reached Westminster. She dreaded saying goodbye to Wolf, missing his cantankerous presence before they even parted company. Facing his imminent departure brought her dangerously close to tears yet again. They'd been through so much together, it seemed she'd known him for ages. What would she do without him?

Kit's arrival at the king's palace was so overshadowed by doubt and desolation, that she could hardly appreciate the wonder of the palace or the fact that the king had summoned *her* to it. She dwelt on the details of getting her bags unloaded and her mare sent to the livery so she wouldn't have to think about leaving Wolf. Once, when she caught his eye unexpectedly, she was certain she saw a spark of...something...but then it was gone so fast, she realized she was mistaken. She knew very well that the light of his eye was *Annalise*...and not a simple *wench* from the country.

Lady Maude Teasdale, a distant cousin of the Lancaster king, greeted Wolf's party in the courtyard and took charge of Kit. As the woman received a brief report from Sir Gerhart regarding their journey, Lord Kendal took Kit aside.

"It occurs to me," he said, "that it may take you some time to adjust to things here in the palace. If any...difficulty arises, you must feel free to summon me. I am not without influence here..."

"Thank you, Lord Kendal," Kit replied, rising on tiptoes to kiss his cheek. His kind words seemed to ease the parting. "I will call on you if I need you."

"And me, Lady Kathryn," William added. "I am also at your service."

"I shall remember," she said with a sad smile. "You and Lady Kendal have been very kind."

"And you, Sir Gerhart?" Kit asked hesitantly, hoping for a kind word, unwilling for him to leave on such unpleasant terms. "Will you also be nearby in case I should have need of you?"

Wolf gritted his teeth. "It would seem that you have an abundance of champions, my lady." His voice was harsh. "You won't have need of me."

Lady Maude whisked Kit quickly away, along with two palace guards and a bearer, into the depths of Westminster Palace. Kit turned back to look once, and saw Wolf standing idly in an archway, scowling, watching her go while Lord Kendal and his son, as well as the rest of the men, mounted and prepared to leave. The expression in his eyes gave Kit to believe that perhaps it had finally occurred to Sir Wolf that they might never see each other again. Swallowing a pang of loneliness and suppressing a sharp aching need to be held once again by Wolf's strong arms, Kit turned and walked deeper into the corridors of Westminster Palace.

"We did not know exactly when to expect you, Lady Kathryn," Maude said, leading a brisk pace through the gallery. "But rooms have been made ready, and you have two well-trained maids who will see to you until his majesty returns."

"Returns?" Wasn't the king here? Why had he sent for her if he wasn't even here?

"Yes. Unfortunately, his majesty is not in residence at the moment, but I understand he is to return within a fortnight. You are certain to have an audience with him then."

Kit wanted to ask what King Henry wanted with her, but feared it unwise to admit she had no inkling of why he'd summoned her. She thought it best not to mention her doubts, but just try to endure her stay in London. Besides, she could use the time to find Rupert. After all, she told herself, that's why she had allowed herself to be brought all this way, wasn't it?

Maude finally led Kit into a large, cheerful chamber that was lavishly furnished. It did not appeal to Kit's simpler tastes, although there were huge windows overlooking a courtyard, now enshrouded in the deep evening shadows. It was on the opposite side of the building from where Wolf had left her so she knew she wouldn't be able to catch sight of him leaving.

"The adjoining sitting room is for your use as well, Lady Kathryn," Maude said as she opened the connecting door. "No doubt the other ladies will be anxious to meet you and to hear of your travels. You may entertain here or do whatever you wish. We were instructed to help you make the palace your home."

"Thank you, Lady Maude," Kit said, sighing. "I am most grateful. But who are—"

"What would you care for first? A bath? Supper?" Maude opened the door to the chamber to admit the two maids she had spoken of before. Both were young and enthusiastic about meeting their new mistress. They curtsied as they gave their names, Meg and Jane.

"A bath would be nice," Kit said, wishing that Lady Maude would just leave her. She felt terrible and wanted to be alone. Not even the thought of seeing Rupert raised her spirits.

"Their majesties have a number of retainers and advisors who reside here at Westminster. Queen Catherine's ladies are here as well as many of the wives and daughters of the king's advisors. We have quite a few other Catherines here as well...such a lovely name.''

''Thank you.''

''You will meet some of the ladies tomorrow, I daresay,'' Maude informed Kit. ''We have all been anxiously awaiting you.''

''You have?'' Kit was somewhat surprised. She wondered if everyone here knew her business with King Henry except her.

''Why yes, of course,'' Maude replied. ''His majesty told us to expect you. Ah, here is your bath.'' Footmen carried several buckets of steaming water into the room and poured them into the hip bath which had been placed near the fireplace. ''I'll leave you in the care of your maids.''

Kit somehow lived through eight of the loneliest days she had ever known.

Henry had given orders that Lady Kathryn was to be cared for and given whatever she needed. Hence, work had been started on several new gowns for Kit, the ladies of the court having made much of her ''quaint'' country fashions. With a twinge of distress, Kit realized how backward and ridiculous she must have appeared to Wolf, who was accustomed to the stylish ladies here at court. Her loose, flowing gowns were not at all in fashion. Fortunately, the Westminster seamstresses were first-rate, and Kit's wardrobe would be completely replaced before King Henry's return.

The king and queen left a large entourage at Westminster. The women often spoke French, which Kit had never needed to learn, and all too often, no one bothered to translate for her.

As she passed the days waiting for the king to return, Kit's mornings were spent walking in the gardens, usually alone, wishing she could get away from Westminster to the countryside. She thought perhaps she might catch sight of Wolf somewhere in the immensity of the Westminster estate but knew in her heart that she would never see him again.

Afternoons were occupied with several of the other ladies of the palace. They had various gentle occupations—sewing and mending, embroidery, and a few of them worked on a huge, colorful tapestry. They chatted and gossiped together as they worked, sometimes with a wandering minstrel in their midst, who played his lute and composed verses as he entertained.

Rupert Aires' name was often mentioned, among giggles, titters and blushes. Kit didn't understand the innuendoes; she only knew that she was put out with Rupert. He was in London, probably quite near, and likely to have heard of her arrival, yet he hadn't bothered to visit. He hadn't even sent a note. Why hadn't he come? And why did all these ladies giggle when his name was mentioned? He couldn't possibly...? No, she shrugged off the thought.

There was even talk of Sir Gerhart among the ladies, and many of them seemed anxious to discover anything Kit could tell them about him. Lady Catherine Montfort seemed particularly interested. "Ooh, Sir Gerhart," Lady Catherine cooed. "He moves so well... He is so fierce... Was he ever...that is to say, did he—"

"Sir Gerhart saves himself for his love in Germany, as you well know," Jacqueline Meaux said in her charmingly accented speech. "He has never—to *my* knowledge—indulged in any...romance with a lady at court."

"I say he has no woman waiting in Germany," Catherine pouted. "He just—"

"*Au contraire,*" Claire retorted. "*Mon père* says he has met the girl and her father. And she is *très belle.*"

"Then will Sir Gerhart return to Germany to wed?"

"Perhaps she will come to England," Jacqueline answered Kit. "Or they may go to Paris. It is said Sir Gerhart has a fondness for Paris."

And so it went on, unendingly for days, with Kit's restlessness increasing by the hour. Kit needed no translator in order to figure what "tray bell" meant, nor any of the other engaging little French phrases the ladies used when speaking of Wolf's betrothed. Kit learned that *Annamarie* was a sophisticated, beautiful lady, and she surmised that Wolf probably resented the time he'd spent traveling from Northumberland to London, away from his betrothed.

On the ninth morning at Westminster, Lord Kendal came to visit, bringing his daughter-in-law with him. Several times Wolf had spoken to Lord Kendal of his concern for Kit, alone in the palace. Kendal promised that he'd look in on her. Why Wolfram couldn't do it himself was an additional puzzle that Lord Kendal intended to solve, though he had his suspicions.

"This place can be a den of vipers, Lady Kathryn," he said knowingly. "Thought you might like a friend."

Lady Charlotte Kendal was slightly older than Kit. She was a tall brunette, with soft brown eyes and a friendly, unpretentious smile. She was nothing like the ladies at court. "I've been anxious to meet you," she told Kit. "Gerhart told us about your journey from Northumberland."

"You saw Gerhart?" Kit's spirits rose at once, yet she felt depressed at the same time. He was so close…

"Yes," she laughed, "we've been overrun with guests, what with Lord Kendal and my husband's brother visiting as well."

"You'll be rid of all of us soon enough when we go to Arundel." The Marquess didn't mind his daughter-in-law's good-natured teasing. She was good to his son and had presented him with an heir just a year ago.

"You needn't trouble yourself on my account," Charlotte replied. "Your grandson thrives on all the attention you men have been giving him. We like having guests."

"When do you leave for Arundel, my lord?" Kit asked.

"Tomorrow."

"Does Gerhart go—"

"Yes, Sir Gerhart rides with us," Kendal said. "I'll be

certain to inform him of how you fare here at Westminster.''

Kit's face fell. Though she hadn't seen Wolf since he'd left her at the palace, she had somehow thought of him as being close by. But now, he'd be far away in West Sussex. Too far away for her to be comforted by thoughts of him.

Chapter Ten

Arundel
Late May, 1421

King Henry V was pleased to see the Marquess of Kendal.
The monarch was in high spirits. His recent marriage to
Catherine of Valois was proving to be a satisfactory match,
and his victories in France had done him a great deal of
good at home. The king was well-disposed to be friendly
and generous to old friends, and Lord Kendal was one of
the most loyal. He had proved it by his fidelity during various difficulties early in the reign of Henry IV and his continued support.

Sir Gerhart's presence with Lord Kendal was appreciated, and the king welcomed the knight's report on Kathryn
Somers' journey to London, though it was with some regret
that he learned of Kathryn's loss of her cousin at Windermere. Henry was given a full accounting of their journey,
including the attack they repelled on the night they left
Windermere.

"How did the lady fare during the attack?" Henry asked,
alarmed. "Was she harmed?"

"No, Your Majesty," Wolf replied. "Though she involved herself in the fray."

''How so?'' The king's hazel eyes betrayed his curiosity.

''She slipped away unseen,'' Wolf explained with a grin, ''and mounted her horse where she *stood astride* and shot stones at our attackers with a leather sling. And her aim was true.''

Henry looked at Wolf in disbelief. He knew of no ladies who used weapons for any purpose. To become involved in a battle where their very lives hung in the balance...

''Tell me more about Lady Kathryn,'' he ordered, as intrigued by the story as he was by Gerhart's tone of fascination when he spoke of the lady.

Wolf was surprised at the king's request, assuming that his majesty knew all he needed about Kit. However, given the fact that Wolf had been told so little about Kit when he'd been sent to fetch her, he quickly realized that King Henry knew very little about the lady himself. Why she had been summoned to London remained a mystery, too. Though they were close, Wolf could not breach protocol by asking the king his reasons.

He had been worrying about Kit for days, trapped at the palace among Queen Catherine's women and the English-women who made the intrigues of court their lives. Wolf was grateful to the Marquess of Kendal for introducing Kit to Lady Charlotte. As desperately as he wanted to see to her welfare himself, he knew he'd be unwelcome, given the nature of their relationship during the last days of their journey. She had probably been happily reunited with Rupert Aires by now, anyway.

Wolf recounted to Henry things about Kathryn that he remembered from their trip. He told the king about Somerton and what he knew of Kit's management of the estates. He also mentioned her stepfather's rough treatment of her. He described the care she gave Bridget and Kit's reaction to the old woman's death. Wolf spoke of Kit's diplomatic handling of the situation at Windermere Fair, when she intervened to prevent Philip Colston from punishing young Alfie Juvet unjustly.

Henry was intrigued, not only with the stories of the young woman, but with Sir Gerhart, the German nobleman who had always seemed so restrained and dispassionate, so coldly logical and reserved. They had become close during the French campaigns, and he had never seen Gerhart so fascinated by a woman before. Kathryn Somers had had a significant effect on the knight, and Henry wanted to know more.

The king withheld a smile as he reconsidered some of his plans and options, especially with regard to Lady Kathryn Somers. There was much to do before his return to France, and he wanted matters secured in England before his departure.

"Tell me of her appearance."

Wolf raked his fingers through his hair. "I haven't ever really *seen* Lady Kathryn, sire," he said, though he saw Henry's puzzled expression and knew he'd have to explain himself. "When first we met, she was wearing peasants' garb—filthy breeches and tunic, and a cape, I think. Her face and hands were covered with mud, and her eye was swollen and blackened. Lord Somers had also battered her lip, so it wasn't possible to tell quite *what* she looked like."

"I imagine she eventually washed her face?"

A strange heat arose around Wolf's neck, under his tunic. Of course Kit washed her face. What was Henry getting at? What did he want to know? That she had eyes as green as the emerald Henry wore on his left hand? Or that her skin was the color of fresh cream and soft as the white satin of Henry's tunic...that her blush was as gentle as a morning breeze? Perhaps he wanted to know exactly how high her cheekbones were or the way her delicately formed chin was dented—

"Her chin is cleft similarly to yours, Your Majesty," Wolf said abruptly. He wished they could get on to other subjects and stop talking about Kit.

Henry seemed taken aback, and Wolf tried to smooth over his reply.

"Her appearance is altogether pleasant, though I don't believe I've ever seen her without a head covering," he said, his sense of frustration increasing. "Her clothing never revealed anything of her shape, though she's about this tall..." Wolf put a hand up to the level of his shoulder, "...and she fits with me in my saddle with room to spare...."

And the knight was enthralled, Henry thought. It was very interesting. From their short conversation about her, the king could easily see that Lady Kathryn had twisted Gerhart into knots.

Gerhart had done well, and Henry was pleased with him. Not just for getting Kathryn Somers to Westminster safely, but for his past years of service. It had long been the king's intention to reward Gerhart for his exceptional service. In light of these new developments with Kathryn, it was entirely possible that Gerhart's reward could serve more than one purpose. He would give it due consideration.

"'Tis good to see you, Kendal," the king said, turning to the Marquess who had remained quiet during Wolf's report. He was as fascinated with the knight's tale as Henry was. "We met your son at Catherine's coronation."

"Yes, Your Majesty," Lord Kendal replied, "we spoke of it. He and his wife were most pleased to welcome Queen Catherine to England. We all wish you well, Sire."

The king nodded his approval.

"As to my reasons for seeking an audience with you..." Lord Kendal laid out the papers and scraps of evidence on the table for the king's perusal and began his opening arguments on Wolf's behalf.

Westminster Palace

Kit happened upon Rupert one sunny morning when she was walking through the west garden. Truth be told, she practically fell over him.

Feeling particularly gloomy and lonely, she had taken one of the less used paths, hoping that the bright scenes would cheer her. A perky little stream ran through that end of the garden, and there were clusters of interesting rocks situated here and there, as well as a bench under a huge old oak.

Kit noticed some herbs growing near the brook beside some wild grasses and she stooped to investigate, thinking she might possibly add to her store of medicinal plants. She made her way along the water's edge, paying little attention to her surroundings, other than the small shoots and wild herbs that were hidden among the rocks.

That was when she tripped over a pair of feet. Apparently, she had been so quiet, or Rupert and his companion had been so occupied, that they hadn't been aware of Kit's presence in the garden until the moment she tripped over them. Rupert sat up abruptly out of the tall grasses and was about to lambaste the intruder when he suddenly realized who she was.

Just then, Lady Catheryn Hayward, whom Kit recognized from court, sat up and brushed bits of grass from her hair and gown. She blushed and donned an embarrassed smile, but couldn't very well avoid facing Kit.

"Well, Kit!" Rupert said, flustered. He got to his feet and gave her a sheepish grin.

At least he appeared to feel contrite, Kit thought. "Rupert," she nodded, acknowledging his greeting somewhat distantly.

She was nearly devoid of emotion, which was surprising. Here he was, finally. And all wrapped up with Catheryn Hayward, a distasteful little idiot who was always whining about something whenever Kit saw her. And here Kit was, face-to-face with Rupert at last, and she had nothing to say. She had thought she'd throw herself into his arms when she finally saw him, that she would tell him all about Bridget and the king and get him to help her figure out why she'd been summoned to London—

"I'd heard you were here." His face had only become more handsome over the last three years, but Kit wasn't moved by his fine features. Looking over at Catheryn's flushed face and puffy lips, she now understood clearly the sly remarks of the women at court and realized that whatever she had known and felt about Rupert in the past was no longer true. He belonged more to *them* than to *her* and she cared not a whit.

"How long have you been back?" she asked.

"What? You mean in London?"

She nodded.

"Oh—well, months I suppose," he replied. "Some of us came in advance of the king."

"You must have been busy here at the palace—"

"Not at all," Rupert said with a devilish grin. "His majesty gave us liberal leaves after our long months in France. It's good to see you, Kit."

"I...we...supposed you'd come home to Northumberland..." It was strange. She should have been upset that he hadn't come for her months ago yet she found herself somewhat relieved instead, that she was not officially betrothed to this handsome rascal.

"No, I don't intend to go north until I must. I prefer London." He smiled rakishly.

"I see," Kit said, glancing over at Catheryn, who had stood and turned around to straighten the bodice of her gown. She thought the rumors among the women at court were that Rupert was pursuing Lady Alice. Yet here he was with Catheryn.

How frivolous he was, she thought. He hadn't taken their promise to each other seriously, nor did he behave responsibly toward his family. He should have at least visited them. Or sent word to his aging father. Thinking about the responsibilities he so easily shirked, Kit's ire rose.

"Kit—"

"Rupert," Catheryn whined his name. "I think it's time you took me back. Mama will be wondering."

"In a minute, Kate," he put her off, even though she'd taken his arm and was hanging on as though unable to support herself.

"Why are you here, Kit?" he asked. "Why did King Henry summon you?"

"I haven't been told. I still await his return to Westminster."

"He'll be here in four days, I've heard," Rupert told her. Catheryn began tugging his arm in earnest. "Well, I suppose I must take the lady back...."

"Goodbye, Rupert."

"Not goodbye," he protested. "We'll surely see each other...."

Though she had turned her back to them and already started walking towards the brook, Kit couldn't help but overhear Lady Catheryn's seductive giggles.

She should have felt sad, she supposed, or even indignant, but Rupert was just as he'd always been: carefree, thoughtless, lighthearted. Now that she thought about it, he'd never shown many signs of responsibility, fewer still of commitment. Why had she ever thought he'd take his betrothal promise seriously? As she walked away, she was immensely relieved.

On the other hand, her one and only certainty in life had ceased to exist.

Arundel Castle

The Marquess of Kendal was beaming. As he traversed the long corridor beside Bartholomew Colston's son, he could hardly contain his smile. Things couldn't have gone better. The king had listened to the case against Philip of Windermere, studied the evidence presented to him and drawn his own conclusions.

King Henry judged that Bartholomew Colston was innocent of involvement in the assassination attempt on his father, Henry IV, during the revolt of 1401. Furthermore, the evidence was irrefutable that Clarence and Philip Colston had been the ones involved not only in the conspiracy to assassinate Henry IV, but also in the plot which resulted in the deaths of Bartholomew and his son as they traveled to Bremen. The withered parchment, completely deciphered, attested to that.

Philip and his father had cleverly contrived to blame Bartholomew for the assassination attempt on the king, thereby ensuring that the earl and his heirs would be discredited and lose all claim to Windermere—in case they happened to survive the attack on the road to Bremen. The king remarked that Wolf's survival was a small miracle, and he graciously forgave the knight the deception involving his identity. He understood Wolf's need to use his German name until he was able to clear Bartholomew Colston of treason.

King Henry quickly dispatched a small army, under the command of Sir John DuBois, to take Philip Colston into custody. They were also charged with the task of finding Lady Agatha. Their instructions were to bring both of them to London where Agatha could be officially questioned, and Philip would be tried in the king's court for his complicity in the deaths of Bartholomew and John Colston. There was also the question of treason, to which Philip would answer alone, Clarence having been dead these last eighteen years.

Wolf took the liberty of sending Hugh Dryden to Windermere to quietly keep track of the doings there.

"What has you scowling now, boy?" Lord John asked as they reached the courtyard. "Your lands are restored, your titles returned and more. You are now *Duke of Carlisle*. Windermere and a half-dozen other estates are yours. What more do—"

"It was too easy," Wolf replied, still trying to absorb all that had happened during his audience with the king. He frowned. "All these years, I thought I'd have to fight tooth and nail for Windermere. It never occurred to me

that…'' he shook his head. ''Well, it doesn't matter now.
Windermere is mine, and I'll somehow pay the price for
it.''

''Windermere, Your Grace?'' the Marquess used Wolf's
new title.

''I didn't expect anything more.''

''But you are so much more now,'' Lord Kendal said.
''A duke of the realm, equal to any of Henry's brothers.''

Yes, he was gratified, even pleased to have been so am-
ply rewarded. He could go to Windermere as master now
and return the castle and his estates to their former gran-
deur.

Henry knew that Wolf was anxious to return to Windermere. However, the king required that the new duke
perform one last service before his departure.

Lord Kendal returned to London the following day with
his son, leaving Wolf at Arundel to assist the king. There
were more plans to be made for Henry and Catherine's
return to France, as well as governmental business in England to see to before they would follow Kendal to London.

''I would speak to you on a matter of some importance
to me, Wolf,'' Henry said as they finished work that afternoon. He was still adjusting to calling his friend ''Wolf.''
Somehow the name suited him, as had ''Gerhart,'' the
name he'd used all those years in Germany. The king saw
Wolfram as a man with strength of character as well as
physical power, possessing nobility and a sense of justice
as strong as his own. Wolf Colston was a man in whom he
could entrust a delicate but necessary task.

''I was recently informed that I have a sister,'' the king
said. ''I don't recall ever having met her mother, but I have
it on greatest authority—a document among my father's
papers—that this sister was conceived some twenty years
ago, soon after my father became king.''

With a quick mental calculation, Wolf knew that old
King Henry's first wife had been dead more than twenty
years, and he had not yet married Joanna of Navarre when

he took the throne from Richard II in 1399. The sister had to have been born between wives.

"Her existence has become known to various parties—the French, and unfortunately, some hostile Scots. She will become a liability unless I can get her situated safely. I cannot allow my half sister to be taken by some band of cowardly Scots, nor can I afford to pay any heavy ransoms for her safety. Even the damnable Lollards have threatened to breach the palace to do what they will. I cannot risk her safety."

"Lollards, Your Majesty?" Wolf asked. He was unaware that the heretical group in London was so militant. "Do you expect violence?"

The king nodded. "There is always that possibility. A few religious fanatics… I've ordered a great deal of protection for my sister, but it will not be enough."

"What do you intend to do?"

"Marry her off. She needs a husband with the power and authority to protect her. Someone with lands and position," the king said. "A duke."

Westminster

Kit could tolerate only so many fittings and only so much gossip. The days dragged and on the afternoon when the king was due to arrive at Westminster, Rupert came looking for her just as she was about to explode from restlessness. He had organized a shooting match near the palace gates with several of Henry's soldiers and thought Kit would like to join in. He knew the men would enjoy the novelty of seeing her shoot a bow. He had a vague recollection that she was rather good at it, he said.

Word traveled fast in the palace. When the ladies heard of Kit's invitation to shoot with Rupert and some of the men, they heartily objected to being excluded and begged Rupert to let them join in. Catherine Beauvais, Katherine

Courtnay, Alice Trevelyan and Margaret Troyes dressed in their most colorful gowns, ordered a picnic and had their horses brought round.

"I wish I had my own bow," Kit told Rupert as they rode toward the downs.

"Don't worry—one of our bows will suit you."

Kit could see the colorfully dressed ladies mingling with the soldiers, long before she and Rupert were even close by. She nearly laughed at them, so afraid were they at leaving Rupert alone with her.

"Ah, good," Rupert said, studying the crowd ahead.

Kit raised an eyebrow.

"The ploy worked." He gave her a sly look and seemed to debate within himself whether to disclose his secret.

"Whatever are you talking about?"

"Jackie Meaux," he tilted his head in the direction of the group ahead. "She's got word that her dear auntie on her mother's side is sick..."

Kit took inventory of the women up ahead. There were Katherine Courtnay, Catherine Beauvais, Margaret and...*Alice!* "Why you conniving rotter!" she exclaimed, understanding dawning. "You sent Lady Jacqueline away so you could seduce Alice Trevelyan without interference!"

"Jackie's a resilient soul," he said, "She'll live through it."

"But that's cruel, Rupert," Kit said indignantly. "You can't just...go through all of the ladies here at Westminster, picking them off one at a time, like targets. It's unfair. Immoral. And plainly inconsiderate. Think of their feelings, their—"

"You're all too tenderhearted, my Kit," he laughed. "Not a one of them has any heart. Each one wants to seduce *me*. In her own way, of course. And I merely let them."

"You are incorrigible, Rupert Aires." She dug her heels into the little mare and rode on ahead. She couldn't let him see that she knew he was right. Many of those ladies actually deserved Rupert.

Kit enjoyed herself tremendously, delving into the sport wholeheartedly to forget her worries. She was aware that the king would be returning soon and that before long she would learn his reasons for summoning her to London.

"You're a better shot than I remembered, Kit!" Rupert said with a laugh when Kit's arrow pierced the center of the target. He squeezed her shoulders, to the consternation of Lady Alice. "Let's see you do that again," he challenged.

She smiled at him, then placed her arrow in the notch. She pulled back and let the arrow fly. Everyone watched to see if it would make its mark.

"Dead center!" Rupert shouted, taking Kit's face in his hands and kissing her.

"I've been practicing since you went away," she replied, enjoying the fun. This was how she remembered Rupert. Lighthearted, laughing. She was so engrossed in the moment that it was some time before she noticed the entourage which was proceeding some distance away, down the thoroughfare towards the palace.

The king and queen rode among three hundred soldiers and several royal advisors. Wolf Colston was next to Henry, half listening to the king speak to his wife about the banquet which was to be held the following evening. Wolf was much more interested in planning his return to Windermere and had decided not to attend the king's affair, if Henry would excuse him.

Wolf's wandering attention was caught by the activity of the archers in the glade west of the king's entourage. There was no mistaking Lady Kathryn in the center of it all, and he witnessed her perfect shot. He also saw Rupert Aires kiss her.

Kit unmistakably put her hands on his arms and kissed him back.

Chapter Eleven

Lady Maude Teasdale informed Kit that the Earl of Langston, Edward Markham, would be calling on her that evening. She told Kit that the earl was one of Henry's most trusted diplomats, who had returned from France only weeks before, and had arrived at Westminster with the king and his party that afternoon.

Langston was a white-haired man, old enough to be Kit's grandfather. In one hand, he held a document rolled up and tied with a gold ribbon. "My dear Lady Kathryn. How good it is to meet you at last," the gentleman said when she entered the room. "I must say—you are the very image of your mother."

Kit's nerves were already wound as tight as a bowstring, and his statement didn't help. His words shocked Kit, but she maintained her composure. Just barely. No one ever spoke of her mother except Bridget.

"How do you do, sir?" she said quietly as she curtsied. She trembled slightly in anticipation of what the earl had come to say. "You knew my mother?"

"I knew both your parents."

She reeled at his words. *Both* her parents? There wasn't a person alive who admitted to knowing her mother's first husband. "I was told you wanted to speak to me," she said in a quiet voice, full of expectation now.

"Yes. The subject matter is somewhat delicate," Langston said as he led Kathryn to a chair. "Why don't you sit while we chat?"

Kit sat in a comfortable chair near the window and was so preoccupied with Langston's visit, she hardly noticed the dramatic flood of deep purple irises growing in a bed of black earth right outside. Kit had no doubt that the earl was about to inform her of the reason for her summons to London, and she tried to master a suddenly queasy stomach. She had an odd sense of foreboding after his words about her parents.

"I knew your mother when she was here twenty years ago. She was a lively thing, and a bit difficult as well. For her father, I mean."

"Are you saying that my mother was willful, sir?" Kit asked, her nerves abating slightly. The earl's manner was direct and friendly and helped to put her at ease.

"To say the least," he chuckled.

"Disobedient?" The very idea was intriguing. Bridget had never said anything negative about Meghan. As far as the old nurse was concerned, Meghan had been perfect. But what did all this have to do with King Henry V calling Kathryn to London?

"Suffice it to say that your mother was a lively girl, and a much-welcomed addition to the king's court. You must realize that it was a difficult time, when Henry Hereford took the throne from Richard. Not everyone was supportive."

Kit wanted to laugh at the earl's understatement. A group of Richard's supporters, who were supposedly loyal to Henry, attempted to assassinate the new king and his sons a few months after the coronation. And then it had happened again nearly a year later. It must have been an explosive time.

The earl continued, "However, his highness Henry IV was enjoying a great deal of success after ridding the country of King Richard. Lady Meghan Russell had arrived from Ireland just before the coronation, and she became enamored of Henry. Of course, there were many who loved Henry at that juncture.''

''My mother?'' Kit laughed somewhat dubiously. It was ludicrous. ''And the king?''

''She...well, she appealed to him,'' Lord Markham continued. ''Many of the ladies vied for his attention, but he cared only for Lady Meghan. You must understand that there were a great many pressures on Henry then. He did not step into an easy role. It was up to the king to uphold the monarchy, to repair the wrongs done at court, to preserve— Well, I've strayed from the subject at hand.''

He untied the gold cord around the document and began to unroll it.

''There is no easy way to tell you this, Lady Kathryn,'' Lord Markham said. ''However, young King Henry desired that I be the one to inform you since I happened to be here at the time...knowing both your mother and the king.''

''Knowing my mother...and the king?'' She looked doubtfully at the document which he placed before her and recognized the royal seal.

''Henry Hereford, King Henry IV, was your father,'' he said.

She shook her head to clear it. ''King Henry Hereford...?''

''Henry Monmouth—Henry V—is your brother,'' he continued. ''Half brother, actually.''

Kit stared at the parchment before her, as if it could speak, as though it could comment on what the earl had just told her. Then she looked up at him, disbelieving. It was impossible. Intolerable. Her mouth went dry. ''No one ever said anything. Why now? Why has his majesty sent for me now?''

''Your father's wishes were unknown until recently, when this document was discovered,'' the gentleman told her. ''The king was unable to marry your mother, though I can assure you that was his most desperate wish then. He chose Somerton as a safe place for both of you. The king was most concerned with your safety, especially since we seemed to be on the verge of civil war at the time. His enemies could easily have taken advantage, had they known of your existence. That is why your identity was kept secret.''

''But now…?'' Kit brushed away a tear that had spilled onto her cheek. All those years of believing her father had been her mother's husband, a nobleman who had died honorably somewhere… Yet Bridget had known, had tried to tell her in the end.

''This document was recently found among the old king's papers. He mentions you, his daughter, several times.''

''Me. His daughter.'' His *bastard* daughter, her heart cried out bitterly.

''Too many people are now aware of your existence. More will soon know your identity. There are many Lancastrian enemies who could take advantage of this information.''

''How?''

''The primary threat, of course, is abduction,'' Lord Markham said.

''Are you saying that someone might try to abduct *me?*'' she asked shakily.

He nodded. ''That was why King Henry had you brought to London as soon as he verified the information in his father's papers. To assure your safety.''

''But why should I believe this…this…paper?'' she asked quietly. ''Why should I accept your word that I…that I am a bastard?''

Lord Markham rolled the document and tied the gold cord around it. He wasn't particularly satisfied with the way the interview had progressed, with Lady Kathryn so obviously distressed. She had mettle, though, he concluded. She hadn't broken down, nor become hysterical. It had to be difficult to learn this sort of thing, though. That one's whole life had been a lie. He certainly didn't envy her.

"I was there, my lady," he replied kindly. "Your father confided in me. Believe me when I say I have no wish, no motivation to cause offense or injury to you."

She could see that his words were sincere, though it gave her little satisfaction. "What now?"

"The king, your brother, wishes that you marry."

"Marry?" Kit cried.

"He has chosen a powerful man, the Duke of Carlisle, whom he trusts as a brother, to wed you."

"I suppose this...duke...knows I'm a bastard?" she cried bitterly.

"His grace has been informed."

"And he agrees?" she asked harshly, blinking back the tears. "He would marry a bastard?"

Lord Markham replied affirmatively.

"What if I refuse?"

"A royal subject does not refuse, Lady Kathryn," he said. "You are the king's sister. He is only doing what he deems best for your welfare, in compliance with your father's wishes."

"Which are...?"

"That you be wed according to your station. That you be protected."

He gave Kit the opportunity to digest the proposal. She had no choice in the matter, and she had to realize it. When she was once more composed, he carried on with the king's instructions.

"His majesty will not be able to openly acknowledge your relationship to him, although many already suspect it. He asks that you say nothing to confirm it, nor must you deny it, either. It is doubtful that you will be confronted to provide confirmation."

"I go on as Kathryn Somers?"

"Rather, as the Duchess of Carlisle."

She nodded hesitantly.

Lord Markham smiled then. "You will meet King Henry tomorrow, before the banquet. He has requested that you sit at his left hand, a place of honor."

She nodded again. What else could she do? She was trapped.

Wolf argued as he walked with his cousin, Nicholas, outside the palace. It was the morning of the banquet, at which his elevation as Duke would be announced as well as his betrothal to the king's sister. Of course, her relationship to the king would not be admitted publicly. Only Henry's brothers and a select few of Henry's advisors were aware of her existence. A few others suspected, but it would never be confirmed.

Wolf had known his recovery of Windermere had been too easy. His marriage to the king's sister was the price. And he was determined to pay it.

"But Wolf—"

"It doesn't matter, Nick," Wolf said. "One woman will suit as well as any other. A close tie to the throne can't hurt me."

"But you've never set eyes on her, Wolf," Nicholas protested. "How could you possibly agree to taking one of these damned Catherines to wife?"

"Just be glad his majesty didn't make *you* duke," he said sarcastically. "Then *you* would be the lucky bridegroom."

"No, fortunately, I've only been made Viscount of Thornton. I can choose my own wife. Does the woman know yet?"

"Yes. I understand the lady was told last night."

They heard voices in the distance. "My God," Nicholas said as he stopped dead in his tracks. His mouth suddenly went dry as he stared straight ahead. "Who is—? Isn't that Kit Somers?" he asked incredulously, indicating a woman sitting with a man some distance down the garden path.

She sat next to a man on a wooden bench with a cloud

of delicate purple forget-me-nots and white irises at her feet. She wore a gown of jade green with a fitted, low-cut bodice, clearly delineating a narrow waist and pale breasts straining fashionably above the fabric of her gown. Her head was uncovered, and her alluring face was softly framed by curling golden tendrils. Cascades of lush blond curls tumbled down her back in total disarray, and the two men watched as her shoulders convulsed with weeping.

The woman in question was definitely Kit and recognition slammed through Wolf like a thunderbolt. She was the beautiful, sensuous woman from Somerton Lake. Chagrined, he realized that she had known who *he* was all along, though Kit had chosen not to reveal her identity to him.

But why? His heart pounded as he recalled that she had responded to his kiss with an abandon and a passion he'd never experienced in any other woman. It had been the same every time he'd kissed her, now that he thought of it. He was frustrated beyond reason as he watched her distraught form clinging to her companion. He wanted to go to her and comfort her as he had at Windermere. But he had no right. He was betrothed now, and she probably was, too, and nothing—Damnation! It was Rupert Aires whose shoulder she was drenching with her tears. Here was Kit's reason for keeping her identity secret, he thought bitterly.

Wolf drew on all his powers of discipline in order to control the urge to go to her, drag her away from Rupert and demand an explanation. His duty was to wed the king's sister, whether he liked it or no and Kit Somers could only make it difficult. He had finally admitted to himself that he wanted her with a passion he'd never felt before, and he knew that his desire for Kit could only interfere with his marriage. He had promised to marry the king's half sister, and Wolf was determined to do it. He would pay the price for Windermere, though it was higher than he had ever thought possible.

He had to get Kit out of his thoughts, or he knew the marriage would be untenable.

Kit soaked Rupert's shirt with her tears. She realized she'd been crying a lot lately, and resolved to stop it. Not even when she was married to the Duke of…whatever… would she allow herself any tears.

"It will be all right, Kit," Rupert said. "You'll see."

"But I always thought I'd wed *you*," she cried. She couldn't bear to tell him the true reason for her tears—the fact that she was a bastard, not the honorable offspring of lawfully wedded parents. That she bore the shame of having been disowned and sent away.

"Marry me?" He was aghast. Kit was more like a sister to him. True, they'd talked as children about being married to one another, but it had only been child's play. Nothing serious. At least that was what he thought.

She nodded. "Until I came here and realized you weren't at all what I thought you were."

"Now, what exactly does that mean?" He feigned offense and pulled back from her. God, she'd grown up to be a beauty, Rupert thought as he looked down at her. Not that he'd want to marry her, but if she had anything else in mind—

"Just that you're not a particularly good choice for a husband."

"Well, that's a relief," he said with a grin, even as she bawled in his arms. "I'd hate to think anyone wanted me for such a horrifying purpose."

"No," she sniffled. "But…"

"But what?"

"Nothing." Kit sat up and wiped her eyes. "I shouldn't be out here crying like this." She wiped her eyes on Rupert's doublet. "If anyone should see us…"

"Don't worry, Kit. No one at Westminster is ever up and about this early."

* * *

Kit had a long, leisurely bath to calm her nerves. Afterward, Jane made some sort of poultice to lay across her eyes to reduce the redness and swelling from her incessant crying spells. Kit finally lay on a pallet in front of the fire and dozed as Meg dried her hair in the heat of the flame and Jane lay out her clothes for the evening.

The maids knew Lady Kathryn hadn't slept much the night before, and their lady was out of sorts all day long. Rumor had it that her distress was due to the marriage arranged for her by the king. It hadn't become common knowledge yet that she was actually Henry's sister—his bastard sister.

When Kit finally awoke, the maids dressed her in the sleek white gown trimmed in gold thread that had belonged to Meghan, the one Kit had promised Bridget she'd wear when she was presented to the king. The golden bliaut had been altered to fit her form tightly, and additional fabric was added to the sleeves to make them fashionably long.

Jane brushed Kit's hair until it was a mass of silken curls. Then she talked Lady Kathryn into leaving it unveiled and entwined it with thin, white velvet ribbons. Since Kit owned no jewelry, she was the epitome of simple, angelic elegance when she went to meet the king.

Queen Catherine was formal and reserved in her greeting, yet Kit sensed no lack of warmth in her. Her light brown eyes sparkled benevolently, and she seemed to have a genuine affection for Henry. Kit noticed that she often laid a bejeweled hand on her husband's arm, and showed other signs of closeness. Her face was long and thin, almost gaunt, though not unpleasant. The style of her crimson gown was the same as that worn by the ladies at court and Kit knew at once whom the ladies emulated.

Looking at her brother, she was struck primarily by the differences in his facial features compared to her own. The only similarities were that Henry's chin was cleft as was hers, and the shape of his eyes was vaguely similar, though his were hazel and hers green.

"At last we meet," he said warmly as Kit curtsied. "I understand you're called Kit." Henry took Kit's hand and led her to a seat.

"But how—"

"The Marquess of Kendal told me all he knew of you," Henry said. "And of course Sir Gerhart's report was quite complete."

Kit blushed. She immediately thought of the incident with Wolf on the stairs at Kendal and wondered if he'd included it in his report.

"He was most descriptive when he told of the attack outside of Windermere," Henry went on, amused by Kit's reaction to Gerhart's name. He poured wine into a goblet and handed it to his sister. "I understand the battle wouldn't have gone so well if not for your leather sling and a few well-placed stones."

"Gerhart said that?" She knew she sounded breathless and forced herself to correct it.

"Of course." Henry sat down next to her. "It's true enough, isn't it?"

"Then why did he taunt me—?" She stopped, preferring not to speak of Gerhart now. It was upsetting enough to know she was the king's bastard sister, about to marry some decrepit old duke. It would be disastrous to think of Gerhart now. "Excuse me, Sire," she said, intending to close the subject, "but Gerhart didn't seem to think my assistance was particularly valuable."

"On the contrary, he made a special point of telling me of your prowess in the battle. He thought your actions worthy of the most seasoned soldier in his troop."

"But—"

"In fact, it is one of the reasons why I decided to betroth you to the duke. Carlisle needs a woman with spirit, one who can see past his faults, his superficial shortcomings. He must wed an equal. Not some simpering, weak-kneed chit—"

"But Your Majesty, perhaps I am not...ready?" It was worth a try.

"Nonsense," Henry laughed. "Our father stipulated that you were to wed a powerful peer, preferably before your seventeenth year. Unfortunately, our father did not see fit to inform me of your existence. I discovered you quite recently and entirely by accident."

Kit took a gulp of her wine. "Couldn't we just ignore our relationship for the time being and go on as before, Sire? No one knows, and I'd prefer to forget it as well if only—"

"On the contrary, dear sister," Henry said, smiling, resigned to the truth. "There are many who do know. And soon there will be more."

"No." It was barely a whisper.

"As king, and as your brother, I have certain responsibilities toward you. We Lancasters—and I stress *we*—have more than our share of enemies. There are hostile factions who plan strategically to achieve their ends, and some are brazen and rash, like the Lollards, who have proven themselves quite unpredictable and dangerous," Henry said. "I had hoped that Langston could make this easier for you, but I realize this sort of revelation must be disturbing, no matter how gently put."

"Disturbing...yes..." Tears were welling up behind Kit's eyes again, and she fought to maintain control. How could she tell the king that she had no wish to be his sister, that she spurned his efforts at making her secure? Let the Lollard fanatics come or whomever else—

"Let me remind you that there are many...illegitimate members of our family. Our grandfather, John of Gaunt, had sons by a mistress whom he later married."

"The Beauforts," Kit said. "Your uncles."

"*Our* uncles."

"Yet *our* father never married my mother."

"He could not, Kit," Henry said. "There were complications. Glendower of Wales, the situation in France, a possible political marriage—'' He waved a hand expansively. ''A king is not always free to choose.''

She drank the last of her wine in an effort to do something, anything to gain a moment to get control of herself.

Queen Catherine touched Kit's shoulder. ''Lord Langston told us that King Henry loved your mother,'' she said gently. Her accent made her voice seem small and delicate to Kit. ''He said the king mourned her death till the end of his life.''

''A small consolation.''

''But true, nonetheless,'' the queen said. ''Try not to begrudge your parents the small happiness they shared so many years ago.''

''I will try,'' Kit said earnestly, though she had no idea how she would ever come to understand the two who had created her. Two people whose love created her and yet could destroy her life.

''Come,'' Henry said, standing. He took his wife's hand and Kit's in each of his. ''Compose yourself and let us go to the banquet. It will be my pleasure to escort a lovely lady on each side.''

''Oh, hell's fire,'' Kit muttered under her breath.

Her brother smiled.

''Your Grace.'' A man's voice drew Wolf's attention from his cousin, who was enjoying the king's ale. He turned to see the Earl of Langston. ''May I be one of the first to congratulate you. Your betrothed seems to be a woman of spirit and substance, and a comely maid as well.''

''Let me offer my congratulations as well, Your Grace,'' added Lord Kendal, who was attending the banquet with his son and daughter-in-law. ''When do you wed the lady?''

''His majesty has planned for the ceremony to take place three days hence,'' Wolf said absently, turning back to Nicholas, only to see his cousin amble away through the thick of the crowd. At least he was amiable while drinking, Wolf thought.

Wolf heard that the king had entered the hall, but he was so far away, he was unable to see the royal couple. He knew he was to be seated next to Queen Catherine, so he took his leave of Kendal and Langston to proceed towards the dais. When the king and queen were finally within view, it was not the two of them who caught his eye. His attention was riveted on Kit, standing next to Henry.

She was a vision, dressed in shimmering white and gold from her chin to her wrists and down to her ankles. Wavy, flaxen hair was uncovered and unbound, cascading gloriously down Kit's back and gently framing her face. She was as beautiful as he remembered, and his mind reeled at the thought of losing her to Rupert Aires. He thought of those long hours she had spent sharing his saddle, with her body so near. His hands recalled the softness of her skin, his lips remembered the way she'd kissed him at Kendal, and his heart pounded in response. She was all he desired in the world, both the fantasy and the reality. Perhaps the king would—

The truth of the situation suddenly crashed into his consciousness. Kit stood in a position of honor at the king's left hand. Bloody hell! *Kit* was the king's sister, the "Catherine" he was to wed.

Yet he had seen her crying this morning, obviously after receiving the order to marry him rather than her beloved Rupert.

King Henry caught Wolf's eye and beckoned him forward. Kit turned to see Wolf approaching, and her heart fairly lurched in her breast. Wolf was so much more than Rupert could ever begin to be, she thought, thoroughly appreciating the way he moved his agile frame through the crowd to reach her. He wore a tunic of deep blue, a color which set off his dark hair and the silver in his eyes. If only...but it was impossible. Even if she weren't betrothed to the old duke, what would Wolf want with King Henry's bastard daughter?

As he came closer, Kit felt the color rise in her cheeks, embarrassed that Wolf was about to learn that she was the king's bastard sister. She wanted to run from the room and lock herself away.

Even as she ruminated over her predicament, Kit distinctly heard Henry's closest knights address Wolf as "Your Grace," and saw them bow formally to him. She hadn't realized that an earl was ever called "Your Grace," and thought only a duke merited that title.

God's blood! Could Wolf be a duke? she wondered. She'd been so certain that Windermere was an Earldom.

Why was everything so muddled now? Kit cast a puzzled glance toward the king who greeted Wolf with one word as Wolf bowed to him.

"Carlisle."

Chapter Twelve

Kit recovered from the faint a few minutes later and found herself alone with Wolf in the gallery outside the banquet hall. She wanted to throw her arms around him, but his expression was forbidding. It was obvious he already knew of her parentage, and he was displeased with the prospect of having an illegitimate wife. She didn't blame him for looking askance at her.

"Don't expect me to believe you fainted dead away, Kathryn," he said harshly. The anger was clear in his eyes. "Remember, I've seen you in worse circumstances than this."

Was he serious? Could he possibly think she'd pretended shock, she who had never fainted before in her life? Damn if she would do it intentionally and damn if she would allow him to treat her like the bastard she was. "Ha!" she said, matching his anger. "There *are* no worse circumstances than this!"

"Agreed," Wolf said. "But we're stuck with each other by the king's command. And I mean to see it through."

"Really!" Kit was furious with him now. How dare he refer to marriage with her as being "stuck!" She stood on wobbly legs with the intention of leaving, but found that her legs were too weak to move. She sat down again but not before Wolf saw her eyes dart toward the door.

''Don't think of bolting,'' he warned coldly. He wondered if she was entertaining some notion of Rupert Aires coming to rescue her. ''We'll return to the banquet as soon as you can walk. Together.''

''I'll return *if* and when I decide I'm ready,'' she retorted, ''and not with the likes of you.''

''But I'm your betrothed, no matter how distasteful that may be.'' There was no mistaking the bitterness in his tone.

Only Henry's personal guards were aware of Lady Kathryn's faint. When Wolf had seen the blood drain from her face, he had moved swiftly to catch her and get her out of the banquet hall before any of the guests could witness her distress. He was at first dismayed by her reaction to seeing him, then angered by her outright rejection. She could do worse than a duke for a husband, but apparently she had her heart set on Rupert.

Well, that was just too damn bad. Kathryn Somers would become the Duchess of Carlisle. And soon. King Henry had decreed that the marriage would take place in three days.

''You brood more than ever,'' Nicholas said to his cousin on the evening before the wedding. ''Did you prefer Annegret so much?'' He goaded Wolf, in an attempt to draw him out. Nicholas knew Wolf had no affection for Annegret, yet his mood since the banquet had been black, and he had refused to say anything about it. It seemed to Nicholas that Wolf should have expressed some relief, if not sheer glee, at finding that Kathryn Somers was the king's sister. Now that Wolf had been made duke, with Windermere restored and Kit as his wife, he should have been more than satisfied.

''Annegret...'' Wolf muttered.

''I realize she would have been more a docile wife, more—''

''Christ's crown, Nicholas! Kathryn prefers another man.''

''Absurd.''

"You saw her with Rupert Aires after being told she was betrothed to me."

"You believe she prefers *Rupert?*"

"No. I'm *certain* she prefers Rupert."

"She would choose one of Henry's knights over you, a duke?" Nicholas scoffed. He finally understood that it was hurt pride that ate at his cousin. He obviously wanted her. "She is not a fool, Wolf."

"No."

"You must convince her, then."

Wolf's eyebrow shot up. "Convince her?" He had never had to convince a woman before. Either she wanted him or she didn't. That was all there was to it.

Nicholas nodded. "*Ja.* Convince her that the king chose well for his sister," he said. "Demonstrate your superiority."

It hadn't occurred to him that he'd be able to win her over. Wolf knew she'd been in love with Rupert forever. How was he supposed to change her mind, her heart? Not that it mattered, he reminded himself. He had always planned on a marriage of convenience, not sentiment. If Kit intended to remain aloof, he could do the same. In fact, he could manage to spend as much time away from her as possible.

Because if he stayed near, he knew he was lost.

She swore she would absolutely not weep again. But as Jane toweled Kit dry after her bath and helped her with all her layers of bridal clothing, the tears threatened again. The day was sunny and green, fresh and new. Perfect for her wedding, yet the circumstances were less than desirable. Wolf was a reluctant bridegroom.

Meg fastened the row of tiny buttons on the back of Kit's gown—they had chosen a gown that shimmered blue-green, depending on the way the light caught it. The gown was one of the newly made ones, and Kit was still amazed by its richness and style. With long, draping sleeves and a tightly fitted bodice, the neckline left her shoulders bare and scooped low across her bosom and back, where the train was attached. A thin gold girdle hung low on her hips and the skirt flared out somewhat, having a tendency to cling to her legs as she walked. It was, without question, the most beautiful gown she'd ever worn.

Kit watched in the mirror as Jane brushed her hair into a thick, cascading mass of pale yellow curls down her back. She thought of Bridget, and wished her old nurse had been the one to help her prepare for her wedding. She had never dreamed she'd be alone this day, without friends, and about to wed a man who didn't want her.

Meg answered a polite tap at the chamber door and admitted a footman carrying a small golden casket. "His majesty sent this gift, my lady," he said as he handed the box to Kit. "He hopes to see you wear it at your nuptials."

"The king will be there?"

"Yes, my lady," the man replied. "Their majesties will both be present in the abbey. King Henry plans to attend your wedding feast later, as well."

"Thank you," Kit mumbled, accepting the box. "Please give my regards and my gratitude to the king."

The man bowed as he left the room and Kit opened the box containing a beautiful necklace of gold. When Meg fastened it on, both maids voiced their approval of the finishing touch. As Kit's heart sank, she could only think that she'd have preferred some small token from her betrothed, rather than her brother.

Wolf watched Lady Kathryn walk regally down the long aisle of the abbey, carrying a single light pink rose, and he was struck again by her effect on him. She was ethereal yet earthy, beautiful but imperfect, sensuous though innocent. Several of the king's guards were flanking her and Wolf was quick to notice, with some irritation, that one of them was Rupert Aires.

After the vows, High Mass was celebrated, and Wolf was

sure Kit looked at him no more than twice during the entire ceremony. Both times she appeared shy and wary of him, even though she had been completely poised before all the onlookers and the archbishop when she approached the altar.

Apparently it was only her husband she was unable to face.

The first time she looked into his eyes was when he placed the ring on her finger. It was a delicate band set with four square-cut emeralds. Kit was surprised that it was anything more than a plain gold band. She had already accepted the fact that he didn't owe her more, and she hadn't expected him to honor her so. It was then that she felt moved to give him the single, perfect rose. Granted, it was not a priceless gem, but it symbolized her hope for understanding between them.

The second time she looked at Wolf was when he kissed her. It was a light, undemanding kiss, but it left his senses reeling. What had she done—bathed in fragrant spring flowers? Swallowed some sweet nectar to make him want her lips even more? He pulled away from her before it was too late, before he devoured her.

He had no idea how she wanted to cling to him, to tell him how sorry she was that he had to be bound to her, by the order of the king, and against his will. Kit wanted him to kiss her as he had at Kendal, or even at Somerton, when he hadn't known who she was. Now that he knew, she saw that he wanted nothing to do with her and a lump the size of an apricot grew in her throat, though she managed to hold back the tears that threatened throughout the ceremony.

The wedding feast was a lavish affair. All the nobility and gentry within riding distance had come to witness the marriage and to see the king once again before his departure for France. There were hundreds of guests present, most of whom neither Kit nor Wolf knew. The bride and groom sat together for the meal and drank a number of toasts that were made in their honor.

Finally, before King Henry decided to leave the banquet, he offered his own toast to the Duke and Duchess and requested that they seal his good wishes with a kiss. Wolf obliged by giving Kit a quick peck on the lips.

"My lord Duke," Henry admonished, with a sly grin, "a pat such as this will not suffice. Give your wife a kiss. As a man would a woman."

Kit's color deepened, knowing that she and Wolf would have to comply with Henry's wishes, even though they were in the presence of hundreds of people. Yet she was very much aware of her husband's appeal and she yearned for him to touch her, to amend the gap that existed between them. She easily remembered how it felt to be consumed by the fire of his touch, since thoughts of that time at Kendal had plagued her ever since reaching London. She wished he weren't so repulsed by her now.

Wolf touched her chin and turned her to face him. There was a heat, almost a fever in his eyes when she looked in them, and Kit had the strangest feeling that he felt some of the same yearnings she did. His lips met hers softly, almost gently. She moaned slightly, enough for him to hear, and he deepened the kiss.

Neither of them heard the bawdy shouts of the crowd as Wolf moved his mouth hungrily over hers, and his arm went around her waist to draw her nearer. Her hands slid up to encircle his neck and she opened her lips willingly, desperately. The heat possessed her as their tongues met, and Kit felt herself melting into her husband.

Just let it be real, she prayed, when Wolf suddenly pulled away. Her heart was beating so hard and so fast. She could hardly breathe. It was impossible to look away from Wolf, whose eyes still burned with the heat of their kiss. The cheers of the crowd gradually entered Kit's consciousness. Embarrassed with their display, she took her arms from Wolf's neck.

But he didn't release her. He was enthralled by her eyes and her swollen lips which gave promise of a sensuous onslaught to come.

"There now!" the king shouted. "If you continue thus, you will likely have heirs for your fine estates!" The guests laughed and applauded appreciatively.

One of Henry's squires pushed through the crowd to the king and spoke quietly to him. Henry frowned, then nodded and stood.

"I must be off," he finally said. Two squires and three guards moved to accompany King Henry. Wolf arose from his place to walk with the king.

"There may be trouble, Wolf," Henry said, noting with satisfaction that Lady Kathryn came alongside her husband.

"Sire?"

"Owen Tudor has information that Lollards have infiltrated the guards," Henry said as they left the banquet hall and entered the gallery. "A few fanatics, wanting to demonstrate their...*displeasure* with my support of the Church. I'll thwart what plans they've made by removing myself. I had intended to take my leave anyway."

"Hold, Your Majesty. Send a party ahead," Wolf said, alarmed. Everything was moving too quickly, and the king was not exercising his usual caution. The gallery was uncharacteristically dark. "Where is the light? Aren't the candles alwa—"

The door to the banquet room slammed behind them, and Kit screamed as she saw the glint of metal swing from on high. They were left in almost complete darkness, but for the one candle that had been dropped by the squire, Owen Tudor. Kit heard swords slashing the air, meeting metal, and in some cases, flesh. In a panic, she picked up the fallen taper and lit the candelabra near the door as she searched the darkness for Wolf.

Unable to see her husband, Kit tried to pull the door to the banquet hall open again, but it was jammed, or locked. She knew there were other entrances to the gallery, but it would take some time before anyone realized something was amiss. They could not expect help from the noisy crowd. She quickly turned back to see what was going on in the dimly lit gallery.

Henry was without a weapon, though Wolf and a guard were defending him effectively. Everything was moving very fast, and there were so many shadows, it was difficult for Kit to determine the number of their attackers, who were conveniently dressed in black. She counted eleven, and knew her side was outnumbered. Again. And she had neither sling nor bow to help.

A guard near Kit ran his sword through one of the assailants, then turned to face another. The fallen man's sword crashed to the floor under him and though Kit had never learned to use a sword, she intended to try it now. She knew it would be too heavy for her to wield as a soldier would, yet she thought other uses could be made if she put her mind to it.

She struggled to push the dead man away in order to get to his sword and managed to get hold of it with both hands just as someone grabbed her from behind. Coming up swinging and yelling, Kit hurled the huge sword and struck her assailant across the side of his head, hard enough to stun him and knock him down. Kit looked over toward the king just then and saw Wolf take a blow to the chest. To Kit's alarm, blood poured from the wound, though her husband didn't fall. He managed to swing a fatal blow, and his attacker dropped before him, only to be replaced by another. Henry, who, like Kit, had grabbed a sword from one of the fallen men, was already fighting desperately and was unaware of Wolf's circumstances.

Kit, enraged and terrified for her weakened husband, circled around the fray and came at Wolf's new attacker from behind. She cried out as she saw Wolf take another strike in the leg, which brought him to his knees. Close enough now, Kit struck with all her might, bringing down Wolf's opponent. She dropped the sword and went to Wolf, who was sinking to the floor. Four black-clad men lay dead around him.

Kit was now able to see the amount of blood flowing from the chest wound, and she was fearful for his life. She eased him down, then ripped her linen underskirts to make a bandage. She pressed the cloth to the wound to staunch the bleeding.

"Kit," Wolf rasped. "Move away. Don't get..."

"Hush, husband," she replied tearfully. "I'll see to your care."

"No—"

She silenced him with a light kiss and tore another bandage for his leg. She would not let him perish before she understood the meaning of his kiss at the banquet.

The battle raged on before them, with men falling before her eyes, yet the king and at least two of his guards continued to fight. Two men in black fell, then another one of Henry's guards. Tears of fear and desperation streamed down Kit's face as she realized that there was nothing more she could do, for there remained at least four enemies hacking at King Henry and the squire, Tudor.

Then Kit heard noise. A lot of noise. Voices were surrounding them, and lights. She looked up to see a group of Henry's men, perhaps twenty of them. Lord Kendal and his son were among them, as were Rupert Aires, Nicholas Becker, and several of Wolf's men. Their strength was more than enough to dispatch the remaining black-clad men.

As the battle concluded, the king made his way to where Kit sat with Wolf's head cradled in her lap. She held the cloth to his upper chest, having tied the other around the wound in his thigh. Wolf's color was pale, but his breathing was steady as he drifted in and out of consciousness. He was unaware of his wife's tears.

Henry motioned behind him for assistance, then ordered that litters be brought for the injured men.

"Come, Kit," Henry said. "We'll have him taken to—"

"Three of our men are dead, Sire," said one of the new-comers.

"And the attackers?"

"All."

"No word of this ambush is to be taken from this hall," Henry said vehemently. "If Lollards were responsible, they are not to know they had even the slightest measure of success. Dispose of the traitors' bodies. Let no one hear of this."

"Yes, Sire."

"Kathryn, we'll move Wolf to—to Kendal's house," Henry said. "Kendal?"

The Marquess nodded his agreement. "Of course, Sire."

"My own physician will see to him," the king continued. "He will be well again, I promise you."

"Your Majesty," Kit said quietly, "he cannot be moved so far."

"I fear she's right, Sire," Nicholas agreed. He bent over Wolf and pulled away the bandage to reveal a gaping wound. "We should not risk jarring him over the roads. At least not until this gash is sewn. And the leg…"

Henry gave a moment's thought, then agreed. "There must be available apartments somewhere in the palace… Who would suspect newlyweds who do not emerge from their chambers for days?" he mused. "It can be carried off."

"My maids, Sire…?"

"You will manage without," the king said. "I trust you'll not object to having a couple of palace guards to do your bidding?"

"No, Sire," she replied, relieved but still worried. Wolf was so pale, so cold. "But I would prefer that my husband's men remain close."

When the duke and his bride were finally missed, no one was surprised. At least a hundred of the guests had witnessed the kiss at the wedding feast, and a number of ribald remarks were made regarding the newlyweds' whereabouts.

Kit watched as Wolf was gently placed on the bed in a large, comfortable chamber. While Kendal saw to it that the physician was brought, his son Robert returned to the banquet to quell any rumors which may have arisen regarding the incident in the gallery.

Rupert and Nicholas remained to help Kit undress Wolf. When Chester appeared with a basin of water and cloths, the two men stayed to assist as Kit bathed his wounds. Wolf still drifted in and out of consciousness. His injuries were serious but did not appear to be mortal, and Nicholas assured Kit that all would be well.

Kit's tears were barely contained. The emotional upheaval of the last few days was nearly too much for her, but she knew she had to muster the inner strength necessary to deal with it. It was terribly disconcerting to see this man who was her husband, so huge, so powerful, lying so close to death. She couldn't bear to lose Wolf...now that she knew she loved him.

"I have seen many a wound such as this on the field of battle," Nicholas said. "Look. The lung is not punctured." Kit looked and saw that it was true. Her husband's breathing was steady and noiseless, but the expression on Nicholas' usually lighthearted face was grave. "And see the leg...only the first layer of muscle is cut. It will mend."

She was much more reassured when the physician, Lord Blackmore, arrived and agreed with Nicholas' prognosis. The bleeding had stopped, so he packed the wounds with some foul-smelling concoction and dressed them, showing Kit what to use and how to replace them if they should come off during the night. "'Tis best not to sew such wounds, for then they tend to fester," the doctor said, "and that's what often kills the man, not the injury itself."

Kendal removed himself once he was satisfied of Wolf's condition. "You have only to send for me if you have need of assistance, my lady," Kendal said to Kit before taking

his leave. ''Your husband and I have strong family ties—
I will tell you about them some day.''

Kit smiled wearily at the Marquess.

''I also knew your father—I will tell you about *him* one
day as well.''

Kit had barely heard what the Marquess had said until
his last words. She blanched and looked up at him, realizing
now that he also knew of her parentage.

''Don't fret, Kit,'' he said. ''No one will learn of it from
me. Least of all, Lady Kendal.'' He smiled at Kit, wishing
that his attempt at levity could help to raise her spirits.

Nicholas took the first watch, only to be sent out of the
room when some of Kit's clothes arrived from her chambers. She changed out of her soiled and bloodied marriage
gown to wash quickly and put on more comfortable sleeping clothes.

Kit sat up for hours, watching Wolf for any signs of
distress. She stayed at his bedside and often bathed his
forehead and neck. He still felt cool to the touch, so she
didn't worry about fever yet, but he was so pale that looking at him made her weep.

''Wolf Colston, don't you dare leave me now.'' She lay
her cheek aside his as she cried.

''I'll try not to, Kit,'' his whisper was rasping. He raised
one hand to stroke her head, then it dropped back weakly.

Later, when it was Nicholas' turn to watch, he insisted
that Kit sleep. Reminding her that the following day was
likely to be a long one and she would need her strength,
he finally prevailed. Hardly able to keep her eyes open any
longer anyway, Kit lay down on the bed next to Wolf and
slept until early morning when it was Rupert's watch. Then
she got up and sat next to a window overlooking the east,
and thought about the morning Bridget had died. She had
sat with Wolf then, watching the sun rise, and thinking that
all she wanted was to be with Rupert.

If only Wolf recovered, she'd tell him she hadn't needed
Rupert at all. Wolf Colston had been the one all along.

Chapter Thirteen

Wolf had only intermittent awareness of his surroundings. At times he thought someone had taken a hot poker to his chest, and his leg throbbed interminably. He knew Kit was with him though, and that was all he really cared about. He felt her tears dampen his face once, and tried to comfort her, but he was too weak. He wanted to assure her that all would be well, but didn't have the breath or strength to do it.

The dawn light in the room was faint and he had some difficulty seeing who was there, but once, he recognized the voice of Rupert Aires, speaking to Kit.

"I'll wager you're sorry now you didn't marry me instead," he said quietly.

"*You*, Rupert?" A bitter laugh escaped her. "It's been some time since I realized you'd make a terrible husband." Fatigue was audible in her voice. "Nay, I've never been so well satisfied of my choice before. If only God will spare him…"

Wolf had very few lucid moments as he battled fever and infection, and Kit worried that it would ultimately overcome him. The wounds were grave and Kit was not ignorant of the worried looks exchanged between the men who attended her husband, in spite of the physician's optimism.

On the fourth afternoon, as Kit knelt next to Wolf's bed,

she nearly despaired. She closed her eyes and prayed to God for his recovery. Though she had a long history of unanswered prayers, Kit still pleaded for Wolf's delivery. Deeply immersed in prayer, she heard a strange, distant voice.

"You look like the wrath of God," it said.

She looked up to see who had spoken, but she and Wolf were alone in the room. Kit sniffled, brushed the tears from her face and sat up, puzzled. Certain that someone had spoken, Kit glanced around the room to see if someone had entered without her knowledge.

"Wrath of God, indeed," she muttered, seeing no one. It had to be her imagination, what with the fatigue and worry—

"It's true, Kit. What ails you?"

She snapped her head back toward the sound and found herself looking at Wolf. His eyes were open and focused, and he was frowning at her. It was his first conscious act in over three days.

"What ails *me?*" she gasped.

"You've been weeping." His voice was weak, his eyes gentle.

Using the backs of her hands, she brushed away the new tears that had sprung from her eyes. Yes, by God, she'd been weeping. It had become a normal state of affairs for her ever since she'd met him.

"Weeping?" she cried. "I've been terrified, not knowing if you'd live—"

Nicholas and Edward, having heard voices in Wolf's chamber, hurried in and stopped short when Wolf cast a dark look at them. He had thought to pursue the moment with Kit to find out what was wrong and why she was terrified that he'd live.

"Nicholas!" She turned to see Wolf's cousin approaching anxiously with Sir Edward alongside. Alfred and Ranulf were not far behind. Kit assumed they all must have heard her startled voice.

"What is it, Kit? Is—"

"He's conscious!" She knelt back at his side and took his hand in hers.

"What's wrong with my wife?" Wolf asked the men. "And why does my chest pain me so?"

"Do you not remember, Your Grace?" Edward asked. Several more of Wolf's men appeared.

"You were injured five nights ago," Nicholas replied to Wolf's question. "The king was attacked as he left your wedding feast. You and several others were trapped with the king outside the hall..."

Wolf tried to recall it, but his memory was faulty. He remembered the wedding feast...beautiful Kathryn...an attack on the king...Kit weeping...Kit lying with him, holding him?

He tried to sit up but Kit prevented him by holding his shoulders. She'd seen the wounds that morning when the physician dressed them, and they had a long way to go before being healed. "Get off my chest, woman," Wolf protested, annoyed and dismayed that his wife possessed the greater strength. "I'll not stay abed any longer."

"You will stay here until your strength has returned."

He gave a grim smile at the determined look on her face. Her fresh-flower scent and the fragile transparency of her skin belied her underlying strength. "Do you dare command a duke of the realm?"

"'Tis a wife's right and duty, Your Grace," Alfred joked, "perhaps even her purpose."

"I see," Wolf said suspiciously, looking around at his knights. They obviously supported Kit in this. Wondering how she had managed to get them all on her side, he turned back to Alfred. "And when did the likes of you—a single man—become an authority on wives?"

"Not 'wives,' Your Grace," Alfred laughed.

"*Your* wife, Cousin," Nicholas said. "She has not left this—"

"Nicholas!" Kit interjected, "Will you send someone to

the king to inform him of my husband's recovery?'' It would not do at all for Wolf to know of her attendance on him, not until she knew how he would receive the information. Though he owned her heart, she could not bear to hand it to him now.

''So I am to be held prisoner until my wife deems me fit to move?'' Wolf was incredulous.

''The king's physician will determine when you are able to be up and about, husband,'' she corrected gently. She realized how it rankled him to be unwell and bound to bed. ''Lord Blackmore has attended you since the beginning.''

''Blackmore?''

''The king's healer.''

''And not you, Kit?'' he asked quietly, half teasing, half hoping, his tone making her heart pound in her breast. ''Had you no hand in my care?''

The intensity of his eyes flustered her, and she hesitated to reply.

''Your wife is the reason you still live, Wolf,'' Nicholas said.

Wolf and Kit's eyes remained locked making her blood heat and course faster through her veins. Finally, Wolf broke the silence. ''Is it your intention to starve me, then?''

''Starve you?'' Kit returned to reality. ''Of course not. Are you hungry?''

''As a bear.''

''Nicholas,'' Kit said, ''would you mind seeing to it? I'm sure that somewhere in all of Westminster, you should be able to find something suitable for a *sick* man to eat.''

''No.'' Wolf protested weakly. ''Bring me some decent food—not some mush meant for—'' But Nicholas had already left the chamber, grinning a ridiculous grin.

Two days passed, and Wolf's strength returned to him gradually. He became surly with the inactivity imposed on him and barked at Kit and the men who served him. Kit refused to take his attitude to heart, forcing herself to re-

member the few tender words he'd spoken when the fever
was at its worst.

When he was well, she was sure they would come to an
understanding. He would realize how she felt about him
and at the very least would accept her as his wife, regardless of her parentage.

Wolf remained dubious, however. Whatever had tran-
spired while he was delirious was unclear to him, and he
didn't know whether he could trust his senses. Had she
really told Rupert Aires that marriage to Wolf had been her
choice? How was he to know he hadn't heard the words in
a dream, that Kit's tears and tender ministrations were not
merely manifestations of his delirium? He even thought
he'd felt her curl up against him in the bed those nights
when he was sick, though now she disappeared into the
next room when night fell. Vague memories of her light
hands upon him, touching, exploring, healing, came to him
and he was unsure whether it was merely wishful thinking
or reality.

He'd also had visions of his father and brother, slaughtered on the road to Bremen; being presented to his mother
after his recovery; his mother's vacant gray eyes as he had
cried in her lap. All of it had seemed quite real.

On the day before the king and queen departed England
for France again, Henry made a visit to Wolf's chambers.
Assured by Lord Blackmore that the duke's health was im-
proving by the day, he decided to speak to Wolf of serious
affairs, to bring him up to date on all that had been hap-
pening since the attack. Finding Wolf and Kathryn alone
in the chamber, Henry sent away his squires and attendants
to speak privately with his sister and her husband.

"We know the attack on the night of your wedding was
perpetrated by Lollards," the king said. "There is some
doubt as to whether or not they intended to kill me. They
may have been completely surprised by the ferocity of our
defense and were forced to fight back just as brutally."

"But—" Kit began to question her brother, but he silenced her with a patient gesture.

"Regardless, they were all killed, and their bodies disposed of. All have been identified. No one need ever know of this ambush to give credence to the Lollard cause and their demands. Steps have been taken as well, to assure that no such incident occurs in the future."

"How did they succeed in getting so close to you, Sire?" Wolf asked.

"They infiltrated the guards," Henry replied. "We know who was responsible, and he was killed in the attack. There are one or two others who remain." The king smiled and waved a hand to dismiss the subject. "We will deal with them directly."

"Thank the saints that Queen Catherine was not with you that night, Your Majesty," Kit said. "If she had been harmed—"

"Quite," Henry said gravely. "Until I could get a weapon, I was helpless. You must be sure to thank your wife, Wolf, for saving your neck." The king grinned. "I don't recall ever having seen a woman wield a sword with quite the same vigor as Lady Kathryn did that night. You were a sight to behold, dear sister."

Wolf raised a puzzled brow, and Kit blushed.

"I knew of your skill with the leather sling, and I've heard of your prowess with a bow. Now I find you can handle a sword that must have been half your weight."

"Sire, I only did what I thought was necessary, and awkwardly at that," she said, embarrassed. "I...I've never actually been taught to use a sword," she added meekly.

"Be that as it may, at least the two of us owe you our lives for your quick action. I thank you."

Kit gave a nod to accept his thanks, unaware of anything she'd done to protect the king. Her actions that night had been solely for Wolf's benefit.

"The next news is not good." The king directed his

words to Wolf. "I forbade your men to speak of it until I was certain of your recovery."

"Sire?"

"Philip Colston has disappeared."

"The Earl of Windermere?" Kit asked.

"On the contrary, my dear," Henry said, "your husband holds Windermere. I sent a small army to take Philip Colston into custody and bring him to London. The men returned three days ago with neither Philip nor Lady Agatha."

"Agatha?" Kit whispered.

"He must have found out somehow," Wolf said.

Henry nodded. "'Tis likely. The servants were questioned, and all of them thought Philip was somewhere within the castle. No one was notified of his departure, yet he most certainly disappeared."

"I'll find him."

"I have every confidence you will, Wolf," Henry replied. "And when you do, deal with him as you see fit. However, until he is found, guard your back. When you return him to London, he will be tried on the evidence you and Kendal presented to me. I have written my opinion on the matter, and of course, I've stripped Philip Colston of the title."

"I am grateful, Sire—"

"Also, be aware that Baron Somers' men have been here and know of your marriage to Kit," the king said. "I understand they returned to Somerton several days ago, so you should be prepared for possible trouble from that front. Kathryn is to be protected from her stepfather, though the man would have to be a fool to offend a duke, not to mention his king. Somerton knows I favor Kit, as did my father who managed to send a man to Somerton once or twice a year to evaluate her circumstances."

Wolf nodded. That would explain the knights who Kit said had visited periodically and had asked about her welfare. Somehow, the blockheads always missed seeing the bruised and battered child.

"Which brings me to my last point," Henry interrupted. "As to your request, my decision is—no."

Kit looked from her husband to her brother, having some difficulty following this part of the conversation. She knew of no request.

"You will remain here in England and deal with Philip Colston, get Windermere back in order and see to your other ducal responsibilities." Henry stood to take his leave. "No, remain seated. Let those wounds heal. We need strength in the north, Wolf, and I rely on you to provide a goodly portion of it."

Wolf acquiesced as the king moved with Kit towards the door.

"You also have a new wife to attend to." He embraced Kit loosely. "Farewell. You shall hear from me from Paris. And of course I wish to be apprised of the situation with Philip Colston."

Nicholas and Chester returned after Henry left. They began discussing Windermere with Wolf and what might have happened to Philip. There was a good bit of conjecture regarding Hugh Dryden, who had been sent to Windermere before the wedding, and whether Wolf's man knew of Philip's whereabouts.

While the men spoke, Kit tried to puzzle out what Wolf's request to the king must have been. Henry insisted that Wolf fortify the north and get Windermere in order. Did that mean that Wolf hadn't intended to deal with Windermere and the rest of it? Had he planned on going somewhere other than his estates, somewhere away from her? Henry had most distinctly said that Wolf had a new wife to attend to, hadn't he?

Her heart was in her throat when the realization struck her. Wolf had asked to accompany the king to France. Without her.

"Philip must have friends—"

"There are plenty of places to hide—"

"A few of us can go undetected—"

"We must get to Hugh—"

The discussion went on, and Kit was oblivious to it. Tears stung the back of her eyes as she twisted the band of emeralds on her finger. She despaired of ever coming to terms with Wolf. He wanted to be away from her. He couldn't stand to be near her, and it was only the king's command that kept him at her side. What was she to do? Perhaps marriage to Rupert would have been better than this—at least Rupert didn't detest her company.

"We'll depart for Windermere in five days," Wolf concluded. "I'll be able to sit a horse by then. In the meantime, four or five men are to ride on ahead. I want them to see that rooms are made ready. They can meet with Hugh, scour the neighborhood, sound out the town, follow up on rumors..."

Chapter Fourteen

Late June, 1421

Wolf's thigh injury was no more than an angry red slash, but the chest wound still needed to be bound, especially when they rode. An army of men accompanied them on the journey, as well as Wolf's core group of soldiers who'd been together as a troop for several years. Most of these had been well rewarded with lands and estates by the king for their service in France, but they were loyal to Wolf and wanted to see him established at Windermere before going off to claim their various prizes. None of them could rest easy with Philip Colston on the loose.

Kit wondered at first if her husband would bother taking her with him to Windermere. He had so obviously wanted to be away from her. She was amazed on the day before they left, when he asked if her things were packed. He told her to purchase whatever she thought she'd need from the London shops, reminding her that there would be no such luxuries in Cumbria as were available in London.

With mixed feelings, Kit prepared to leave Westminster. There was nothing more she wished to purchase in London. She had already enlisted Rupert's help in finding the craftsman in town who could create the one item she wished to buy—her wedding gift to Wolf. And while Wolf was in the throes of delirium, she almost believed she'd never have the opportunity to give the precious package to him.

By the day of their departure, Wolf walked without a noticeable limp, but Kit could see that when he moved his upper torso, he was not without some discomfort, and she was concerned whether it was wise for him to sit in the saddle all day. She had ordered her mare from Windermere to be saddled but before she was able to mount, Wolf called to her.

"Nicholas will lift you, Kit," he said as he rode towards her. "You ride with me."

"But your wound—"

"Doesn't trouble me enough to be slowed by your pretty mare." His tone was gruff. "Our journey to Windermere will take six days as it is. I'll not be delayed."

And so Kit was settled in front of her husband, and they were off.

Kit enjoyed her closeness to Wolf all day as they rode, even though he rarely spoke. There were things she wished to say to him, but found she didn't know how to breach the gap between them. So she said nothing, and they traveled over the miles together in silence. His arms felt just as secure and comfortable around her as they had on the trip from Somerton. Kit tried to make herself believe that he wasn't as dissatisfied with her as he seemed. Perhaps in time, he would accept her, though Kit began to think she'd need to implement some kind of plan to win him over.

Wolf relished her nearness. Her scent, as always, reminded him of fresh flowers. She was soft and sweet and he gathered her close as they rode, thankful that Henry had not agreed to his request to return to France. It was before his marriage that he had asked to go along in Henry's retinue, unwilling to remain close to a wife who was so clearly displeased with her marriage. Yet he knew now that he couldn't have stayed away from her. Kathryn Somers would be a wife to him as soon as they reached Windermere. And she would learn to accept it.

The weather was fine every night, so they camped outdoors, without bothering to set up the small tents and tarps they'd brought in case of rain. Kit always fell asleep looking at the black sky, gazing at stars and plotting ways to make her husband notice her. Wolf managed never to lay his blanket next to hers until she was sound asleep, and he was always gone before she opened her eyes in the morning. Kit was sure it was intentional.

By the fourth night, Kit was discouraged and frustrated. They rode together as they had from Windermere to Kendal, with hardly any words between them. Kit sensed an asperity in Wolf that she doubted she'd ever be able to overcome, no matter how she tried to win him over. She couldn't imagine why he had ever agreed to Henry's demand that he wed her. He had never seemed to be a man who'd easily do another's bidding, not even the king's.

They finally stopped at the crest of a small ravine. It was a likely place to camp and Wolf lowered Kit down from Janus' back to Nicholas, who waited to assist her. When she glanced back up at Wolf, Kit was dismayed by his grimace of pain. His wound was obviously troubling him, and she meant to have a look at it as soon as he dismounted. Wolf rode Janus over to the area where the rest of the horses were to be tethered and dropped down to his feet.

Kit was right behind him carrying a water bag and her satchel of medicines and bandages, much of which had been provided by Lord Blackmore.

"Let me dress your wound while there is still some light, Wolf," she said.

"This dressing will do," he said, wary of removing his tunic, unwilling to suffer the touch of her gentle hands. She had ministered to him daily at the palace and on the road, nursing him carefully. But the more she touched him, the more he wanted her, and this was not the time or place to show her to whom she belonged.

''The dressing will *not* do,'' she asserted. ''You're in pain, and I would see why.''

Had he been in better spirits, Wolf would have thought it comical the way Kit—nearly half his size—seemed to think she was actually dragging him by the arm to the clearing.

She led him to a spot out in the open, away from the thicket of trees where the men were making camp, a place where the fading light was in its greatest abundance. She insisted that he sit on the trunk of an ancient tree which had been torn from its roots in some long forgotten storm. As he removed his tunic, Kit opened her bag to get the salve and the clean bandages she would need. She was amazed that he came along with her so docilely and decided that his improved temperament was because he'd been in the saddle all day, an occupation he seemed to enjoy.

Kit stepped between his thighs, trying to remain unaffected by his half-naked presence, and unwrapped the long linen outer dressing from his chest. She reached around him, coming close with every turn made by the long cloth.

Just at the point when Wolf thought he couldn't bear her nearness any longer, she gasped.

''You've been bleeding!'' Her look of dismay surprised him more than the bleeding itself. He had felt the warm ooze some time ago, but had no idea she would react so. Kit pulled off the saturated inner dressing and looked at the injury. ''I should never have let you leave Westminster so soon!''

''*You?* Should never have *let...?*'' Kit was so distraught that she didn't notice the signs of mirth in his eyes.

''That is correct, *Your Grace,*'' she avowed as she washed the wound and examined the extent of the damage. Only a small area at one end of the injury had bled, and Kit was relieved. She felt that the salve, liberally applied, would control the bleeding if he were careful. ''As it is, we will not turn back since we have already come so far and—''

He laughed. Though it was a pleasant sound which she hadn't heard in weeks, Kit did not appreciate her husband making sport of her. True, they were bound together by the king's order, but she did not feel it was her duty to become the brunt of his humor. As it was, she didn't know how she would be able to live with the knowledge that she was not Wolf's first choice—that he cared for another, that he had wanted to leave her at the first opportunity.

"—we will reach Windermere soon so it is pointless—"

"I've always thought you had a talent for giving orders like a duchess," he chuckled, then winced as she slapped the medicinal paste into the sensitive torn area.

"You needn't laugh at me."

"I'm not laughing at you."

"I *am* a duchess, in case you've forgotten." Her voice had become very quiet.

The laughter faded from Wolf's face when he saw traces of moisture beginning to gather and glisten along the lower lashes of her eyes and that telltale tightening of her lips. Oh, how it wrenched his heart to see her cry. He didn't blame her for it at all. By all the saints, it was bad enough for her to have been ordered to marry against her wishes and now, she was being dragged across the country again to a dank and dreary old castle with an ominous history with a man whom she had never in a thousand years intended to wed.

Damn Henry! It was obvious that Kit couldn't abide being his duchess, and Wolf thought the least Henry could have done was to ascertain his sister's opinion on the subject of matrimony before making an irrevocable decision on it. Wolf didn't know how to make things easier for Kit, but he realized it was up to him to try.

"Yes, you are a duchess. But a princess first," he said as Kit wound the bandage around his chest. She stopped abruptly and left the bandage dangling.

"You mean a *bastard* princess," Kit said as she whirled around and stalked away from him.

Bastard princess? *Bastard?* What did he care who her parents were? Why should she, for that matter? But it obviously upset her tremendously. He hadn't missed seeing the quivering of her chin just before she'd stormed away from him. Was this the reason for her behavior? That she was ashamed her father never wed her mother?

Impossible. He quickly cast the notion aside. It was ridiculous.

He moved quickly and caught her before she got to the thicket of trees.

"Kit."

She shrugged his hand off her upper arm and kept on walking.

"Wait, Kit." He took hold of her arm again and turned her. He saw that her eyes were shimmering emerald pools about to overflow, though she seemed determined not to weep. He touched her cheek with one hand, then brought up his other hand to caress her hair away from her face.

Wolf hesitated for only a moment, then his mouth brushed hers gently. She trembled at the light touch. He moved his head to caress the notch below her ear with his lips, then pressed a soft kiss on her temple. He felt warm tears course down her face and rubbed them gently away with his thumbs.

"Is it me, Kit?"

She saw the uncertainty in his eyes and couldn't fathom his reasons for it. She'd expected his scorn perhaps, or even complete rejection, but not hesitancy and doubt. Not gentle caresses and tender kisses.

"No," she cried. "Not you. Never you."

Both his arms dropped to her waist, and he pulled her close. His mouth came down on hers hungrily. Insistently this time. It was a hot, demanding kiss, a sensuous blending of lips and tongues. Kit sighed with a growing wonder as she parted her lips, meeting the thrusts of his tongue with her own. She felt his heat now, his incredible, exciting fire and wanted him to consume her, yet she knew he would end it. He always did.

Nevertheless, Kit slid her hands up his bare chest, past the bandages, then higher to thread her fingers through the hair at the back of his neck. Wolf pulled her ever closer, tightening the contact between them, fitting his length to hers.

She recognized the expanding knot of desire as she moved against him. He moaned, and the sound inflamed her even more. Jolts of pleasure shot through her, and Kit realized she wanted his hands all over her. She wanted him to touch her as he had at Somerton Lake and on the road to Kendal.

Wolf felt the tips of her breasts harden as they pressed through the cloth of her gown against his naked skin and knew she was as aroused as he was. He trailed hot kisses down her throat and cupped her breasts with his hands, gently raising the nipples with his thumbs.

God, how he wanted her, but not here, not among his men in this rough camp. He would make her his wife in nothing less than the duke's bed.

Wolf wrapped her in his arms and kissed her ear, his warm breath causing her to shiver. "Do you know how desirable you are?" His voice was low and harsh with wanting. Kit barely squeaked a reply. There was confusion in her eyes, and her lips were swollen and yearning to be kissed again. But Wolf restrained himself. "Our first time together must be special…"

Wolf pulled her hands away from his shoulders, held them against his chest and looked at her. He was surprised by the raw desire he saw in her eyes, and his heart soared. God, she wanted him! But she was too inexperienced to understand his hesitancy.

"Kathryn, I would bed you properly," he said gently. "Not here, not with all my men about."

She looked down, embarrassed by her wantonness. What

could he possibly think of her? What did she know of how a wife should act?

He lifted her chin, and she looked into his eyes. She saw not only desire there, but tenderness, too, and she realized that what he said was for her benefit. ''We must wait 'til we reach Windermere. Only then will I make you my wife.''

Kit leaned forward and kissed the notch where his neck met his breastbone, and it was nearly his undoing. Then she stunned him, her words nearly breathless. ''I think I've waited nearly all my life for you, my lord. Two more days should hardly matter.''

When he finally lay down next to her that night, he was certain they would be two of the longest days of his life.

Kit was determined to make the marriage work. They had already taken a giant leap forward, but Kit realized they still had a long distance to go before they had a marriage between them. She didn't expect Wolf to fall in love with her right away, but she intended to make him forget *Annalise* and every other woman in his past. She knew he'd been enamored of the woman at Somerton Lake, a fact which bolstered her courage, giving her the nerve to attempt to seduce her husband, scant as her seductive skills were.

That night was clear and pleasantly cool after the sun set. Kit lay on her blanket and looked up at the star-filled sky. She watched as the smoke from the small cook fire dispersed in the air and wished that Wolf would come and lie down soon. She fully intended to remain awake until he came to her. When Wolf finally finished speaking with the guards and came to take his place next to her, he settled down on his blanket without a word and turned his back to her.

Wolf would have liked to hold Kit as she slept, as he had every other night, but he didn't dare, not after her passionate response to him when he kissed her in the clearing.

Chester and Alfred were not more than five feet away. Alex, Claude and Nicholas weren't far, either, and Wolf did not care to be tempted by his sweet wife beyond his endurance. Just being this close was trial enough, without even touching.

Kit, undaunted by her husband's lack of consideration and unaware of his reasons for turning away, turned to him instead. She put her arm around his waist and fit her length to him, pressing soft parts against the very solid, but sensitive wall of his back.

He was certain he could feel every detail of her flesh.

"Sleep well, husband," she breathed in his ear.

The heat of the sun still burned when they stopped the last night on the road. It was terribly humid, with the threat of a storm in the air and Kit couldn't wait to peel off her sticky clothes and bathe in the secluded lake they had seen nestled in the wooded dale on their approach to the valley. The men set up camp again while Kit hiked down the hill toward the water, carrying fresh clothes.

The small lake was situated in a thicket of willows and old, gnarled elm trees. Reeds grew up at the muddy banks and the beady eyes of little green frogs peered from their hiding places all along the edge. It was not much of a lake for swimming, and Kit knew it would be foolish to try it alone in unfamiliar water. She glanced around and verified that she was alone, then took off her shoes, tied her skirts up around her hips and stripped naked down to the waist. Then she waded into the water to wash. The cool water felt heavenly, though the muck at the bottom, oozing through her toes, was barely tolerable.

Wolf had seen Kit slip away a while before, and didn't at first realize what she had in mind. He was setting up camp with the rest of the men, and it wasn't unusual for Kit to find a few moments of privacy whenever they dismounted. But then he remembered seeing the lake, and it occurred to him that she'd been carrying a spare gown when she'd headed down the hill. He began to worry that she might try swimming in the strange lake alone, knowing she had a propensity for the water. He dropped what he was doing and followed her tracks through the long grass down the hill and entered the lonely little woods.

When he reached the water and saw Kit, his feet rooted in place. She was just as he remembered her at Somerton Lake. She was his golden lady, but this time only partially naked, alluringly so, and her face was clearly visible in the light of the brilliant pink sunset.

She lifted her hair and drizzled water from a cloth down the back of her neck, then the front. Wolf watched her nipples harden as the cool water made her shiver and felt himself hardening as well. There would be one more grueling night and another difficult day in the saddle until they reached Windermere. He'd already decided to wait until then, but...

The argument raged within him, and he knew he'd have to be patient. She'd be too tender to ride on the morrow if—

"Come and I'll wash your back, husband," she said, astonishing him with her awareness of his presence. Her voice was husky, inviting.

Wolf walked slowly towards her, watching her turn to face him fully. She continued sensuously rubbing her arms and breasts with the wet cloth, nearly driving him mad. He had never seen a woman move so erotically before. She was beautiful and seductive. And she was his. He was impatient to test her sensuality in his arms. God, how he wanted her.

Kit felt an urgency to touch him, to have him touch her. His eyes grazed her skin heatedly, and she knew he was just as anxious. Wolf moved toward her, and Kit began to tremble in anticipation. He pulled off his doublet and tunic as he walked, dislodging the bulky dressing that had served him well enough throughout the long day.

Bare to the waist, Wolf was an impressive man. Wide,

powerful shoulders and an expansive chest tapered to a trim and narrow waist. Kit appreciated the play of his muscles under the mat of coarse, dark hair that covered his chest and trailed to a point where it slipped into his chausses. He came to her slowly, purposefully, and when he reached her, Wolf turned to present his broad back for her ministrations.

His flesh rippled as she moved the cool, wet cloth across it, less affected by the motive of cleanliness than the sensations caused by her cool hands. Kit stretched up to apply the cloth to his shoulders, and Wolf clearly felt the brush of her breasts against his back. Unable to restrain himself any longer, he turned all at once and took her in his arms.

"What sweet torture is this?" he asked, pressing hot kisses to the column of her throat, his lips trailing down.

"Not torture, my lord," Kit replied, shocked by the sensations caused by his mouth on one nipple, "only—ooh…"

His mouth found hers again, and a shudder ran through her as their tongues met. He lifted her up, ignoring the stab of pain from his wound, and carried her to a patch of soft, green moss near a stand of elms. The ground felt cool on her back, and Wolf's lips were hot on her skin.

The sky was streaked with brilliant pink and wispy clouds raced past, presaging winds and storms to come. They barely sensed the change in the air. The vivid colors framed Wolf's face as he leaned over Kit, and she watched as his silver eyes turned to dark gray. His mane of hair was wilder now than ever and she tugged on it, drawing him down, willing him to take possession, to make her his wife.

"This is not what I intended—"

"How could a duke's bed be more suitable," she murmured into his hair, "or more stately?"

Without experience to guide her, Kit's instincts ruled. She ran her hands slowly down his back and buttocks, then across to his chest and down. She loosened the cords at his waist, freeing him to her touch.

"I wanted to pamper you…" His hand cupped her

breast, then toyed with the nipple. His lips nuzzled her throat.

"I only wanted *you*..."

Spurred on by her words, and the sensations of flesh meeting bare flesh, Wolf's hand moved down; caressing, raising Kit's level of arousal. A tremendous tension grew in her, and the muscles in her legs flexed. He pushed her dampened gown off her hips and drew his hand back up her thighs, pausing to stroke her intimately at their junction. Kit shuddered once, then relaxed and opened herself to him.

A maelstrom grew around them. Leaves shot past, and Wolf was stung by more than one sharp twig as the wind drove dust and debris across the ground and through the air. Rosy skies turned vermilion. Dark, low-hanging clouds moved in. Hands, lips and tongues explored new territory.

"Touch here..."

"Don't stop..."

"You're so hot, so incredibly—"

"Please. Wolf..."

Her plea was dwarfed by a distant rumble of thunder. Neither Wolf nor Kit heard it, so completely absorbed were they by the overpowering sensations they shared. Every nerve, every fiber of her being was alive, and his touch ignited her to flame. Rational thought did not exist, only desire and an intensely mounting pleasure.

"Sweet Kit," he rasped, "I fear I will hurt you."

"You can hurt me only by holding back," she said, her lips and tongue exquisitely torturing his ear. "Teach me. Show me how to give you pleasure..." He took one of her hands and showed her while his mouth and tongue ravished her, bringing her to the brink of ecstasy.

She moaned with need as he positioned himself over her. Kit laced her hands around his neck and met his fierce thrusts with a passion born of desire and love. The splendor of their joining burst like lightning, crackling electrically through loins and limbs, shuddering out of control.

"You are not too tender?" Wolf asked much later, caressing a flaxen lock near Kit's ear, marveling at the wonder of her. Her head was nestled in the curve of his arm, and they were still curled around one another on the deep green moss. Lightning flashed in the distance, and Kit heard the low growl of thunder in the still faraway storm. She raised herself up on her elbows and studied her husband.

"No. And you, milord? Have I bruised you?" she asked with a wicked grin.

"Aye." He gave her a wolfish smile.

She caressed his nipple with her lips and felt him shudder in response. "Pray tell, how would you have me remedy the problem?" She teased the sensitive skin with her lips and teeth.

"I'll leave that to you," he said with a groan as her head moved. "I'm entirely at your mercy."

Chapter Fifteen

When it became clear that the storm was headed their way, the men moved camp from the hill, down into the shelter of the woods. A tent was set up near the lake for Wolf and his bride, and several tarps were hung from the trees to shield the men from the worst of the rain. Wolf stayed out and helped see to the animals and the supplies before the storm broke, rejoining Kit in their tent only after everything was secure.

He found his wife dozing in the center of their little shelter, amid the furs they'd brought in case of such weather. A pale yellow candle in a clay bowl flickered and sputtered, casting changing shadows on her face. Wolf shucked off his clothes and settled in under the furs, next to her bare skin. He wrapped an arm about her waist and pulled her close.

Kit stirred at the gentle intrusion, then came awake hazily.

"It's started to rain," he said. His voice seemed a caress in contrast to the harsh, irregular pattering on the fabric of the tent. She could feel his warm breath ruffling her hair.

"I hear it," Kit replied, glancing around their dry nest. She felt as though they were alone in the world, nestled in a warm cocoon. There was a wonderful security in being wrapped together in fur pelts, with the sound of the rain pouring down all around them. The scent of the tallow candle and its flickering light in the tent added to the snug atmosphere. She could stay this way for days, as long as Wolf was with her.

He traced the line of her jaw with a finger, trailing it down her neck and across her collarbone. "Are you warm enough?"

"Um-hm." She stretched her arms and legs. Warm and content.

The way she snuggled her soft curves into his side sent tremors of need down Wolf's entire length. He worried that everything was happening too quickly for Kit's good. Though he'd made love to her only an hour before, he wanted her again.

He bent his elbow and propped his head on his hand. Determined to get his mind off her very desirable body, he asked her about one of the statements King Henry had made before they left London.

"You haven't told me how you saved my life the night of the attack."

"The king exaggerated."

"I think not," Wolf shook his head. "If anything, Henry's a master of understatement."

"Yes, I suppose…"

"So, what happened, then?" he asked. "I remember it was dark when we went into the gallery, and they came at us from all quarters." His finger traced back from her clavicle, then up to the curly wisps of hair at her ear. His eyes seemed almost black now, with lashes dark and thick as soot. His face was smooth too, Kit noticed with delight. She didn't recall any other occasion when he'd shaved in the evening.

"Henry was without a weapon," Kit answered. "You defended him until he finally picked up a sword from one of those men. The Lollards."

"But then I was hit."

"In the chest—yes," she said. "We were outnumbered.

There were two of them going at you, and I couldn't see how you'd be able to defend yourself...." She shuddered, remembering the gush of blood from the wound. "...and I was afraid you'd be killed..."

"And...?"

Kit told Wolf how she'd managed to pull a sword out from under one of the dark-clad men and use it to defend herself until she could make her way to him.

"...then I whacked the man—"

"Whacked?"

"Yes, I *whacked* the one who cut your leg," she said, emphasizing the silly word. "I swung the sword as hard as I could and hit him in the side, just under the ribs."

"You whacked." He was amused and impressed with her ingenuity and daring. He doubted there was another woman in all of England who would have come to his rescue with a sword she could barely lift.

"Really, Wolf," her tone was that of a scolding mother. "My technique may have been lacking, but the end result was to my satisfaction."

He grinned. "Mine, too."

"My beautiful gown was ruined," she said quietly. "You bled all over it."

"I seem to remember someone crying..."

"You weren't meant to hear."

"Why?" His hand moved absently back to her jaw, and his finger traced a featherlight line across her lower lip and down to the cleft in her chin.

"I always thought you shouldn't cry in front of a dying man," she said with a smile. "Makes him give up hope."

When Kit awoke, she was alone. Morning light edged through the tiny cracks of the tent as she dressed in a clean gown. She emerged from the shelter and stretched, glancing around among the trees to find no one about. Somehow, eighty men had disappeared without making a sound. At least not enough sounds to wake her.

One weathered tarp remained, strung between two stout trees, and a small fire burned underneath, shielded from the misty morning. Kit heard a sound in the distance and saw Janus, hitched to a tree. Snorting and prancing, the stallion was anxious to move.

She made her way down to the water's edge and washed quickly, all the while wondering where her husband was. Kit even had a moment's pause when she thought Wolf might have left her, but immediately knew how foolish that thought was. She would have liked to believe he couldn't leave her after the previous night's intimacy and passion, but knew that duty was his reason for staying. His pride and sense of duty wouldn't allow him to lose a wife, no matter how little—or how much—she meant to him.

She returned to the fire and sat on a soft, dry spot of grass to brush and plait her hair. And as she did, Kit prayed her thanks to God that the Duke of Carlisle hadn't turned out to be the decrepit old Duke of her premarital imaginings. Her conscience told her that she should be confessing her shame for her night of wild abandon with Wolf, yet her feelings for her husband canceled out any guilt she might have felt.

Wolf had sent most of the men on ahead, unwilling to awaken his sweet wife to face the saddle so early. He was aware that their progress might be slow and he wanted to savor this time alone with her, before they arrived at Windermere, before all his new responsibilities closed in.

While Kit still slept, Wolf stationed a troop of twelve men up on a ridge to their southeast, to await his departure from the lake area. The men were instructed to follow the duke and his wife at a discreet distance, providing protection at the rear while Kit and Wolf rode on at their leisure.

He returned to the lake and found Kit on the matted lawn near the fire, brushing the long wavy hair that he knew would smell like flowers when he pressed his face to it. Her skirts were spread about her, and Wolf read a look of amusement on her face. He patted Janus as he walked by and saw Kit look up. The smile she gave him warmed his soul.

"Are you hungry?" he asked when he reached her. He had left a bowl of food, covered and warming near the fire.

Kit blushed and looked down when he spoke to her, and he was chagrined to lose any of the unexpected intimacy they'd experienced during the night. Not allowing her embarrassment to come between them, he crouched down next to her and took the hairbrush, then laid a hand at her cheek and kissed her brow.

"Here's a bit of meat left from the night's meal. Old Darby, our cook, saved this for you."

She broke her fast as Wolf resumed brushing her hair for her, sending shivers down her scalp and neck at the sheer pleasure of it.

"Don't bind it today, Kit," he said. "Your hair pleases me. I prefer it loose."

It seemed that she was still uneasy with him, and he had no intention of letting her continue so. Yet he was unsure how to proceed. Women were so different. What would help to put her at ease? More touching? Conversation?

"What were you thinking of just now?"

"Thinking of?"

"Yes. When I came back, you were smiling as you brushed your hair. You seemed amused about something."

She blushed again, remembering her thoughts. "It was nothing."

"Come now. Surely not 'nothing'?" He sat next to her and set the brush down, then caressed a curl behind her ear. "Kit, last night—"

"No, no," she interjected, clearly not wanting him to think she'd been dissatisfied in some way. "It wasn't that at all." Her brows settled back to a relaxed position and the look of vague amusement returned to her deep green eyes. She looked sweet and innocent, yet he remembered with fresh awareness, her sensual abandon during the night.

Wolf didn't think he'd ever get enough of her. He never knew it would be like this, with an insatiable hunger for her.

"I was remembering something…"

"Go on."

"When the Earl of Langston told me that I was to marry the Duke of Carlisle, I assumed Carlisle would turn out to be a wrinkled-up, moldy old man."

"You mean he didn't tell you *I* was Carlisle?" His hand stopped toying with the stray golden tendrils.

"No, Wolf," she said. "No one told me. Why do you think I fainted when I saw you the night of the banquet?"

"Why, Kit? Why did you faint?"

"I…I don't really know," Kit replied, embarrassed that she *had* fainted and taken aback at Wolf's sudden intensity. "I'd been upset ever since learning about King Henry. The old king, I mean—being my father. I'd always been led to believe my father was an honorable man…wed to my mother…that he'd died on the continent before my birth…" She shivered, having to face again the lie that had been her life and the truth that could ruin it forever.

Wolf moved closer and put his arm around her. Could it be true that she hadn't known he was the one to whom she was betrothed? That when he'd seen her crying on Rupert Aires' shoulder, it wasn't because she was distraught over the prospect of marrying him?

"I discovered in one day that I was…a bastard…*and* promised to some old duke—"

He interrupted by turning her face and kissing her gently.

"—and…so I was smiling this morning because I'm…I am well pleased that my husband turned out not to be a broken-down old tyrant of a duke—"

He kissed her a bit more fervently then.

"—but merely Sir Gerhart, a knight most pleasing to the eye—"

His lips moved down her throat as his hands unfastened

her lacings and pushed the bodice of her gown down, over her shoulders to her waist.

"—considerate to a fault—"

Wolf's fingertips brushed over her nipples, causing an immediate response.

"—and immensely...talented..."

She never finished the thought.

Wolf situated her in front of him on Janus, sidesaddle, for the ride home—to Windermere. She was a bit tender, though not unbearably so, and they rode comfortably together, without a trace of shyness between them now.

"Tell me about Windermere, Wolf," she said, nestled against his chest as they rode in the late morning mist. The ground seemed greener and the tree trunks blacker, and Kit felt content and secure encircled in her husband's strong arms.

"I was born at Windermere," he said, his warm breath gently stirring the hair at the top of her head. Wolf never cared to speak of his past or his family, but he found that he wanted to tell Kit. In some undefined way, his past was now hers. And once he'd told her, he hoped they could close the door on it together. "I was the youngest son of Bartholomew and Margrethe Colston. John was my eldest brother, six years older than me, and there was Martin, who died of lung fever when he was around twelve. I must have been about seven or eight at the time.

"My mother left England after Martin died, to stay for a time with her parents. John and I were no comfort for her, and I don't suppose my father was, either, though I was too young at the time to understand much of what happened."

For months, Margrethe's melancholy over Martin's death deepened to a degree that worried Bartholomew. Thinking she might benefit from a change, he had his wife taken to Bremen, to spend time with her parents, and hopefully to recover from the death of her young son.

The plan might have worked, but when Bartholomew and John were lured to Bremen and killed during their journey several months later, Margrethe's fate was sealed. She never recovered from her grief, and spent the subsequent twenty years wasting away, bit by terrible bit.

"But she had you, didn't she?" Kit asked. "Didn't your survival give her a reason to—"

"No, Kit," he said quietly. "It didn't."

They rode on in silence for a while. Kit held in her mind an image of her husband as a boy, experiencing the loss of his father and brothers, needing to share his own grief with his mother. But Wolf's mother had withdrawn into herself and had no room for him. Kit vowed that she would always be there for Wolf. And their children.

"Who was responsible for the ambush that killed your father and John? Was it ever found out?"

"The Marquess of Kendal, who was my father's closest friend and ally, tried to investigate the attack and the rumors that followed my father's death," Wolf explained. "But he was put off every time by the king. Henry—your father—was tremendously insecure at the time, with plots and threats and small revolts going on all around him. It was years before Henry knew whom to trust, and even then, he couldn't be sure.

"Kendal said he felt certain that Clarence and Philip Colston had been behind the attack, but he could prove nothing—not until I showed him the parchment we found outside Agatha's window at Windermere.

"Just about the time Bart Colston and his sons departed England for Germany, an assassination attempt was made on King Henry. The cutthroat who was hired to carry out the deed fumbled it, but managed to escape capture. However, though he escaped, the man accidentally dropped a purse containing a few gold coins and a missive bearing the old Colston seal. The contents of that purse became conclusive evidence in Henry's mind, that the Earl of Windermere was responsible for the attempt on his life. Further incriminating the earl, the Colstons all 'fled' England right at that time, presumably in case the assassination attempt failed.

"One of Henry's scribes at Westminster deciphered the document. Kendal had already recognized the seal as that of the Welshman, Owen Glendower, but most of the words were faded and distorted—nearly impossible for us to make out."

"What did it say?"

Wolf's voice was cold. "In the letter, Glendower merely congratulated my Uncle Clarence and his son, Philip, for their ploy to be rid of Henry and gain an earldom in the process. He fully appreciated the twist of fate ensuring that Windermere fell into Clarence's hands as well as placing the blame on Bartholomew for Tommy Tuttle's handi-work."

"Tommy Tuttle!"

"The man hired to kill King Henry. I never did find Tuttle himself," Wolf said, "but some of his cronies still hang about London. I gathered that he was a nasty piece of work with Welsh connections, but I couldn't find anyone willing to talk about his activities with Glendower twenty years ago."

"But you didn't need him to prove your case to Henry?"

"No, though I wanted to present every bit of evidence I could find. I did discover, however, that Tuttle could not read."

"That shouldn't have been a great surprise, Wolf. There are not so many who can—"

"No, it wasn't a great surprise. But why would an illiterate felon carry with him a note giving explicit instructions on murdering the king, along with methods of escape and then conveniently drop the purse with the note and the pay-ment inside?"

"Hmm. I suppose Henry also concluded that your father had been falsely implicated?"

"Aye. He did."

"What about Philip now? And Agatha?" They leaned a little to the left in the saddle to avoid some branches that hung low over the track.

"Well—Agatha," he said. "We had always assumed she'd been part of it."

"We?"

"My grandfather and I," he replied. "He is Rudolph Gerhart, Margrave of Bremen."

So Bridget had been right, Kit thought. Wolf was the grandson of a prince.

"When Hugh got me to the abbey after the attack—"

"Hugh?"

"Hugh Dryden. You know him, Kit. He accompanied us from Somerton."

Yes, of course she remembered Hugh. He was a powerful but wiry man, possibly a few years older than Wolf. He was rather plain-faced with dull brown hair and piercing blue eyes. Kit remembered that Hugh was never far from Wolf, though it occurred to her that she hadn't seen him in weeks.

"It was Hugh who saved my life and got me to the abbey of St. Lucien after we were ambushed. As a youth, he'd been sent to foster with our family, so he happened to be with us when we were attacked and he hasn't left me since. But I digress.

"It was my grandfather who believed that Clarence and Philip were responsible for the deaths of my father and brother." His voice was thick with emotion, but he went on. "I was too young to understand it then, but when I came of age and started talking about returning to Windermere, he told me his suspicions."

"And that's why you used your grandfather's name when you returned to England?"

He nodded. "I couldn't very well come back declaring I was Wolf Colston, heir to Windermere, could I?"

Kit agreed.

"My grandfather never really believed I'd ever prove

anything against Philip, but since I am not Rudolph's heir, it didn't particularly matter to him when I left Bremen. He never had much use for me. As for Nicholas..." one side of Wolf's mouth twisted up, "...he was never a favored grandson, either. Old Rudy will likely turn up his toes when word reaches Bremen that Nick is now a viscount."

Kit smiled, though she didn't really understand why Wolf's grandfather would be chagrined to find that his grandsons had done well.

"My plan was to serve Henry and win his trust, then go to Windermere and find a way to expose Philip. I'd never had any idea that Agatha would turn up the evidence I needed. There were rumors that she died years ago, but you saw her. And you didn't believe she was a ghost?"

"No. She was flesh and blood."

"Well, whether or not she was involved in the conspiracy with Clarence and Philip, she apparently recognized me when we were at Windermere—"

"I couldn't tell you at the time, but she called you 'the wolf.'"

"Ah?"

"Or '*my* wolf,' actually. I think she may have told me you were the rightful earl, but she spoke in riddles and rhymes. I think she's mad."

"Well, for some reason, she wanted to see Philip fall from grace," he said. "I can't think of any other reason why she would have given you my father's seal."

Kit shrugged.

"I don't doubt she and Philip have been on tenuous terms since Clarence's death. In fact, John Beauchamp thinks Agatha may have been a virtual prisoner in that tower room for years."

"I wonder if anyone else knows of the secret door."

"I doubt it," Wolf said. "I spent the first nine years of my life there, exploring every corner of the castle and *I* was surprised when you told me of it."

"I wonder what happened to her."

"Frankly, I'm more interested in what happened to Philip."

"And Hugh," Kit asked. "Where has he been these last few weeks, anyway?"

"At Windermere," Wolf said. "Keeping track of my cousin, Philip."

Chapter Sixteen

They had ridden several hours when Wolf finally led Janus off to the side of the beaten track near a broken-down, uninhabited stone hut. He swung off the beast's back and reached up to help Kit slide down.

They walked west through a heavily wooded area with rugged hills and huge granite outcroppings scattered among the trees. Wolf took Kit's hand, and they made their own path through the thick underbrush of the woods. It was a bit like a fairy place, Kit thought, with beads of moisture still on the thickly growing ferns. The sunlight filtered in through the tall shafts of the trees and reflected on the sparkling water droplets. It was misty in the higher ground and craggy hills jutted up out of the haze like gnarled old fingers of a long-forgotten troll.

Wolf cleared the way as they climbed one such wet, rocky hill, and Kit heard the sounds of flowing, splashing water as they moved higher.

"Where are we?" she asked as they made their way to a wide ledge carved out of the hillside. Kit wondered if they were going to climb to the top.

"Windermere land," Wolf replied as he led her around to the far side of the rock. "There's a place I want you to see."

Kit picked up her pace and followed more closely,

warmed by the thought of Wolf bringing her to a special place. He'd said nothing of his feelings on the marriage, yet she sensed acceptance in him. In fact, if his pleasure during their encounters the previous night and in the morning came near to matching hers, she was certain he couldn't help but have some tender feelings for her. The thought brought hope that the marriage would yet prove satisfactory.

They finally came to a broad, flat clearing carved into the hill. It was bordered on her left by a sheer rock face where a thin sheet of water slid down the wall and flowed into a gentle brook, high above the surface of the forest.

"Where does it go?" Kit asked, enthralled. It was a beautiful place; a world apart.

"Come and see."

They walked on, and a bit farther, Kit could see where the burn traced a downward course until it too, became a waterfall. "It's beautiful," she breathed. It was bright and sunny in the high clearing where they stood, with rich green moss and clumps of pink sundew growing in tufts of soil that seemed to have been left accidentally in the clefts of the rocks.

They were high enough to be able to see beyond the trees. Wolf stood behind Kit, put his hands on her shoulders and turned her to face north.

"Windermere Castle," he said.

In the distance, Kit could trace the narrow track they'd traveled as it turned into a more reputable thoroughfare, moving through the valley closer to the town and the castle. Surrounded by fertile, well-tilled fields, the pretty town huddled below the castle walls. The dark gray fortress itself stood on elevated ground with a tall, thick stone wall surrounding it. Three towers were visible in the distance, and a flag flew from a staff on the highest of the three towers.

It was a breathtaking view of Windermere.

"My mother called this place 'the earl's nook'," Wolf said.

Kit leaned back into him, and he slid his arms around her. There was a wistful tone to his voice, and she knew he was remembering his last days with his family.

"My brothers and I...sometimes we came here with my father..." His voice was quiet, and they listened to the gentle sound of the water meandering past at their feet. "The last time I was here...well, this is the route we took when we left for Bremen that last time. My father and John and I climbed here for a last look at Windermere before we left. This is the first time I've been back since I was a child."

She felt the steady thud of his heart through her back.

"Kathryn." His breath was warm at the top of her head. "My cousin Philip...as long as he's at large, I'll worry. You must have a care. Always keep an escort with you."

Kit was pleased to think he'd worry about her, but didn't want to be a burden to him. "Do you really think he'd cause me any harm?"

"There's no question," he said, turning her in his arms. She looked up and saw fierce determination in his eyes. "Philip isn't to be trusted. Do you understand? I'll not risk your safety."

"But Wolf, I've managed so far to take care of myself—"

"You don't understand, Kit. You don't know him as I do."

She saw that he meant to have his way in this. "All right, then," Kit said. "Tell me what you want me to do."

He was relieved. He knew that John Beauchamp had been right when he'd said Philip was *twisted*. Wolf remembered enough incidents as a child when Philip had proven it.

Wolf led Kit to a cool ledge cut into the rock wall and sat down with her. He picked up one of her hands and kissed her knuckle. "First of all, don't ever underestimate Philip. He's dangerous and he's vicious, no matter what he seemed to you when you met him."

"He seemed cold and unfeeling to me," Kit said.

"That's the least of it." He braced his elbows on his knees and leaned forward, turning to look at her. "I don't know where he's hiding, though perhaps Hugh has found him by now. If not, I want you to be on your guard. One of the men will go with you whenever you leave the castle. Don't go riding alone, or into Windermere town by yourself. Let someone know where you'll be if you're going to an unlikely place in the—"

"But Wolf," she protested a bit hesitantly, panicked at the thought that he would leave her at Windermere and go on to some other place without her, "where will *you* be?"

"Me?" He smiled and her heart nearly melted.

"Yes," she said, a little breathlessly. "I have no wish to remain at Windermere if you are not…that is, if you—"

"Kathryn," he took her hand again and looked into her worried eyes, "do you think I could ever leave you again?"

"Again?"

"I left you once in London…"

"Yes, you did," she whispered, remembering her desolation at Westminster, wishing he would come back, realizing that Rupert was not the man she wanted. Knowing the man who was…

Wolf wrapped one of her curls around his forefinger, then pulled it down gently, straightening it. She was so unpredictable, so impertinent: so different from everything he'd always thought he wanted and needed. He dropped an arm to her waist and pulled her close. He kissed her forehead and breathed in the fresh, flowery scent of her hair.

"Your hair…you never left it uncovered before we came to London."

"I was afraid," she said simply. His chin rested on the top of her head. "I thought you'd recognize me from that night at Somerton Lake. And at Kendal…well, at Kendal, when it was just *me,* you made it quite clear you didn't—"

"Kit—it was only that I couldn't claim you for my own," Wolf said.

"But I thought—"

"It wasn't true," he said, "whatever you thought...it was...well, it was not easy for me to turn you over to Rupert Aires in London. I thought it best to make you angry. To stay away from you...to keep some perspective—"

Kit stood abruptly and folded her arms around herself. Her mind cautioned her to be wary, yet her heart yearned for what he said to be true. She wanted to believe he'd put distance between them only because he knew it would prove difficult giving her up to Rupert.

But what about *Annamarie?* She wondered if Wolf's past hesitancy was due to some tender feelings or loyalty towards his former betrothed.

Kit watched the water as it dropped from the cliff's edge to blend with the shining waters of the brook, and wondered whether to tell him of her despair at Westminster; despair that she would never see him again, that her life would be forever empty without him.

"I missed you terribly," she finally said in a small voice. She felt him standing right behind her; his warm body close by, his breath near her ear.

"I had no idea..." How he'd hated having to abandon her. All those weeks she'd spent in London, alone, with only the shrews at court for company. "I thought you and Rupert—"

"Rupert was my mistake," Kit said, turning to look at Wolf. "I quickly realized he was...he was not quite what my imagination had made him out to be over the years we were apart."

"Kit, what are you saying? ...You don't regret giving Rupert up?"

She shook her head. "And I told him as much," Kit said with a wistful smile, "though I think I rather insulted him."

She walked over to the stream and crouched down to draw some water up in her hand, letting it spill back into the burn. "I daresay I was somewhat distraught that morning when I told him. I'd met the Earl of Langston the night

before, and found out about my mother, my birth...and I
happened to run across Rupert in the garden. I couldn't bear
to tell him about Meghan and Henry...so I told him about
my betrothal to you—or rather, the Duke of Carlisle.''

The sunlight was fading, and Kit looked out at Windermere Castle as her shadow lengthened out beside her. She
had no idea what her revelation meant to Wolf—that her
tears that morning hadn't been because she was fated to
wed him.

"I told him I'd always thought he and I would marry,"
Kit said. "Of course, he was quite appalled by the thought,
until I told him he would make a very poor husband."

"That's true enough," Wolf said, putting a hand under
her elbow to raise her up, away from the water. "But what
about me?" His voice was soft, seductive. "What kind of
husband do you suppose I'll make you?"

Kit searched his eyes and wished for an easy answer.
She didn't know how a powerful knight like Wolf would
react if she spoke the truth, that she found him warm and
tender, gentle and considerate with a new and uncertain
wife, a wife who knew she was not his first choice.

She reached for the small leather pouch in her belt which
she'd worn all the way from Westminster. She'd kept it
close, intending to bring it out when the moment was right.

"I had this made for you in London," she said, handing
it to him, hoping he would understand her answer to his
question.

Wolf took the soft brown pouch and loosened the draw-
string, then drew out a small wooden casket. He looked
inside and took out the gold ring that Kit hoped would
become the signet of the Duke of Carlisle. Framed together
within the circle of the signet were the head of a wolf and
a rose, neatly engraved on its chest. A modest-sized ruby
was on each side of the band, below the circle. When he
finally looked up at Kit, comprehension was clear in Wolf's
eyes.

"Kit..."

She leaned up and touched his lips with her own, silencing him with a searing kiss, opening her mouth, inviting him, inciting him to respond with a fierceness that made her breathless. His arms encircled her and pulled her tight against him, and there was no mistaking his desire, his need.

Before they started their descent from the earl's nook, Wolf caught a glimpse of men in the distance on horseback, riding south from Windermere. There seemed to be six or so, and they rode with an urgency that raised clouds of dust on the trail behind them.

"Who do you think it is?" Kit asked, following his gaze into the dale below.

Wolf's eyes narrowed as he shook his head. "Can't be certain from this distance, though it looks like Nicholas in the lead."

Kit believed he was right. She thought she could identify his head of light blond hair and the white horse—Nicholas' usual mount. But the situation being what it was at Windermere, Wolf was right to be cautious.

"What do you think is amiss?" she asked worriedly. "Their haste—"

"Perhaps they've found Philip and are merely anxious to inform me," Wolf replied. "Then all our apprehensions would be resolved."

Kit doubted it, but appreciated Wolf's attempt to reassure her. They climbed down the trail in the hill and made their way back through the thick woods to get to the place where Wolf had tethered Janus.

"Come. We'll move up here so I can get a better look at them," he said, moving the big horse back up into the woods to conceal him. Kit walked alongside Wolf, until they reached the higher ground and a good vantage point within the trees.

"Our escort will meet whoever approaches—"

"Escort?"

He smiled down at her and nodded. "We've a dozen good men guarding our backs. They'll meet the riders if we don't intercept them first."

Twelve men? Following them? Kit blushed, remembering their leisurely ride to the earl's nook, with her husband nuzzling her and pleasantly tantalizing her with gentle fingers. She was mortified to think that twelve men had been close by—perhaps even within sight of them—when they were on the cliff near the dual waterfalls.

"Don't fret, Kit," he said, reading her thoughts. "I handpicked the few who understand the meaning of the word 'privacy.'"

"I don't fret," she said irritably. "I never fret. But you might have told me you had men all around us."

"Not all around us," he chuckled, amused by her perspective. "Seventy-three men ahead of us in three groups to clear the way, and twelve behind—a fair distance behind—to protect the rear."

"Hmm."

"Look. 'Tis Nicholas." He gave her a quick kiss, took her hand and headed toward the road. "He's got Douglas, Alfred and Claude with him—three of the men who came in advance of us, days ago. Shall we see what devils they have biting at their heels?"

They ambled along, picking their way back toward the road, and the riders who were rapidly gaining on them. A gray dusk had fallen, and it was becoming quite dark in the woods, though Wolf led faultlessly through the damp underbrush and bramble. His surefooted stride reminded Kit of the time—it seemed so long ago—when she'd run away from him, and he'd carried her back to camp in the dark.

The riders slowed when Wolf and Kit appeared on foot with Janus following behind. The two walked north as the riders continued towards the hills on their southerly course. They finally met where the road became a rough track, near the edge of the woods. The eastern side of the road was bordered by high cliffs and as the sun dropped beneath the level of the trees to the west, the group was enshrouded in shadow.

All eight men dismounted.

"All is...ah...well...Your Grace?" Sir Edward asked, casting a sidelong glance at Nicholas. Kit suddenly realized that they had some idea where she and Wolf had been, and what they were doing, and she blushed.

Wolf looked them over. Every one of them was squirming.

"All is most definitely well," Wolf finally said, good-naturedly. His smile unnerved some of the men—they were so unaccustomed to it. "What dire news do you bring that you travel at breakneck speed? Did I not bid you farewell just this morn, Nick? What tidings do you bring of Windermere?"

"There is a great deal to discuss, Wolf," Nicholas replied, his manner now less embarrassed and more serious. "As dusk approached, some of us became concerned by your absence. To begin, no one has seen Hugh Dryden in three days."

The men all looked grim, and Wolf lost his smile.

"Second, a couple of Philip's cronies have been seen about town, but they always manage to disappear before they can be apprehended," Nicholas said. "I will not be at ease until you and your lady are safely behind the castle walls."

"Tell me the rest as we ride," Wolf said as he gave Kit a lift up to Janus' back.

Before mounting his horse, Nicholas said, "Baron Robert Wellesley and his daughter await you at Windermere, as well as Baron Thomas Somers and three of his men."

"Somers!" Wolf exclaimed. "I should have known—"

"Wolf!" Kit screamed as an arrow shot past her, impaling the leather satchel on the saddle in front of her. Janus reared up and Kit leaned forward, into his thick mane, but couldn't manage to get a grip on the animal. In the instant before Wolf regained control of the massive horse, another arrow flew past, and Kit was thrown to the ground and knocked unconscious.

Fearful that she would be trampled in the fray, Wolf quickly threw Janus' reins to Nicholas and ran to pull Kit away from the horse's hooves. He picked her up from the ground, then carried her to the trees, shielding her with his body as the arrows continued to fly all around them. Most of the men made for cover as well, leading their horses swiftly to the woods. Three men circled around on foot to the east to pursue the archers concealed in the trees on the cliff. Some of Wolf's men were already returning arrows to the eastward heights, but there were no human targets visible. The trees and their long shadows covered their attackers quite adequately.

Wolf eased himself down to the ground, holding Kit. She came around quickly. "Kit, are you all right?" he asked. His big hands gently smoothed the hair away from her forehead.

"Yes." She grimaced as she moved. "I'm just bruised a bit." Her head ached where a lump had started. Her left ankle, hip and shoulder were sore, too, but Kit had suffered worse in her lifetime. She would manage to survive this little episode as she had all the others.

Wolf was not so philosophical. Unbidden visions of the ambush and slaughter of his family twenty years before came to mind. He wanted to bellow with rage that his men—possibly the best-trained unit in England—hadn't been able to protect Kit from injury. He vowed never to be in such a vulnerable position again.

"Where are you hurt, Kit?" he asked gently, probing the back of her skull.

"My head aches some, but the rest is nothing, Wolf. I'll be fine."

"Show me."

"No, Wolf. Not here—with your men all about."

"No one is near, wife," Wolf insisted. "Show me your bruises."

Kit adjusted her bodice so her husband could inspect her shoulder blade. Then she rearranged her skirts to view the damage done to her hip and ankle.

"See? Not so bad. I've lived with worse than this," she said brightly. "And I heal quickly."

Wolf gritted his teeth, furious that Kit had been a victim—again.

"It will mend," she said. "Even when Lord Somers broke my…"

Wolf's face darkened and Kit realized she shouldn't have mentioned her stepfather right then. She hesitated to go on.

"Broke your what?"

"Well, I just meant to reassure you that I will be fine. I heal quite easil—"

"Somers broke your *what?*"

She hesitated before replying. "My two fingers," she finally said quietly, holding up the first two fingers of her left hand. "It was *years* ago, Wolf."

Kit saw a muscle tighten in Wolf's jaw and wished she'd said nothing. With Thomas Somers awaiting them at Windermere, it was not wise to have given Wolf further cause to hate him. No, the villain at hand was Philip Colston. Not Lord Somers. And Kit knew it was important to remember that.

"How is she?" Nicholas asked as he knelt next to Wolf, beside Kit. "A bit pale… Otherwise able to ride?"

Kathryn nodded as Wolf fumed.

"Then it's time to take your bride home, cousin."

Chapter Seventeen

Windermere Castle
July 1, 1421

The twelve men who Wolf had assigned to bring up the rear pursued the attackers on the cliff while the men who'd come from Windermere escorted the duke and his bride to Windermere Castle. Wolf rode with Kit practically on his lap, going as slowly as he dared, conscious of her swelling bruises, but making as much haste as possible to stay ahead of further trouble. It galled him to run away from an attacker, but Kit's safety meant all to him.

Wolf seethed with anger that she could be hurt—especially in his presence, and he was plagued by the surprisingly clear childhood memories of the fatal attack on his family as they traveled to Bremen. He'd been in plenty of skirmishes and battles—massive, full-scale, bloody battles, yet the sight of his precious Kit, lying unconscious on the road beneath Janus' hooves was nearly his undoing.

When they reached Windermere, Nicholas led the way through the castle while the rest of Wolf's men saw to the horses. Wolf carried Kit and followed Nicholas up the huge stone staircase, through the great hall and up another flight of steps until they reached the master's chambers. Groups of curious servants assembled along his route, and Wolf called orders to them as he made his way.

Nicholas pulled back and tied the exquisite blue brocade curtains that surrounded what was now the duke's massive bed, then lit all the candelabra in the room. The chamber itself had been cleaned and stripped, then refurnished to the duke's tastes. There existed none of the dark, ominous corners of the chamber Kit had shared with Bridget when they'd visited Windermere before. The master's chamber was light, clean and sparingly furnished. Kit wondered how Wolf had managed to have a chamber so quickly prepared to his liking.

It was so unlike any other part of Windermere that she had seen before. There were no dank tapestries on the walls to conceal hidden doors or passageways. The rushes had been swept out and replaced with strange, thickly woven floor coverings such as Kit had seen only in the king's chambers at Westminster. A large vase of fresh, red roses stood on the trunk near the window and another was on the mantelpiece, reminding Kit of her rose garden at Somerton. One corner of her mouth turned up, and she glanced up suspiciously at her husband.

"The situation is not good, Wolf. No one at the castle remembers seeing Hugh Dryden," Nicholas said, once they were in the privacy of the duke's chambers. "But a man answering Hugh's description was seen in town one week ago. I don't know where he was prior to that time, but we've verified that Hugh set himself up at Prudhomme's tavern—the man keeps a small inn as well—and spent several nights there. Then he disappeared."

"Disappeared?" Wolf stopped where he stood, disbelieving. "How does a grown man *disappear?*"

"Who can say?" Nicholas replied. "All we know is that his packs and horse are still at Prudhomme's place. And Hugh is no longer there. It's been three days now."

"And what of Philip?" Wolf asked as he stepped up and lay Kit gently on the bed. He sat down next to her and took her hand, absently rubbing his thumb across her palm. Just that light touch sent shivers of pleasure through Kit's body, overshadowing her various aches and pains. She didn't want to think of Philip or Hugh or Windermere.

Nicholas shook his head. ''Apparently, when John DuBois and his men arrived over a fortnight ago, Philip was here—at least the servants all believed he was on the premises.''

The king's men, under the command of Sir John DuBois, had arrived late one afternoon and were greeted by the earl's housekeeper, Blanche Hanchaw. The woman bid Sir John to wait in the hall while she located his lordship. A quarter of an hour later, the earl was still not to be found. The housekeeper gave her apologies to the knight, and said she was certain that, in his absence, the earl would want them to enjoy the hospitality of Windermere before their return to London in the morning. She hoped that—wherever he had gone—the earl would return to see them off by morning. However, she gave them to believe that the Earl of Windermere often left the castle without notice. Where he might be, Mistress Hanchaw could not venture to guess.

Sir John, not of a mind to return to the king without Philip Colston, and not entirely trusting of the housekeeper, produced a warrant and ordered his men to search the castle and all the grounds for the earl. Their search resulting in failure, John sent men to scour the town, but the earl still eluded them.

The commander posted men in strategic places on the roads, in the town and about the castle. They stayed several days, but Philip never turned up. Defeated, John DuBois finally returned to London with news that Philip Colston was still at large.

''Philip's possessions are still here,'' Nicholas said. ''When our men arrived to set Windermere in order for your coming, they cleared out this room—packed everything in trunks. However, Claude Montrose said that if

Philip had actually been here when DuBois arrived, he must have left in haste. It appears that he left all his belongings here.''

Wolf glanced around for the first time and found the room to his liking. Nothing of Philip remained. The chamber had been cleared out and scrubbed, the rugs laid and pitchers of roses arranged the way he remembered the flowers in Kit's room at Somerton. He knew she was partial to roses.

''Post men all over the castle and in town,'' Wolf said. ''I want complete surveillance of the area. It is highly doubtful that Philip would be foolish enough to reveal himself. But we might catch sight of one of his henchmen. I want them followed if they're seen—not apprehended. And I want it done discreetly.''

''I will see to it,'' Nicholas said. ''What of Somers? He requested an audience as soon as you arrived.''

''He can wait. It may be days before I am ready to see him,'' Wolf replied tersely.

''But Wolf—'' Kit started.

''You're not to get anywhere near him, Kit,'' Wolf interrupted her. ''I don't trust him.''

Nicholas nodded, satisfied. Wolf was not the only one who abhorred Kit's treatment at the hands of her stepfather.

''Has Stephen Prest been located?'' he asked Nicholas. Prest had been Bartholomew Colston's loyal steward years before and Wolf had given orders that the man was to be found. Wolf knew of no better candidate for the position of steward to the Duke of Carlisle.

''Not yet.'' Nicholas answered a knock at the door and allowed two servants to carry in Wolf's packs and Kit's satchels. ''We've heard he's at Elton Manor, two days' ride from Windermere. Chester and William have ridden to Elton to see if they can find him.''

''Good. Hallmote will be held as soon as he returns,'' Wolf said, ''or after I name another steward, if that becomes necessary. I'll have my vassals swear fealty as soon as possible and we'll begin to repair the damage Philip has done over the years.''

''*Ja,* cousin,'' Nicholas said.

''And find a healer, Nick. Send her here—to Kit,'' Wolf said.

''I believe the gardener is—'' he replied.

''I don't need Will Rose,'' Kit said. ''These bruises are nothing. I just—''

''Find him and send him to us.''

''I'll do that,'' Nick said with a broad smile as he headed toward the door. ''Welcome home, Wolf.''

''Nicholas—'' Kit said before the viscount left the room.

''Your Grace?'' he said with a grin.

Her cheeks reddened at his use of her title. ''Thank you. For everything.''

He responded with a tilt of his blond head. Then he was gone.

''How do you feel?'' Wolf asked Kit when they were finally alone. He gently smoothed a stray curl back from her forehead.

''Like a sack of peaches—that have been tossed down a hill,'' she replied, grimacing. But on seeing his worried look, she amended her words. ''Oh, it's not so bad, Wolf, really.''

Kit pulled her skirt back above the thigh and twisted around to look at the damage to her hip. The bruise seemed to have increased in size since she'd last looked, and Kit wondered if the same was true of the one on her shoulder blade.

''Help me with this, will you, Wolf?'' she asked, trying to unfasten her dress.

''Lie still, Kit, and rest until the healer comes.''

''There is nothing Will can do for this,'' Kit retorted. ''I just want to see how bad it is.''

Will Rose insisted on treating Kit's bruises with leeches. Kit had never seen Brother Theodore use leeches for bruises at Somerton, but Will assured her that the nasty little creatures were often able to draw off blood from the bruise, limiting its size as well as some of the pain. She wished she'd known about the practice years ago. There had been plenty of times she could have used it.

When the leeches were glutted, they fell off, and Will collected them in a small earthen pot. "Ye'll be fine in a couple o' days, Yer Grace," he told her. "Best to stay off that ankle 'til the swellin' goes down a bit, though."

"I'll do that," she yawned as the man turned to leave. She was so tired, she didn't think she could keep her eyes open any longer. "Thank you, Will." Kit sank back into the soft mattress of the bed, and Wolf pulled the coverlet over her.

"Rest now," he said. Then he blew out most of the candles in the room.

A quiet knock brought Wolf to the door. It was Nicholas, along with Sir Edward, who had been out searching for the archer among the cliffs. A quick glance at Kit and Wolf knew she was asleep.

"Your Grace," Edward said quietly after Wolf hushed him. "We lost the archer on the hillside. We believe there was only the one."

"What!"

"We killed him, actually," Edward amended. "Inadvertently. We had him surrounded on three sides, with only a high cliff behind him. There was absolutely no means of escape. He tried to run—the men closed in."

"Go on." Wolf clasped his hands behind his back and paced to the window and back.

"He started heading in the opposite direction, then all the men moved in. Cornered him. He was shouting at us as he backed up. He stumbled…a hell of a fall…"

"Who was he?" Wolf asked at length. "Do we know?"

"Turns out he was Philip's bailiff," Nicholas said. "A man called Broderick Ramsey."

"No clues on the body where we might find Philip?"

Nicholas shook his head.

"Have you any idea yet, how many men are still loyal to Philip?" Wolf asked. "And how many might still be in the vicinity of the castle or Windermere town?"

"Not yet, but our men are questioning everyone. We should have some ideas—"

A rap at the door interrupted them. Nicholas opened the door to a footman who carried a huge wreath made of fresh leaves and flowers, intricately woven onto a light birch frame.

"What's this?" Wolf asked.

"'Twas brought by a young lad and his parents, my lord," the footman replied. "Townsfolk."

"Who are they? What are their names?"

"Why, 'twas Master Juvet with his wife and their boy, Alfie, my lord."

"Bid them to stay," Wolf ordered. "Have them wait for me in the hall."

"Yes, Your Grace," the man replied. "Also, Your Grace, Baron Somers…er…*demands* to see you."

"You can send *him* back wherever he came from," Wolf replied angrily. "I'll not be seeing him tonight."

"Yes, Your Grace."

"Come then," Wolf said. "Let's go see the Juvets." They left the room, and Wolf left a guard at Kit's door.

"Have you spoken to Somers?" Wolf asked Nicholas.

"Only briefly."

"What does he want?"

"He doesn't say," Nicholas replied. "Though he was sober before you returned. And civil enough."

Wolf knew he would need to prepare himself before meeting with Kit's stepfather. It would take all his self-control to avoid beating the man to a bloody pulp. Blackened eyes, split lips, broken collarbones and fingers…he hated to think what more the bastard had done.

"And what will you do about Baron Wellesley?" Nicholas asked.

Wolf paused on the stair. He had pushed the baron to the back of his mind. "I don't suppose he's said what he wants, either?"

Nicholas shook his head. "No. Though he appeared quite anxious to welcome you home."

"It seems strange, does it not, that he should come to welcome me to my own home?" Wolf asked. "Is he trustworthy?"

"I don't know. He may wish only to cull your favor—"

"I have no intention of trusting anyone in this castle yet, until I determine whose loyalty lies where. Especially not Thomas Somers," Wolf said to Nicholas as they continued down the stairs and moved towards the great hall. "But I'll need someone to tend to Kit…"

"Not the housekeeper?"

"Mistress Hanchaw least of all," Wolf replied.

"Not Somers—"

"Ha! I'd sooner let Kit near a wild boar."

"What about Baron Wellesley and—"

"He may favor Philip."

"And his daughter?"

"Lady…?" Wolf was at a loss for her name.

"Christine. We met her at Windermere Fair. As I recollect," Nick added with a grin, "she took a liking to you—a strong liking."

"I'm not in need of another wife, Nick," he answered, taking his cousin's meaning.

"No, but Lady Christine is here. Mayhap Baron Wellesley is unaware that you were wed in London."

"Well, he'll learn of it on the morrow. Why don't you try to persuade the lady to favor *you* instead," Wolf said with a grim smile. "Good night, cousin."

Nicholas and Wolf split up, then Wolf went on to meet Alfie's family alone. The Juvets were a young couple, clean and well dressed, certainly not wearing the simple rough tunics of peasants. Freemen, Wolf thought. An idea took root in Wolf's mind, and he wondered if the Juvet family's obvious prosperity would prevent Madam Juvet from accepting a position in the duke's household.

Alfie was the first to speak. He stepped forward, glad to see Wolf, yet nervous at the same time. "I was hoping to see yer lady, sir," he said," to give her the wreath we made and…to thank her…for…" He twisted his hat in his hands.

"My wife is indisposed," Wolf said. "She took a fall just outside of town, though I'm certain she'll recover quickly."

"Thank the saints for that," Alfie's mother said quietly, crossing herself.

"Is it bad, milord?" Alfie asked, swallowing hard. "I mean, is she…does it hurt her very much?"

"Well, yes," Wolf said, "it seemed to hurt quite a bit. But I daresay she'll be up some tomorrow."

"Your Grace," Master Juvet said, "may I say that we— in town—were disturbed to hear of the attack upon your person and the duchess' fall. There are a number of men in town who wish to assist you…to bring justice…er…to those who would do you ill."

"Your efforts are appreciated, Juvet," Wolf replied. "All I ask of you now is to inform me if any of Philip Colston's men are seen about. Perhaps one of them can lead us to my cousin."

"Yes, Your Grace," Juvet said. "May I also say how pleased we…that is to say, all of us in town were pleased to learn that it was you—Sir Gerhart—who is Wolfram Colston, Duke of Carlisle. And we just heard of your marriage today when young Alfie here—well, Alfie was the one who learned you'd wed Lady Kathryn. Your lady is a most gracious, generous—"

"Lady Kathryn will always have my undyin' gratitude and loyalty, Your Grace," Alfie's mother said, mustering her courage to speak. "What she did that day at the fair— for my boy—"

"The townspeople remember Sir Gerhart well from the day you came to the fair, Your Grace," her husband interrupted. "They never met a man—an outsider—who was so interested in their work, or their fields and crops. The earl himself never cared much, so long as he got his workweek from us," Juvet said, choosing his words cautiously. After all, it wasn't every day that a common freeman addressed a duke, and he had been chosen by the townspeople to be the one to represent them, to test the waters in their new lord's home. "Ever since King Henry's men came to arrest the earl—well, the old people have been talking about your father, Lord Bartholomew, and the way things were in the days when he was earl. I must tell you that the mood in town has changed a great deal since we learned that *you* were returning as Lord of Windermere."

"Thank you, Juvet," Wolf said. "I am pleased to be home."

"About Lady Kit," Alfie said. "When can I see her? When—"

"Hush, lad!" his mother scolded him and pulled him back behind her.

"I would venture to say that my wife will be able to see you tomorrow, Alfie," Wolf said, "if you don't present yourself too early. Not before noontime at least."

Alfie smiled and nodded. "I'll be here!"

"There is one problem, though," Wolf said, turning his eyes to Madam Juvet. "Lady Kathryn is in need of a companion...a trustworthy woman to spend days here at the castle with her—"

"Oh, Your Grace," Madam Juvet interrupted without hesitation, "I am just the one for it!"

"You, Madam Juvet?"

"Oh, yes," she replied. "I owe your wife a debt, and I'd gladly be companion to such a merciful, courageous lady. If not for her—well, I hate to think what would have happened to my Alfie if she'd not interceded for him." Madam Juvet beamed at Wolf.

Emma Juvet agreed to begin her duties the following morning. Alfie would be permitted to come along for a short visit because Wolf knew how pleased Kit would be to see him.

Wolf was anxious to return to his chambers to see about Kit. He gave orders for bathwater to be sent to his room and was about to mount the stairs when he encountered Thomas Somers, lurking in the shadows near the steps. Lines of dissolution crinkled the skin around his eyes and mouth, and Wolf felt an immense distaste for the man who had so abused Kit when she was helpless to defend herself.

"Won't see me, eh?" he slurred drunkenly, poking a finger into Wolf's chest. "Can't spare a few moments' time for your *precious* wife's father?"

"Since you cannot claim the honor of being my wife's father— *No!*" Wolf replied forcefully, reining in his temper. "Leave Windermere at once, Somers. You have no business here."

"Well, I won't leave 'til I've seen her," the baron sneered. "Don't know why the king wanted her in London, but *you* owe me. You went off to London and you *took* her. Preyed 'pon her innocence. Don't try to deny it. And don't think I don't know what the lying whore's been tel—"

Wolf's fist smashed into the baron's face, sending Somers crashing to the stone floor, and rendering further speech impossible.

Somers raised himself up on one elbow and touched his face gingerly with his other hand. His eyes were teary with the force of the blow and a steady stream of blood trickled from one nostril. With gentle fingers, the baron reassured himself that none of his facial features had been knocked loose. He glared at Wolf with a chilling and obvious hatred in his eyes, but the duke turned and left the sprawling baron to his own devices.

Wolf headed up the steps to his chamber, unaware of a witness in a nearby alcove.

* * *

Wolf sat down next to Kit on the bed. Her eyelashes lay thick on her cheek, and she stirred only slightly when he touched her face. Wolf's heart twisted, seeing her lying there so pale, so vulnerable. At least he had been able to keep her safe from her contemptible stepfather.

Servants arrived and laid a small fire in the grate to take off the chill of the evening. Then they set up Wolf's bath in front of the fireplace. Wolf bid them to leave one bucket of hot water near the fire, and gave orders that he was to be disturbed by no one—with the exception of Nicholas Becker. He stood up and stretched, looking back down at his wife.

Aye, she was weary. He'd kept her up most of the previous night, he recalled with a tender smile, then he'd kept her in front of him in his saddle all day. Even without the terrible fall she'd taken, it was no wonder that she slept.

Wolf shucked off his clothes and settled into the bath with a long sigh. He was home, though it felt like home only because she was with him. His Kathryn. He shuddered to think what his life would have become without her. He'd have gained Windermere and Carlisle and the rest, but what would have been the worth of all the holdings in England without her?

Wolf indulged in a long soak, then washed and got out of the tub. After drying himself and stoking the fire in the grate, he carried the bucket of hot water and a cloth to the bed.

Kit slept soundly, even as he removed her clothes and washed her gently, taking care of her various aches and bruises. Her only signs of life were an occasional sigh or moan.

When the water and cloth were discarded, Wolf finally extinguished all the candles in the room, then slid into bed next to Kathryn. He drew her in close, and she unconsciously fit herself into the curve of his stomach and chest.

"I'll take care of you, love," he whispered to her slumbering ears. He turned the new signet ring on his finger. "We're home now...a wolf and his rose..."

Chapter Eighteen

Kit slept the night through, and the morning as well. Wolf hated to leave before she was awake, but two of the men who had been out scouring the hillsides with Claude Montrose returned with evidence of men living in rough camps south of the castle. It was the first lead they had on Philip, and Wolf was anxious to follow up.

He didn't give a second thought to Baron Somers who had cleared out of Windermere before midnight.

"Be certain not to leave my wife alone, Madam Juvet, unless Sir Ranulf is nearby," Wolf instructed quietly, speaking to the woman in the gallery outside his chambers. Ranulf was assigned to the castle for the day in order to be available in case Kit had any need. The tall knight gave Emma Juvet a nod of his head.

"Do you expect trouble, Your Grace?" Emma asked, frowning back at the duke.

"No," Wolf replied. "Just a precaution—no doubt some of the servants are resentful of what happened to Philip…"

"Aye, Your Grace," Emma said knowingly. "I take your meaning."

"I won't take any chances with my wife's well-being." Wolf said as they entered the bedroom quietly together. He bent over Kit and kissed her forehead as she slept, then smoothed a few wisps of hair back from her cheek. She turned over and sighed, but didn't awaken.

Mistress Juvet sat next to the open window, mending her son's long stockings by the early afternoon light. A soft breeze stirred the dark hair at the nape of her neck, and she glanced up at Lady Kathryn's bed again.

The lady's eyes were open this time. And lovely grass-green eyes they were.

"Good day to you, Your Grace," she said as soon as she saw that the duchess was able to focus.

Kit propped herself up and glanced around the room, looking for Wolf.

"Your husband left with his men this morning, I'm afraid," the woman said. "He left orders that you weren't to be disturbed. I'm Emma Juvet—from town," she said. "Young Alfie's my boy."

"Ah...Alfie," Kit remarked. Oh, how her body ached. But not nearly as much as her heart. Why had he left her? All had seemed well between them yesterday, but in the light of a new day, Kit felt anything but secure in his affections. There was no legitimate reason for him to keep a vigil over her, but she would like to have seen him when she awoke.

"Last night we came—my husband and the lad—to pay our respects," Emma said. She set her mending aside and filled a basin of water from a clay pitcher on a wooden stand. She brought it over to Kit. "The duke asked me to spend the day with you—he seemed not to want you...left alone, Your Grace. Leastwise not until you get a maid of your own choosing."

"I see," Kit answered, finally gaining some understanding of Wolf's reason for sending Alfie's mother to her. Philip was still a threat.

"Did my husband say when he'd return, Madam Juvet?"

"Please call me Emma, Your Grace, and no," Emma replied. "He didn't say."

"Was there any word about Philip?" Kit asked. "Any sign of him?"

"Only that it seems somebody's been hiding out in those woods to the south of town," Emma reported. "The duke went with some men to go see."

"Oh." Kit was disappointed. How she wished she had awakened with him. She didn't even remember sleeping with him in their bed last night, though in her dreams, he held her close and she could feel his warm breath in her ear. She pushed that foolish fantasy to the back of her mind.

"The bowman who put his arrow in your saddle is dead."

"They killed him?"

"Not as I hear," Emma replied, after taking the water away and helping Kit to dress. "He fell from a cliff they say. Broke his neck in the fall."

Kit shuddered.

"It was Broderick Ramsey, Lord Philip's bailiff," Emma said. "Never was much of an archer. That's why the shaft pierced your saddle—and not your husband's neck, I'd say."

The duke had not mentioned any restrictions on Kit's activities, so Emma didn't protest when Kit asked to be helped down to the hall. Though she felt like an old woman, hobbling down the stone staircase with Emma's help and some unexpected assistance from Sir Ranulf, Kit made her way gingerly into the great hall. Young Alfie was there, and he made much over "Lady Kit" and her return to Windermere.

Once she was ensconced in a large, comfortable chair, several of the servants came to Kit to ask after her comfort and also to introduce themselves.

"I imagine most are pleased to have a mistress about the place now," Emma said after everyone had left, "and none too sorry to see the last of Philip Colston."

"Windermere certainly needs work, doesn't it?" Kit

asked, looking around the hall. It truly was as shabby and gloomy as she remembered it.

"Aye, that it does."

"Are there weavers in town, Emma?" Kit asked as an idea presented itself.

"That there are, Your Grace," Emma replied.

"And how about carpenters and masons?"

"Aye, we've got the lot."

Kit knew Wolf was preoccupied with locating Philip, and she didn't know how much time that would take. The castle needed work, and Kit decided to begin the task herself. After all, she was perfectly capable of managing a household and felt confident that she could take on a task of this magnitude. Within the hour, Kit had Gilbert Juvet in the hall, helping her to decide how to go about procuring the goods and workmen to get the primary jobs done.

Philip hadn't had a steward in residence for several years, and Kit took it upon herself to begin an examination of Windermere's ledgers, which recorded the expenses and income from the lord's demesne and the various fees and rents from the town. By the time the men filtered into the hall and took their places for the evening meal, Kit had a good grasp of Windermere's financial state, and she had organized the initial phase of restoring order to Windermere Castle. In fact, several tradesmen from town were coming to meet with her after supper to discuss the specifics of her plan.

A small table was brought to Kit at the hearth both for her convenience and comfort, and the Juvet family joined her for the informal evening meal. Old Darby, a weather-worn soldier, came to serve them himself, and on Kit's bidding, sat with the mistress for a spell while she ate and joined in the discussion of the needed renovations.

Kit and her group were so preoccupied with their discussion that when Baron Robert Wellesley and his daughter entered the hall, she didn't notice them.

Mistress Hanchaw was aware of their presence, though,

and guided the two to the main table on the dais, where the duke's and duchess' places were vacant.

"What? His grace is still absent?" Baron Wellesley demanded.

"How very disagreeable of him to stay away so long," Lady Christine remarked petulantly.

"His grace, the duke, was here until noon, my lady," the housekeeper responded as the baron and his daughter took their seats.

"Yes, but we had to leave *so* early to visit Baron Edward at Brington," she complained, casting a dark glance toward her father, "I was certain the duke would be here to sup with us."

"Yes, well, let's make the best of it, dau—"

"The best of it?" Christine demanded. "How is there to be any 'best of it' without Sir Gerhart—his grace—present?"

Kit overheard most of the conversation and she cringed, well aware of the faux pas that had been committed. Nicholas had mentioned that the Wellesleys were guests at Windermere, and Kit had completely forgotten it. She knew it was terribly discourteous of her not to have acknowledged them, yet she'd ignored them so long already, the Wellesleys could easily construe her hesitation as a deliberate slight.

"Mistress Hanchaw," Kit called. "Please have places set for Baron Wellesley and his daughter over here, near me," she said firmly, conscious that the housekeeper had been aware of, yet done nothing to correct the faux pas. "It will not do for our guests to dine there on the dais when I am unable to join them."

Blanche Hanchaw pursed her lips almost imperceptibly and returned to the dais. She ordered servants about, then led Robert and Christine Wellesley to Kit's table, not without some muttered protestations from Lady Christine who thought it suited her ill to be seated among servants and freemen from town.

"Please accept my apologies, I'm having some difficulty getting about…" Kit said warmly, inviting the castle guests to be seated. "I am Kathryn Colston—I believe we met here in spring…?"

"Ahem, ah…yes, Your Grace," Baron Wellesley said, the first to recover from his surprise. He and his daughter had not been privy to the rumors that were rife among the servants, and weren't certain that what little they'd heard was factual.

"So, it's true, then?" Christine asked.

"Hush, Christine," her father reprimanded, and Christine merely raised her chin stubbornly.

"Yes, it's true," Kit replied to the beautiful redheaded woman. "We were attacked yesterday on the road, and I took a fall—"

Christine started to laugh, and her father's face reddened to the ears at his daughter's inappropriate response. Kit looked from one to the other and suddenly realized that she and the Wellesleys were discussing two very different things.

"Please forgive my daughter, Your Grace. She—er—well—"

"Yes, I…I see," Kit said quietly, understanding her error immediately. "The duke and I were wed last month in London."

There was a long pause at the table which verged on becoming uncomfortable. Finally, Christine Wellesley broke the silence, having regained her poise and control. "Pray, tell me how it feels to be injured in battle, Your Grace," she said as she focused her eyes at Kit. "I've always been jealous of the men and their adventures in war."

"It's vastly overrated," Kit said with a wry smile. Though Lady Christine might never be a true friend, at least a truce had been called.

Nicholas pulled up a chair next to Kit and joined in the meal with her unusual group. She introduced him to her

companions. "Nicholas, you may remember Baron Wellesley and his daughter, Christine, from our last visit to Windermere."

He greeted them, then turned back to Kit. "Has Wolf
not yet returned?"

"No," she replied, unnerved by his words. "I thought
he was with you—only delayed—"

"No. Wolf headed east, I took the south."

"Where could he be?" Kit asked as she clasped her
hands in her lap, betraying the nervousness she had masked
quite well up 'til now. She'd thought of her husband at
least a hundred times throughout the day and anxiously
awaited his return.

"Don't worry, Kit," Nicholas tried to reassure her. "All
will be well. Your husband is more than capable of routing
his unsavory cousin. But I don't expect they'll meet just
yet. My hunch is that Philip won't be found very easily."

"You can count on that," Wellesley said. "I always had
my suspicions about the earl. Struck me strange."

"Strange, indeed," Nicholas remarked. "Baron, you
know this neighborhood better than we do. If you were
Philip Colston, where would you hide?"

Robert Wellesley sat back in his chair and pondered the
question. "Well," he finally said. "Philip has always enjoyed hunting to the west of Windermere, near the caves
along the coast. There is a lot of well-stocked woodland,
and it is even rumored that one of the caves is arranged
with lamps and furniture as well as a stocked larder for the
earl's comfort."

"So you believe he's hiding in his cave?"

"Not necessarily, but perhaps," Wellesley said, frowning. "Philip is a secretive sort. I always sensed something
about him when we stayed here at Windermere. That he
was somehow skulking about even when he was said to be
away...I don't know exactly..."

* * *

There had definitely been men living out in the forests. Wolf found plenty of evidence of it. But none of the men.

It was well after the evening meal when Wolf returned to Windermere castle. He had worried about Kit ever since he'd left, wondering if her bruises pained her much, if the swelling in her ankle had gone down, how she tolerated staying abed...

He intended to go directly to their chamber to see how she fared. His own meal and all of Windermere's other problems would have to wait until he could be sure Kit was safe and receiving the proper care. As he entered the great hall, Wolf vowed never to leave her side until all was well with her again. He chastised himself for leaving her all day so he could chase shadows in the forest. He should have let his men spend the day in the search without him—

Unbelievably, there Kit sat, near the fireplace, in the midst of several people, most of whom Wolf did not recognize. She had a long piece of parchment on her lap and was writing furiously, conferring with Gilbert Juvet. Two other men were nodding agreement, and a third pointed to the stained glass window at the far end of the hall. Emma Juvet sat at Kit's side with young Alfie curled up on the bench next to his mother, sound asleep with his head in her lap.

Wolf approached the group, having difficulty believing his eyes. Kathryn appeared to be in good health and high spirits. Her cheeks were suffused with her usual soft pink tinge, and her brow was furrowed in concentration—not pain. The quill moved rapidly across the paper with Kit stopping only to ask a question here, or define a problem there. When she finally looked up and saw her husband, the smile she bestowed on him set the blood coursing like fire through his veins.

God, she was beautiful, he thought as he crossed over to her. He stood behind her chair and placed a kiss on the top of her head, then came around to her side. The men all got to their feet to greet the duke, but Wolf bade Emma to remain seated so as not to disturb her sleeping son.

Kit introduced Wolf, naming the tradesmen who had come from town on Gilbert's summons to estimate the amount of time and the cost involved in cleaning up and repairing the great hall, the kitchen and the staircase.

Now that Wolf was here, Kit began to have second thoughts about her plans for restoring Windermere to its former glory. What if he didn't approve as she'd supposed he would? What if he took it amiss that she'd initiated the plans on her own? His frown when he'd first appeared gave her some pause. She hoped he wouldn't dismiss the Juvets and tradesmen out of hand until she had the opportunity to discuss the project with him.

"I've learned there is a solar in the north tower where some of the women from town can work on your new banner," Kit told him.

"My new banner?"

"Y-yes," she said. "And Edward the carpenter says work can begin here in the hall day after tomorrow."

"Work in the hall..." He glanced around, as if seeing the place for the first time.

"Would you like to look over the estimates, Wolf?" Kit lifted the parchment for her husband's edification, but he only glanced at it.

"That won't be necessary. Whatever you decide will be acceptable, Kathryn," Wolf said at length, putting one hand on her shoulder. "Windermere is in your capable hands."

Kit exhaled, her relief nearly palpable. Not only had he come home safe to her, but he was entrusting her with making Windermere majestic again as it must have been in the old days. He may not love her yet, but at least he had confidence in her ability to get the work done. It was a start.

"I take it you were no more successful than me," Nicholas said.

Wolf shook his head.

''Your duchess supped tonight with Lord Wellesley. The baron may be of assistance to us, Wolf,'' Nick said. ''The man knows the territory and I don't think he was overfond of your cousin.''

''We'll discuss the search on the morrow,'' Wolf replied, then turned to Kit. ''You've had a busy day, wife,'' Wolf said, amused with Kit and pleased to find her so fit. ''Can I persuade you to leave this group and join me in our chambers?''

''You must be fatigued, my lord,'' Kit said as she set her quill and parchment aside and started to rise from her chair. ''Please excuse us now, gentlemen. It grows late, and I must see to my husband's supper.''

Wolf wouldn't allow her to stand on her own two feet, but swept her up into his arms. She blushed at being so treated before the townsmen, yet relished the sensation of being in his arms. She had missed him so much all day.

''I'll see you tomorrow, Emma?'' Kit asked before Wolf had a chance to move away.

''Yes, milady,'' Madam Juvet replied, smiling at the duke's impetuous treatment of his wife. ''Bright and early!''

Wolf crossed the hall carrying Kit. She wrapped her arms around his neck and snuggled closely, laying her head against his breast, enjoying his nearness.

''What did you find on your hunt?'' she finally asked as he climbed the staircase.

''A trail—nothing more.''

''The men in town want nothing better than for you to find Philip and his men,'' she said.

''We just might—with their help.''

They entered their chamber, and Wolf sat down on the bed with Kit in his lap. He was reluctant to part with her so soon—they'd been separated all day.

The room was already prepared for them. The bed was turned down, the candlesticks lit and a fire glowed in the fireplace. Wolf couldn't take his eyes off Kit's mouth, the desire to kiss her nearly unbearable. But one kiss would lead to another and another and his sweet wife was too badly bruised, too new to the physical aspects of loving...

"I could have walked, you know," Kit said quietly as she traced his lips with her fingers. She hadn't realized how desperate she'd been for his touch.

"Could you now?" He could hardly believe the sensuousness of her fingertips moving softly on his mouth, and his pulse quickened. Did she have any idea what she was doing to him?

"Mmm," she assented, moving her knuckles across his whisker-roughened chin. "But I've grown lazy at Windermere with so many here to serve me." She pulled his head down so that his lips met hers but it was too gentle a kiss, and it left her unsatisfied. He was treating her like a piece of fragile glass—worried that she might break. And if he didn't touch her soon, if he didn't make love to her, she would surely crack into a thousand pieces.

"Kit, I—"

"Kiss me, Wolf," she said. "Touch me..."

"If I touch you, I won't be able to stop," he said, nuzzling her neck. God's breath, her eyes were so beautiful; there was a lively, sensuous sparkle in those emerald depths.

She slid her hands down his chest. "Let me undress you, husband," she said with a thickness to her voice. She untied the laces that held his tunic together, then opened his shirt and pulled it down past his shoulders and off his arms. His wound was completely closed now, though it was still a fierce red scar across his upper chest. Kathryn kissed the spot and moved off his lap and over to Wolf's side, somehow pushing him down on the bed. She urged his legs onto the mattress, then pulled off his boots as she knelt next to him.

She removed his belt. Then Wolf stayed her hands, torn between a fierce desire to bury himself in her heat and an equally powerful inclination to hold her in his arms, carefully, gently all night. Surely it was necessary to take care with her bruised and battered body. Women were said to be fragile creatures.

Undaunted, Kit sat back and unfastened her bodice at the shoulders and slid out of her gown. Clad only in the thin white chemise which revealed more than just a vague impression of her body within, and with loose shimmering curls of gold framing her face, Kit leaned over him and dropped a light kiss on his lips.

"Shall I have Darby send you your supper?" she asked in a breathless voice as her lips caressed the scar on his forehead, then moved down to where it sliced the skin below his eye.

"Kathryn," he rasped, unable to answer her question.

Her hands were braced on either side of his head, and he felt the gentle tease of her breasts grazing his chest.

"Kit…" Her lips, her tender touch were driving him to distraction. He couldn't make love to her now—her bruises were too raw, too tender. So he used every ounce of his control to keep his hands off her, aware that she was too inexperienced to understand her effect on him.

"Perhaps you would like to sleep now," Kit breathed, kissing his neck, certain now that she could seduce him to the point of forgetting about sleep. Her head descended tentatively; testing, tasting, relishing every groan and sigh she elicited from her husband.

"I missed you so…" She could feel his heart slamming in his chest and it urged her on. She prayed he would soon respond.

"Kit—"

"I've been waiting for you…" she whispered. There was a fine sheen of perspiration on his forehead now. Moving farther down, she teased him unmercifully, using her lips and tongue, then her teeth on him.

"I longed for you…" Waves of sensuality washed through her. "I…I want you so very badly."

His restraint was finally shattered.

Chapter Nineteen

No more signs of Philip's presence were reported, nor did Wolf's men come any closer to determining what had happened to Hugh. Furthermore, it was said that Baron Somers and two of his men were still in Windermere town, staying at Prudhomme's, but there were no disturbances associated with his presence. Wolf didn't care to flatter Kit's stepfather with any further attention and just assumed the broken nose would suffice.

Over the next few days, Kit and her husband pursued the different tasks they'd assigned themselves. Wolf made a thorough inspection of the castle and battlements, with an eye to determining what areas needed to be fortified. He met with town leaders to narrow down his choices for reeve and bailiff. He surveyed his demesne and looked over Philip's accounts for himself. There was much to deal with those first few days, and Wolf hardly saw Kit until after dark. Only fleetingly and from a distance did he see Kit about the hall, wearing work clothes—an old gray gown with a dingy apron tied about her waist and her hair wrapped up in a cloth.

He found her presence a bewitching, yet stabilizing force in his life—something his restless soul had missed.

Workmen constructed scaffolding in order to make structural repairs in the hall as well as to clean the stained glass windows that were dull with years of grime and grease. Only the workmen from town worked on these high scaffolds, though Kit enlisted all the castle servants in the task of cleaning up the rest of Windermere.

Never had she felt so useful—or so needed. The household servants looked to Kit for their orders and found her way a refreshing change from the imperious manner of Blanche Hanchaw, whose directions were often vague and downright silly. As far as Kit could tell, Windermere hadn't undergone a decent cleaning in decades, and she wondered exactly what Philip had used his housekeeper for—if not for keeping house.

The search for Philip continued, but after four days, there were still no signs of the former earl. Conjecture ran high that he had somehow escaped to the Scottish Highlands or possibly to Ireland, but no one could say for certain. However, it was not in Wolf's nature to trust that Philip no longer posed any danger. Scouts still scoured the countryside daily, hoping to find signs of Philip or some of his men.

The days at Windermere Castle were full, and they passed quickly and productively for Kit. She missed Wolf when he was away, but knew full well that there was a tremendous amount for him to accomplish in a short time, and without the assistance of a steward. Besides, every evening he made up for his absences when they retired to their chambers, and all her jealous thoughts about Christine Wellesley fled through the window. Until the next time she saw them together.

Kit and Emma took a break from their work in one of Windermere's high turrets to enjoy a small midday meal. They stood leaning against the wall, looking down into the courtyard below. Most of the servants and workers were taking their meal as Kit and Emma were doing, and enjoying the lovely sunny afternoon.

''Look, 'tis the duke, your husband,'' Emma said, pointing.

Kit watched as Wolf rode into the courtyard with Baron Wellesley on his right and Lady Christine to his left, smiling and batting her obscenely full eyelashes. Kit didn't particularly care for the way Wolf leaned towards Christine, paying particular attention to whatever she was saying. He'd been more than courteous to the lady these last few evenings at supper as well, Kit recalled, even though Christine had naught but the barest civilities to exchange with her. And it rankled.

"What is it, milady?"

"Nothing, Emma," she replied, turning away from the courtyard as Wolf helped Christine down from her mount.

"You don't like seeing your man with that red-haired one, do you," Emma asked.

Kit just scowled.

"She's very beautiful," Emma said, "though your husband has eyes only for you."

"Oh, he doesn't..." Kit sighed.

"Give him the test then, eh?" Emma said confidently. She'd been around the duke and his wife enough these last few days to know how he felt about his lady. "I'll wager he wouldn't give a hill o' beans for that one down there."

"What do you mean?"

"Get his attention. See what happens, milady," she told Kit. "Lay your claim. It's what I'd do."

Kit gave it a moment's thought. Emma was right. Wolf was her husband, and she was not the least inclined to share him. She loved him.

Kit pulled off the dusty cloth from her head and let it drop to the ground. Wolf and the others saw it, and both he and Lady Christine looked up to the turret that rose high above them.

Wolf grinned. As he moved away from the baron and his daughter, he tossed off a couple of words, hardly aware of what he said. Kit was smiling down at him, her hair blowing in loose tangles in the breeze and Wolf felt something rare. A warm welcome. Welcome home.

Christine Wellesley turned away angrily, unwilling to watch the Duke of Carlisle make a fool of himself over his little blond slip of a wife. Kathryn was so unsuitable, it was impossible to understand how Wolf could tolerate her. The woman actually wore coarse grays and browns and dirtied her hands right along with the servants. With a bit of luck, Kathryn Colston, Duchess of Carlisle, would succumb to some fever or other. After all, no noblewoman was meant to slave as she did...

Wolf took the stone stairs two at a time and wound his way down the corridor to the turret where he'd seen his wife. He found the place easily, stepped outside and motioned quietly for Emma to leave them.

"Emma, do you suppo—" Kit said, her shoulders sagging unhappily as she turned. "Wolf! You came!"

Here was the imp he'd rescued from Somerton, he thought, smiling. Her lovely face was smudged with soot and her green eyes were direct and challenging as always. Delight was there, too. She was glad to see him, and Wolf's heart soared. A few quick strides and he was at her side, taking her into his arms. He wondered in passing if she had any idea that through this marriage she had rescued him from a life of utter predictability and indifference.

"What sort of temptress are you, that the mere sight of you draws me up here to taste you?" he asked, after a searing kiss.

"Temptress?" she laughed, pulling away to look at him. "Me? Your eyes deceive you, my lord. I am not blessed with russet hair, nor sky blue eyes—"

"Nay. Your golden curls and emerald eyes have ruined me for any other."

Kit shivered with pleasure upon hearing the words, but still, she was unsure of him. Lady Christine was everything Kit could not be.

"But I fear you have been saddled with a dull wife. Bruised, unable to ride...slow-moving...a woman reduced to dropping stray rags from towers to gain your attention, sir.''

''You have my complete attention now,'' he said as he nuzzled Kit's neck.

''I love you, Wolf,'' she breathed. ''God knows how I love you.''

She looked into his deep gray eyes and struggled with the silence she met. Then his hands began to move again, caressing her neck, her back, her hips.

''I never thought to hear you say it,'' Wolf said as his lips met the sensitive skin on her throat. ''And there is nothing in this world I'd rather hear.'' His voice was tender, and he pulled her closer. ''Because I love you, too, Kit. I love you, sweetheart, as I'd never thought possible.''

Emma brought a single candle into the small storage room where Kit was struggling to pull out rolls of old, dark, mildewed tapestries. They had worked their way some distance from the great hall which was the main work area, but Kit was determined to clear out all the refuse from two centuries past and start afresh. After all the tragedy in Wolf's life, she felt compelled to clear out the dreary trappings of what had been. She would make his house bright and clean, efficient and cheerful, with none of the old ghosts of Windermere lingering to haunt him, as she knew they must.

Kit was determined to make Windermere and herself his present and future. Together, she and Wolf would make a family—something neither of them had, but had always yearned for.

''This is a funny sort of room, wouldn't you say, milady?'' The candle cast long, flickering shadows across the walls, which were made of rough-hewn wood and were completely unfinished.

Kit frowned as she looked about. ''Help me with this, will you, Emma?'' she said. Emma placed the candle on an overturned wooden crate and reached up to help Kit pull out a huge, heavy roll. "Yes, it's a strange place, all right. I wonder why none of this old rubbish was ever discarded. What's the point of keep— What's this?"

"What?"

"Look here," Kit said as she picked up the candle and took it to the back wall. "It's a hidden door, just like the one in the room I shared with Bridget last spring."

"Ah, yes, your cousin—the one that died…"

"I wonder where it goes."

"We'd best get some of the men to look this over, Your Grace. Why don't I—"

"Nonsense. Come on," Kit said. "Let's try it. I assure you, nothing untoward happened the last time. In fact, it was only a passage leading to— Here. Come on and help. This door is heavy."

Kit pushed at the heavy timber door and was able to move it only by inches. Emma's curiosity was aroused and the two women slipped into the passageway and peered into the darkness, trying to illuminate it with the single candle.

"Hold the candle, Emma. I'll just— Ouch!"

"What is it!"

"Damnation, it's the door! Slammed on my ankle."

"Here…are you all right?" Emma asked, looking down at Kit's injured ankle.

"I'm fine. Just help me pull the bloody door back," she said, wrinkling her nose. "It smells rank in here. Cold and damp."

They pulled, but the door didn't budge.

"Look. It's a staircase, milady," Emma said after they'd tried their best to pull the stubborn door open.

"Umm. But it leads down this time. I wonder what's under this part of the castle."

"I don't know. Mayhap we should try the door again."

"You're right," Kit replied, shuddering. "Let's."

The door still didn't move. They were stuck behind it, in the strange passage that Kit realized was only vaguely similar to the one she'd seen leading from her room to

Agatha's tower room. That other stairway had been made of stone and though the passage had been cool, it did not smell of rot the way this one did. And here, it led down, to somewhere under the castle itself. She shivered.

They began to pound on the door, hopeful that someone passing by would hear and rescue them. Both women fought panic and attempted to stay calm, with their wits intact.

At length, they gave up on pounding. Kit picked up the candle and held it high. "Maybe there's a way out if we follow the stairs," she said, trying to keep her voice from quaking.

"No, Your Grace," Emma protested urgently. "We must stay here. Your husband will surely find us—"

"How? No one can hear us or else someone would have gotten this door opened by now," Kit said as she eyed the narrow wooden steps. "We've got to try to find our way on our own."

"Do you suppose...?"

"What, Emma?"

"Er... Nothing."

"Tell me."

"Well, I was just thinking—wondering—if maybe someone up there...closed the door behind us," Emma said. "Your husband didn't exactly trust everybody..."

"You mean someone might have locked us in?"

Emma nodded.

Kit chewed her lower lip and considered the possibility. There were certainly servants enough around to have done the deed...and if someone locked the door, they would have closed up that storage room as well, just so it would take longer to discover, once she and Emma turned up missing.

She took a tentative step, not trusting the wood to bear her weight. The wood hardly creaked when she stepped, so she continued on, with Emma right behind. The stairs continued for what had to be at least another two or three flights and when they finally ended, she and Emma stood in a small, crude chamber consisting of an earthen floor and walls.

A slight movement in a corner startled the two, and they hugged each other closely.

"Rat!"

"Aye. There must be food down here."

"Milady, this doesn't seem to be the way out, if you'll only—"

"No, look, Emma. Another passageway."

"That's what I was afraid of," Emma muttered.

"Come on," Kit admonished good-naturedly. "Don't be so fainthearted. I doubt anyone's been down here in years."

They followed the narrow passage in hopes of finding another hidden door. Kit kept the candle raised as high as she dared, desperate to find a way out, but fearing that the faint wind currents would extinguish it.

"I wonder if there's more than one tunnel," Kit said. "This breeze must come from somewhere... They proceeded cautiously and moved farther into the tunnel.

"Ooh, the smell is getting worse." Emma covered her mouth and nose with her hand.

"It certainly is," Kit replied with a grimace. "I wonder whatever— Why, this seems to be another chamber. Look, Emma, there's a torch up here in the wall. Thank God. I'll just light it—"

Emma's echoing scream broke the subterranean quiet. Kit whirled around, and in the full glare of the blazing torch, her shocked eyes lit on Lady Agatha, Countess of Windermere, sitting on the dirt floor, her wrists in manacles, chained to the wall.

Biting back a scream of her own, Kit's hand covered her mouth. Here was the source of the putrid odor. The countess had been dead for several weeks at least, and had Kit not recognized the old woman's shapeless black gown and her twist of gray hair, she would not have known Agatha.

"God in heaven, 'twas Philip," she whispered. "Philip did this."

"Aye," Emma's quivering voice assented, holding onto Kit's arm. "We must find our way out now. Quickly! Please, milady—"

"We will," Kit said, distractedly, her eyes adjusting to the light. Covering her mouth and nose, she looked around the room and saw that there was more here in the gruesome chamber than just the pair of manacles that held Agatha's body dangling. There were three skeletons, one appallingly small. Small bundles of rags were scattered about on the floor, and Kit was wary of finding out what lay underneath them. A low, wooden table displayed several grotesque cutting instruments. Kit found herself letting her breath out slowly. "It's just a matter of— What was that? Did you hear that sound?"

"Let's go back, Your Grace. Please—"

Kit walked to the other side of the wooden table on the opposite side of the horrible chamber, with Emma hanging on to her from behind. Emma collided with Kit as she stopped abruptly.

"Holy mother!" Kit gasped, looking down at one of the bundles of rags. "It's a man! And he's alive!"

"Dear Jesus, Mary and Joseph," Emma whispered as Kit knelt next to the crumpled figure on the ground. "Who could it be?"

"Hugh! Oh, God, it's him! Hugh, can you hear me?" Kit swallowed hard and repeatedly to keep from vomiting. The injuries done to her husband's friend were atrocious, and it took every ounce of courage to look at him. She could hardly bear to face what had been done to him, and tears welled up in her eyes as she tried to focus on the dirt floor next to the man's head.

Hugh groaned weakly.

"I don't think he's aware."

"Thank heaven for that," Emma said. She clutched at

Kit's sleeve, trying to bring her mistress away from the man.

"How will we get him out of here?"

"How will we get ourselves out?" Emma asked desperately. The man was obviously near death and dragging him back up those steps was clearly not feasible.

"Hugh, if you can hear me, it's Kit. Lady Kathryn," she said through the lump in her throat. "We'll go for help. We'll get you out of here."

"What now, milady?" Emma asked. "Do you suppose there's a passageway somewhere that leads out?"

"Oh, lord."

"What?"

"Oh, my God."

"What is it?"

"What a fool I am!" Kit swallowed hard. "Philip! He's probably hiding in here somewhere!"

Chapter Twenty

Sir Alfred had been assigned to see to Lady Kathryn's security, but he had found there wasn't much to do, with the lady working among the servants, scrubbing the place like a common washerwoman. So he'd stayed at the huge table in the great hall, sharpening and polishing his various blades and paying little attention to his surroundings. If Philip Colston mounted an attack, the former earl would have to get past him, and Alfred was confident it couldn't be easily done.

At length, when servants began organizing tables in the hall for supper, it finally occurred to Alfred that he hadn't seen either the duchess or her companion in quite some time, and he became curious. He made a cursory search of the hall and the surrounding rooms, but Lady Kathryn was not to be found.

Then he became worried. The Duke would have his hide if anything happened to his lady. Alfred went to check the lady's chambers, but she was not there either, nor in the solar where the weavers were putting away their materials. The turrets were empty, and so were the living quarters nearby.

As a last resort, Alfred left the castle to search the court-yard and grounds, in hopes that Lady Kathryn and her maid had slipped out another door and were enjoying the early evening. It was even possible that they were waiting for Mistress Juvet's husband to come fetch her.

Wolf returned to Windermere just before dinner. Kit wasn't anywhere in sight, but that was not unusual since the day after their return to the castle. She worked at a furious pace, determined to whip Windermere into shape in the least possible length of time. He marveled at her ability to organize the work force and to pitch right in with them. He wasn't so sure it was appropriate for his wife, a king's daughter, to be on her hands and knees working her skin raw. But she was doing it for him.

She loved him. His beautiful, unpredictable, brash Kathryn loved him and his heart fairly twisted in his chest when he thought of her saying the words, "I love you, Wolf."

"Hot water to my chamber," he said to a servant as he walked through the hall. Workmen were climbing down scaffolds and putting away tools, making ready to return to their homes for the night. The great hall already seemed more habitable, Wolf thought as he mounted the stairs. Layers of grime were disappearing, and it was even possible to see clouds through some of the windows.

He wondered if he would find Kit in their rooms awaiting him. He fervently hoped so. There was nothing he'd like better than to share a hot, sensual bath with her. Not that she could get any hotter or more sensual if she tried.

Wolf had never felt such a burning desire for a woman in his life, such utter contentment. And it was entirely due to his sweet wife. The restlessness he'd always felt before was gone. Home now was wherever Kathryn was. She possessed strength and endurance, and Wolf knew with certainty he could rely on Kit's love no matter what happened.

The only imperfection in Wolf's world now was that Philip was still at large, though the threat of his presence was diminishing by the day. It was almost possible to believe his cousin had taken ship for Ireland and would never return, though Wolf was not so naive as to think his problems would be resolved so easily.

The bathwater arrived without Kit, so Wolf bathed alone. At length, when he was dressed again, and just lacing his boots, a knock sounded at the Duke's chamber door.

"Greetings, Your Grace," Chester Morburn said as he entered Wolf's room.

"Chester! You're back!"

"Aye," Chester replied with a smile. "And we brought with us a very willing guest."

"Where is he?" Wolf asked, grinning.

"Sir Stephen is in the hall, Your Grace, awaiting you."

Stephen Prest was very much as Wolf remembered him. His formerly vivid red hair was now a duller shade, more like rusted iron, and there were plenty of white strands interspersed. Otherwise, he had hardly changed. His intelligent face was endowed with the same astute, piercing blue eyes, a long, dignified nose, and a mouth readily given to laughter. He was easily as tall as Wolf, though not as brawny, and his movements were confident and economic. Seeing Sir Stephen again brought back memories of the past. Of happier days at Windermere.

"Welcome home, Your Grace," Prest said as he placed a hand on Wolf's shoulder. His voice was full of emotion. "'Tis a day I thought I'd never see."

"It pleases me greatly that you returned with my men."

"Not half so much as it pleased me, Your Grace. And you a duke now..." he said with a laugh. "Your father would have been so proud."

"Thank you, sir."

Chester went to give orders for an early meal for Sir Stephen while Wolf questioned William Guys about their trip. "Problems on the road, William?" Wolf asked, concerned they might have been ambushed the way he and Kit had been.

"No, Your Grace—"

"No. No problems other than the fact that I am no longer

a young man,'' Prest said with a sigh. ''It's been years since I've traveled much. Not since your father's day...'' He looked up sadly at Wolf. '''Tis *good* to have you back at Windermere.''

A small table was laid for Stephen, and Wolf sat with him, drinking a mug of ale while the steward took his meal. They reminisced only a little, Wolf being anxious to bring Stephen up to date on the events since meeting Philip at Windermere in the spring.

Stephen shook his head sadly. ''I suppose I should seem more surprised by what you say... Tales of some of Philip's evil doings even reached us at Elton. Clarence and Philip were two of a kind, you know. Ambitious. Greedy. Cruel. I tried more than once to have your father remove his brother's family from Windermere, but the earl wouldn't hear of it.''

''My father was too trusting.''

''Your father was a fair and just man,'' Prest said, ''and he assumed everyone possessed some degree of honor.''

Wolf brooded quietly over Stephen's remarks. Bartholomew had lost Windermere and gotten himself and John killed due to misplaced trust and loyalty.

''I'll not be making those same assumptions here, Stephen.''

Prest studied the new lord of Windermere for a moment before speaking. ''I thought not,'' he said quietly. He could see that Wolf's scars went deeper than the superficial ones that marred his face, though Stephen sensed a glimmer of hope in the silver-gray eyes.

''My wife met Lady Agatha last spring.''

''Oh? It was our understanding that the lady died some years ago. Soon after Clarence, in fact.''

''Kathryn assured me that the woman she met was flesh and blood,'' Wolf replied. ''A trifle mad, perhaps, but alive, nonetheless.''

''And might I ask where Lady Agatha is now?''

Wolf shrugged. "We've no more trace of her than we have of Philip. She's disappeared."

"Philip was never on good terms with his stepmother," Prest remarked. "I am somewhat astonished to learn she's been living here with him all these years."

"Well, by the looks of things, their relations were strained," Wolf said. "He was keeping her prisoner in a tower room at the west end. Apparently, Agatha was able to escape her room by means of a hidden staircase. That's how she made her presence known to my wife."

Prest nodded. "Your parents were always worried about you boys getting into one of the secret passages, and becoming lost. Some of the hidden entrances were sealed permanently. Your mother was especially fearful…"

"I never knew of any passages."

"They deliberately kept you ignorant of them."

"You say there are other hidden passageways?"

"Oh, yes," the steward replied. "I'll be happy to show you the ones I know tomorrow. In daylight."

"Secret staircases?"

Stephen nodded.

"Hidden chambers?"

"Intriguing, isn't it? The first Earl of Windermere—your father's grandfather—was rather eccentric. Liked to have a handy means of escape wherever he was."

"I suppose it has its advantages."

"That it does, Your Grace," Prest laughed. "Tell me about your plans here. It looks as though someone has taken a hand to making the place fit."

"My wife."

"Organized all this?" Prest asked, looking around at the scaffolding and the progress made thus far.

Wolf gave a nod.

"Your wife is an able woman," Prest said. "It requires a good bit of experience and skill to organize a task of this magnitude."

"Lady Kathryn is experienced, Stephen," Wolf said. "In fact, she managed her father's estate before our marriage."

One of Prest's thick eyebrows rose a notch. "How unusual. A woman...managing an estate?"

"You'll meet her soon," Wolf said. He asked one of the servants to locate his wife and request that she join him in the great hall.

"And what of Philip's accounts?" Prest asked.

"My wife and I have both been through the ledgers and everything is in order," Wolf replied. "But there are some obvious abuses."

Nicholas came looking for Wolf and found him sitting with the old steward in the hall, near the hearth, where a space had been cleared of all the tools for cleaning and repair. He sat down with the two and Wolf made the introductions.

"Where's Kit?" Nicholas finally asked.

"Someone's gone to fetch her."

"She's probably found some new little nook to repair or to scrub," Nicholas said with a grin. "Or perhaps there's a chandelier that needs rehanging or—"

"Possibly," Wolf laughed. "She might be doing any of those things. But at least she's occupied within the castle and not an easy target for Philip."

"*Ja.* That's true, Wolf. And she's dedicated to renewing Windermere. I shouldn't make a jest of it."

"My wife, when you meet her," Wolf addressed Stephen, "will not appear as you would think a duchess ought."

"So I gather, Your Grace."

"She has taken it upon herself to organize—"

"Gerhart!"

The three men turned to face the voice.

"Wolf, sir...Your Grace!" It was Sir Alfred Dunning, approaching quickly. His dark visage boded ill and there was a sickly sheen of sweat across his brow. That he had been so rattled as to call Wolf by the pseudonym Gerhart—

A sense of dread exploded in Wolf. He stood so abruptly, his chair fell behind him. Nicholas and Stephen followed suit.

"What is it—?"

"Your lady, my lord—"

"What—?"

"I cannot find her." Alfred looked ill.

"What do you mean—you can't find her?" Wolf demanded, already on the move.

"Lady Kathryn was working with Mistress Emma down toward the kitchens," Alfred said almost breathlessly. "I was here—in the hall. She couldn't have gotten past me. Yet she's gone."

Nicholas glanced up at the windows. "It's nearly dark, Wolf. I'll gather men and begin searching the grounds."

"I've been through the courtyard and the west garden."

"Tell me again," Wolf said. "Where were you and where was my wife?"

Alfred led them to the huge table in the great hall where his sword and dagger still lay with the sharpening stone and polishing cloth. "I stood here," he said, planting his feet exactly where he'd been working on his sword. "Workmen were all about, and Lady Kathryn was down through there—" he gestured down the hall towards the kitchens "—with Mistress Emma. I could see them very well from here." He was clearly puzzled by their disappearance.

"What were they doing?" Stephen Prest asked as he walked towards the area where the two women had last been seen.

"Mucking about with some old tapestries somewhere over there…"

Stephen approached a dark, scarred wooden door and tried the latch. It was locked. "Near here?" he asked.

Wolf walked over to the old steward, his brows furrowed

ferociously, his eyes betraying his fear. He raked his hand through his hair in frustration. All his thoughts and hopes of a future were quickly receding. There would be nothing without Kit.

"Who would have the key to this room, Your Grace?"

"The housekeeper, Stephen. Why? You don't suppose they're locked—"

"Your pardon, sir," Stephen said. "If memory serves correctly, this is a small storage room—"

"Quite possibly. But the question is—"

"I believe there is a false wall within. A secret passage, if you will?"

"Here?" Wolf glanced over his shoulder and called to Alfred. "Bring light!" Then he turned back and demolished the door with one solidly placed kick.

Debris on the floor nearly tripped them as they entered the dark little room. When light arrived, Wolf realized the huge lumps were hastily rolled tapestries, thrown haphazardly on the floor. "Where, Stephen? Where is it?"

"Let me see…"

Stephen walked to the back wall and pressed his palms against it, hoping to feel it give way. He was uncertain after so many years. "I believe your parents had this one sealed because it opens to a long staircase to the dungeons."

"This is it, all right," Wolf said. "I've seen another just like it." He found the latch exactly like the one in the room where Agatha had visited Kit and tried to spring it. "This is no use. It's been jammed somehow."

"Intentionally, by the look of it." Stephen's thick brows came together worriedly.

Wolf put his shoulder to the door but was unable to budge it after two tries. "Alfred," Wolf commanded, "come here."

It took another two blows before the two huge knights were able to force down the door. The crashing sound seemed to be swallowed up by the dark depths beyond. A cool, dank wind assailed Wolf's nose as he stepped through the portal, and he shuddered thinking of Kit down there. In Philip's lair.

"Stephen," Wolf asked, holding the candle in the void, "do you have any idea where this passage leads? Are there any other exits that you can remember?"

"Two that I know of."

"Send someone for Chester and William. Have them gather as many of my men as possible. I want a guard posted outside this door as well as at the other two entrances. You'll have to show them where, Stephen."

"Of course, Your Grace."

"Come on, Alfred," Wolf said.

Alfred recognized the urgent edge to his lord's voice and didn't hesitate.

Kit stood perfectly still. She could hear her own breath as well as Emma's, and her heart was pounding in her ears. They both felt as though they'd traversed miles of pitch-dark tunnel, but were no closer to finding a way out than before.

Their movements were muffled by the packed dirt of the walls and floor but Kit was certain she heard something behind them. She caught a look in Emma's eyes and knew the other woman had heard it, too.

They were being followed.

Kit tightened her fingers around the knife she'd brought from the room where Hugh lay maimed and near death. She raised the blade, poised to strike. A chill ran through her when she heard the sound of muffled laughter in the distance.

Dear God, she hoped Wolf was on his way, but Kit knew he couldn't always be there to protect her. Poor Wolf, she thought as her panic rose, stuck with a wife who so often needed rescuing.

Kit sensed someone moving through the dark toward her, and she commanded Emma with a nod to move. Quickly.

Better to keep going than to be trapped in this maze of tunnels.

They retreated back the way they came, and Kit searched the walls on the left for the marks she'd scored in the dirt at eye level as they came through the first time. The torch was starting to sputter though, and it was difficult to see. Kit wanted to get back to the room where Hugh was. Perhaps they would find another torch there.

She hoped desperately that the torture chamber would be a better place to try to defend themselves. Perhaps they could find their way to the storage room door if they first got to the room where Hugh lay. Kit was not averse to trying the door again, or even standing at the top of the stairs and yelling her lungs out.

The sense of being followed continued even as they entered the chamber where Agatha still sat hideously, hanging by the chains in the wall. No ominous pursuer entered after them and Kit looked at Emma, wondering if she'd imagined having been followed.

"I don't think there is any other way out," Kit whispered as she placed the dwindling torch in the rough wall sconce. "We'll be without light soon—let's see if we can find anything else that will burn."

Hugh lay silently on the ground, and Kit knew he was still alive only by the rasping sounds of his shallow breathing. His lips were dry and cracked, and he was covered with sores. One eye was swollen shut and crusted with dried blood, and Kit was unable to tell whether the eye was still in its socket. Bones were probably broken, and she was afraid to move him for fear of hurting him further.

"D'you think anyone will know to look for us down here?" Emma asked, keeping her eyes averted from Hugh Dryden. She didn't know how Lady Kathryn could stand to touch him, to gently smooth back his hair.

"Of course," Kit replied shakily. "I mean, certainly. Sir Alfred knew we were working in the storage room, didn't he? And he's bound to miss us soon."

"But if the door's locked...and hidden from sight—What's that?" Emma gasped, her fears increasing with the precipitous fading of their one measly torch.

"Dear God," Kit whispered, "it's a rat." She wished she had her sling.

"I can't find anything in here that will burn, milady. These old rags lying about are all too damp."

"Well, we can tear up our skirts and our shifts if we must," Kit replied absently, eyeing the rat in the flickering light. She bent down and unlaced her shoes.

The rat crept close to Hugh's outstretched toes and Kit let her shoe fly, hitting the rat squarely. It skittered away to hide in some dark corner. Kit kept the other shoe in her hand and at the ready. Emma was already tearing her skirt into strips to add to the flame of the torch.

"I'm glad I've been wearin' my oldest rags to the castle for the cleaning."

"I'll give you a new gown, Emma. Two of them!" Kit replied quietly as she began to tear strips from her own shift.

"Sir Alfred is bound to be investigating the storage room door right now. Even as we—"

Both women shrieked as the torch fell to the ground and was deliberately stamped out. The darkness was absolute, and the chill in the air was even more pronounced now that they were unable to see.

Neither Kit nor Emma breathed or moved a muscle other than to clasp each other tighter. They had seen a dark booted foot trounce on their only source of light, but it had happened so quickly and so unexpectedly that they saw nothing of their assailant. They heard the laugh, though. A man's laugh, deep and throaty. Unmistakably wicked and cruel, echoing horribly against the walls of the tunnels.

Kit pulled at Emma's waist, and the two women sidled back towards the opposite entrance. She moved cautiously, frantically trying to remember the exact location of the objects in the room that could trip her up.

"I felt, from the moment I met you, that you were a resourceful woman," the eerie voice whispered. Philip's voice. "A worthy...consort...not at all like my weak, little Clarisse." That awful, quiet laughter grated on Kit's ears again, and then she bumped into something at knee level and lost her balance. She fell.

Emma screamed and fell away with a loud thud. Kit was left alone in the darkness to wonder what had happened to silence her companion so abruptly.

A cool hand crept up her ankle, and even as Kit was aware it could be Emma's hand, she was reviled by the touch. Instinct told her it belonged to Philip, not Emma. She pulled away, but he was fast. He grasped her ankle and yanked, knocking her flat on the ground and effectively stopping her retreat. Kit struggled to turn and crawl away, but Philip managed to pin her down, his sense of awareness in the dark much better developed than hers.

"If your doting husband ever finds you, he'll never want you again," the harsh voice whispered through the dark. "I'll make certain of that." He wrapped his hand around Kit's hair tightly enough to make her cry out. Did he intend to maim her as he had done to Hugh?

She kicked—and missed any worthwhile target. But the move brought her leg into contact with the knife in her pocket. She had forgotten about it, but it would do now, she thought, forcing herself to be calm. Kit increased her struggles with both legs and one arm, reaching into her pocket for the knife. Then it was in her hand, and her fingers tightened securely around it.

Philip held her down with all his weight, but he stilled suddenly and pulled away from her for an instant to listen. "Damn his hide!" He spat the words.

Kit could hear nothing but their combined breaths and she panicked, certain Philip was aware of the knife. She struck quickly with the blade, and he screamed.

He grabbed her and yanked her up so abruptly that she

dropped the little knife. Kit tried to reach down for it, but Philip yanked her hair brutally. "Oh, no you don't!"

Then suddenly, with a groan of frustration, he shoved her. Hard. She lay still, knowing she'd wounded him, yet awaiting his next attack. Then there was loud breathing, rasping and muttering...and the sounds were receding. He was going away! Probably to light a torch, she told herself, and braced for the bright light to blind her momentarily.

Yet nothing happened. The sounds of Philip's retreat continued and then dissipated somewhere beyond, in the tunnels. There were other sounds now, confusing, muted sounds and Kit hoped to God that Philip wasn't going to attempt another attack.

Kit reached out for Emma, certain she couldn't be far. Inching her fingers across the deathly cold, packed earth, Kit finally found flesh. Emma's warm flesh. She moaned when Kit touched her, but Kit hardly heard the sound. The other, very distracting noises were coming from the short tunnel behind her, beyond which were the stairs to the storage room. A faint light cast ghostly shadows on the walls of the vile chamber, growing stronger and brighter as it rapidly drew near.

"In here!" It was Wolf's voice, and Kit rejoiced. She looked over at Emma, who was just coming round.

"My God, Kit, are you all right?" Wolf dropped the torch on the ground and crouched down next to his wife. She was covered with blood and sheer terror seized his heart.

"Wolf—" her voice trembled in spite of her effort to sound calm.

"Go after him, Alfred," Wolf ordered harshly. Then he turned to Kit and spoke in a gentle, controlled voice. "Where are you hurt, sweetheart? Tell me where he cut you," His hands were actually shaking.

"I cut *him*, husband," Kit said, shuddering.

"Please Kit, don't jest now." He pulled her against his

chest, cherishing her, vowing never to let her out of his sight again. ''Tell me—''

''I don't know how badly he's wounded, but I know I cut him. It was Philip.''

He pulled away from her momentarily to study her face. She was pale, and her eyes bore a haunted look. ''You mean this isn't *your* blood?''

''Nay, Wolf. Philip suffered the damage,'' she said grimly. Her voice broke then. ''And Hugh. He's here.''

And then, for the second time in her life, she fainted in her husband's arms.

Chapter Twenty-One

Wolf carried Kit out of the dark hole as servants swarmed behind him, helping Emma Juvet up the stairs and tending Hugh Dryden. Anger and frustration seethed just below the surface of his calm facade. He reached the storeroom—there was no doubt now it had been locked intentionally—and continued walking through the great hall until Nicholas Becker caught up with him. Together, they mounted the next flight of steps and moved through the gallery toward the duke's chambers.

Nicholas was shocked by Kit's bloodied appearance. "How is she?"

"I don't know yet," Wolf replied dismally. "Before she fainted, she told me she was unhurt."

"But the blood—"

"She said it was Philip's," Wolf replied. "She stabbed him."

"Good for you, Kit," Nicholas gave a grim smile of appreciation, even though she was still limp and unconscious in Wolf's arms. "How badly?"

"No idea. She fainted before she said much."

"I've seen Hugh," he said, his stomach turning, just thinking about what had been done to the man. "It's unspeakable, the things your butcher cousin did..."

"Summon the gardener and priest to tend to him."

"I've already sent for them," Nicholas said. "And I've posted guards at the entrances to the underground caverns."

"Did you see Alfred?"

"No, but Chester went down with me through one of the outside entrances. We scoured one of the passages and came up right behind you," Nicholas explained. "Chester and Claude are still down there helping Alfred to comb the tunnels," Nick replied. "It may take some time—"

"Send more men," Wolf shouldered open the door to his chamber and went in. "Search every possible hole and find out if there's a possibility of other escape routes— routes Stephen would be unaware of. I want Philip *tonight*. One way or another."

"But Wolf, Stephen showed us all the exits! And we had them under guard before you even got down the dungeon steps. We should have caught the monster—"

"In twenty years, my cunning cousin has likely added to his cavernous network as well as making new, less accessible exits." He laid Kit gently on the bed and smoothed a few wisps of hair back from her face. "Either he managed to escape somehow—through an exit unbeknownst to Stephen—or my cousin remains down there, somewhere under the castle," Wolf said, his voice filled with a quiet bitterness. "Waiting, like a foul spider in his lair."

Nicholas chewed out a curse in his native tongue. "I'll see if there's a chance he got out some other way," he said as he left the room.

Wolf sat down next to his wife and leaned over her. He pressed a soft kiss to her ear and her temple, and waited for her to regain consciousness. A niggling fear worked its way into Wolf's mind that Kit would never truly awaken again. That when she opened her eyes, the shock of her experience in that underground dungeon would render her stuporous, like his mother.

But Kit had spirit. Wolf knew Kit had a strength and tenacity his mother never possessed. Mayhap if Margrethe had had some of Kit's strength, she wouldn't have given up on life, given up on *him*. "Come back to me, love," he whispered. "Don't slip away from me now that I know you're mine."

He framed her face with his big hands, and Kit winced when he touched a fresh bruise on her jaw. That was a good sign, wasn't it? Kit stirred a bit more, but didn't awaken. Wolf peeled her bloodstained gown from her skin and discarded it, all the while, praying silently that she would return to him.

"Kit, sweetheart," Wolf prodded quietly. "Open your eyes. Wake up for me. You're my life, you know. Windermere and the rest of it..." His voice was unsteady, and he let out a ragged breath. "It's nothing without you."

When she was undressed, he lay down next to her, pulled a cover over them and wrapped himself around her limp body to warm her.

She moaned.

"Come on, my love," he kissed her forehead, her eyes, her lips. "Come on..."

Another moan and she was moving her legs. When her eyes opened, there was a look of panic, but it was quickly gone. In its place was recognition and relief. And when her memory returned, she began to tremble, as he had known she would.

"Kit?"

A violent shudder overtook her.

"It's over. You're safe now. I won't let anything happen to you—"

"Where's Philip?" she asked. "Is he—"

"Not yet," Wolf replied. "Nicholas and the rest of the men are still searching. He can't be far."

"And Hugh," she whispered, curling closer into her husband's warmth. "What about poor Hugh?"

Wolf let out a long, somber breath. "He's alive. Barely."

"Oh, Wolf—"

"Philip won't have the opportunity to harm anyone else,

I promise you.'' He kissed her above her ear. ''When I think how close he came...''

She shuddered again.

''Are you all right, Sprout? Are you sure you're—''

''Hold me.''

She still trembled but the horror and revulsion of Philip's deeds were kept at bay by the sensation of her husband's strong arms closing around her, his powerful legs anchoring hers. ''Aye, love,'' he said. ''I'll hold you. All night and all day if necessary.''

''You told me Philip was dangerous,'' she breathed. ''You said he wasn't to be trusted... D-did you know? Did you realize then what he was capable of?''

''I knew.''

''Really. I'm fine, Wolf,'' Kit insisted later as she wrapped herself in the blanket. ''Go with Nicholas and find Philip.''

Wolf hesitated. There was nothing he'd like better than to go out with his men and hunt Philip down, but he was reluctant to leave Kit on her own.

''You've had a terrible shock—''

A timid tapping at the door interrupted him, and Wolf walked away from Kit to open it.

''...er, Your Grace,'' Maggie stammered, ''I brought up some bathwater. I saw Lady Kathryn before and...''

Wolf opened the door wide and admitted the girl, who came in and arranged the tub, then poured the hot water into it.

''Please, Wolf,'' Kit said. ''Go on. I'll be all right. I'll bathe and wait for you here.''

Wolf pulled on his doublet and sheathed his sword and dagger, still debating on the advisability of leaving her. He knew all his men would be involved in the search, except for whoever Nick had assigned to sit with Hugh. He looked over at Maggie, who had seemed more trustworthy than any of the servants and decided to go. But just for an hour or two.

"In case of trouble, you can call to the guard in Hugh's room," Wolf said. "I won't be gone long, Kit."

"I know you won't." She smiled and knelt up on the bed for his kiss.

"I love you, Sprout."

"Just come back to me quickly," Kit whispered, clinging to him tightly for a moment and releasing him. Then he was gone.

"It's ready, Your Grace," Maggie said, indicating the tub. She had set out Kit's scented soap, towels and clean clothes for afterward.

Kit sat down in the hot water and prepared herself to wait.

"Seems you've got a few more scrapes and scratches, Your Grace," Maggie said, using a wet cloth on Kit's back, careful of the yellowing bruise on her shoulder. She seemed to want to say more, but didn't press it. Kit was too preoccupied to give it much thought.

"Where is Emma?" she asked.

"Gone home," Maggie replied. "With her husband."

"Is she all right? Did any—"

"Nay, she's well," Maggie reassured Kit. "Only shaken up a bit is all."

"I'd like to see her—see for myself that she's all right."

"But the duke, Your Grace," Maggie protested. "He wouldn't be wanting you to leave here. Not now. Not 'til—"

"No, I don't suppose he would."

Maggie sighed with relief, and Kit finished her bath without further talk of going anywhere. She helped Kit towel herself dry and argued only a little when Kit insisted on dressing in a presentable gown rather than her nightclothes.

"I won't sleep until my husband returns, anyway," she said, "so I might as well be properly dressed. When they bring Philip back, I'll…"

"Yes, Your Grace," Maggie replied. "Would you be wanting me to find you some supper? Old Darby's like to have something warming in the kitchen..."

"Supper?" Kit hadn't thought about food at all until that moment, and she realized with some surprise that she was famished. "Yes, I suppose I'd like that, Maggie."

"All right, then," the maid said, gathering up the wet towels and Kit's soiled gown. "I'll be back before you know it, my lady."

It seemed unusually quiet to Kit, now that she was alone, and it began to unnerve her. She wondered how long it would take before Maggie returned, and found that she was anxious for the girl to get back. As she sat brushing her hair, a door closed somewhere within her hearing and startled Kit so she nearly jumped off the chair. The shadow she cast in the flickering candlelight brought a gasp to her lips and sent her heart pounding.

This was ridiculous, she thought, jumping at every noise and shadow. Philip was certainly not lurking about these chambers, waiting to do his worst. But the very thought of Philip sent a new onslaught of chills and without even thinking about it, she went over to the chest and rummaged through the items neatly stacked until she found her small dagger—one that Rupert had given her years before.

Only after Kit had sheathed the dagger and slipped it into her bodice did she feel more secure. Though she did her best to convince herself that Philip was nowhere near, she didn't care to encounter that villain again, weaponless.

Another door closed somewhere, and Kit heard footsteps approaching. Expecting to find Maggie on her way back with a tray, Kit opened her chamber door and stepped out to see Lady Christine Wellesley coming towards her.

"Lady Kathryn!" Christine said, taking Kit's arm. "I just heard of your terrible ordeal. How glad I was to learn of your rescue before that fiend, Philip was able—"

"I'll wager not half as glad as I was..." Kit muttered. She turned and walked back into her chamber with Christine following. "My maid has gone to fetch my supper, if you'd care to sit?"

Pressing a hand to her breast, Christine said, "We can't. Your husband sent me for you."

"Wolf?" Kit asked, puzzled. Why would Wolf have sent Christine Wellesley for her? That didn't make any sense, but Kit came out the door and into the dim corridor. "Has he found Philip? Oh, Lord—is he hurt?"

"No, no," Christine said, following right behind. "He wants your help."

"My help?"

"I can't explain," Christine said, with a shrug of her shoulders.

Kit wondered why Wolf would want her in this distant wing of the castle. No one ever went as far as they were going.

"Didn't you see what it was he wanted help with?"

"No," Christine responded. "He just said to hurry."

"He must be hurt," Kit said more to herself than to Christine. "I can't imagine him needing—"

"In here. Quickly."

Christine opened the door to a chamber lit by one meager, flickering taper, and stepped aside for Kit to go in. Wolf was nowhere in sight. "But—?" Before Kit could complete her question, Christine gave her a shove and left, closing the door behind her. "What the bloody hell...?"

A movement in the far shadows caught Kit's attention. It wasn't Wolf, but there was definitely a man hidden there, and he was approaching.

"Well, Kit," Baron Somers slurred, coming out of the shadows. He smiled wickedly and staggered only slightly. Two black eyes and a nose bent and swollen out of proportion gave him an ominous appearance. "That's no way to greet your loving father."

Kit gasped, backing up to the door. "I...I don't understand."

"You thought your devoted husband would be here?"

His hand lashed out and slapped her viciously. His other hand came around and grabbed a fistful of hair, near the scalp. He pulled her so that her face was inches from his. He reeked of drink. "You idiot! So gullible!"

"Please…"

"That's right! Beg! Beg me for mercy!" he said, twisting the hair till tears welled up in Kit's eyes. "Your husband will not be back to rescue you this time."

"Wh-what do you mean?"

Somers laughed drunkenly. "Philip Colston will destroy him."

"How?" Kit demanded, forgetting her fear. "How will Philip destroy Wolf?"

"The duke's gone alone to confront him—Philip has a tidy little nest under the bridge on the western end of town." Somers laughed again. "He will slay your precious duke—"

Kit turned immediately and tried the door, which would not budge. Locked, of course. He didn't intend for her to escape this time.

"And Lady Christine?" Kit tried to keep the trembling from her voice. "What has she to gain by all this?"

Somers' drunken laugh was even more evil now. "The high and mighty Lady Christine believes all that will happen is you'll be out of her way. She intends to wed your husband when he is properly widowed."

"Wed my husband!" Kit cried. "She—"

"She doesn't know that even now, at this very moment—Wolf Colston is headed into Philip's trap!"

"I must go to him!" Kit snapped. "You must—"

"I must do as I please!" He slapped her hard again, knocking her off her feet. "You will learn proper respect for your father!" he growled, losing his balance and staggering a little. "You and that damned husband of yours—ruining Somerton! Your fault. All your fault."

Kit got to her knees, a confused expression on her face.

"I've had to punish them and burn some of them out!"

Somers ranted. "The villein—they try to cheat me! There's no respect anymore. They think I don't know it, but I see them laughing up their sleeves. At me!"

His speech was slurred, and he moved menacingly toward Kit again. She saw the cruel glint in his eye and knew that he was more vicious than ever. He'd always been at his worst when he'd been drinking.

"I'll show them." He staggered toward her. "And *you!*"

Kit got up to her knees, then her feet and backed away from him. There were no weapons of any sort to be seen, nor did the baron wear a sword or a knife. At least she had a fighting chance of escape. She knew she would have to get her own knife out of her dress somehow, and a plan to do so formed in her mind.

Somers struck her again, and Kit went down hard. But this time, she rolled away from him and lay still. She wanted him to think she was grievously injured. Without making any outward movements, her hand slipped down quickly to retrieve the knife that was hidden in her bodice. And she waited, unsure of what Baron Somers would do. He might kill her with a vicious kick, but it seemed more likely that he'd want to prolong the punishment.

Kit knew her knife would have to be accurate this time. No fumbling it like she had the night they were attacked on the road to London, no stabbing blindly the way she had with Philip Colston. She would have to be deadly sure this time. Wolf's life was going to depend on her escape.

He came for her then, yanked Kit onto her back and fell on her. Straddling her, he took her head in both his hands, but only had a chance to knock it into the floor once, stunning her, and causing a screaming pain to shoot through Kit's skull. In spite of the haze, Kit rammed the knife under Somers' rib cage. She pushed with all her strength, sickening when she felt the knife pierce through living flesh. She heard his grunt of pain and felt the flow of blood covering her hands and soaking her clothes.

He fell heavily onto her, and Kit squirmed out from under his weight, pushing him away. Her head still hurt, but she was over the initial shock of pain and knew she had to move quickly. She went to the door and tried it again, even though she knew full well it was locked.

Reluctant to even look at Thomas Somers and what she'd done to him, Kit forced herself to kneel down next to him. His breath was coming in short gasps, and his color was poor. He looked up at her with uncomprehending, glassy eyes, and she knew he was dying.

"You gave me no choice!" she cried shakily.

He turned his head away.

"Where is the key?" Kit demanded.

He made no reply.

"I'll find it, damn you!" Searching him ruthlessly, ignoring the blood which still flowed freely from his wound, Kit finally found the key tucked into a pocket of his doublet. She started to rise, but on second thought turned back to Somers and pulled her knife from his belly.

A half-moon and a sky laden with stars lit her way down the unfamiliar path. Kit had only been in town once, and that seemed like a lifetime ago. As she made her way through the deserted, narrow streets, Kit fought tears and desperately tried to remember the bridge at the west end of town. She had to approach it without attracting unwanted attention, but Kit couldn't remember the place well enough to make a plan. Were there buildings on either side? Was there merely a bank at the river's edge? How would she be able to get to Wolf before Philip was aware of her presence? How would she be able to incapacitate Philip if he discovered her?

It was hopeless, Kit thought with despair. She brushed her tears away and considered her situation. There was no way she would be able to outfox and outmaneuver Philip. Even if she could sneak into his hiding place, Philip would discover her before she could release Wolf. She had to have a better plan than just storming Philip's hideout.

Kit dismounted when she came to a familiar-looking lane and led the horse on foot while she considered her options. It wasn't long before she recognized the cottage where young Alfie had taken her to clean her cloak after the incident at the fair in the springtime. The windows were not shuttered, and Kit could see that there was still light in the house. Maybe this was her solution. She dismounted and went up to tap on the door.

Alfie answered. His eyes registered his second shock of the night—the first having been his mother's shaky return from the dungeons of Windermere Castle.

"Da! It's Lady Kit!" Alfie held the door open wide, allowing Kit to pass.

"Gilbert." There was an unmistakably urgent edge to her voice.

"Your G-Grace!" Juvet stammered, coming in from the other room of the cottage. It was a shock not only to see the duchess in his cottage, but to see her covered with blood. "Dear God, what has happened?"

"I need your help," Kit cried, unable to keep her tears under control any longer. "Philip...my husband..."

"Sit yourself down here, my lady," Juvet said, guiding Kit to a kitchen stool. "Alfie, get a mug of ale. Be quick, boy!"

"He may already have my husband!"

"Now, tell me clear...Philip has the duke? Where?"

"M-my stepfa-father—Baron S-Somers—"

"Aye? He's a bad one, he is... Go on..."

"He said Philip l-laid a trap for W-Wolf," Kit said, taking a gulp of ale. "He's got him somehow under the bridge at the west end of town."

"The west bridge?"

"I was going to go there myself," Kit cried, "but I don't know if I—"

"No, my lady," Gilbert said. "You done right. You'll have help, and plenty of it." He turned to Alfie. "Run, boy, and get Daniel Page and Robert Abovebrook. Have

Robert send his son for William Smith and Kenneth Gamel. Be quick and be quiet about it.''

''What are you going to do?''

''I'm not exactly sure, Lady Kathryn,'' Gilbert Juvet said, chewing his lower lip. ''You might tell me what you had in mind. I doubt Philip can have more than three or four men in his favor. And I can get you any number to back your husband, the duke.''

Kit rose from her seat. Every moment's delay might mean Wolf's death, yet undue haste meant certain failure. ''Do you know the place under the bridge where Philip has my husband hidden?''

''Nay. I can't say as I've looked closely...the river widens and becomes quite shallow along there... I suppose a cunning devil might carve himself a cozy den under that bridge if he'd a mind to.''

''Do you think we can draw out Philip's men somehow?'' Kit asked. ''Can we get them to leave Philip unprotected so I can go in and free Wolf?''

''Well...I'm not so sure as I'll agree that you should—''

''But I must!'' Kit implored him. ''You don't know the things he'll do! You didn't see—''

''Aye. I know,'' Juvet swallowed hard. ''Emma told me.''

''So you understand the need for haste,'' Kit felt the knife tucked securely at her waist. She spoke soberly and with a fierce determination. ''I've killed one man already tonight. I've no compunctions about dealing Philip *his* death blow as well. I mean to free my husband—no matter what the risk.''

They turned to the sound of men approaching Juvet's cottage. The door was ajar, and two men let themselves in after a quick tap.

''Daniel, Robert,'' Juvet greeted them.

''Alfie told us what's afoot,'' Daniel said. ''The others will be here presently.''

''Good,'' Gilbert remarked. ''Now, all we need is a plan. And a quick one, to boot.''

Chapter Twenty-Two

It was raining earnestly now, and Kit was glad of it for it washed away the odor of stale blood that she'd been carrying with her since her encounter with Thomas Somers. The townsmen, all twelve that they'd gathered, were in place now, near the bridge, waiting.

Only a few minutes ago, Gilbert and the blacksmith had come down quietly and confirmed that there was a trapdoor in a hole at the base of the bridge. The whole thing was concealed by lilac bushes and small scrub brush. Kit and the men ran through their hasty plan and Kit, along with Tom Partridge, began to implement it.

Tom chased after Kit as she came down toward the bank of the river. He caught up to her, grabbed her arm and swung her around.

Kit screamed and punched at his chest, but the man only laughed at her puny efforts to escape his powerful grip.

"Let me alone!" she cried. "Somebody help me! I can't—ugh!" She slipped in the mud and fell flat on her back.

"Oh, milady," Tom whispered in a panic. "Let me—"

"Errah, ye bloody sod!" Kit yelped, kicking at him. "Get yer raunchy hands off me!" She made as much noise as possible, hoping to attract the attention of the men holed up under the bridge.

Tom, realizing at once that Lady Kathryn was all right, made as if to slap her while she was down. Kit cried out and fought him fiercely. Poor Tom would have a number of bruises for his efforts.

She got up and ran toward the underhang of the bridge where the lilacs grew abundantly, but couldn't see any sort of passageway. Damn Philip Colston and his underground hovels! The man was a snake! A mole! A worm!

Tom followed her up the incline, his eyes sharp for the opening under the bridge. The charade with Lady Kathryn was going well, but it couldn't go on forever. At this point, Tom and Kit both realized they'd have to practically fall into the hideout to get any response from the occupants.

"Oh, no ye don't!" Kit screamed and shoved Tom into one of the bushes. Tom, a little stunned by Kit's strength, moaned. He couldn't bring himself to curse before a lady, though he sorely wanted to. Instead, he groaned even louder and turned to the side. Even in the dark, he could see the hidey-hole from where he was perched awkwardly among the sharp branches. "Think to maim me, do ye?"

Tom clapped his hands once, making it sound like a slap. Kit let herself fall to the ground at the root of the large bush.

"Ooh, yer a mean one, Tom Partridge!" Kit wailed. "Ye'll not get away with this! I'll see that ye—"

"Here, here!" a man's voice interrupted Kit's tirade. "What goes on here?"

"Who are you?" Tom wrestled himself out of the lilac bush and poked a finger into the intruder's chest. "And where'd ye come from?"

Kit backed away from Philip's man, whom she knew full well had come out through the trapdoor. She'd seen him, and where he'd come from, but she was certainly not going to let him know that fact. Let him think she was afraid of him. Let him come after her—oh, please God, let him come.

"Did ye think to share her?" Tom's eyes gleamed with

evil intent as he pushed the man back. He hoped his suggestion would be taken seriously, because then the plan might just work.

Without warning, Philip's man punched Tom square in the face, knocking him down and out cold. It was a maneuver Tom hadn't bargained on.

Kit ran up the embankment, her pursuer hot on her heels. She turned and continued running until she heard a crash and a curse behind her. Heart pounding, muscles sore, Kit turned to see Gilbert and two of the other townsmen holding Philip's man down. The man struggled, only to be rewarded by a stiff blow to the jaw.

She drew her knife and approached him.

"I can do it, my lady," Kenneth Gamel said. "I done some soldiering…"

Kit nodded to him, relieved not to be responsible for any more bloodshed now. Contrary to what she'd thought before, she'd already had her fill.

"Lady?" Philip's man said, recovering, finally recognizing her dirt-crusted face. She had uncovered her hair, as well. "Bloody Christ, I should've known—"

"Shut yer bloody mouth, Tuck," the blacksmith said.

"Her ladyship will be tellin' you what you should or shouldn't be doin' now," Kenneth said.

"Who's in that nest under the bridge?" Kit asked.

"Ye mean, besides the earl and your husband?" Tuck said, smirking.

Daniel Page kicked him in the side. "None o' yer insolence!"

"Answer the duchess, Tuck," Kenneth almost whispered, but the knife he held at Tuck's ear spoke loud and clear.

"Or what?" Tuck rasped. "Yer all just a bunch o' townsmen. None o' ye could—"

The knife began a slow slice.

"All right! Stop!" Tuck cried, trying desperately to keep from moving his head. "I'll tell ye! I've nothing to lose!"

"Naught but body parts..." Kenneth had a determined look about him.

"Speak!"

"There's only the earl and...and Saladin with him," Tuck said, tears rolling out of the corners of his eyes.

"And my husband?"

"Aye! He's there as well."

"Alive?" Gilbert Juvet asked the question Kit was unable to ask.

Tuck grunted. "Philip plans to keep him alive like he did with Dryden. He knows how. He'll be careful."

"What condition is the duke in now?"

"He's—he's—"

Kenneth positioned the blade next to Tuck's other ear. "I'm havin' some trouble believin' you, Master Tuck," he said. "It seems a bit...imprudent...for Lord Philip to be down in his hole with only the two of you."

"No! No! That's all!"

The knife moved.

"Stop! I beg you!" Tuck cried. "You're right! Jack Hartford's down there, too!"

"Hartford!" Kit gasped. Jack Hartford was one of the Windermere liverymen. He must have lured Wolf into the trap.

"We were going to let the earl do as he liked...there's no stoppin' him, anyway— Ouch!" Kenneth had moved the knife only to be sure Tuck bore it in mind as he spoke. "Be careful with that blade!"

"Tell me more."

"We were going to get on a ship bound for Ireland—all of us—his lordship included," Tuck said. Perspiration flowed freely now, and the man frequently squeezed his eyes to shut out the sight of his captors. "He only wanted to...wanted to... It's just the duke! He hates the duke!"

"Bind his hands," Juvet said. "Quickly, lads.

"Lady Kathryn." He took her aside. "Are you up to this?"

"Yes—I'll continue, Gilbert," she said. "I'm going in after my husband."

"I thought you would," he muttered. "Come on, let's move!"

Tuck cooperated nicely. Gilbert figured he was partial to keeping his ears. Kit figured nothing. She was just grateful things had gone so well this far. It still remained to be seen whether or not they'd be able to get Wolf safely away from Philip. She hoped he hadn't had time to do much damage. Wolf had only left her—when?—two hours ago? Surely not enough time...

Kit forced back visions of Hugh Dryden and moved on down the embankment. The rain let up to a steady drizzle, but no one noticed. Two men went to each side of the underground passage and waited.

"Call them," Kenneth said quietly. "Make it sound like you found something...like you need their help."

"Wh-what are—?"

"Just do it!" Kenneth Gamel let Tuck feel the sharp tip of his knife at the base of his neck.

"Saladin! Hartford!"

"That was real nice," Gamel said. "Now let's get them out here."

"Come, help me with this!" Tuck cried. "The bloke's too heavy for me!"

Two men scurried out of the hole. "Damn yer eyes, Tuck," one said, "will ye shut yer face? The earl don't—"

His words were cut short as he was attacked and easily subdued by the two men to his left. Two men on the right took the second man out of the hole, and both Saladin and Hartford were silenced.

William Smith motioned Kit to follow him. He was the biggest of the townsmen and likely the strongest, and it made perfect sense for him to lead the way. Kit had insisted on being the first one into Philip's hideout, but was persuaded—by reason and common sense—to let the burly fellow lead them. With luck, Philip would be down there alone with only the duke, and there would be little or no danger to Lady Kathryn. William wasn't counting on it, though.

Kit drew her knife and followed the big man closely.

Once Smith had crept a couple of feet past the door, he stopped abruptly, holding one arm back to keep Kit from falling over him. She peered past him and realized that the passage took a sharp right turn. They could stay indefinitely at the entrance without being detected. There was a dim light emanating from the right and they assumed there was some sort of chamber there, concealed within the structure of the bridge.

William Smith got down to his knees and slowly, carefully, moved his head to peer around the corner. Kit was anxious to do the same, but William restrained her. She knew he was concerned about her reaction to what she might see, and if truth be known, Kit was worried, too. If Philip had done any of those terrible things to Wolf—well, Kit didn't know what she would do. It was certain that she'd give them away, though, and there would be nothing either of them could do to prevent Philip from killing Wolf quickly.

Smith moved back enough to give Kit a chance to look into the room. There was only the light from one torch, but it was a small compartment. Easy to see every corner. Water dripped down in several places, and the floor was a muddy mess. Kit's eyes riveted on Wolf, slumped in a chair at the far end of the chamber. His hands were bound behind him.

Blanche Hanchaw stood at the far left, wringing her hands while Philip went over to Wolf and grabbed him by the hair above his forehead, pulling his head up.

"Look at me!" he crowed as he splashed a dipper of water in Wolf's face. Blood poured cleanly from a diagonal slice across his cheek. His left eye was badly bruised and swollen shut. "I want you to see me! I want you to be...full aware of what happens here. It's not the least amusing if you sleep—''

''My lord,'' Blanche said anxiously, ''what can be keeping those fools?''

''They're probably all having a go at the wench,'' he sneered. ''Idiots. Blundering fools.''

''I don't like this, Philip,'' Blanche said. ''Anyone might see them.''

''Don't worry. You know perfectly well this little hidey-hole has served me time and time again.'' Philip gritted his teeth and gave Wolf's hair a brutal yank. ''And when I'm through here, it's off to Ireland we go.'' He picked up a long iron rod that had been worn to a sharp point at one end and studied Wolf. '''Tis a pity we can't have a fire in here…''

Kit could see that Philip was mad. He wasn't merely twisted, as Wolf had called him, he was actually out of his senses. She thought of Hugh and knew no one in his right mind would set out intentionally to commit those horrors. Kit bit her hand to keep from crying out. Smith turned and whispered almost soundlessly in her ear.

''We'll have to move fast,'' he said. ''Especially ye, mi-lady.''

She tightened her grip on her knife and nodded.

''I'll go for the earl while ye keep the woman occupied. She's likely to see ye before the earl is aware aught is amiss. Gilbert and the lads'll be along any minute now.'' William said. ''Are ye able?''

A quick nod of her head and a fierce look in Kit's eyes were answer enough. Together they stormed the chamber, Kit wielding her knife, William brandishing a cudgel from his shop.

Wolf was fully conscious, though brutally beaten, but he realized from the start that it was to his advantage to appear incapacitated. Philip might let down his guard—might even unbind his hands. And now that Wolf knew his cousin preferred a fully awake victim, he was not about to comply with his perverse wishes.

However, it was time to make his move. Philip's cronies, including that bastard Hartford, who had lured him into Philip's trap, were gone. Wolf was well aware that the men could return at any second, so as Philip stood looking down at him, contemplating exactly how he was going to use the iron pike on him, Wolf swayed to the side and fell off his chair.

It was exactly the diversion William and Kit needed as they sprang into the chamber. As Philip leaned over his fallen cousin, Wolf kicked savagely, catching Philip full in the chest with his heel, knocking him over. William quickly brained him with the cudgel, rendering the evil earl unconscious.

Blanche screeched when she realized what was happening and tried to make a run for it. Kit tripped her, knocking her face-down onto the muddy floor, and sat on her. Blanche struggled to gain her feet, but Kit held her securely.

"William!"

"Aye, milady?"

"Is Philip—?"

"Out cold!"

"Then come deal with this woman while I see to my husband!"

Wolf lay in the mud on the floor, bruised and sore, still bound tightly and very uncomfortable. "Kit!" His voice was a thin rasp.

"Aye, husband," Kit replied tearfully, cutting the bindings at his wrists. "I've come for you." She helped him to sit up, then wrapped her arms around him.

"But how—?"

"Baron Somers saved your life," she said, looking up at him. "Oh, Wolf—your eye. And this cut—it needs stitching."

"'Tis nothing," he said.

"'Tis not," Kit returned. "You forget I know firsthand of these things."

"Where is Somers?" Wolf growled as he got to his feet. "I swear by all the saints I'll kick his weasly arse all the way across Cumbria—"

Then Gilbert Juvet was there, along with three or four townsmen—as many as could fit in the small compartment.

"Tom!" Kit cried as Tom Partridge made his way toward her. His nose was a bloody mess but he seemed otherwise unharmed.

"Your Grace," Tom said to Kit, "I...I ought to apologize—"

"Apologize?"

"For knocking you down out there..."

Kit laughed. "'Twas your job, was it not?" she asked, taking his arm. "We drew them out, didn't we? Just as we intended."

"That was you?" Wolf asked. He'd heard some sort of commotion, of course, but it hadn't meant anything to him other than the fact that it had drawn Philip's cronies out of their murky nest, giving him his chance to overpower Philip.

"We couldn't figure any other way to get Lord Philip's men out of here," Gilbert said.

"So we created a disturbance," Kit finished.

"Where are Hartford and the other bastards?" Wolf asked.

"We have them all, Your Grace," Gilbert said. "More than half the town is out there waiting to see Philip dragged from this hovel."

"Disturbed the lot of them, did we?" Kit asked, laughing now through her tears.

"Aye, ye did, milady," Daniel Page remarked as he and another man doused Philip Colston with water and yanked him to his feet.

Philip was quick to regain consciousness. His eyes narrowed to slits, and he spat and cursed everyone present, especially Wolf. The townsmen merely laughed at Philip, a comical figure now, covered in mud, foaming and spewing at the mouth. The men weren't gentle with him as they led him away, each man cursing him in return and striking him as it pleased them.

"Take charge here, will you Juvet?" Wolf requested, following the men and their prisoners out of the hovel. "I'd like to get my wife home…"

"Aye, Your Grace," Juvet replied, clearly pleased at the authority given him by the duke. "By the way, John Carpenter went off in search of Lord Nicholas. If he's found him, I'd imagine he'll be here soon."

"My thanks, Gilbert," Wolf said, "for helping my wife save my life…" He put his arm around Kit's shoulders and squeezed. Gilbert shrugged and walked ahead of them out of the little room within the structure of the bridge.

"I don't suppose your *Annalouise* would have done as well?" Kit couldn't resist making the remark, though she'd vowed never to mention the other woman to Wolf.

"Who?"

"I know you were betrothed before Henry ordered you to—"

Wolf laughed out loud. "Annegret? I was never betrothed to Annegret…"

"Annegret," Kit muttered. "Whoever."

"And Henry didn't order me to wed you," Wolf told her. "He ordered me to wed his sister. If I'd known from the first that *you* were his sister, he'd never have had a chance to give the order."

"Are you certain, Wolf?"

He kissed her soundly. "Annegret represented an alliance to my grandfather. She meant even less to me."

Kit sighed with relief. The last of her worries was resolved.

"There could be no other wife for me, Sprout," he said, holding her for a moment before they left the hovel.

So many torches were lit that it seemed more like dawn

than the dead of night. Giving truth to Gilbert's words, at least half the town had turned out to see Philip brought low, so unpopular was the former Earl of Windermere. A huge crowd of people waited on the opposite side of the bridge, cackling and jeering at Philip, and throwing over-ripe fruit and vegetables at him, while Philip screamed back at them. Blanche merely cowered as she was pulled along ahead of her former master, unsure of what her fate was to be.

Wolf and Kit stayed back, savoring a moment alone while the crowd at the other end feasted on Philip's downfall. The emotions of the hour finally overcame her, and Kit was unable to restrain her tears any longer. Wolf held her until her weeping subsided.

"I must get you home and see to these injuries," Kit said, sniffling.

"Aye," Wolf smiled. "For the first time, I'll be able to rest easy in our bed at Windermere. And time enough to tell me how—"

"What's going on up there?" Kit asked, looking up at the bridge, wiping the last of her tears away.

There was no longer any commotion. The townspeople were quiet and Philip was raving madly. It was impossible to understand all of his words though Kit and Wolf were able to glimpse a scuffle taking place in the center of the bridge. Then there was a frantic shout and a man flung himself from the highest point, down into the shallow water beneath the bridge. Kit gasped and covered her mouth with her hands.

Philip. It had to be Philip.

Wolf walked down the embankment into the darkness and waded into the knee-deep water. The crowd spread out along the bank of the river to watch silently as the duke pulled his hated cousin out of the water. Not a single person hoped for his survival, nor gave up a silent prayer for his salvation.

Chapter Twenty-Three

Windermere Castle
October, 1421

A fire blazed in the huge hearth of the great hall where a beautiful new banner hung from the high wooden beams over the duke's table. Clean, herb-scented rushes were spread about the floor. In daylight hours, the sky was clearly visible through clean windows. All traces of soot and ash were gone, and the dust was kept at bay by a throng of well-directed, faithful servants. Dried flowers in pitchers adorned each table, and a huge wreath of them hung over the mantel of the largest fireplace.

The tunnels beneath Windermere castle were still being filled in. It was a huge task, filling the barrows with earth and carting them down the dark passageways. But Wolf was determined to wipe out any trace of Philip and his depravity. He would keep no reminders of Philip's hideous reign over Windermere.

Luckily, Maggie, the dark-haired maid who was so devoted to Kit, had only suffered a lump on the head the night Christine Wellesley had sought to trap Kit with Baron Somers. She was discovered the following morning locked in a garderobe near the duke's chambers, suffering with a miserable headache and worried to death over Kit's fate. She became Kit's personal maid and companion as soon as her head mended.

Lady Christine Wellesley left Windermere in disgrace.

Baron Somers was returned to Somerton for burial.

Blanche Hanchaw and the men known to have been Philip's cohorts were taken to London to stand trial on several different charges. All were found guilty and hanged except for Blanche. The Hanchaw woman was bound and sentenced by the court to spend the rest of her wretched days in a dungeon in Wessex, under a moldy old castle never used anymore by its lord, the Duke of Carlisle.

Hugh Dryden's wounds began to heal with time and great care, though it would still be some time before he'd be able to claim his own estate.

Kit stifled a yawn. It was late and though she was tremendously hungry, she could easily have returned to bed. In fact, Kit even considered asking Maggie to bring a tray to her chamber. Wolf had vetoed that notion, though. He wanted his duchess at the evening meal, for they were having guests and he said he had a few announcements to make.

Maggie came to help her dress for dinner. Kit had just had a nap and couldn't understand her continued fatigue. "I brought you a little snack," Maggie said. "I've, er...noticed as how you've been especially hungry lately..."

"'Tis strange, isn't it?" Kit asked. "I don't remember ever having such an appetite before."

"I don't suppose..."

"What?" Kit covered another yawn with her hand.

"Well, I only wondered if..."

A gentle tapping at the door interrupted their conversation. Maggie answered it and let in Emma Juvet.

"Sleeping again, are you?" Emma asked, embracing Kit. Gilbert was now the reeve of Windermere, and his position

brought the Juvets into frequent contact with Kit and Wolfram Colston.

"I just don't understand it," Kit said as Maggie fastened
up her gown. "I've already rested once this afternoon, and
I'm ready to sleep even more."

Emma laughed. "You'd figure it out if you gave it the
least little bit o' thought."

"I'd figure...?"

"Have you considered the possibility of a babe?"

"For heaven's sake, I...I've..."

Emma and Maggie stood there smiling foolishly, waiting
for Kit to draw her own conclusion.

"I'm with child?" Kit asked, a bit bewildered by the
prospect. She had never kept track of her menses, though
she knew that their lack usually indicated pregnancy. It's
just that she and Wolf hadn't ever discussed children. And
with all the activity these last months since their coming to
Windermere, she hadn't given much thought to having ba-
bies. Though now, the idea was very appealing.

They would have a child. She and Wolf had made a child
together.

The two other women nodded. "Of course that's it,"
Emma said.

"But I'm never sick," Kit protested, worried that it
might not be true, "and I remember quite distinctly hearing
that—"

"I was never sick with Alfie," Emma interrupted. "Not
a once."

"So you mean it's possible?" Kit asked, her eyes gleam-
ing. "Truly?"

Emma nodded. Kit wondered what Wolf would say when
she told him about the babe. She would plan the telling for
a quiet, romantic time...perhaps first thing in the morning
when the sun was bright and she would be able to see her
husband's face. He was usually in an amorous mood upon
awakening...

Kit was the last to arrive in the hall. Wolf was just about

to leave his guests to go fetch her himself, but then she arrived, looking sleepy…and a little bit bewildered.

"Kathryn," Wolf said as she greeted him with a kiss. "Are you well?"

"Of course I am well. What could be amiss?" Kit replied with a smile. She turned and nodded to Wolf's companions. They were dressed in their finest tunics. "Nicholas, Edward, how festive you look…"

"Come. All is ready," Wolf said, leading Kit to their table. The others followed and took their places as well. Musicians came into the hall and began entertaining as the servants brought in the first courses of the meal. Kit ate ravenously, happily aware that she was providing sustenance not only for herself, but her babe, too.

When Wolf finished his meal, he stood and garnered everyone's attention. His announcements began with awards of land to those of his men who would go. They were Kenneth, Egbert and Chester, all men who intended to marry and establish homes of their own.

"I would not wish for these three to leave me now, but their estates are nearby and we will see them often," Wolf said. "I can also say that I now understand the attractions of home and wife. Lady Kathryn and I wish you well." He raised his glass and everyone toasted the knights who intended to leave Windermere.

"Next, we must bid my cousin, Nicholas, Viscount of Thornton, farewell," Wolf said. There were calls of protest from the lower tables, but Wolf went on. "It is time for him to claim his title and take his estates in hand. I have selfishly relied on him long enough." Wolf picked up a parchment from the table where he'd sat for the meal. "Besides, I recently received this missive from our grandfather in Bremen. It warns that if the bastard grandson does not soon claim what is his, King Henry will surely come to his senses and revoke what was given. He urges you, Nicholas, to get to Thornton in all haste." A great deal of laughter accompanied Rudolph Gerhart's warning, and Wolf noticed the look of shock in Kit's eyes.

"Did I ever mention that my uncle never wed Nicholas' mother?" Wolf asked Kit.

She shook her head, still stunned.

"Nick's worth is greater than all the legitimate cousins I've ever had, and I love him well," Wolf remarked. His voice was loud enough for Nicholas and everyone at the duke's table to hear. "We have been as brothers these twenty years and will continue another forty."

"Hear, hear!"

"Lastly," Wolf began, "I invite all of you to return in the month of May for the christening of our firstborn child."

At this, a cheer went up, and Kit looked at Wolf with her jaw agape. He knew! He winked at her, grinning.

"Of course, I cannot give you an exact date, but the birth will occur in the spring."

Later, after the candles were out, a cozy fire had been banked in their room, and they were snuggled together in their big bed. "When did you realize I was carrying our babe?"

He smiled. "I think it was the morning when you finished your own porridge, and then started on mine."

She poked his ribs.

"Or was it that day a couple of weeks ago when you slept till noon, had a nap and then retired just after dark?"

"Rascal!"

"Oh, Kit, how I love you." He laughed and gathered her into his arms. "I know that your monthly courses ceased soon after we arrived at Windermere. That means you'll bear our child late in April. It would please me if she were born on the anniversary of the day I took you from Somerton."

"She?"

"Of course," Wolf said. "I want a daughter exactly like

you. She will have a father who loves her and dotes upon her.''

''And what of sons?''

''You may have as many as you like,'' he said, grinning, ''as long as you give me my daughter first.''

Then he turned and unfastened the ties of her gown. He kissed her mouth, then her throat and shoulders. Kit shuddered, overcome by feelings of warmth, security and love.

''I love you, Wolf.''

''I know,'' he said.

''My life would have been nothing if Philip had—''

''Hush, love,'' he said, easing her down onto the bed. ''You rescued me, and all is well.''

''Better than I'd ever hoped...''

''Feel free to rescue me any time,'' he murmured and showed his wife that she was well and truly loved.

* * * * *

Don't miss your chance to read
award-winning author

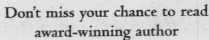

PATRICIA POTTER

First Scottish historical romance

THE ABDUCTION

An eye for an eye. Clan leader Elsbeth Ker longed
for peace, but her stubborn English
neighbors would have none
of it—especially since the
mysterious Alexander had
returned to lead the
Carey clan. Now the
crofters had been
burned out, and the
outraged Kers demanded
revenge. But when Elsbeth faced her enemy,
what she saw in his steel gray eyes gave her pause....

Look for *THE ABDUCTION* this March 1999,
available at your favorite retail outlet!

HARLEQUIN®
Makes any time special ™

Look us up on-line at: http://www.romance.net   PHABDUCT

Look for a new and exciting series from Harlequin!

HARLEQUIN Duets™

Two __new__ full-length novels in one book, from some of your favorite authors!

Starting in May, each month we'll be bringing you two new books, each book containing two brand-new stories about the lighter side of love! Double the pleasure, double the romance, for less than the cost of two regular romance titles!

Look for these two new Harlequin Duets™ titles in May 1999:

Book 1:
WITH A STETSON AND A SMILE
by Vicki Lewis Thompson
THE BRIDESMAID'S BET
by Christie Ridgway

Book 2:
KIDNAPPED? by Jacqueline Diamond
I GOT YOU, BABE by Bonnie Tucker

2 GREAT STORIES BY 2 GREAT AUTHORS FOR 1 LOW PRICE!

Don't miss it! Available May 1999 at your favorite retail outlet.

HARLEQUIN®
Makes any time special.™

Look us up on-line at: http://www.romance.net   HDGENR

COMING NEXT MONTH FROM

HARLEQUIN
HISTORICALS